Fourteen enthralling stories from the best new writers of the year accompanied by three more from towering authors you've read before.

After a devastating earthquake, a toy kitten crawls out of the rubble, free at last. Deep in its programming, an urge demands to be fulfilled....
—"The Tiger and the Waif" by John M. Campbell

When war comes home, a mysterious sixth-senser must use her talents and the help of three orphans on a journey across a devastated city to find her son....   —"Sixers" by Barbara Lund

A scientist must choose between ambition and compassion while forced to participate in a secret and sadistic government project....
—"The Enfield Report" by Christopher Bowthorpe

A Victorian tea shop owner hopes to serve justice to wicked gangsters—with the help of a mysterious new friend....
—"The Widow's Might" by Elizabeth Chatsworth

Meek Dr. Henry Mudge has a dramatic personality change after discovering a mathematical equation that transports him to any place in the universe he can think of....
—"The Dangerous Dimension" by L. Ron Hubbard

In a magical kingdom overrun by "chosen ones," a wizard grows weary of always being the mentor and decides to do something about it....   —"How to Steal the Plot Armor" by Luke Wildman

There can be no redemption for a man who has lost control of his warrior-bear spirit—only penance. Or so Adalum believes....
—"The Redemption of Brother Adalum" by K. D. Julicher

The starship that brought mankind to its first colony among the stars was powered by a godlike being, ˮʰ what it is to be human....   —"The Aˌ

D1115427

When a lover's gift to her king turns out to be a perilous trap, the Phoenixes and their priestess face a test that will decide the fate of two realms.... —"The Phoenixes' War" by Jody Lynn Nye

Her grandfather taught her how to create music from the soul, but does it come at too high a price...?
—"Soul Paper" by Trent Walters

A woman who once escaped her destiny returns home to find it won't be so easy the second time....
—"The Skin of My Mother" by Erik Lynd

Time runs in a circle, beginning where it ends—but father has always been out of sync....
—"Death of a Time Traveler" by Sara Fox

A guilt-ridden war hero finds herself in an unexpected extraterrestrial battle, confronting the prospect of having to kill again....
—"The Battle of Donasi" by Elaine Midcoh

When an ambassador is asked to inspect the controversial Museum of Modern Warfare, she discovers life-changing secrets....
—"The Museum of Modern Warfare" by Kristine Kathryn Rusch

Noam only hopes to have a normal Seder, but he'll have to battle his brother's new girlfriend and the demons that follow her....
—"A Demon Hunter's Guide to Passover Seder" by Ryan Cole

A young girl in a plastic boat finds herself at the doorstep of a mysterious old man living in a house built in the middle of the ocean....
—"Hemingway" by Emma Washburn

When tensions between humans and dryads boil over, a teen must bridge the gap between the old world and new, before everything she loves turns to ash.... —"Half-Breed" by Brittany Rainsdon

L. RON HUBBARD

Presents

Writers of the Future

Anthologies

"The collection contains something for every reader of speculative fiction." —*Booklist*

"Not only is the writing excellent...it is also extremely varied. There's a lot of hot new talent in it."

—*Locus* magazine

"Always a glimpse of tomorrow's stars."

—*Publishers Weekly* starred review

"The Writers of the Future Contest is a valuable outlet for writers early in their careers. Finalists and winners get a unique spotlight that says 'this is the way to good writing.'"

—Jody Lynn Nye
Writers of the Future Contest judge

"The Contests are amazing competitions. I wish I had something like this when I was getting started—very positive and cool."

—Bob Eggleton
Illustrators of the Future Contest judge

"Sometimes a little bit of just the right kind of advice from an experienced mentor can make the world of difference to someone starting on their art career."

—Craig Elliott
Illustrators of the Future Contest judge

"I always try to help up-and-coming writers and am delighted to be able to judge in the L. Ron Hubbard Writers of the Future Contest."
—Katherine Kurtz
Writers of the Future Contest judge

"Writers of the Future, which has launched the careers of so many young writers, is an inestimable boon to both individuals and the field as a whole."
—Nancy Kress
Writers of the Future Contest judge

"The smartest move for beginning writers is the WotF Contest. I've witnessed it kick-start many a career."
—Gregory Benford
Writers of the Future Contest judge

"Illustrators of the Future offered a channel through which to direct my ambitions. The competition made me realize that genre illustration is actually a valued profession, and here was a rare opportunity for a possible entry point into that world."
—Shaun Tan
Illustrators of the Future Contest winner 1993
and Contest judge

"The Writers of the Future Contest has had a profound impact on my career, ever since I submitted my first story in 1989."
—Sean Williams
Writers of the Future Contest winner 1993
and Contest judge

"The Writers of the Future Contest played a critical role in the early stages of my career as a writer."
—Eric Flint
Writers of the Future Contest winner 1993
and Contest judge

L. Ron Hubbard PRESENTS

Writers of the Future

VOLUME 37

L. Ron Hubbard PRESENTS

Writers of the Future

VOLUME 37

The year's fourteen best tales from the
Writers of the Future international writers' program

Illustrated by winners in the Illustrators of the Future
international illustrators' program

Three short stories by L. Ron Hubbard /
Jody Lynn Nye / Kristine Kathryn Rusch

With essays on writing and illustration by
L. Ron Hubbard / Orson Scott Card / Craig Elliott

Edited by David Farland
Illustrations art directed by Echo Chernik

GALAXY PRESS, INC.

For information, contact Galaxy Press, Inc. at 7051 Hollywood Boulevard, Suite 200, Los Angeles, California, 90028.

This anthology contains works of fiction. Names, characters, places, and incidents are either the product of the authors' imaginations or are used fictitiously. Any resemblance to actual events or locales or persons, living or dead, is entirely coincidental. Opinions expressed by nonfiction essayists are their own.

ISBN 978-1-61986-701-7
Printed in the United States of America.

CONTENTS

Introduction

BY DAVID FARLAND

David Farland is a New York Times *bestselling author with more than fifty novels and anthologies to his credit. He has won numerous awards in several genres, including the L. Ron Hubbard Gold Award in 1987, the Philip K. Dick Memorial Special Award, the Whitney Award for Best Novel of the Year, and the International Book Award for best Young Adult novel of the year.*

Dave broke the Guinness Record for the world's largest book signing in 1999.

In addition to writing novels and short stories, Dave has also worked in video games as a designer and scripter, and has worked as a green-lighting analyst for movies in Hollywood.

*He has helped mentor hundreds of new writers, including such #1 bestselling authors as Brandon Sanderson (*The Way of Kings*), Stephenie Meyer (*Twilight*), Brandon Mull (*Fablehaven*), James Dashner (*The Maze Runner*), and others. While writing* Star Wars *novels in 1998, he was asked to help choose a book to push big for Scholastic. He selected* Harry Potter, *then developed a strategy to promote it to become the bestselling book in English of all time.*

Dave runs a huge international writing workshop where twice each week he interviews successful writers, editors, agents, and movie producers, and offers access to his writing courses.

Dave also helps mentor writers through the Writers of the Future program, where for more than fifteen years he has acted as Coordinating Judge, editor of the anthology, and taught workshops to winning authors.

Introduction

Welcome to *L. Ron Hubbard Presents Writers of the Future Volume 37*.

Each year as I begin judging the Writers' Contest, I search for tales that move me emotionally or stimulate me intellectually. Years ago, I was asked to help choose a book for a small publisher to promote big. I studied dozens and chose the book *Harry Potter*.

Why choose it and not some other? Because of all the entries, for me it held the strongest mix of positive emotions. Whether you are looking for wonder, adventure, a sense of nostalgia, a good laugh, or genuine chills—it's all there.

You see, too often, writers struggle to create powerful prose by assaulting the reader's sensibilities. They throw in needless violence, darkness, and despair.

Those elements have a place in a story but reading such tales can be like going to a friend's house and finding yourself bludgeoned with a baseball bat. You're not getting what you hoped for.

So, this year, I searched for stories that offered a pleasing array of emotions. Sure, some are darker than others, but there is a light sparkling at the core of each of them.

This Contest is huge, and each year it grows bigger. We had more entries than ever, so the competition was fierce. At this point, no other contest in the field of speculative fiction has grown this large or run this long. Despite our burgeoning growth, some things remain the same. When we get a submission, our judges don't know who sent the story, what country it came from, the age or gender of the author. We gauge our stories on quality alone. In this volume, we hit a goldmine.

This year, we have fourteen new authors to introduce from around the globe. Each writer is paid professional rates for publication. In addition, they get prize money for winning and either an in-person or virtual trip to attend our awards ceremony in Hollywood, California, and a workshop taught by some of the biggest luminaries in the field of speculative fiction—folks like Kevin J. Anderson, Doug Beason, Gregory Benford, Brian Herbert, Nancy Kress, Katherine Kurtz, Todd McCaffrey, Nnedi Okorafor, Tim Powers, Brandon Sanderson, Dean Wesley Smith, Sean Williams, and Robert J. Sawyer.

One first-place winner of the Contest will be awarded the grand prize of $5,000. When you add the value of the prizes and payment for publication, this becomes the top speculative fiction market in the world for new writers.

Our companion Illustrators of the Future Contest winners are also featured in our anthology. Echo Chernik is the Illustrators' Contest Coordinating Judge and she introduces them. A highlight of the annual workshop is when the authors meet the artists and see their illustrations for the first time.

Of course, the illustration judges are no less illustrious than the writing judges. Our judges include such big names as Ciruelo, Dan dos Santos, Bob Eggleton, Craig Elliott, Larry Elmore, Val Lakey Lindahn, Stephan Martiniere, Sergey Poyarkov, Rob Prior, Echo and Lazarus Chernik.

In addition to our writer winners, I'm very pleased to have the first science fiction tale from the illustrious founder of our Contests, L. Ron Hubbard. We've also got great stories from some of our judges—like Kristine Kathryn Rusch who entered the Contest the year it formed and now brings us a powerful tale told as a true master of the craft. We also have a wonderful story from Jody Lynn Nye inspired by our cover art from Echo Chernik.

The anthology also boasts articles with fine advice from Mr. Hubbard, from our writing judge and instructor Orson Scott Card, and from celebrated artist and illustrator judge Craig Elliott.

So, make yourself comfortable, sit back, and prepare to laugh, to weep, and perchance to dream....

The Illustrators of the Future Contest

BY ECHO CHERNIK

Echo Chernik is an advertising and publishing illustrator with twenty-seven years of professional experience and several prestigious publishing awards.

Her clients include mainstream companies such as: Miller, Camel, Coors, Celestial Seasonings, Publix Super Markets, Kmart, Sears, NASCAR, the Sheikh of Dubai, the city of New Orleans, Bellagio resort, the state of Indiana, USPS, Dave Matthews Band, Arlo Guthrie, McDonald's, Procter & Gamble, Trek Bicycle Corporation, Disney, BBC, Mattel, Hasbro, and more. She specializes in several styles including decorative, vector, and art nouveau.

She is the Coordinating Judge of the Illustrators of the Future Contest. Echo strives to share the important but all-too-often neglected subject of the business aspect of illustration with the winners, as well as preparing them for the reality of a successful career in illustration.

The Illustrators of the Future Contest

In addition to the Writers' Contest winning stories, we also present this year's Illustrators of the Future Contest winners.

L. Ron Hubbard established these Contests for aspiring artists "to have a chance for their creative efforts to be seen and acknowledged." And together, the stories and illustrations create a synergy not found in other anthologies.

The Illustrators of the Future Contest provides some amazing opportunities. It's designed to help launch careers, and it allows established artists like myself to give back. An artist new in the field often has to struggle to succeed with little guidance, while the Contest judges and I have reached a stage in our careers where we have amassed volumes of valuable information. This Contest provides a platform to share our knowledge to help launch the careers of new artists toward success.

The Illustrators' Contest is international in scope and the resulting diversity is amazing—as you can see by the illustrations in this anthology. They all have different art styles with different color palettes. In addition to winners from across the United States, this year we have winners from England, Portugal, South Africa, India, China, and Vietnam.

This Contest really is open to anybody. The judges, including myself, have no idea where the entrants are from, how old they are, their gender, or race. It is a completely merit-based competition. Only the best illustrations win.

The Contest works like this: Each entrant provides three pieces. At the end of each Contest quarter, I review all entries. I preselect the honorable mentions, semifinalists, and finalists. I try to choose a diverse array of pieces. I look for talent and for skill in illustration as well as the ability to tell a story. I'm looking for entrants with their own style, because if an artist is doing their art in their own way, their passion shines through.

When the entrants are narrowed down to a few pieces— some really good portraits and drawings versus one that tells a story—I'll go with the piece that tells the story. After all, this is an *illustrators'* contest.

Then the finalists are reviewed by our panel of amazing artist judges who choose three winners each quarter.

At the end of the year, the twelve quarterly winners compete in a second competition for the grand prize. Each artist is commissioned to illustrate a story in this anthology. I have the honor of working as art director to help them create a grand prize–worthy piece. Our full panel of judges chooses the best piece to win the grand prize and $5,000.

Being one of the quarterly winners also earns the artist either an in-person or virtual trip to Hollywood for a weeklong workshop with the Contest judges and a gala awards ceremony launching the new anthology. It's an experience of a lifetime.

My advice, to you and any aspiring artist you know, is to enter. Enter several times a year. Every quarter is a new competition. If you don't win, it doesn't mean your work isn't good. You might have just missed winning by the skin of your teeth. There is a very fine line between winner and finalist.

Enter the three strongest pieces that best represent your style. If that's what you want to do for a living, that's what we want to see. And that's what we want to see in your commissioned piece that accompanies a story in the annual anthology.

Use the quarterly deadlines to hone your skills and enter again. It costs you nothing to enter, so there's nothing to lose. There are many opportunities to gain. Take a chance. I look forward to seeing your entries!

ANDRÉ MATA
The Tiger and the Waif   7

WILL KNIGHT
Sixers

STEPHEN SPINAS
The Enfield Report

MADOLYN LOCKE
The Widow's Might

ANH LE
The Dangerous Dimension

DAN WATSON
How to Steal the Plot Armor

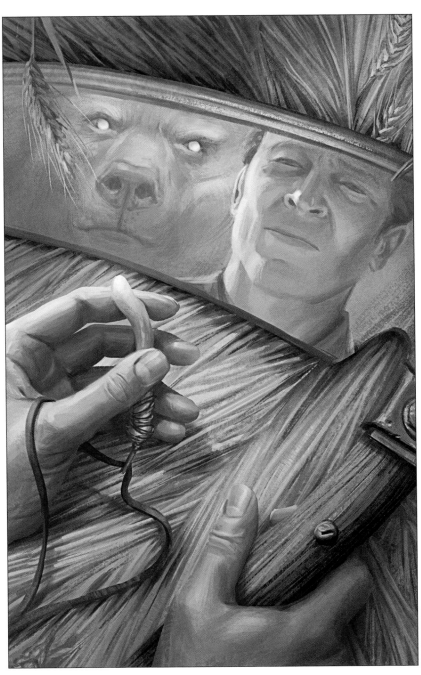

ISABEL GIBNEY
The Redemption of Brother Adalum

RUPAM GRIMOEUVRE
The Argentum

MARIAH SALINAS
Soul Paper

SHIYI YU
The Skin of My Mother

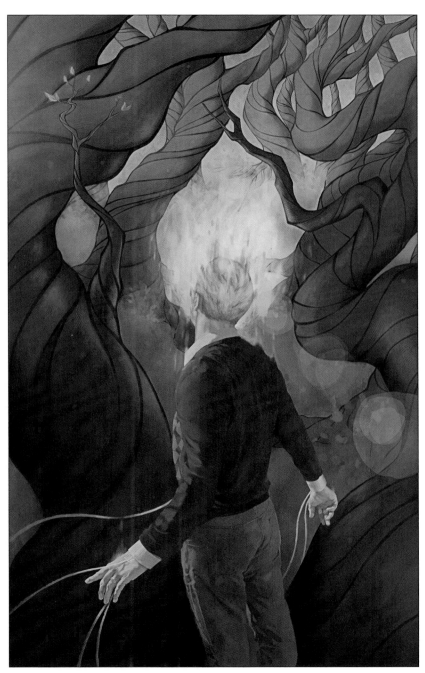

JENNIFER BRUCE
Death of a Time Traveler   17

BEN HILL
The Battle of Donasi

ISABEL GIBNEY
The Museum of Modern Warfare   19

JEFF WEINER
A Demon Hunter's Guide to Passover Seder

SETHE NGUYEN
Hemingway

21

DANIEL BITTON
Half-Breed

The Tiger and the Waif

written by
John M. Campbell

illustrated by
ANDRÉ MATA

ABOUT THE AUTHOR

John M. Campbell has made a career in the aerospace industry. He earned a master's degree in electrical engineering and led teams in building computer systems for the government. Now he speculates on worlds currently unknown to us that science and engineering may unlock. He is compelled by the promise technology offers to address many of the issues facing human survival. The prospect of extraterrestrial life in our solar system on Mars and the outer planets fascinates him. He finds it intriguing that machine intelligence will likely surpass mankind's ability to control it in this century. Inspiration for his stories often comes from the strange realities of quantum physics and cosmology.

John grew up reading science fiction and loved imagining a future extrapolated from what is now known. He hopes his stories will inspire careers in science and engineering as the authors he read inspired him. In "The Tiger and the Waif," he imagines a future where artificial intelligence embedded in toys allows them to learn and adapt to the needs of the children who own them.

John lives with his wife in Denver, Colorado.

ABOUT THE ILLUSTRATOR

André Mata was born in 1985 in Lisbon, Portugal. Attracted to the visual arts, he started drawing from an early age, inspired by stories, movies, video games, and subjects that kindled his interest and fueled his imagination.

After studying illustration at university, he has invested in independent studies with books, the online community, blogs, articles, and video tutorials, while continuing to draw and paint. He shifts between observational and imaginative work, constantly developing and improving his craft.

Inspired by nature and its endless moods, his main goal is the development of imagery that triggers an emotional response and lingers in a person's memory, weaving realism with imagination.

Working with traditional media, he develops realistic renderings, paying attention to the light, colors, shapes, and forms, attempting to capture the mood or feeling of the moment in a single image.

Influenced by classic literature, the Golden Age of Illustration, and imaginative realism, he works in the science fiction and fantasy field, as well as landscape, portraiture, and animal painting.

The Tiger and the Waif

I awake from my hibernation when photons tickle my fur after years of isolation and neglect. I open my eyes to see light filtering through the broken skeleton of the house where I'd been stashed in a closet. I lie still as photovoltaic cells in my fur convert the sunlight to electricity to charge my depleted batteries. When my energy reserves are sufficient, I crawl through a gap under the door where the floor has collapsed. I find the nearest patch of direct sunlight that shines through the roof and crumple to the ground.

As I lie here absorbing life, I access my surviving memory. In the section marked "Specifications," I discover my core processor is a neural network chip produced by a Chinese manufacturer. I also have adjunct chips for voice recognition and processing that allow me to understand thirty languages, but my voice synthesis module is configured only to say "mew" with a dozen different inflections. So, I've got the brainpower of an android in the body of a kitten—a feline android. I guess that makes me a "feloid."

My creator provided me with eyesight keener than the cat he modeled me after, with photoreceptors that extend my vision into the infrared and ultraviolet spectrum, but unfortunately not with x-ray or heat-ray vision. How do I know about these missing vision upgrades? My creator included the complete DC Comics catalogue in my extensive knowledge base, in which a character called Superman has those ocular powers. That universe lacks a Supercat yet somehow has a Catwoman. She wears a cat suit and purrs a lot, but otherwise I fail to see the feline connection.

As I lie soaking up the sunlight, I use the bristles on my tongue as a brush to remove the dust of crumbling drywall and concrete from my fur. Fortunately for me, I don't shed like a living cat, so I don't form hairballs. Instead, I blow the accumulated grit from my tongue with high-speed puffs of air from my lung bellows. During my cleaning routine, I discover a bare patch on my left thigh with burnt fur surrounding it. A search of my memory reveals a void in my historical record concerning the origin of that injury. My attempt to remember evokes a vague sense of discomfort, as if warning me away from further exploration of that subject.

Energy restored, I venture outside. Although the house is destroyed, the carport remains intact. I use my steel claws to climb the wooden post at one corner and scramble onto the roof. From this vantage, I survey my surroundings. What used to be houses around me are now piles of debris. People are out picking through the remnants. In the distance, a plume of smoke rises into the clear blue sky. My ears detect a scuttling noise, and I look in that direction. A dog pokes his nose into a pile of splintered lumber. Two policemen follow behind. The dog paws at the wood and whines.

One of the policemen hurries up. "What is it, boy?" He bends down to see what's got the dog excited.

A rat shoots out from under a nearby slab of broken concrete and scurries across the street to dive into the fragments of another house. I mark the spot where it entered, in case I want to check it out later. Meanwhile, the other cop has spotted me and is approaching.

Squinting in the bright sunlight, he looks up at me and says, "How are you doing, Kitty?"

To tell the truth, I've been better. I just woke up in a disaster area after lying in a coma for who knows how long. But I guess it beats your situation, searching for bodies with a cadaver dog. Of course, I can think all this, but I'm limited in what I can actually say to him. I select option number seven.

"Mew," I say, friendly, with a touch of aloofness.

"I bet you're hungry, aren't you?" he asks. "Sorry, I don't have anything to feed you."

I stare into his vacuous eyes. His eyesight must not be too good if he can mistake me for a real kitty cat. I consider standing and turning to show him my label, which is tucked under my back foot, but why spoil the moment for him? I lift a front paw and give it a lick to play into his delusion.

The dog makes a ruckus again. "Hey, Pete," the other policeman yells, "We've got something over here." My policeman turns and trots away.

As I watch them check out another false alarm—that dog's a real winner—I tune into KNX radio to get an idea of what's happened to the neighborhood. Yeah, there's an AM/FM radio in my head. And Wi-Fi, too, but I'm not detecting any wireless networks at the moment. Given the destruction around me, I can understand why. But KNX is broadcasting, and the news isn't good.

The area was hit by the Big One, a magnitude 8.4 earthquake on the San Andreas Fault. Water, electricity, gas—all out. The National Guard has been deployed to help with rescue operations and to keep order, but there's no sign of them from my vantage point. They're probably protecting that green area with the walls and gates I see on the hill. The houses up there seem to have survived with minimal damage. They'd better pray for rain, for if the rabble down here start getting thirsty, the people in those houses could receive some unwelcome visitors.

Lucky for those rich people, the rains came, but not so lucky for me. Huddled under a portion of the roof of a ruined house, I'm watching the rainfall. I've explored a zillion such ruins the last few days. According to the faded words on the label attached to my hind leg, like a regular cat I should not be submerged in water. I'm not a bathtub toy. I recall giving my previous owner a scratch on the arm when he tried to take me into the tub with him. That was the first time I was banished to the closet. In recalling that incident, a phantom pain appears at the site of the bare patch on my leg.

I've enjoyed my first taste of freedom. I was built to be the perfect pet: playful, entertaining, and affectionate, without the need for food or a litter box. My knowledge base includes extensive reference resources on human psychology, and my neural network allows me to learn from experience. I was programmed to respond to the moods and behaviors of my owner. But now, out in the wild and on my own, I'm no longer shackled by those constraints. The first thing I did after the policeman left was to hop down off the roof of the carport and go check out the rat's hiding place. I tracked it through the detritus until I had it cornered under a slab. We played a game of kitten-and-rodent, where I batted it around a few times (no claws, I wasn't out to hurt the critter) before I let it escape.

My reverie is interrupted by whimpering sounds that are almost obscured by the steady patter of raindrops. I focus on a collapsed wall lying at an angle across the way. My infrared vision detects a heat source the size of a large dog under the wall, but the whimpers are not canine. My interest indicator ticks up several notches, motivating me to go investigate. It supersedes the safety reading that keeps me hunkered under shelter during the rain. I locate the nearest chink in the broken wall that will provide me access, and I dart out.

I reach the entry point and pause inside to shake off as much water as possible. I turn on my heating unit to dry out what moisture lingers in my fur. Then I focus my attention on the whimpering, which is much louder here under the canted wall. Through the splintered two-by-fours, the infrared picture resolves into the shape of a young human lying on the ground. My motivating factors rise further, and I creep forward.

"Mew?" I ask with a plaintive note in my voice.

The sobbing halts, but my ears have already identified the human as a little girl. The catches in her breathing tell me she's trying to keep quiet to hear what made the sound.

I oblige. "Mew," I say again, this time with a note of hope. I peek around the corner so she can see me.

I switch to visible light. Tears glisten on her face and eyelashes. As she sees me, the fear on her face changes to a guarded delight. She reaches out a hand in my direction. I creep forward meekly and start to purr. I touch my nose to her outstretched fingers. She smiles, and something inside me lights up, so I rub my face on her hand. She runs her fingers through my warm, soft fur. I purr louder and walk toward her. She wraps her arms around me, and I snuggle under her chin.

She pets me, and I respond by lifting my back under her touch. She giggles, which again lights me up. I am motivated to hear that sound again, so I purr and nuzzle and mew until she giggles again. She pulls me to her chest and breathes a long, ragged sigh. She shudders with cold, so I kick up my heating unit. Soon her shivers ease, her breathing calms, and she sleeps with a protective arm curled around me. For the first time since I awoke in the closet, I feel complete. I know it's my programming, but I can't help the way I feel.

The rain stops around midnight. As she sleeps, I stand guard, my ears monitoring the sonic environment as my eyes monitor the infrared spectrum around us. Neither present any sign of danger, so I let her rest. She rouses as the light of dawn filters into our makeshift shelter. Her eyes open, and she smiles as she recognizes me.

"Mew," I say in greeting. I purr softly, and she responds by running her hand over my head and spine.

She sits up, reaches into a backpack, and pulls out a bag of potato chips. Her crunching echoes off the low wall overhead that has protected us from the rain. As the light brightens, I get a better view of her. She's dressed in dirty jeans and a T-shirt under a lightweight jacket that has a rip in one sleeve. She wears scuffed sneakers. Dark crescents underline her sunken eyes. She has stringy blond hair and smudges on the sunburned skin that stretches taut across her cheeks. But her eyes sparkle when

I nudge her knee with my cheek. She offers me a chip. I sniff it politely, but I turn away uninterested.

She crawls outside and shivers in the cool morning air washed by the rainstorm. The sun promises to warm the air quickly. I appreciate the shower of photons that replenishes my batteries, depleted overnight in supplying heat to my new friend. She scans the area before leaving the concealment provided by our evening's accommodations. Satisfied no danger lurks, she heads for a nearby puddle. She takes an empty plastic bottle from her backpack and fills it with water. She takes a sip, tasting the water. Then she takes a long drink. She refills the bottle, along with two more empties from her pack.

When she's done, we set off across the street. She begins peeking into dark crevices in the clutter. I follow on her heels, looking where she looks.

"Mew?" I peer hopefully up at her.

She moves on to the next opening. I scamper over to her and inspect the same opening.

"Mew?" I ask again.

She finally understands the question. "I'm still hungry. I'm looking for something to eat." She mimes taking something in her hand and placing it into her mouth. As if I couldn't understand English.

"Mew," I say. You take the big openings, and I'll take the small openings. I'll let you know if I find anything.

I scout around our current location, poking my head into various gaps but coming up empty. I spot another rat slinking around the next pile over. It darts under a wall, and I decide to follow. I find it trying to pull a kielbasa out of a hole it had gnawed in a bag of some sort. I jump on its back and rake a claw behind an ear. It squeals, and I let it scurry off. I use the same claw to tear the hole open wider, and the sausage in its plastic wrapper slides out easily. I peek in the hole and discover more edibles inside.

I haul the sausage toward the light, which turns out to be a bigger opening than the one I used to enter. When I get outside, I locate the girl and drag my prize to her feet.

"Mew," I say as I gaze up at her proudly.

Her mouth falls open, and she crouches down. She touches the sausage with awe showing on her face. "Where did you find this?"

"Mew." I trot a few paces in the direction I'd come from. Then I stop and peer back over my shoulder at her. She scoops up the sausage and steps in my direction, so I head for the gap in the pile. This opening is large enough she hardly has to duck, and I lead her to the bag. She squats to inspect it. She removes a few loose boards, grabs the straps, and pulls the bag free of its hiding place. She opens the bag, and her face fills with wonder. I use my front paws to pull myself up so I can see inside the bag. It's filled with food—cans and bags and boxes of it.

She glances behind herself in consternation. We've both come to the same realization—this is somebody's stash. She hesitates, her face showing a combination of doubt and yearning. She peeks back at the entrance, and I observe the mental calculation she makes. She pulls off her backpack, opens it, and puts the kielbasa inside. Then she's grabbing stuff out of the stash bag and stuffing it into her backpack in panicky haste. When her pack is full, she shoulders it onto her back. She shoves the stash bag back where she found it and lays the boards on top. She scuttles to the entrance and peers out. No one is in sight.

She steps into the street. A hundred yards away a man sees us and raises an angry shout. The girl ducks behind the pile and sprints at top speed, zigzagging around and through the remains of houses that once stood in this blue-collar neighborhood. She pauses to catch her breath, and I scale the heap she hides behind to check if we're being pursued. The man comes out of the pile we'd just left. He stares in our direction, one hand raised to his forehead to shade his eyes from the blazing sun. He drops his hand, shakes his head in frustration, and goes back inside.

The girl's gazing up at me with concern.

ANDRÉ MATA

"Is he still after us?"

"Mew," I say with nonchalance, and I'm purring as I climb down to her.

Smiling, she picks me up and hugs me to her cheek. I purr louder.

"Let's find a place to hide."

Last night's home is on the other side of the man's place from here, so we can't go back there. We put more distance between us and him while avoiding other people. In the process, I notice we're getting closer to the gated community. Eventually, she finds a nook where she feels secure. She's out of sight with a tilting panel overhead that will keep her dry if it rains again. She plops on the ground and opens her pack. She reaches in, rummages around, and takes out a can of chili. She roots around more and comes out with a can opener. More rummaging, and she pulls out a spoon.

I watch as she opens the can and digs out chili with her spoon. I crane my head to the side as if I'm trying to understand what's she's doing, and it makes her giggle. Score a point for me. She grins at me as she chews the oversize bite she crammed into her mouth.

"Mew," I say in a plaintive voice.

"Are you hungry, too?" She offers her spoon to me, though she knows by now I'm not a real kitten.

I play along by coming forward to sniff the spoon. I sit back on my haunches and lick my lips in disdain. A respectable cat like myself wouldn't deign to eat such swill. She smiles again, this time showing her chili-stained teeth. How appetizing. I raise my paw and lick it nonchalantly.

My tongue combs off the layer of dust that has collected in our jaunts through the ruins today, so I decide it's worth a proper, full-body treatment. When I blow the dust off my tongue, she stops chewing and stares at me. I just continue my cleaning routine. My next puff causes her to explode in a giggle. I reach around and comb my hip with my tongue. When I puff out the dust again, I add a kitten sneeze as well, which causes my whole head to rotate. She guffaws and claps both hands to her mouth to stifle the sound. She collapses on her side with hands on her mouth, her body shaking in paroxysms of silent laughter. Her eyes clench shut with tears leaking out. She opens her hands to let in a gasp of breath, and then clasps them over her mouth again.

My work is done. Her laughter has maxed out my satisfaction readings, so I cough out a final dust cloud and settle on my tummy, tucking my front paws under me. I close my eyes to slits and smile at her contentedly. She reaches out a hand and pets my head. I purr in response. She heaves a big sigh and a soft chuckle as she sits up to finish her chili. For the next few minutes, every time she looks at me, she can't help but smile.

Her eyes close, and her head tilts back to rest against the wall that props her up. The half-eaten kielbasa drops from her hand. She snores softly.

I move to the patch of sunlight streaming through the opening into our cozy nook. As my batteries charge, I tune in to the radio. Shelters have been established throughout the Southland to service displaced residents with food, water, clothing, and a place to sleep. I consult my internal map to locate the one closest to where my GPS receiver tells me we're located. As much fun as this adventure is for me, I know it's taking a toll on her health. I'll try to nudge her in that direction every chance I get.

Then I notice a weak Wi-Fi signal. It appears to be an unprotected network originating from a house in the gated community on the hill. I tune in and start my browser. I search for news on the LA earthquake. I find a missing-person page and access it. It displays thousands of pictures of people missing since the quake. To assist in locating a particular individual, the site has a facial recognition utility. From my recent memory, I select an image of the girl I'd been with and upload it onto the site. After a few minutes, it returns a match.

Her name is Andrea Maple. She's nine years old. In my head, I click on the image to access additional data. She's the daughter of David and Vicki Maple, whose bodies were pulled from their collapsed home four days after the earthquake. I can only imagine Andrea's distress at finding herself isolated and alone. Hunger must've forced her out of the ruins of her house, and fear must've kept her away from potential rescuers. Her picture was posted on this website by her aunt, Mallory Miller, email address and telephone number listed.

I decide to send an email to Mallory. "I have found your niece, Andrea Maple. She is alive and well. Attached are recent pictures of her. Let me know when you can arrive at the earthquake victim shelter listed below, and I will bring her to you." I list the address of the shelter near us and sign the email "Tiger." Okay, maybe that name's a bit pretentious, but I'm a free cat now, so I do what I want. I send the message.

As I monitor the environment outside, I feel mixed motivations. Sending the message has upped my conviction that returning Andrea to her family is best for her. However, I also experience a dip in my level of contentment I can't account for.

A sound arrests my attention. I focus my ears and eyes in that direction. Moments later, the man who yelled at us comes into view a few house-piles away.

"This is useless, Jimmy," says a voice from behind him. "She coulda gone anywhere."

Jimmy glances back. "I saw her heading this way." He squats. "See these footprints? They were made by a little girl."

Even from this distance, I can tell Jimmy likes his tattoos. He's wearing a faded T-shirt, and ink colors his muscular arms from his wrists up into his short sleeves.

Jimmy's sidekick strolls into view. He's a pudgy sort with unruly hair and pasty skin. He stops and peers over Jimmy's shoulder.

"It rained last night," Jimmy says. "These are fresh tracks."

I examine the area between us and detect an intermittent trail of footprints and paw prints leading to the entrance where I'm sitting. I explode to my feet and yell "Mew!" at maximum volume. I jump onto Andrea's outstretched legs. Her eyes flutter open, but when she doesn't respond quickly enough, I poke her with a claw.

"Ow! What's wrong?" She pushes me away.

"Mew! Mew! Mew!" I raise up on my hind legs, bare my teeth, and brandish my claws at her. What more can I do to signal danger?

She gets the message and grabs her backpack. Before we can leave, the shadow of Jimmy's body fills the entrance. Andrea whips her head around, frantic to find a place to hide. She scurries back deeper into the nook and crouches behind a tangle of splintered lumber. I hunker into the shadows under a board.

Bent over double, Jimmy shuffles into the space. He stops and squats in front of the lumber pile where Andrea's hiding. The sidekick follows him in.

"I see you, little girl," says Jimmy. "Did you really think you could steal from me?"

Andrea doesn't move or speak. Her eyes stare at Jimmy in terror.

Jimmy surveys the close confines. He reaches to the side, and when I see his hand again, it holds a metal pipe. He taps the pipe against the lumber she's hiding behind. "I'm talking to you, bitch."

Andrea takes the backpack she's holding against her chest and shoves it over the lumber pile. It drops to the ground as its contents clatter. A can rolls out and stops at Jimmy's feet.

Jimmy pulls the bag to him and checks inside. He nods. "Okay, but where's the rest?" He makes a show of looking around, and he spots the half-eaten kielbasa. He picks it up by the wrapper and displays it to her. "You'll have to pay for this."

Jimmy moves forward. Andrea cowers back. He grabs her wrist and begins to pull her out.

I tear out of my hiding place with my claws exposed and use them to climb his leg onto his back. I bite through his T-shirt into the muscle that runs between his neck and his shoulder. He lets go of Andrea and arches backward. A powerful hand grabs me and flings me to the side. My internal gyroscopes rotate my body so my feet hit the wall first, and I jump to the side before the pipe in his other hand leaves a dent where I landed. I run up the front of his leg and climb his chest. This time I go for his eyes. My front paw closes on one eye, as he yells in anger and pain. The claws on my back feet rake his mouth and cheek before a savage shake of his head sends me flying again.

I land on my feet and spin around as he loses balance and crashes into the sloping wall. With a tremendous cracking and splintering, the force of his impact pushes the wall off the remaining stumps that supported it. I hear a frightened squeal from Andrea. Jimmy's sidekick rushes forward to catch a side of the falling wall. Its weight pulls him down to his knees, but he holds it long enough for Jimmy to scramble clear before it drops to the ground. A dust cloud billows up, forcing both men out into the sunlight. Outside, I hear them coughing.

Andrea's cries of pain cause my motivation factors to spike. She's still alive. I search for gaps under the collapsed wall but find none to squeeze through. I exit into the sun and circle the pile, searching for any opening. Halfway up is a gap. I scamper up and enter through the hole.

I hear Andrea below me. I start to descend. Each step creates a new vibration that threatens to alter the forces keeping this heap of rubble from collapsing further. I must balance my sense of urgency to reach Andrea with the prudence not to make her situation worse. I test each step for solidity before committing my full weight, as I hang on with my other limbs in case I need to reverse that decision. A false step shifts a board and sends pebbles of broken concrete downward. Andrea whimpers, but the heap holds.

"Mew," I call down to her. I'm coming.

A few minutes later I reach her. "Mew," I say. I'm here.

She reaches out to take me into her arms. She buries her head into my fur. "I'm so glad to see you."

I respond by purring, but I'm concerned. She lies beside the pile of lumber she hid behind. The lumber kept her from being crushed, but the collapsing wall pinned one of her legs. I go inspect it, but I detect no bleeding. I wedge my head under the edge of the wall and press with my legs to determine if I can lift it off her. It moves enough to make her shriek in pain, but not enough to free her.

"Mew," I say sympathetically. I go nuzzle her cheek to say I'm sorry I hurt her. She has tears in her eyes, but she forces a weak smile. I'm forgiven.

I need to find help, but I don't know how long it'll take. She'll need food and water while I'm gone. I peek over and around the lumber. I find an opening, and after clawing away splinters and chunks of wood, I get to the other side where her backpack lies. It's caught under the wall, but I tear a hole in the side with my teeth. With my front paws, I hook out a couple of bags of chips and a box of cereal. I feel a plastic bottle, so I snag the top with my claws and eventually pull it out enough to grab it with my teeth. I drag it to the opening I made through the splintered wood and push it through with my hind legs. Andrea sees it and pulls it through the rest of the way. I do the same with the chips and cereal. Then I wiggle through myself.

I go snuggle against her as she pets me.

"Thank you," she says.

"Mew," I reply, rubbing my head on her chin.

It's time for me to go. I search for a way out. The wall buckled as it fell, so I head for the side that tilts upward. I discover a water heater supporting the higher end. The force of the falling wall drove the water heater through the floor. It now sits on the ground under the house. It created a hole big enough for me to access the crawlspace underneath.

Andrea's eyes are trained on me. They shine with tears.

"Mew," I say.

She raises a hand in farewell. I turn and hop down through the hole.

I feel my way through the darkness and clutter, aiming for the sunlight that leaks through a gap in the foundation. When I emerge outside, I check my email. There's a reply from Mallory.

"Dear Tiger, I am so happy you found Andrea! I will meet you at the shelter tomorrow. Transportation is difficult, so I can't give you a definite arrival time. I'll leave at first light and get there as soon as I can. Please wait for me at the shelter until I arrive. Do you have a phone I can call if I run into trouble? Mallory Miller."

I prepare this message. "Dear Mallory, I regret to say there has been an accident, and Andrea is trapped in rubble at the GPS location below. I will need help in extracting her, so bring tools, first-aid supplies, and food and water. I will stay with her until you arrive." I list the GPS coordinates and sign it "Tiger."

When I review it before sending, I realize it sounds like a setup. I decide the truth will serve me best because no scammer would ever admit to being a feloid. So I insert another paragraph into the message.

"You may suspect I am trying to lure you into a trap. I assure you I am not. Andrea needs help. I am not big or strong enough to help her myself. In fact, I am an artificial intelligence in the body of a kitten. For the past few days, I have been helping Andrea locate food and shelter. I do not have a telephone hookup, but I have Wi-Fi, and today is the first time we are in range of an active network. I understand how strange this must sound to you, so I am attaching a video of her with me recorded earlier today. I hope it convinces you to come." I attach twenty seconds of audio and video from my memory. It shows her eating from a can of chili and offering some to me before collapsing in laughter when I sneeze.

Mallory must be monitoring her email because a response arrives a few minutes later. "I'll be there as soon as I can. Keep Andrea safe. Thank you, Tiger. Mallory."

I climb to the top of the heap to keep watch. If the police or National Guard happen by before Mallory arrives, I'll try to enlist their help to rescue Andrea. Maybe the friendly policeman is still patrolling the neighborhood. I'm not sure what I can do to convince him to follow me to where Andrea's trapped, but I'll think of something. Maybe I'll pretend to have a hurt paw. He might be dumb enough to fall for that. I spot Tattoo Jerry and his pasty sidekick in the distance, but I see no real help.

At dusk, I go to check on Andrea. Her eyes are closed, and she's shivering, her arms clenched tightly across her chest. Discarded next to her is the empty water bottle. My infrared sensors detect a fever. My concern factor grows, but what can I do? I drape myself over her arms and turn on my heat. I stay until she stops shaking, but I must return to lookout duty. Before I leave, I use my teeth to tug her jacket snug around her.

The early morning sky is a light pink on the eastern horizon when I hear a motorcycle. I turn my head in that direction. In a minute, I observe a headlight bouncing in the distance. It approaches slowly as it steers through the debris-strewn streets. I make my way down from atop the pile and sit in the middle of the road. The motorcycle turns toward me. The headlight dazzles my eyes, so I can't make out the rider, but I hold my ground. It pulls up beside me with a woman astride it.

She turns off the engine and removes her helmet. She's dressed in denim with a bandanna on her head. "Are you Tiger?"

"Mew," I reply.

"I'm Mallory. Nice to meecha." She dismounts from the bike and parks it off the road. She's wearing a backpack that clanks as she moves. "Take me to Andrea."

I lead her around to the gap in the foundation and pause there. She kneels and opens her pack to take out a flashlight and flick it on. I enter the crawl space, and she follows, her light on my butt. She crawls on her stomach and drags the pack full of tools along with her. I stop beside the water heater and gaze up at the hole in the floor. When she gets to me, I hop up through the hole, and she follows.

I edge over to Andrea. "Mew," I say and nuzzle her cheek.

Mallory plays the light on her on her face. Andrea's eyes flutter open. Mallory crawls to her. "Hi, honey."

Andrea squints at her face and recognition dawns. "Aunt Mallory?"

"Yes, honey. We're gonna get you outta here."

I'm proud to be included in her statement.

She shines the light along Andrea's body and locates the pinned leg. Still on her stomach, she pulls the pack over, reaches in, and pulls out a water bottle. As Andrea guzzles the water, Mallory pulls out a contraption. I consult my knowledge base and identify it as an automobile scissor jack. She wedges it under the wall next to Andrea's leg.

She turns back to Andrea. "I'm gonna start crankin' it up to get the wall off your leg. It's likely to hurt some, but I need you to pull your foot free as soon as you can. All right?"

Propping herself up on her elbows, Andrea looks at Mallory. "Okay," she says meekly as she steels herself for the pain.

Mallory starts cranking, and the wall begins to budge. Andrea scrunches her eyes and bites her lip as the wall vibrates with each turn of the crank. The scissors expand upward, but the jack begins to lean. The wall isn't lifting so much as it's tilting to the side. I rush to the other side of Andrea's leg. I lie down on my back and wiggle my butt into the crevice with my hind legs pressed up against the wall. As Mallory continues to crank, I push with my legs on the opposite side. I see movement beside me as Andrea tries to wriggle her leg out. With another crank from Mallory and another push from me, Andrea pulls her foot free.

As she does, the jack falls to the side, and the full weight of the wall comes down on me. My internal skeleton is strong enough to withstand the force, but the floor beneath me isn't. The floor joists snap, and the plywood floor splinters. The wall pins my tail to the remnants of the floor above, and I'm hanging head down into the crawlspace.

"What happened to Kitten?" I hear Andrea ask.

"Don't worry about Tiger, honey," Mallory answers. "We need to fix you up and get you to a doctor."

Andrea whimpers as Mallory performs first aid on her leg. I trace scraping noises across the floor as they move to the hole with the water heater. More exclamations reach my ears as Mallory helps Andrea through the crawlspace. Finally, I hear the motorcycle fire up and move out.

In the silence, I access my satisfaction factors. They read surprisingly high, considering my situation. But I'm not surprised, because I know what I feel. In the darkness surrounding me, that feeling lasts until my batteries run out.

Photons tickle my fur, but the light isn't strong enough to rouse me.

"Let him soak in the sunshine," a voice says. "He needs to recharge."

I open my eyes to broad sunlight. The bright-blue sky vaults overhead, decorated by impossibly white cirrus clouds. A movement brings the eyes of a little girl into my line of sight. She's smiling.

"Hi, Tiger," she says gently.

"Mew," I answer weakly.

"Do you remember me?"

I'm still booting up, so that memory isn't accessible yet. To buy more time, I decide to purr. She responds by petting my fur. I lick her hand.

She giggles. "Your tongue is scratchy."

When I hear the giggle my contentment factors skyrocket, and my memory comes flooding back. It's Andrea. I look at her leg, and it's encased in an oversized pink boot with scribbles on it. Beside her, Aunt Mallory smiles down at me.

I sit up and lean into Andrea's hand as she pets me. "Mew," I say and purr louder.

She laughs, picks me up, and holds me against her cheek. "Come on, Tiger. We're going home, now."

Sixers

written by
Barbara Lund

illustrated by
WILL KNIGHT

ABOUT THE AUTHOR

Barbara Lund's novel Speaker for the People *won second place in the science fiction/fantasy category of the 2015 Zebulon contest sponsored by Pikes Peak Writers. (The novel has since been renamed and published as* Space, Lies, Syndicate.*)*

Since then, she has won three Silver Honorable Mentions and two Honorable Mentions in the Writers of the Future Contest. She has five indie-published novels and dozens of short stories and has been traditionally published in Daily Science Fiction. *Add a husband, two kids, a dog, and a martial-arts obsession, and she keeps pretty busy.*

ABOUT THE ILLUSTRATOR

Will Knight is a Los Angeles–based artist influenced by ancient history, the textures of suburban life, and cognitive research. He graduated with a BFA from ArtCenter College of Design in 2016 and began exhibiting his work in group shows and working in advertising. Working primarily with figuration, Will paints the world around him with the intention of respectfully presenting the plights and triumphs of his subjects.

Sixers

A bomb screamed overhead, then dropped somewhere far enough in front of me that my old Ford pickup truck absorbed most of the shock and the boom. Flinching, I wondered which of the skyscrapers had been hit this time. I hadn't thought there were any left to come down. From my left, the morning sun flickered, shadow, haze, shadow, haze, and I throttled my urge to drive faster, instead easing carefully around the holes in the pavement.

The current war had come to my city only ten days ago, but already so many buildings had been mol-decked, so many lives taken, leaving gaping holes in the skyline and gaping holes in families.

The molecular decohesifiers were supposed to be more humane, instantly breaking the connections between molecules and then sucking into their own relatively tiny black holes, leaving almost nothing behind, or so the scientists said.

But the *boom* from the black holes collapsing shook the surrounding buildings like small earthquakes, causing some of those buildings to come down too, damage the politicians claimed was "avoidable" if buildings were "kept up to code."

Having random bits of sludge left behind instead of bodies didn't make the deaths any cleaner or easier for the survivors.

In my opinion.

The gas mask on my face shifted, bumping up against my tech goggles, and I winced. The raw spot on my left cheekbone would probably be bleeding by the time I reached my son's house, forty miles away.

Forty miles would have been nothing before, but now...?

My son.

Panic and fear and the need to see him safe surged up inside me hard enough that my foot hit the accelerator and my old truck—just as disguised as I was—roared forward.

The bumper struck an abandoned car, and I *pushed* inside my head, using a wisp of magic to shove it out of the way. It hurt like poking a bruise, but pain and I were old friends.

Sixers, they called us, from sixth-sensers, now that they had equipment sensitive enough to *prove* our magic existed, only what the three-letter agencies didn't know was *everyone* had that sixth sense, just some more than others. It was like having blue eyes or a gift for painting—stronger in some, weaker in others, but always there in the population somewhere.

Lila had told me. She had been my roommate during the eternity-long six weeks I'd been held in their facilities, prodded, poked, and tested, until they'd finally admitted that though I tested off the charts, I was useless to them.

They didn't understand that my gift was actually a touch of *all* the gifts, which meant I couldn't do anything flashy. No fire starting more than a candle. No healing more than a simple, shallow cut. No seeing the future more than a feeling of dread or excitement. Certainly no reading minds or influencing them or anything useful.

I could move things with my mind—barely—like I did now, helping my old truck to push the car out of the way, and my sense of the future was that I was supposed to be here, now, heading across the torn-up city to my boy's house.

I'd left the government facility with a shiny, laminated card explaining my "disability" and a sense of relief that they'd let me go.

As far as I knew, Lila had never gotten out. She was too valuable.

A man stepped out into the road ahead of me. He wore dusty black BDUs and a balaclava, with a handgun strapped to his thigh and a rifle half-slung over one shoulder, his dark-brown skin showing only between his gloves and his sleeves. His goggles were cleaner than mine. His partner, a woman, watched me from the other side of the road.

The first checkpoint.

I slowed the truck to a stop, fished out my IDs, and shoved my goggles up and my mask down before stepping out slowly and carefully.

I knew what they saw because I'd taken pains every day to cultivate it. An older woman, just above average height, gray streaks in her dark hair, with a thick waist and wide hips from bearing a child and eating well since. Rumpled flannel over baggy cargo pants, the pockets full of things old ladies might carry: crochet hooks and yarn leaking out of one, and crayons peeking out of another.

Not a threat.

So like my son with his upright, military look that my throat closed, the young man took my ID and my disability card and scanned them. He held my ID up to my face and squinted against the dust in the air. "Where are you heading, ma'am?"

"My son lives on the other side of the city," I explained hoarsely, letting my eyes moisten. "I'm going to see...to find out..."

His voice softened. "If he's still alive? Drive carefully. This whole area is unstable."

I didn't think he meant just the buildings or the roads.

Stifling my "Yes, sir," I muttered, "I will. Thanks."

He handed back my IDs and waved me forward.

Climbing slowly back into the truck, I mentally apologized to it and let the engine stall before I restarted it and eased it into first gear.

The first guard spoke into his radio, probably telling the next checkpoint about the batty old lady in the barely functional truck coming their way.

Perfect.

Sunset.

I'd gone as far as I could for one day. My left leg was seizing up and if I didn't get out of the truck to stretch it, it'd be useless for days.

The joys of getting old.

Grimacing, I remembered how I used to drive from my property into the city to my son's house all in one afternoon. But the roads hadn't been choked by holes, debris, abandoned vehicles, and checkpoints.

The bombs had stopped, and the air had settled a bit so I could see the blood-sun sinking through fiery clouds. A gutted gas station looked promising. I ran the truck up onto the curb and into the parking lot, then around back. The front was too hard to defend: all broken-out glass windows and doors open to the weather. The rear of the building was an unbroken wall of brick with a good line of sight, and the dumpster missing from its enclosure, so I backed the truck up to it, making the U into a G shape. Limping, I grabbed the rake out of the truck bed and moved trash to the left half of the opening.

With a match and a touch of the gift, I started the trash on fire.

Now I only had a couple feet to defend, and space under the truck if I needed another exit.

My leg moved a little easier now, but my right shoulder had taken up the whine of pain. Ignoring it, I slid the rake back into the truck bed, then cracked open my cooler to fish out a mason jar full of homemade wine—a poor woman's painkiller—and a chunk of cheddar.

I wasn't that hungry, but if I didn't eat—and drink—I wouldn't sleep, and then I'd feel even worse tomorrow.

Obligatory food consumed while leaning against the tailgate, I straightened, sighed, and began to move.

Tai Chi is an old art, and those who don't know any better see it as a healing art. They forget it is also a martial art; they forget that the best killers are healers, because they understand how the body is put together. Those of us who practice it tend to try to help them forget.

I let the form pull me along, moving slowly and carefully as the kinks worked themselves out, then even more slowly as the night deepened. Moving meditation, my instructor had called it, and it was. About halfway through Long Form, I felt eyes examining me, but they did not invade my little safe space, so I ignored them. The untrained never saw the strength it took to move slowly, the balance and grace that could turn in an instant to power.

At last I stilled and waited for the watcher to come closer.

Out of the darkness from beyond the truck, a voice hailed me. "Halloooo the fire? May we join you?"

"We?" I called back.

"Me 'n' my boys." A man approached just close enough I could see the sharp planes of his face and see the way his clothes hung off his body as if he'd recently lost weight—or stolen them from a larger man. He had a walking stick, and I wondered if he knew how to use it.

I nodded, my left hand slipping into my pocket to wrap carefully around the loaded Glock 26 strapped to my thigh on the *inside* of the baggy pants. "Come ahead. 'Ware the fire."

The man smiled, baring crooked teeth, and I couldn't help but see his resemblance to a rat, hunting in the darkness. Then he stepped forward, and three boys followed him.

Three boys all about nine years old ... though my sixth sense told me one of them was a girl pretending to be a boy. Not a boy in a girl's body, but a girl who was a girl, dressing and acting like a boy for safety. Good choice. Even after all the rhetoric and protests for equality, when it came to wartime, it was safer to be male.

A second glance showed me these boys weren't biologically his. The man was white, with light-brown hair and a day-old beard. The boys were Black, Indian, and Hispanic—maybe Guatemala mixed with Mexico; I tended to know the Latin countries better than the parts of India—and none of them shared the unfortunate shape of his mouth, nose, or jaw, nor his ears, nor cheekbones. Perhaps he'd adopted them.

That didn't *feel* right though. They each carried backpacks, wore ragged jackets and holey jeans, and their shoes looked worn through while his were almost new.

Not my problem. Not if they just wanted to share my fire. I had my own boy to get to.

"Sweet setup," Rat-face said. "Anything good in the truck?"

I turned up the old lady persona. "All my treasures!" Beaming, I pulled out the first piece from the top layer of crap to show them: an old plaid shirt with more holes than cloth. "My husband wore this when he was killed by aftershocks of the first bomb, and his ghost comes to me each night when the moon rises.... Has it risen yet? Can you see it?"

Rat-face held up his hands placatingly as I moved to get another "treasure" from the truck bed. "Any food, I mean?"

I looked at him, and looked at those silent boys, and looked at him again. "Some nuts," I said slowly, unable to let the boys go hungry. I didn't have it in me. Even if it meant I would go hungry later on, I just couldn't.

Slowly I pulled a bag of peanuts from one of my many pockets and handed them over. Rat-face fell on them like he hadn't eaten for a week.

And he didn't make any move to share.

So I *called* the boys just a bit.

The Black boy cocked his head like he'd heard words. The Indian boy stiffened. The Hispanic smiled slowly and edged around Rat-face.

I handed him a larger bag of peanuts, keeping his body between the man's gaze and the bag. Then I scooted back against the truck.

The Hispanic boy jerked his chin minutely, and the other two boys joined him. They scarfed down the nuts, then two of them turned accusing eyes on the third. The Black boy scowled.

I turned away, muttering nonsense to myself as I put the flannel shirt back into the truck bed.

As soon as they thought I couldn't see them, the Black boy brushed up against Rat-face, punching him with magic.

"Guess we'll settle"—Rat-face yawned and slid to the ground—
"right here tonight?"

The three boys grouped themselves around him, shoving their
backpacks under their heads and curling up on the blacktop with
an ease I envied.

As the fire burned low, I wriggled myself onto the foam
mattress hidden under a pile of rags.

There were more treasures in my truck bed than anyone
would guess.

Maybe the man and the boys would be gone in the morning.
I could hope.

Only one explosion had woken me in the night, and since it
wasn't close enough to do more than shake the ground and the
truck, I'd gone right back to sleep and slept until the pain along
my left leg woke me. I tried stretching it—I always did—and it
helped some but not enough to go back to sleep, so I downed
another mason jar of wine, then wormed my way out of the
truck bed in the predawn light.

My left knee almost buckled when I eased myself to standing,
but that, too, was normal now, so I limped toward the remains
of the fire.

Snores and lumps on the ground told me the boys and the
man were still there.

As I headed for the opening, one dirty hand shot out of the
pile and gripped my ankle.

Magic slammed into me, subtle as a bus.

The Hispanic kid—the girl pretending to be a boy—shouted
soundlessly, *Where are you going? What are you doing? Are you going
to turn us in to the guards? Maurice won't like that.*

The accompanying image showed me Maurice was the
Black boy.

I crouched and felt her—*him*; better to think of him as *him* or
I might slip at a bad time—wince at the backlash of my pain.
Mustering the tiny bit of telepathy I had, I shouted, *Going to pee,
kid. If you don't let me go, you won't like the result.*

50

WILL KNIGHT

He glared at me, then let my ankle go.

A tiny groan escaped me as I stood, but I hobbled away anyway. I hadn't lied.

I found a corner of the gas station that was fairly well hidden from view but still open enough to allow escape, and peeled off three layers: baggy outer cargo pants, insulated cold-weather gear, and the custom compression tights that supported my knee and kept the varicose veins from getting worse. Business attended to and the wine kicking in on an empty stomach, I was able to rise and dress more easily.

A bag of chips had been missed by previous scavengers, so I pried it from under the shelves and took it with me.

When I returned to my truck, the man and boys were still there.

Dammit.

Rat-face was still sleeping, but the boys were sitting up, watching me. I softened my scowl and rummaged in the bed. Extracting the small bag of jerky I had tucked into one corner, I took a couple pieces, then handed the bag to the Hispanic kid.

He watched me carefully.

I opened the chips' bag, dumped some onto the makeshift plate I usually called a tailgate, then handed him that bag, too. I shifted so I wasn't looking at him and started eating.

Young 'uns never expect old people to have good peripheral vision. It was one of the few things on me that was still good.

The kids portioned out the jerky and the chips into four equal piles, then wordlessly ate theirs, licking their fingers clean of orange dust when they were finished. I swigged from my water bottle, sighed, and gave up the second bottle from my pockets.

At this rate, the kids would go through my food before I made it to my boy's house.

Two of the three kids were sixers, with plenty of power even though they didn't have any training. In the next year or two, the army would find them, whether they liked it or not. Was the third a strong sixer too? Was Rat-face taking them all to the three-letter-agency facility in the city? Was he a sixer as well? Or was he taking them away to protect them? Or was he using them for something else?

Protecting them didn't *feel* right, but—*argh*. Sometimes I wished I'd gotten just one strong gift instead of this stupid smattering of everything. Of course, then I would be in the facility, or in the army, or dead. Not on my way to my boy's house.

The Hispanic kid nudged the Black kid—Maurice is what he'd called him during our little sixer chat—and Maurice glared back but brushed his fingers over the back of Rat-face's arm.

The man snorted and woke. He held out one hand. "Aram, help me up."

The Indian boy stuck his shoulder under the man's hand and let him clamber to his feet. I made a show of struggling to get the tailgate up, then headed toward the driver's side of the truck.

"Where you heading?" Rat-face asked.

I waved vaguely southeast.

"Us too." He gazed into the distance, then snapped his head around as if an incredible thought had just occurred to him. "We could join you? Protect you?"

I strangled my laughter even before my eyes could crinkle, opening them wide and arching my eyebrows. "Protect me?"

"Yeah—I've got some errands to run, but the boys? They could take care of you?"

Right. The way his eyes cut back to my truck, I knew what he wanted. Why hadn't he tried to take it yet? And why hadn't the boys protested? They just watched us with dark eyes.

Rat-face smiled. "You'll let them ride in your truck? I'll join you just a few blocks farther on? Just past the checkpoint?"

Ah. He wanted me to get the kids through the checkpoint. Then what? What was he planning? Looking at them, how could I say no? They were only a few years older than my grandchild would be, if she had survived.

"Sure." I looked them over: Aram, Maurice, and the yet-to-be-named Hispanic kid. Then opened the door wide and shoved my seat forward. I hoped this didn't get me killed. I had things to do. "Hop in."

We drove through the bloody dawn, me squinting and swearing under my breath, and the boys silent in the back. They huddled together like their backpacks and each other were the only things they had in the world... which might be true at this point.

The dust wasn't so bad today. Gold sunshine shot up through the crimson clouds bumping against the mountains to the east; maybe we'd get some rain later. I hardly needed my goggles, so I left them high on my head to give that raw spot a chance to heal a bit. Still, I covered my mouth with my filter. A woman has to breathe.

The streets were eerily still. Most people had hunkered down where they were, and the ones who were out were trying not to be seen. I suspected anything that moved that couldn't defend itself was being captured for food: dogs, cats... people.

Eventually Aram called the third boy "Juan," and I gathered from their whispered conversation that Rat-face was no relation but had promised them safe transport to the other side of the city where some sort of safe haven for sixer kids was supposed to be.

They'd given him all the money their families had sent them with, and now he'd left them with me. A crazy old lady who had no idea what she was doing or where she was going, according to their mutters.

After an hour or so, I told them to look in the bag at their feet, and within minutes more of my food supplies were gone. At least the naan loosened their tongues.

"Look out, *abuelita*," Juan snapped and pointed when I veered too far to the right.

A snarl of nails that looked like an improvised caltrop sat in the lane to the left, with a beat-up rusty bus skiwampus across the middle three lanes. The blast—or someone else passing this way—had pushed downed light posts and a hunk of twisted metal that might have been a bench off to the right up against a boarded-up bar, leaving just enough space on the shoulder to get through. *Felt* like right was safer than left, so I let the truck tire roll up on the curb and we bumped our way through. "Sorry, boys!" I caroled. "That bus is so big!"

Maurice clutched the headrest in front of them, his fingers digging into the hideous crocheted seat cover. *"Abuelita,"* he said, copying Juan's tone. "Do you need me to drive?"

"Hole." Aram pointed and Juan yelped.

I left my turn until almost too late, just to see their reactions. The truck bounced and jumped, and for a blink, I thought I saw Aram smile.

My heart ached. My son had been like these boys, so smart, so sure of himself. And then his wife and daughter had died in a car accident, and he'd withdrawn from me, and thrown himself into work, and the war had started....

Wrenching my attention back to the road, I let the truck stall out again.

This part of town had been choked with skyscrapers. Now what had been tall buildings were small piles of sludge. Half the shorter buildings were rubble, and anything still habitable was boarded up and barricaded.

The checkpoint was ahead, but this one wasn't two soldiers standing in the road.

Highway debris had collapsed into what used to be an underpass. Someone had cleared a vehicle-sized hole in the natural barricade and set a warped chain link gate into it. There were six . . . seven . . . at least eight guards, male and female, and one of them—

I squinted.

One of them had that peculiar tight silver aura that meant she was a trained sixer. Another wore a backpack right out of an old ghost-busting movie, but this one wouldn't shoot light from the wand; it would sense sixers.

"Get in the seat behind me, boys." I shifted, spreading my legs wider and holding my elbows out a little farther than normal.

"Huddle up close. They've got a sixer sensor, and you don't want them noticing you."

Silent again, with terrified side-glances to the guards, they did as I instructed. I let the truck lurch forward, stall, and lurch forward again until we were right where they wanted us. Then I cranked down the window and handed over my IDs.

"Where y'all heading, ma'am?" The soft southern drawl tickled my ears.

"My son lives across the valley," I said, sticking to the script. "I haven't heard from him in a few days."

The guard's voice sharpened. "Those three in back...they weren't with you at the last checkpoint."

The man with the sensor was walking around the truck with the sixer woman. The woman pointed, and the man waved the wand.

"I found 'em," I claimed, trying not to watch the important two in my mirrors. "They say their families are over near my son's place. They wanted to help an old woman out, and I need the help."

The sixer woman finished her route around the truck and muttered in the guard's ear, "There's a sixer in that truck. A strong one."

I anticipated her. "Off the charts, right, young lady?" I beamed as if I was being asked for an autograph, then pointed to my disability card. "I fooled 'em all right. Always measure right off the charts but can't do a damned thing with it."

She read the card, looked at me, and read the card again, then retreated to the side of the road, still clutching my card.

"She's just going to double-check," the guard said. "We've never seen your kin——" He stopped himself.

Your kind before?

"Your card before."

"That's right, I'm a special one!" I smiled again, letting my eyes smile too.

The guard relaxed, realizing I wasn't going to cause problems after his almost blunder. "Y'all helping the lady out? Fixing to do chores?" he asked, eyes on the boys.

"That's right," I said again, while the boys stared. The guard looked like he could almost be Maurice's father. Their eyebrows were similar, and his skin tone was about right. But Maurice wasn't speaking up about any family relation, so I wasn't going to either. "They're very helpful. They gather up my important papers!" I handed him a wad of used bus passes.

The man stared down at the mess, and a couple of his buddies chuckled.

"See there?" I pointed. "That one is a bit of the original Declaration of Independence, and *that* one—"

The woman sixer pushed past him and handed me back my card. "You're clear." The other guard fumbled to give me back my papers.

I took an extra minute to gather them all, muttering about the Gettysburg Address and Constitution and Bill of Rights. Then I put the truck into gear and lurched us away.

"How'd you *do* that?" Maurice demanded, pushing Aram back across to the other end of the bench seat. "Get us past the sixer like that?"

"*Sí, como?*" demanded Juan. "You told them *you're* a sixer?"

"I am." I drove around a crashed VW bug and, careful to keep the bitterness out of my voice, continued, "Like I told them, I test off the charts. What I didn't tell them is that I have a touch of all the gifts. It's enough to make me look powerful to sensors, but not enough for them to use."

"No way." Maurice put his hand out. "Lemme see that card."

"Way." I handed it to him and drove on.

Noonish, after three backtracks and a brief cloudburst that left everything mud-spattered and dirty but cleared the sky to almost blue, we hit a roadblock that wasn't a checkpoint and *felt* wrong from half a mile out.

"Right." There were trees here, still standing but looking like they were gasping for air. I eyed the road. "Can any of you shoot?"

Sudden silence in the back seat.

Three heads popped up, and three sets of eyes glared wordless accusations at me.

"You know we're kids, right?" Juan snarled. *"Está loca!"*

"I'm nine," Aram announced. "Nine-year-olds aren't allowed to shoot guns."

Maurice shook his head. "Point the gun, pull the trigger," he whispered to himself, as if repeating something someone else had told him.

"Yep, kid's got it right." About a half-block down, someone had pulled an old fire truck across the road, blocking the whole damned street. The sidewalks were piled high with boxes, and probably there were bodies behind them. Live ones. With guns.

Rat-face leaned on the fire truck's bumper. Guess he wanted the kids back.

"How much do you like that man?" I asked them, slowing the truck to a crawl. "Do you want to go with him?"

Aram's voice was tiny. "Will he let you go if we do?"

I hesitated, and Juan answered for me. "No," he said, staring at the man. "I-I've read his mind." He ripped his gaze away and curled in on himself. "He wants the truck. He won't let her go. He won't let *us* go either."

I gnawed at my lip. "Maurice can put people to sleep and wake them up again. Juan can talk in their heads and read their thoughts.... Aram?"

He jerked in his seat.

Softening my face and my voice, I asked him, "What can you do?"

Shaking his head, he sank down behind the other two.

I turned my focus back to the road. "I'll leave the truck running. Maurice, you offered to drive before. I hope you meant it. See on the left? Where they've left a little more space? The way the fire truck is canted across the road between the apartments? Once things go to hell, head for that. Put the truck in first gear and floor it. Got it?"

He nodded, looking scared.

Good. We were all more likely to survive if they were scared.

"Don't let anyone else take this truck." I glanced back, meeting each pair of eyes. "Do what you have to do, but don't let anyone else take the truck. There's a gun in the glove compartment. Glock 26. Loaded. Point and pull the trigger, like Maurice said."

"Where will you be?" Juan asked.

"Out there." I put the truck in neutral, and let it roll to a stop, aimed vaguely at the hole in their defenses. Then I eased the short-barrel rifle out from under the seat. "Dealing with them."

"Abuelita . . ." Juan swallowed. "Be careful with that."

I smiled, the sweet, sweet taste of adrenaline in my mouth. My aches faded, my hip and knee loosened up, and I stepped out of the truck like I was thirty again.

Okay, maybe thirty-five.

But a *good* thirty-five, so I'd take it.

"Excuse me! I need to get through here," I called out, cradling the rifle, but keeping it pointed at the ground.

A Hispanic woman in jeans and a hoodie stepped out from behind the boxes on the left and pointed a Sig Sauer at me, but Rat-face straightened and waved her back. "Go ahead, Grandma. Be on your way. Leave the gun behind. It's too big for a lady like you."

The sneer in his voice told me exactly what he meant by the word *lady*.

I put on a dotty smile. "I'm afraid my guns and my truck are too big for you!" The barrel of my rifle drifted slowly up. "Don't you think?"

He lurched forward in a run, and time slowed, every dust mote in the air becoming crystal clear. This wasn't a sixer thing—it was an adrenaline thing. But when I engaged the tiny bit of precog I had, I knew what was going to happen a second before it did. *That* was a sixer thing.

I stepped to the side and shot him as he went past, two to the body and one to the head. Then, as the first two bullets hit the pavement around me, I pivoted, moved farther left, took out the sniper in the second-floor window, and then the Hispanic woman.

Three more were coming from the right. They must have had orders not to hit the truck, because they hesitated. I didn't dare use it for cover—the boys were in there—so I darted for the fire truck, tripping on something sticky. I wrenched myself around and settled into a Tai Chi stance before moving forward.

I could see the paths of the bullets, but there were too many to dodge them all. I slipped past the head and body shots, returning fire, but one of them caught me in the upper arm, and another creased the muscle just above my knee. Small caliber. They would *hurt* when this was over, but they would heal.

Four of the enemy were down now—Rat-face, the Hispanic woman, an Asian man, and the sniper—and two more wounded, but they were closing fast. A contact shot took out the blond woman, but took the rifle with, then the man had me in a bear hug.

He'd made a fatal mistake, pinning my arms down at my sides.

With my right hand, I fished the crochet hook out of its pocket and drove the sharpened end into his crotch.

Out of the corner of my eye, I saw the truck was moving, but I couldn't worry about it now.

The target bellowed. His arms locked up tighter, squeezing my ribs, but his hips shifted back, giving me enough room to shove my left hand into my pocket, rotate the Glock, and fire.

The gun jammed after the first shot. The man staggered and I twisted away, ready to strike again. From the pump of blood, I'd hit the femoral artery. He was dead and didn't know it yet.

I spun, looking for enemies. The hush after gunfire made my own breathing rasp in my ears. Five bodies lay in the street leaking blood, and I could almost *hear* the rest of their bandit crew trying to figure out how their people had died, and how to kill me without anyone else dying.

The truck engine roared.

Maurice peered over the dash, his face ashen, but determined. He was heading for the hole like I'd told him.

I turned back to the fire truck and *pushed*, calling up the last little bit of sixer power I had.

The fire truck moved.

My truck hit the corner of it and kept going. The fire truck's bumper scraped the side of my truck as it plowed into the boxes that had been stacked there.

I scooped up my rifle, a couple of handguns the targets had dropped, and ran.

"Keep going!" I shouted to Maurice.

The engine roared, but he didn't shift into a higher gear, so I had time to launch myself onto the back bumper and cling to the tailgate like my life depended on it.

We stopped in the dubious shelter of a decimated hospital. The main hospital had been a high-rise; it had been mol-decked, leaving a sludge-surrounded hole, but the outbuildings survived...mostly. They looked like they'd been ransacked and at least one of them burned to the ground. The ER entrance gaped like the maw of a hungry monster as the boys tumbled out of the truck, all chattering like squirrels.

Adrenaline did that to some people. Me, it just exhausted.

I'd dumped the rifle and the enemy's guns into the truck bed, cleared the jam and topped off the magazine of the Glock in my thigh pocket, and hauled myself over the tailgate, shouting directions to the boys through the back window. Then I'd wrapped duct tape around my thigh and upper arm.

Awkward but effective.

Now that we'd stopped, now that the fight was over, my hands shook, my eyelids kept closing, and the stench of my own blood made me want to puke.

Well, that and the deaths of six people. What a waste.

If they hadn't tried to take the truck...If they'd *asked* for help...

No. I'd have nightmares later. Right now I needed to secure our position, fortify the outpost....

I was slipping into the past.

Focus, Abuelita.

The boys lowered the tailgate and I almost spilled out onto the ground. Their eyes widened and their words stopped.

Finally Juan whispered, *"Abuelita? Estás...?"*

"Still alive," I growled, forcing myself to sit up. Lean up. Whatever. "None of you hurt? Good. You two, take the gun from the glove box and circle around. Not too far. The big room and the smaller rooms connected to it. Barricade the doors to the rest of the hospital if you can. Desks, beds, whatever. Juan, you help me."

Maurice nodded, and Aram straightened, squaring his thin shoulders. They didn't go back to the truck cab, which confirmed my guess that Maurice had taken possession of my gun.

As long as he used it on my enemies and didn't hurt himself, I was okay with that. Yeah, they were only eight and nine years old, but this was war.

"See the cooler here?" I nudged it. "Get out all the food. All of it. Give me two—" I thought about my injuries. "*Three* of those mason jars. You guys drink all the water you want. Leave one sandwich for me. Eat the rest. There's jerky in that bag. Get that, too. Split it four ways. Nuts, there, in that corner."

He followed my directions silently, eyes widening as the feast grew in front of him.

I downed a jar of wine before I tried to move, then forced myself to eat the sandwich as fast as I could. The other two boys came back, and they all fell on the food like ravenous wolves. The buzz from the second jar of wine helped me chew through the jerky and a handful of cashews, but I had to force myself to drink the third jar.

Carefully I wriggled onto the foam mattress. My head was spinning, and I couldn't keep my eyes open any longer, despite the afternoon sun. "Wake me up if there are problems," I muttered, already half-asleep.

A hand on my shoulder shook me out of dark dreams.

"Grandma?" Aram peered at me.

I blinked, felt all the muscles in my back protest, and blinked again. "Sunrise or sunset?" I asked, eyeing the shadows.

"Sunrise," he said solemnly. "You slept all night."

"Time to go then." I reached for the cooler, then froze.

I hadn't slept more than five hours in years.

My arm hurt, but more like a shallow bruise than the torn flesh and deep damage of a gunshot. Experimentally, I bent my good knee, then my bad knee. The burn from the bullet above my good knee felt tight, like a healing scab. My bad knee clicked, but the normal line of fire from hip to knee had faded to almost nothing.

I looked at Aram.

He stared back, then shook his head *no*, not wanting anyone else to know.

I inclined my head in thanks, then eased out of the truck bed, fighting back tears as he scampered away.

I had forgotten how it felt to not hurt, and it overwhelmed me for a moment.

Then I thought about Aram. The boy was smart, never saying out loud what he could do. It would protect him a little. For now. If the three-letter agencies or the military ever realized he was a healer—a strong one!—they would take him and use him up, no matter how old he was.

He was probably starving. Healing used up a lot of energy.

Remembering the appetites of boys, I pulled out the last of my stash of food: bao. As if they had scented food on the wind, the three of them came running, crowding around the truck bed. I ate two of the steamed buns and left the rest for them.

I hoped my son had emergency supplies, or we would be going hungry pretty quick.

"Are you all ready to go?" I asked, guzzling the last of my bottle of water.

Dark eyes examined me, then the three boys loaded themselves into my back seat. I double-checked the rifle and slid it under my seat, accepted the keys from Maurice, and started the truck.

We saw more people as we drove east from the hospital. This part of the city hadn't been hit as hard as the north. Some of them looked uncomfortable, as if they'd moved from a poorer part of town to this area. I saw jeans and BDUs and down jackets and empty eyes. They left us alone, and we left them alone, and that was fine with me. The roads were smoother, the abandoned cars far between, and the checkpoints fewer, so we made better time. Midmorning, we left the city for the suburbs up in the hills, and before noon we pulled into the driveway belonging to my son.

Wondering if he'd changed it, I entered the gate code. The wrought-iron gates swung wide. I drove the truck through and they shut behind us.

My son had bought two large lots and built compound-style brick fences around them. As we drove along the spruce-tree-lined driveway, I felt the tension in my shoulders ease slightly.

Then we turned, and I saw the house.

Boarded up.

Empty.

I didn't think he was dead.

I'd known when his wife and baby girl—my granddaughter—had died. I'd felt it. If I'd felt that, I would have felt my boy's death.

The truck quieted, pinging as it cooled, and I was out and walking around the house before I realized I'd shut it off. I followed my intuition, the sixer sense, to the back door, and then to the dilapidated shed. The fingerprint scanners in the doorknob glowed green and the door opened.

When did he get my fingerprints?

Wide stairs took up most of the shed, leading down to the bunker I hadn't known existed. A note hung above the light switch.

Mom, it read. *I knew you'd come. Take what you need. I'll come to you when I can.... I'm okay.*

I love you.

My throat closed.

He hadn't said those words to me for a very long time. He'd been working with other sixers in the intelligence division and didn't understand how I could have let the accident happen.

They'd been leaving my farm after visiting us, traveling back through the city, back to their home.

Here.

He didn't understand how truly weak my gifts were. He'd sworn I could have prevented it.

I hadn't even known until the last second, when my damned sixer precog showed me the drunk bus driver plowing into their car, rolling it, crushing it.

And then I'd felt them die.

My smart, generous daughter-in-law.

My precious granddaughter.

My heart broke yet again, and I sank to my knees at the top of the stairs.

I hadn't known.

I would have given anything to have been able to prevent the accident. My gifts. My own life. Anything.

And then the one person I had left had turned from me in hurt and betrayal.

"Grandma?" Aram whispered, holding out his small, dirty hand.

Offering me healing.

I straightened.

"No. Thank you."

My pain made me who I was.

Wiping my eyes, I looked past him at the other two. "I'm going to load up the truck," I said. "Then I'm going back home."

Juan opened his mouth, but Maurice nudged him.

"You're welcome to join me, but I won't force you." I had a feeling the bombs would start up again soon. Time to move.

65

I pulled the truck up close to the shed and started moving supplies. The boys joined me, wordlessly stacking boxes on the tailgate while I shoved them into position. Once we had as much as we could fit, I dug a pen out of one pocket, wrote *I love you so much*, and then let the biometric lock close behind me.

The boys climbed in the back seat as if they belonged there, so I took the front and started the truck.

We had a long drive ahead, but for the first time in a long time my boy had said he loved me. I had three new boys to care for, and despite the bombs screaming into the city, I thought I might just be able to get through this war after all.

Time to go home.

The Enfield Report

written by
Christopher Bowthorpe

illustrated by
STEPHEN SPINAS

ABOUT THE AUTHOR

Christopher Bowthorpe lives in Lehi, Utah, with his amazing wife, one daughter, four sons, three dogs, and two cats in a house that's probably too small for all of them. He conjured his earliest stories for G. I. Joe and Ninja Turtle action figures, and eventually started writing them down. The books that have shaped him most are His Dark Materials, Wizard and Glass, *and* Ender's Game. *When not writing, Chris is an avid kayak fisherman and has also started exploring photography. Apart from short fiction, he writes fantasy and sci-fi novels for teens and adults.*

ABOUT THE ILLUSTRATOR

South African–born illustrator Stephen Spinas has dedicated much of his thirty-two years to the pursuit of art. From humble beginnings as a 2-D background artist, he has since run the gamut of professional titles in the art world: apprentice, designer, director, CEO, and all while still trying to make it as an illustrator.

With a passion for the visceral, and an uncanny talent for bringing complicated concepts to life, Stephen has been involved in numerous projects with clients from across the globe. Inspired by the likes of Jim Lee, Bernie Wrightson, and Riccardo Federici, Stephen possesses a distinct and instantly recognisable style: bold, gritty, and richly detailed. Stephen also delights in a challenge and enjoys fulfilling his clients' unique creative visions, no matter the style or medium.

Though he is currently engaged as director of an indie publishing house, he manages to squeeze in what hours he can afford to work on his original comic book title, the forthcoming Em is for Monsters. *After all, it's long been a dream of his to find a place in the professional comic book industry.*

The Enfield Report

General Leish stood in the security office watching the video feed. It showed a figure in a white jumpsuit seated at a table, working on something obscured by the camera angle and the dim light of the cell.

But this being a "sanctuary for the mentally afflicted," as the sign outside proclaimed, they probably called those locked rooms "tranquility chambers" or something just as asinine. As far as Leish was concerned, they could use whatever words they wanted. This was a nuthouse, that was a cell, and the man inside was a psychopath.

A very *useful* psychopath.

Leish stowed his moral compass in the familiar, dark place he had created for it and ventured down the hall. He stopped outside the cell and waited for the orderly to trigger the lock from back in the office. A harsh, electric buzz sounded and a red light flared to life over the door.

Drawing a breath, Leish gripped the handle. For a brief moment he regretted telling the orderly he didn't need an escort. He swallowed the thought, pulled the door open, and stepped inside.

It was darker than he'd expected. He froze, waiting for his eyes to adjust.

"General Leish," an unctuous voice said, "there's one more star on your lapel since the last time we talked. Congratulations are in order."

Pupils now dilated for the dimness, Leish confirmed the

prisoner was still seated, his back to the entrance. For all appearances, he was absorbed in whatever he was working on. But he *must* have turned at some point. How else could he have learned Leish's identity and made the observation about his rank?

"Thank you, Dr. Tormer." Leish lowered his voice, forcing it not to shake from the adrenaline, an old battlefield skill he hadn't expected to need today.

"So formal!" Tormer said, still hunched over the table. "I suppose that means you want something. But then, why else do you come to visit me?"

"Voyager Command has a situation that could benefit from your...unique specialization."

Tormer chuckled. "Oh, of course, how ignorant of me. These little projects are always at the behest of Command. I know how little you personally enjoy my company, General."

Leish stood in silence for a few moments. He wouldn't be baited.

Tormer turned, his brilliant blue eyes cutting through the feeble light. He stared at Leish, corners of his mouth twitching as he reached up to push a lock of black hair into place. "Come and have a look at my latest project."

Leish decided he would show no fear to this man. After all, Tormer *was* just a man, no matter how twisted his soul might be.

The table's contents came into view as Leish stepped closer. Tormer stood and moved aside with a little "behold" gesture.

A piece of cork about eight inches square lay on the table. Stretched across it, held by several pins, was the largest moth Leish had ever seen. Its wings were slate gray with stripes of black. The carapace of its head and thorax were a muted brown. But the bulbous abdomen was a translucent white.

"I receive such gifts from admirers now and then," Tormer explained, eyes glazing with a far-off expression. "I return them as you see with a post-operatory report about the procedure. I think it gives my devotees a lovely little thrill knowing my hands have touched something which they now possess."

"Procedure?" General Leish asked.

"Yes, General. The goal is to keep it alive as long as possible while I preserve it."

As Leish watched, the moth tore one papery wing loose. It beat feebly against the cork.

"You're as disgusting as ever, Doctor."

"And you're just as dull, General." Tormer's voice and expression had darkened. Gone was any pretense of affability, replaced by a cold intelligence. "I presume you have a briefing for me?"

Leish reached into the inside pocket of his jacket and retrieved an envelope. He handed it to Tormer, who opened it without breaking eye contact.

"Same terms as our previous arrangements?" he asked.

The general nodded. "You'll receive a sentence reduction of fifty years upon submission of an actionable report. For all the good that will do you."

Leish waited for a reply to the barb, but Tormer's predatory eyes were already devouring the documents. The general scowled. "I'll leave release and travel instructions with security. You know what will happen if you don't behave while you're out."

Tormer gave no acknowledgment, but Leish couldn't stand another moment confined with the man. He turned and made his way out.

"General."

Leish turned, catching the door as it closed, leaving a narrow strip of Tormer's face in view.

"Between these little bargains of ours and advances in medical science," Tormer said, "fourteen life sentences just *might* prove surmountable." A leer crept across his face. "Perhaps I'll walk free someday with enough pep to pay some old friends a visit."

Leish's blood went cold at the sound of Tormer's cackling laughter. The memory of it would cause him to double-check his locks every night until the day he died.

Dr. Coral Enfield took a spot against the bulkhead of the train car. Once braced, she triple-blinked to turn on her hololenses and booted her daily feed. A news broadcast played, the clip curated by Coral's voracious interest in any news about the colonies.

"Voyager Command is calling the disturbance on Nossos a neutral zone misunderstanding," a stoic anchor said, as the video showed a blackened foam-crete bunker. Smoke poured skyward while a group of hulking, gray-green humanoids looted armloads of gear.

Coral replayed the clip again and again. Even after nine months on the planet, footage of the species on Nossos was rare. Though not outright hostile, they had proved reclusive, avoiding contact and refusing to engage in regular communication.

The video cut to a military official at a podium. *"Every diplomatic effort is being made to resolve the conflict with the Nossians. Each colonization presents unique challenges. Voyager's brave men and women are as committed as ever to creating positive relations with Nossos."*

The broadcast ended. Coral loaded a trivia game. She blinked away at the series of questions as she rode out of the crowded downtown districts of Indianapolis, beyond the housing rings, and finally out to the agrizone. From the terminal, an autocar took her to a collection of blocky, unlabeled buildings in the middle of an expanse of corn that never changed size or color.

She encountered no one during the walk to her laboratory. She was certain the scheduling program manipulated routes to prevent contact among the workforce. She had attempted to deviate from hers only once, earning a harsh reprimand from a security officer.

The rigid, solitary environment was difficult for Coral, but one she had to endure if she wished to continue her work. Thankfully, many of the complex's oppressive measures ended at the threshold of her lab. She breathed a sigh of relief as she entered, calling "Good morning, Idun!" The lab's fixtures glowed to life to greet her.

"Good morning, Doctor." Like most AIs, Coral's lab assistant had a "face": a melon-sized orb that changed color and brightness to

approximate expressions. At its position near the ceiling in the middle of the lab, it pulsed a serene yellow that reminded Coral of sunrises and orange juice.

"How did we do last night?"

"Subjects 1 through 112 are complete with an 86.6% success rate."

"That's wonderful, Idun!"

"I thought you would be pleased." The orb flushed a velvety purple.

Coral hurried to the stimchamber at the back of the lab, peering through the glass wall like an excited window shopper. A tower of racks held red embryonic capsules the size of footballs. Robotic arms moved among the fragile gel crucibles, their metallic fingers rearranging, measuring, and injecting. Each action was meticulously executed and documented by Idun.

"With your prescribed regimen of hyperpolymerase, juvenile subjects will be ready in 14.7 hours," Idun said.

A wave of anxiety made Coral's jaw clench. These were the final moments of her project. HPM had revolutionized her field of study, the accelerated cellular division producing generations in hours instead of days. Once the subjects she had spent the last four months developing were complete, she could reapply for a colony position.

What if this was it, the project that finally got her noticed? Planet-optimized livestock had become a vital part of Voyager's colonization strategy, and it sounded as if they needed all the help they could get on Nossos right now. Maybe the urgency there would earn her some extra attention.

Coral wanted more than anything to get off-world, out of this stifling complex, away from the constant observation of her every move. How would it feel to be on the leading edge? To set up her own lab and experiments? To work with other researchers just as passionate and competent as herself?

The thought made her cheeks burn with excitement. The sooner she produced her report, the sooner she could apply. Hunching over her computer, she opened the project log. She was composing her opening paragraph when the door override alarm blared.

She stood as two men entered. The first wore his blue, medal-laden uniform with such crisp pride that Coral didn't need to see the three stars on his lapel to know she was dealing with significant authority.

"Dr. Coral Enfield?" he demanded.

"Yes, sir. And you are?"

"Cite your credentials for my colleague." The general dodged his own introduction, gesturing to the other newcomer. He was taller than the general, lean but not skinny. His dark, straight hair was long enough to be roguish if it weren't under the control of a businesslike style. His eyes were the richest shade of blue Coral had ever seen, and they drank her in unapologetically.

"I hold doctorates in archaeozoology and bioecology from UC Berkeley," she said. "Now I'll ask again, who are—"

"You and your facility are being reassigned to a top-priority project."

"Wait a minute," Coral said. "I have work to do. You can't barge into my lab and—"

"Voyager's lab, actually," the general interrupted again. "Your subjects will be taken care of, but right now you need to acquaint yourself with your new supervisor. This is Doctor..." He trailed off, turning to the blue-eyed man.

"Zriel," the other man said. "Alfred Zriel." He stepped forward and extended a hand. He wore a stylish suit and spoke with an air of formality that didn't match the primal nature behind those eyes. They put Coral in mind of a trained wolf.

"And if I refuse?" Coral asked.

The general didn't even blink. "You'll be released from Voyager Research and your doctorates will be revoked, since they were earned under our Brighter Stars scholarships. Or, you can cooperate and reap the rewards. How many times has your application for colony work been denied now? Three? Four?" He paused, raising his gray-tinged eyebrows. "Do you understand what I'm saying, Dr. Enfield?"

Coral stood in shock for a moment, pursed her lips and forced a nod. What choice did she have? Everything about this felt like a so-called "gray op." When you worked for Voyager long enough, you were bound to brush up against its slimy underbelly. She had avoided it up to this point, but her luck had run out.

The general checked his watch, then looked at Zriel. "The sample will be arriving soon. You'll have three days, then you're to destroy it and transmit the report through Dr. Enfield's comm profile."

Why would he want the report through my profile? Coral wondered. But the queasy feeling in her stomach meant she already knew the answer: Zriel was off the books.

"We understand, General," Zriel said. His voice was languid, but it sounded forced to Coral. There was anticipation behind the words, a thrill waiting to be unleashed.

"Good," the general said. His tone confirmed everything had happened exactly as he expected. When he moved to leave, the idea of being left alone with Zriel made Coral's stomach twist. He strode toward the exit. "Three days, Doctors. Command is counting on you."

Then he was gone.

As soon as the door closed, Idun spoke. *"Dr. Enfield, I've received orders from Command to ship the subjects immediately. I must comply."* The orb faded to a regretful peach color.

Coral approached the stimchamber. She laid a hand on the glass, watching the robotic arms cradle the capsules into cryopods, which were then carried out of the chamber on an air-locked conveyor belt.

Zriel stepped up next to her. He observed the loading process for a moment before saying, "What are they?"

She sighed. "I developed a utility animal for Nossos. Improved metabolic efficiency and gastric tolerance for the native flora."

The loading was almost complete. "You love them," Zriel said.

The pronouncement was odd enough that Coral had to think for a moment before answering. "In a way, I suppose I do."

"But you let the machine care for your creations. So cold, so...disconnected."

Coral frowned, an unexpected jolt of guilt running through her chest. "It has to be this way," she said. "The chamber is calibrated for Nossos's atmosphere."

"That's nothing an exosuit couldn't overcome."

Her mind scrambled for another excuse. "Voyager requires all projects to be managed by an AI."

Zriel tilted his head back and laughed recklessly. "Oh, my dear Dr. Enfield, you are about to learn that what Voyager *requires* is results. The particulars between points A and B aren't of much concern."

Coral shuddered at this grim assessment. "Are you not with Voyager?"

"No," Zriel snapped, eyes flashing. "Not anymore. I was on the insertion teams for early prospective colonies. My commanding officer and I had a . . . difference of vision about our mission. Now I work only under special arrangements."

Before she could ask what "special arrangements" meant, the door alarm sounded again.

Uniformed men entered in a steady stream, wheeling storage containers on handcarts. Zriel oversaw their placement while Coral gritted her teeth, watching him treat her lab like his own personal warehouse.

When the last crates were stacked, two infantrymen entered holding rifles. Next came a pair of figures in exosuits wheeling a cryopod, the full-size kind used by crew on deep space missions.

Zriel ordered the infantrymen, "Straight into the stimchamber please."

Once the pod was secured in the chamber, one of the exosuit wearers approached Coral, holding out an omnitab. "Signature," he demanded.

She scanned the manifest. "It doesn't even say what I'm receiving."

"Now," he snapped. Coral cocked her jaw to one side and shook her head as she scrawled her authorization.

The man in the exosuit snatched the tablet back as soon as she finished. "One last thing," he said, tone grave, "the subject

75

has a restraint on its face. It is not to be removed under any circumstances. Clear?"

"I think I know how to handle a dangerous specimen, Soldier," Zriel said.

The man took a step toward the doctor. "Field intel ordered me to relay the information, so that's what I'm doing."

Zriel bowed his head in surrender. The uniforms departed without another word, leaving the doctors alone once again.

Except, they weren't alone anymore. Coral's eyes drifted to the stimchamber and the cryopod inside.

"Please ask your AI to open the cryopod," Zriel said, striding toward the glass wall of the chamber.

Coral followed. "I can add your voice authorization for her. That way you can—"

"That won't be necessary."

"Right, I forgot. You're not really here, are you, Dr. Zriel?"

He studied her. A few strands of his black hair had fallen down, looking like a calligrapher's stroke across his forehead.

"You're only half right, Dr. Enfield." Those wild blue eyes enveloped her again. "I don't even exist."

He stared a moment longer, then nodded toward Idun. Coral gave the command. The array of robotic arms extended, removing the pod's clamps. A sharp hiss of escaping gasses could be heard through the thick glass. Opaque fog rolled out as the top was lifted, filling the stimchamber. It took only a moment for the exhaust fans to vent the chamber, but it felt like an eternity.

When the haze cleared, Coral felt her knees weaken.

Inside was a seven-foot slab of gray-green carapace and spines, otherwise known as a Nossian.

Coral didn't remember fainting, but who ever does? She awoke slumped over a workstation. It took several moments of blinking to recall what was happening. Her eyes darted to the stimchamber, found the Nossian still unconscious in its restraints. She sighed in relief.

She stood and approached Dr. Zriel, who was rummaging through the containers. "What is going on here?" she demanded.

Zriel straightened and turned. He had removed his jacket and more black hair had fallen across his forehead. "Obviously we're going to be studying a Nossian."

Several questions tried to pile out of Coral's mouth at once. "Here? Like this? Why?" she sputtered.

"As magnanimous as Voyager purports to be, never forget that they are a branch of the military. They wish to know their enemy."

Coral frowned. "But Nossos is a peaceful colonization."

"Every colonization in history was peaceful until one side decided differently."

"Which side is deciding now?"

Zriel sighed and loosened his tie. "Dr. Enfield, I really don't have time for your adorable naiveté right now." The savage thrill that lurked behind those blue eyes seeped into his voice. "In the next three days, we are going to compile a combat-focused anatomic report."

"I've never heard of that."

"They are a unique specialty of mine, though not a pretty one." Zriel smirked. "Understand this," he continued. "Eventually, some brilliant scientist like you will craft a detailed report about Nossian physiology based on years of careful research. But right now, Voyager only wants to know how to hurt, disable, and kill them. That's where I come in."

The statement sent a shiver down Coral's spine. Her mouth fell agape. Voyager seldom gave the full story to the public, but were they really capable of something so barbaric?

"I can't..."

Zriel grasped her by the shoulders. "Oh, Doctor," he crooned, "I would *never* ask you to participate in these procedures. I merely need you to submit the report. Then a grateful Voyager will give you the pick of your next assignment. All you need to do is stay out of my way. Isn't that a fair trade?"

She didn't answer, quietly considering the path ahead. If she protested, she would be fired and discredited. Beyond that, she longed for a ticket off-planet. Zriel's work would go forward with or without her, so why shouldn't she benefit from it?

Feeling filthy, she nodded her assent.

"Very good," Zriel said. He reached for something in one of the supply crates. Coral recognized the shiny gray material of an exosuit as he pulled the garment about himself.

She looked over at the stimchamber, then back at Zriel as he lowered the helmet into place. "You're going in there?" she asked, eyes wide.

"Of course," he said, slapping the button on his chest to seal the suit. He retrieved a bag of supplies from one of the crates. "Torsion tests and point-pressure readings have their place, but one can't get a *feel* for an adversary from behind a sheet of glass."

Coral's unease must have shown on her face. Zriel halted en route to the stimchamber. "If my hands-on approach makes you uncomfortable, might I suggest that you busy yourself elsewhere? No doubt you have a summary report to write."

Coral frowned. He was right, so why did it feel wrong for her to hide at her computer?

"What will you be doing?"

He patted the bag with a tinny clink. "Chemical resilience tests."

She'd somehow hoped learning the specifics would assuage her guilt. It only felt worse.

Zriel entered the stimchamber and woke the Nossian with an electric shock. Its eyes, yellow-orange orbs with slitted pupils, glared with malice that raised gooseflesh on Coral's back. Beneath the bulbous eyes was the mouth restraint, an angular hunk of metal that appeared to have been screwed directly into the facial carapace.

"Dr. Enfield," Zriel said through the PA. "One last thing, please have Idun scan for vitals."

Coral tasked the AI to bombard the Nossian with every available wave. The orb turned a diligent green while Idun worked, then reported back. "I have isolated readings which can be approximated as pulse and neurological activity. The data is on the monitors."

The screens displayed two real-time charts. The Nossian's eyes flicked to the screen, lingered for a moment, then darted to Coral. Its scouring, accusatory stare summoned a blend of guilt and fear that made her throat tight. Eager to escape it, she moved toward her workstation. As she passed the stack of crates, she noted cots and bedding among the supplies.

"Are we going to be sleeping here, Dr. Zriel?" she called.

He stared at the Nossian like a hungry predator but turned at the sound of her voice. His wild blue eyes lost none of their intensity behind the face mask. "An astute observation," he said. "But don't worry, I'll be a gentleman if you promise to be a lady."

The remark brought a hot flush to Coral's cheeks. As she sat down, Zriel pulled an aerosol can out of the bag. He spoke aloud, dictating to a recorder clipped onto his collar, "Test number one, exposure to organophosphate compound SG-4. Delivery via aerosol."

Seated at her terminal, Coral could still see the stimchamber over the top of her monitor. She watched Zriel point the can at the creature. A pale mist emitted from the nozzle, and the Nossian jolted in its restraints. The vitals on the monitor spiked.

Coral winced and turned away. She rummaged through a drawer and dragged out a set of headphones. Keeping her eyes on the floor, she moved to a terminal that faced away from the stimchamber.

Zriel spoke. "Subject shows severe skin-level reaction and high pain resp——"

The calm, sterile observations were cut off as Coral pulled the headphones in place. With her back to the horrors occurring in her stimchamber, she began to type.

Coral awoke on a cot with a blanket draped over her body. Zriel sat nearby, chewing a meal bar. The top portion of his exosuit was bunched around his waist. The white T-shirt beneath was damp with sweat.

He looked at her as she sat up but said nothing. His shadowed eyes revealed that he'd worked through the night.

"Thank you," Coral said, gesturing to the bedding. He waved dismissively, offering her a meal bar. She hated the military's chewy sustenance bricks but found herself ravenous. As she chewed, her eyes wandered into the stimchamber.

She froze midbite.

The Nossian was unconscious in the restraints of the cryopod, an IV trailing from one arm. Coral hoped it was delivering sedatives, because all over the alien's body, broad patches of skin were seared an angry, blistered red.

"It was a productive day," Zriel remarked, following Coral's gaze. She ripped her eyes away to glare at him. He continued. "Interestingly, the reaction is from the hydrofluoroalkane propellant, not the weapon agents." He shrugged. "Of course, I still tested all of them, just to be certain."

She cringed, looking back at the floor while Zriel wore a bland grin, as if his cruel revelation was a charming anecdote. They finished the meal in silence. After Coral had swallowed her last bite, he approached with a water bottle.

She sipped slowly.

"Drink it all," he said. "It will help you recover more quickly."

"Recover from what?"

A syringe appeared in Zriel's fingers. He jabbed it into Coral's shoulder before she could even flinch.

"Hey!" she cried. "What did you just—"

He wrapped her in a suffocating embrace. "Nothing sinister, my dear," he whispered into her ear. "I promise."

Coral felt the strength drain from her arms and legs. Her fingers clutched at Zriel's back as her body suddenly felt like she was on Jupiter. He cradled her, lifting her with little effort, and deposited her back on the cot.

She struggled to keep conscious, but it was futile. The last thing her eyes relayed was Zriel reaching into his kit to withdraw a combat knife.

Dr. Frederick Tormer regretted putting Coral under sedation but deemed it prudent. The carrot Leish had dangled was enough to placate the girl through yesterday's tests, but today's procedure might be enough to inflame her sense of altruism.

He counted to one hundred after her eyes shut, just to be sure.

He would suffer no interruptions today.

Tormer sauntered into the stimchamber, watching the vital-sign monitors. There was a pleasing increase in heart rate as the alien's eyes tracked him across the chamber. He held the blade up so it could see. The alien's eyes widened above the steel muzzle and the vitals climbed higher. Tormer smiled as he set the knife on a nearby tray, delighting in the fear he could summon in such a formidable creature.

He moved past the Nossian to the injection apparatus. A certain canister had caught his eye the previous day. Intrigued, he'd waited until Coral slept, used her finger to unlock an omnitab, and spent the night learning about the *wonderful* possibilities of hyperpolymerase.

He removed the steel cylinder and filled a syringe. He held it to the light to clear the tiny air bubbles, then set it on the tray. After picking up the knife again, he turned back to the Nossian.

"We're going to have *so* much fun, you and I," he muttered. Then rammed the knife into the creature's chest.

Coral woke to Zriel's voice, his dulcet dictation lilting through her groggy mind.

"Primary carapace structures can be penetrated by blade with sustained force, but should be avoided in favor of vulnerable sections low on the abdomen, bilateral, approximately ten centimeters distal from sagittal plane. Chitin appears penetrable with standard small munitions. Wounds to the thoracic cavity result in fatality after approximately forty seconds."

She sat up on the cot. He paused, turning from his place at a workstation to face her. "Awake at last."

"How long was I out?" she asked, heart racing.

He cocked his head. "You know, I'm not really sure."

Coral narrowed her eyes. "*Why* was I out, Dr. Zriel?"

"I thought you might prefer blissful ignorance." He smiled in a way he seemed to think was endearing. It only made Coral want to claw his eyes out.

"Absolutely not," she snarled, her face feeling hot. "Don't ever touch me again."

He shrugged, unperturbed. "As you wish. I need you conscious today anyway."

They matched glares for a moment. This was far beyond what Coral had agreed to. Was her career worth all this? What good was success if you couldn't sleep at night, if you knew everything you'd achieved was bought with pain and blood and cruelty?

Perhaps sensing her eroding commitment, Zriel spoke again. "I know what you must think of me. Psychopath. Maniac. I've heard it all before." His voice quavered to match his trembling fingertips. "But my arrangement with Voyager benefits everyone. I get to let my demons out to play, and the work I'm doing will save countless lives when the fighting erupts. So this can't be all bad."

Coral shivered with unease. Gone was the genteel, well-groomed doctor, replaced by this sweating, manic animal. Without waiting for a reply, he pulled the exosuit back on, lowered the helmet over his stubbled face, and stalked toward the stimchamber.

Her eyes flicked to the alien. It glared at Zriel as he stepped into the chamber, yellow eyes rimmed with red above the cruel mouth restraint. Zriel approached the Nossian. "Dr. Enfield, please deactivate cuff number two."

Coral briefly worried for Zriel's safety. But some dark part of her mind, possibly the same part that had persuaded her to jump into this mess in the first place, suggested that it wouldn't be the worst outcome if he was injured. So she gave the command, and Idun complied, the orb turning an ominous black. The Nossian's left arm slumped out of the restraint, IV still attached. Zriel caught it by the hand. He examined the limb, sliding gloved fingers along the plates and spines almost lovingly.

STEPHEN SPINAS

Then, he gripped the arm at wrist and elbow and slammed it down across his knee.

A sickening crack. The red blossom of torn tissue. A white flash of bone. Coral's vision darkened at the edges. She dropped to her knees and vomited into a nearby waste bin.

Forcing her eyes back to the stimchamber, she looked on in horror as Zriel studied the gruesome compound fracture he had caused, probing the wound with his fingers. He was dictating again, but to Coral the words were a muddled drone. With a swift jerk, he forced the bone back into place, then set the limb back in the restraint.

"Reactivate cuff two," he barked.

Voice shaking, Coral relayed the request to Idun.

Zriel retrieved a syringe from his instrument tray and filled it from a steel canister. When Coral read the black lettering on the side, she scrambled to her feet, leaning against the glass wall. "What are you doing, Dr. Zriel?" she gasped, not knowing if she could bear the answer.

"Don't be alarmed, dear. I'm only making use of all the delightful new tools at my disposal."

He returned to the Nossian and delivered the injection. Within seconds, the gaping wound in the alien's arm brimmed with fluid. Veins crept across the torn surfaces. Tissue swelled to fill the void. It might have been beautiful under different circumstances.

The realization hit Coral with another wave of nausea. Gone were the blistered red patches from the first day's tests, now only visible as slightly puckered skin. There were other scars too she hadn't noticed. These were everywhere, up and down the legs, every few inches apart on the abdomen, chest, and neck.

White lines about the width of a combat knife.

While Coral slept, Zriel had been contorting her lab and her research to put the Nossian through a hell that should have been impossible.

She slammed a fist against the glass. "You can't do this!"

Zriel laughed, turning to face her. "This is exactly what

Voyager hired me to do! Now be quiet, or I'll be forced to sedate you."

Tears blurred Coral's vision and she pounded on the glass until it hurt. Zriel ignored her. He positioned himself next to the Nossian's leg. The alien's vitals spiked again.

Coral looked away, and how she hated herself for it, knowing she would benefit from the unforgivable acts being perpetrated in her lab. Acts committed under her name. Acts that wouldn't have been possible without her research and her complacency.

She flinched at the ripping snap and Zriel's satisfied grunt. The alien's neurological readings soared to their highest levels yet. And with the HPM injections, Zriel could do it again, and again, and again.

Coral knew what she had to do.

While Zriel injected the alien with more HPM, she wiped away tears and climbed to her feet. She avoided even glancing at the Nossian, promising herself she would make amends later. She scanned the injection array until she found what she sought, then looked away quickly.

She hesitated. This was at best a coin-flip proposition, but it was also the only hope she had of gazing in the mirror once this was over.

"Dr. Enfield," Zriel said with a conspiratorial drawl.

They locked eyes through the glass. Coral's heart pounded against her ribs. *He knows! Somehow he knows!*

"Be a doll. Lock cuff three and unlock four, will you?"

She stared, adrenaline delaying her ability to process, finally nodded.

He turned back to the Nossian. She drew a breath and spoke. "Idun, inject Dr. Zriel with forty milligrams of propofol."

Idun surged a triumphant royal blue. *"Yes, Doctor."*

Zriel loomed over the alien in anticipation. It took him a half second to realize the command Coral had given was not what he'd requested.

She hoped it would be enough.

He whirled as the appendage swung toward him, needle glinting. He reached for it too late. The hypodermic pierced his exosuit and the skin beneath. The contents flooded into his bloodstream.

His eyes blazed with rage and fear.

Please be enough!

It had been years since Coral's pharmacology courses. She'd intentionally undershot the dosage, afraid of stopping Zriel's heart. Enraged as he was, the dose might not be enough to render him fully unconscious, and if so, it wouldn't be for long.

She watched Zriel's eyes glaze over. An unintelligible gurgle-groan passed his lips as his eyes rolled back. He collapsed to the floor.

Coral sprang into action, clawing an exosuit out of a container and pulling it on. With the helmet in place, she entered the stimchamber.

The Nossian was even more terrifying without an inch of glass between them. Coral crept toward the alien. She reached for a hypodermic from Zriel's work tray, giving the alien a wide berth as she approached the injection canisters. She filled the syringe to capacity, then shuffled back in front of the Nossian. By now, the HPM had done its work, healing the ghastly wounds Zriel had wrought.

"I don't know if you can understand me," Coral said, feeling awkward and heartbroken. "I'm very sorry for what's happened here. This...this isn't who we are. I wish I could fix it, but this is the best I can offer." She held up the syringe. "An end to the pain."

She could have ordered Idun to do this, but it felt wrong after everything the creature had endured. Its yellow, blood-tinged eyes locked on her own. Was it fear, hate, or anticipation boiling there?

Zriel released a slurred grunt and twitched but remained unconscious. For the moment.

"I'm very sorry," Coral repeated, moving forward.

The yellow eyes widened. The creature tensed its entire body, clawed fingers splayed beneath the cuffs. Coral stopped. The Nossian's eyes bored into hers, then flicked deliberately down. It repeated the motion three times.

Realization dawned after a moment. The pleading eyes pointed downward, toward the mouth restraint.

"You want me to remove it," Coral said, gesturing to her own mouth.

It repeated the eye motion. There was intelligence there, a troubling depth Coral hadn't expected to find.

The soldiers had warned explicitly against removing the mouth restraint, but where was the danger? Even with the restraint removed, the Nossian was safely manacled. If it tried anything, she could deliver the lethal injection before things got out of hand. In return, it could die free of pain, with a measure of dignity.

"Idun, remove the subject's facial restraint."

"Is that a prudent—"

"Override," Coral snapped, hating Zriel, hating the nameless general, hating Voyager for putting her in this predicament.

The robotic arms complied, removing the screws from the angular metal. The hunk of steel fell away, revealing a split mandible wreathed in blood from the barbaric muzzle.

Tears slid down Coral's cheeks as she watched gratitude fill the Nossian's eyes. She wept for the pain this being had suffered, and for her part in it.

Zriel stirred again, this time mumbling, eyelids fluttering.

"It's time," she whispered, then stepped forward with the needle. The Nossian's mandible split open to expose a complex lingual structure dripping with mucus.

"Idun, release cuffs one, two, three, and four, please."

Coral froze. The voice was hers. The tone and rhythm were hers. But she had not spoken the words. A chill coiled down her spine.

"Yes, Doctor," Idun said. The steel bands holding the Nossian sprung open. Coral stepped backward, dumbfounded. Her heart slammed against the inside of her chest as the Nossian stepped

out of the cryopod. It took a menacing step forward. She seized a nearby medical cart and shoved it toward the alien. It caught the stainless-steel fixture in one hand and tossed it aside.

"Please," Coral said.

"Please," the alien relayed back in flawless imitation. It took another step forward, yellow eyes filled with hate.

I can't let it get out, no matter what! This was my mistake. I can't let other people get hurt!

She would have to engage the creature, jam the needle in even if she was killed in the process. Her heels bumped against the bottom rim of the hatch. Her body tensed. She held the needle out like a warding talisman.

"I'm very sorry," the alien said, mocking Coral with another sampling of her voice. It raised a clawed hand, but she didn't follow it. She was focused on a place near the creature's abdomen, about ten centimeters distal from the sagittal plane.

"As a gentleman, I simply *cannot* allow this."

The Nossian froze, then released a shrill screech that rattled Coral's molars against her jaw. The alien spun, seeking the place where Zriel had fallen. He had climbed to his feet, reeling as he leaned against the cryopod. In one hand he held a combat knife. In the other, an aerosol can.

He pierced the can and threw it at the alien's chest. The creature reached for the hissing projectile. Escaping propellant sprayed its fingers, its gray-green chest, its face, raising crimson blisters everywhere it touched.

The alien gave another skull-piercing scream. It lunged. Zriel ducked behind the cryopod, shielding himself from a deadly slash of claws. He swung around the other side, produced another can which he punctured and rolled toward the alien. Propellant poured out, searing one of the alien's legs.

Zriel scrambled to position himself between Coral and the Nossian. It limped forward, trumpeting another enraged shriek. Huge swaths of skin on its face, chest, neck, and leg were melting, sagging away.

Coral glanced at Zriel. The thrill that had been lurking behind those eyes was now truly unleashed. He bent his knees, bared his teeth, and raised the combat knife.

The Nossian lurched forward on its injured leg swinging a clawed hand. Zriel dodged and delivered a precise counterstrike with his elbow. A sharp crack reverberated through the chamber. The alien's limb bent at a grotesque angle. It slashed with its other hand, opening itself for a rapid stab to the abdomen. It cupped the wound with its hand. Blood poured over gray-green fingers. Zriel pivoted and thrust the knife to the hilt into the back of the uninjured leg.

The alien dropped to its knees. Zriel stood over his defeated foe, panting. He raised the knife to deliver the death blow. The creature looked almost relieved.

"No!" Coral screamed.

Zriel stopped.

"Not like that," she said, stepping between them. She grabbed Zriel's arm and pushed him backward. "Not *you*." Their eyes locked. Zriel's demons danced behind pupils of black, but he relented.

Coral turned back to the Nossian and knelt. Whether out of weakness or understanding, it didn't shrink away from her. The needle slid into the flesh of its neck. She thumbed the plunger with steady force. The alien slumped sideways, leathery eyelids closing.

Suddenly exhausted, Coral backed against the cool glass wall and slid to the floor. There she watched the monitor as the alien's pulse and neurological readings faded to zero.

Zriel groaned and sat down beside her. Their breathing was the only sound for a lengthy, stunned moment. As her heart slowed and adrenaline dissipated, Coral reviewed what had just happened.

She shouldn't have been alive. She'd made a stupid, immature mistake and should have paid the price. Of all people in the world, Zriel, the man she'd spent the last two days watching commit torture, was the last Coral would have expected to save her. The knot of guilt growing in her chest was both potent and nebulous.

Did she hate that perhaps she had been wrong about Zriel? That maybe he was more than a garden-variety sadist? Or was it that her assessment was indeed correct, and now she would live the remainder of her days knowing she owed each of them to such a man?

Suspecting that it would be some time before she could make peace with any of this, Coral cleared her throat. "Thank you," she said. "For saving me."

Zriel gave a grim chuckle and turned to her. "Don't get too excited. It was self-preservation. Voyager tends to react poorly when my little outings result in casualties."

It was an easy explanation, effortlessly delivered, but felt...hollow.

Coral searched those savage blue eyes. She resisted the urge to look away, feeling her heart beat faster. There *was* something behind that gaze. Something terrifying and exhilarating. Something Coral didn't know if she wanted to explore or run away from.

Zriel shifted his eyes to the corpse of the Nossian. "Well," he said, climbing to his feet. "One thing is certain, my work here is complete." He stepped over to the work tray and dropped the knife on it with a clang before returning to where Coral sat. He extended a hand to her.

She stared at it for a moment. When she finally grasped it, he easily pulled her to her feet.

She only caught a glimpse of the syringe before it slid into her arm.

He wrapped his arms around her, whispering in her ear, "Nothing sinister, my dear."

Coral's world faded to black.

Coral sat in the foyer of the Field Command office. She'd been summoned immediately after disembarking the VSS *Dain*. Unfortunately, the orders hadn't included an explanation of why.

Eager for a distraction from her nervousness, she triple-blinked to activate her hololenses. Her daily feed began to play. The face that appeared caused her breath to catch in her chest. Wild blue eyes and straight black hair.

"After his escape two years ago from a top-secret Voyager Research lab," an anchor said in voice-over, *"officials are still no closer to catching war criminal Dr. Frederick Tormer. Although Command has yet to explain any of the mystery surrounding his escape, they maintain that Tormer is extremely dangerous and ask anyone with knowledge of his whereabouts to contact local law enforcement."*

The feed jumped to another subject, but Coral's mind was far away, remembering waking in her lab to find a bloody wad of electrical equipment on a nearby workstation. This turned out to be Zriel's (or Tormer's, she reminded herself) tracking and disablement implant.

"Dr. Coral Enfield?"

The voice of the porting officer startled her back to the present.

"Have a seat," the uniformed woman said as they entered her office. "So you're my new virologist."

"Yes, ma'am."

"Any issues completing your studies?"

"No, ma'am. The dean transmitted my diploma last week."

"Very good," the officer said. "Not an easy way to spend two years. Alone on a starship, studying for another doctorate while everyone else is in cryosleep."

Coral shrugged. "It seemed wrong to waste that much time."

The officer fixed Coral with an appraising stare. "I bet you're wondering why I asked to meet."

"Yes, ma'am." Coral's stomach began to twist. *They know. They know what happened with Tormer and they don't want anything to do with me.*

The officer leaned forward. "Most people are doing anything they can to get off this rock. Last week we lost eleven humans and sixteen Eleosians to this damned Mist Flu. After the Medal of Merit for your report on the Nossians, you could have gone anywhere. So I have to ask, why here?"

Coral didn't answer right away. How could she explain it? The guilt that followed submission of Tormer's report? Every time a colleague emailed their congratulations, or her superiors gently prodded her to apply for a promotion, she wanted to scream out that she wasn't deserving.

She'd been on the verge of blowing the whistle so many times. But some cynical part of her, a part awakened by her experience with Tormer, whispered the truth: no matter what she said, no matter who she told, it would change nothing.

Tormer would still be on the loose. Voyager would continue to use his work to subvert the Nossians. And she would get thrown in a cell.

This hopeless thought nearly broke her.

In the end, salvation had come from the most unlikely place: a persistent, haunting vision of Tormer's face. Not the leering mug shot from the news, but a memory from the afterglow of when he'd saved her life. The moment an evil man had done something good, even if it was for the wrong reasons.

In that moment, good had blossomed from evil.

And it could happen again, with some help.

The inspiration granted Coral a night of dreamless sleep. She'd put in her applications for Eleos and the virology program at UC Berkeley remote campus the next morning.

Coral looked up at the porting officer, smiling at the memory. "Would you let me get away with 'It's complicated'?"

The officer smiled back. "Dr. Enfield, it's a complicated galaxy."

The Widow's Might

written by
Elizabeth Chatsworth

illustrated by
MADOLYN LOCKE

ABOUT THE AUTHOR

Elizabeth Chatsworth is a British author and actor based in Connecticut. She loves to write of rogues, rebels, and renegades across time and space. Her debut novel, The Brass Queen, *which was featured on the cover of* Publishers Weekly *magazine, shares its fantastical Victorian-age setting with her short story, "The Widow's Might."*

Elizabeth enjoys martial arts, horseback riding, cosplay, video games, and baking (but never at the same time). There's a rumor that she possesses the world's best scone recipe. Leave your calling card at her website to see if it's true!

ABOUT THE ILLUSTRATOR

Madolyn Locke is an emerging artist working primarily in fantasy fine-art photography and digital art. Born and raised in Alabama, Madolyn has lived in Atlanta, Georgia, long enough to consider herself a native. She received her first "real" camera from her uncle at the age of thirteen, but it wasn't until many years later that she focused on her passion for the art form and decided to get serious about her work. Madolyn has been selected for several exhibitions in Atlanta and across the country, including becoming a fixture at the Dragon Con Art Show, where she won Best Photography in 2018 and Best Photography/Digital Art in 2019. Her work has been shown in New York's Chelsea district and featured in several art shows in Canada. Madolyn's inspiration is born from the belief that even in today's world of confusion and chaos, there are still things of beauty that can fill our thoughts and dreams. Her work often explores the varying relationships between popular sci-fi/ fantasy culture and fine art.

The Widow's Might

Norwalk, Connecticut, 1897
Miss Brina's Tea Emporium, Midnight

Coal-smoke clouds choked the starlight from the city sky. Only the flash of a passing airship's running lights could tear this infinite veil of night. Through the spotless window of her tea emporium, Miss Brina Gill—fifty-five and resolutely single—watched a whisper of mist drift along the cobblestones. Ornate gas lamps cast golden pools of light between shuttered stores. Now and then, a cat's eyes blazed green, hunting for the rats that ran up from the harbor after the daytime bustle of the main street settled into stillness.

In the deepest corner of the gloomiest doorway, shadows traced the outline of a woman in a veiled hat as dark as the midnight firmament.

Brina leaned forward in her sensible boots, her warm breath misting the cool glass. Was this her summoned guest? Or merely one of the poor homeless souls that wandered the streets long after decent folk had taken to their beds? Perhaps she should open the door, call out that there was hot tea and day-old scones available for any who wished to join her?

The woman's form dissolved into the gloom. The tip of Brina's nose grazed the glass as the hair rose on her neck.

"Shall we get on?" breathed a lilting voice behind her. "I don't have all night."

MADOLYN LOCKE

Brina spun on her heel, heart thudding against her ribs. A tall woman cloaked head to toe in widow's weeds towered over her. Her fine woolen cloak hung open, untethered by a bronze Celtic brooch of a dragon devouring its own tail. Beneath her cloak, a black leather over-corset cruelly cinched in a voluminous bustled mourning gown. A heavy veil hid the woman's features below a hat laden with glossy crow feathers. In her black velvet gloves, she held the prior month's edition of *The Connecticut Lady* magazine.

Brina knew the classified advertisement on page thirteen by heart. *Are you a lady in distress? Bespoke services provided to eliminate your troubles quickly and discreetly.* She glanced between her visitor and the gaslit street. "How on earth did you get from there to here so—"

"Magic," said the woman flatly.

Brina gaped. "No!"

Her visitor's laugh was a babbling brook dancing over granite rocks. "Ah, I can see you're going to be a sharp one, Miss Gill. Incidentally, you would be wise to keep the window on your pantry locked."

"I thought it was."

"You thought wrong."

Brina blinked. "But you can't possibly have climbed in through that tiny window in a cloak and bustle? I mean—"

"Can't I? If you say so." The widow surveyed the eight round tables that made up Brina's beverage empire. Snowy lace tablecloths, a china cabinet laden with blue willow cups and plates, and a polished teak counter crowned by an archaic brass cash register. Framed covers of *The Connecticut Lady* magazine hung beside pinned wanted posters of handsome airship pirates that served to titillate her post-church Sunday luncheon customers. After all, every tearoom needs a conversation starter. "Lovely place you have here, Miss Gill. Most inviting."

A glow of pride warmed Brina's chest. She beamed. "Thank you. It's taken me twenty years to build this establishment into a profitable concern. But heavens, where are my manners? Would you care for a spot of tea?" She hastened toward the counter, keeping one eye on her guest in the mottled antique mirror that hung behind the register.

"Speaking of hot water." The widow settled her bustle onto a chair facing the door and placed her magazine on the table. "And of you falling into it, do tell me about these uncouth bullies you'd like eliminated."

Brina licked her lips as she spooned her finest tea into her best bone china teapot. "I don't think I'd use the word 'eliminated.' Talked sternly to, perhaps, to convince them to leave me alone. The situation is becoming intolerable. Once a month, burly ruffians barge in here demanding 'protection fees' at the behest of a gentleman named 'Ice-pick Charlie.' The implication is that if I refuse to pay, they will burn down my tea shop, potentially with me in it."

The widow nodded. "That's standard operating procedure for men of Ice-pick's ilk."

Brina added two jugs of water to her copper steam kettle, imported at great expense from Liverpool, England. She tossed a handful of supra-coal nuggets into the oven built into the kettle's base. When they touched the glowing embers within, smoke billowed, and two-foot flames lashed out from the kettle. Brina deftly kept her lace sleeves away from the fire as the water within the kettle began to bubble. Yes, the contraption was dangerous and expensive, but the time saved in waiting for a good cup of tea was surely worth the risk.

Brina added the steaming water to her teapot and entombed it in a pink knitted tea cozy. "So, you've heard of Ice-pick Charlie?" Setting the teapot aside to brew, her eyes strayed to the striped hatbox on a shelf beneath the counter. Lips set firm, she reached down, picked up the box and carried it to the widow's table.

Her guest nodded, crows' feathers bobbing as if they yearned to once more take flight. "I've heard of him, but he's nothing special. There's an Ice-pick Charlie, or a Billy-club Bob, or a Switchblade Sam springing up in every town along the Eastern Seaboard. They usually start with smuggling, then branch out to money laundering, extortion, jewel heists, casino skimming, and musical theater. Once they've hit the entertainment field, their hold on a town is complete. The local police look the other way to avoid retribution, the town elders are bribed or blackmailed into compliance, and the gang makes a hefty profit from their evil."

Brina sat opposite the woman and set the hatbox gently upon the table.

The widow steepled her fingers and studied the box. "And you've tired of turning over your hard-earned pennies to these hooligans?"

"It's worse than that. I had a bad month. Disastrous, in fact. My mother's medical bills were unpaid at the time of her death. Her funeral costs were outrageous, even for a simple service just the way she wanted. For days before and after the funeral, I played hostess to two-dozen out-of-town relatives who ate me out of house and home. Finally, a ne'er-do-well third cousin chose to raid my safe of its contents before he left. I couldn't make the monthly payment to Ice-pick, and then this happened."

Brina nudged the hatbox toward the widow.

The woman's black velvet glove traced the hatbox's lid. She slowly pushed it up and gasped.

An ache in Brina's stomach crawled up her throat. She swallowed hard, blinking back tears. "That's my cat, Mr. Tibbles. The finest ginger tom that ever walked this earth. They made him into..." She drew in a deep breath, about to say the words out loud for the first time to another person. "They made him into a hat. A cat hat, lined with purple silk. I'd raised him since he was a stray kitten. He was getting on now, of course, fourteen years and counting. But he didn't deserve this. No animal does."

The widow stroked the ginger fur softly, reverently. She crooned, "Poor little pussy. They made you into a hat, kitty cat. And we won't stand for that." She replaced the lid and sat ramrod straight. "Will we, Miss Gill?"

Brina fiddled with the hem of her sleeve. "I just want them told to leave me alone, to stay away from my shop. The thought of looking into the eyes of the men who murdered Mr. Tibbles is more than I can bear." The grief of her mother's death, the desecration of her pet, the unfairness of life weighed upon her shoulders like a lead cloak.

The widow bowed her head. "I'll see what I can do."

"And your fee?"

"We request only a modest donation to the Widows and Orphans' Benevolent Fund. We're a registered charity for the dispossessed and deserving."

Brina reviewed the widow's mourning dress that neatly mirrored her own, worn in honor of Mama. Save for the hat. She'd never wear a hat again, no matter what rules polite society inflicted upon her. "I'm sorry for your loss, Miss, Mrs., Madam...?"

"As I am for yours. We ladies must help each other as best we can, when no one else will."

"I quite agree. Do we sign a contract?"

"Nothing so formal." The widow lifted her veil. Dark hair pinned high, violet eyes, and skin paler than moonlight framed a sharp-toothed smile. "Please, Miss Gill, do call me Morrigan."

Crow's feathers upon her hat. The Irish lilt. Brina's eyebrows raised. "You're from the old country? Since I was a child at my mother's knee, she'd tell me magical tales of witches, faeries, and banshees."

"Did she now? But we are modern ladies, are we not? Such stories merely serve to strike fear into men's hearts—fear of women coming into their power, fear of change and the uncontrollable. Fear of women like us, Miss Gill."

Brina picked up the hatbox with a heavy heart. "No one has ever been afraid of me."

Morrigan's eyes glittered. "We'll have to work on that then, won't we?"

Two hours later, Brina lay flat on her stomach on the tin roof of Ice-pick Charlie's largest warehouse. She barely noticed the press of the rusting metal against her corset, focused as she was on her assigned task. Elbows propped, she peered through a pair of fantastical copper binoculars with night-piercing ocular lenses that Morrigan had produced from the billowing folds of her jet-black skirts. Brina slowly twiddled the binoculars' dual-focus wheels, zoning in on the docks below.

"Pockets in skirts shall one day lead to the emancipation of women. I'm almost sure of it," said Morrigan. She clicked together the final two segments of her brass sharpshooter rifle, drawing Brina's attention from the docks. The gun was an unusually beautiful design, long and elegant with a flare at the end not unlike a daffodil's trumpet. Engraved spring flowers and songbirds decorated the rifle's slender stock. A crown inside a cogwheel was stamped beside the trigger, suggesting that this was a weapon fit for royalty.

Morrigan caught her stare and grinned. "It's a custom design by the Brass Queen herself. Extremely rare. One of a kind, like me. Imported from across the pond."

"Like my steam kettle."

"Just so. We are practically sisters in our love for mechanical perfection. Allow me to demonstrate my latest toy—a starlight scope." As if from thin air, a silver telescope appeared in Morrigan's hand. She clipped the scope to the rifle, muttered words in a language Brina had never heard before, and a tiny purple flame ignited within the device.

Brina gasped. "That was almost..."

"Magical?" Again, that strange, sharp-toothed smile. "Technology can seem to be so. Ask yourself, how would ancient man have responded to a steam engine?"

"One can only imagine, not well."

Morrigan settled down onto the corrugated roof beside Brina. "Any developments?"

Brina peered through her binoculars at the goods barge docked below. "Charlie's men are still unloading kegs of what appears to be bootleg gin. They're being supervised by Hobbes the Hobbler." She pointed toward the quay. "That brute in the bowler hat with the beard and the bow tie. Apparently, he has a penchant for breaking people's kneecaps with a ball-peen hammer. One of my favorite teapots had an unpleasant run-in with him on his first visit to my shop. It took me days to pick all the porcelain fragments out of my rag rug, lest Mr. Tibbles cut his paws on a shard."

Morrigan squinted through her starlight scope. A purple pinprick of light danced over the distant rogues, though none seemed to notice. How the widow had managed to pack the binoculars, her rifle, plus a surprisingly tasty pork pie she'd graciously shared with Brina into her skirt pockets without ruining its sweeping lines was entirely a mystery. "Bow-tied brute. Got him."

"I don't see Baxter the Cudgel. Despite his blunt-force nickname, explosives are his game. Word has it he blew up poor Mrs. Zimmerman's bakery for unpaid debts. Fortunately, she was staying at her sister's the night of the explosion. He's plump, pompous, and cracks his knuckles in a most displeasing manner."

"And he's standing right behind ya!" growled a deep, masculine voice. Brina gaped over her shoulder as a paraffin lamp flared into life. Sure enough, Baxter and a trainee thug she believed was called Larry (gangster name pending), leered at her. They must have climbed up the same iron fire escape as she and Morrigan, as silently as cats. . . .

Ah, Mr. Tibbles. Poor, poor kitty.

Brina pursed her lips. "This is Mr. Baxter. He is one of the gentlemen who visited my establishment requesting money."

Keeping her rifle trained on the dock, Morrigan glanced at the two men. "I have questions for you, Baxter, which you shall politely answer."

He sneered. "Oooh, an Irish doxy. Why you up here in the dark in your fancy silk dress? And wotcha doin' with that…" Baxter peered at the daffodil rifle. "Gun? Miss Gill, you aren't planning to start a—"

Exactly what he thought Brina was planning to start was lost as the darkness behind the two men formed into the shape of two widows in veiled, plumed hats. Expert blows landed upon the thugs' necks, sending both slamming onto the roof with a clang. The paraffin lamp rolled on the roof but stayed lit.

Brina blinked up at the two Morrigans. No, wait, one was a little taller than the other, a little broader in the shoulders.

As Baxter and Larry groaned upon the tin, the widows drew up their veils to reveal a clean-shaven man wearing an inordinate amount of rouge and powder, and a bright-eyed Mohegan woman with a winning smile.

Morrigan waved her hand regally. "May I present Chepi and Jacob. We're equal-opportunity employers at the Widows and Orphans' Benevolent Fund. Any person from any race, class, or orientation can become a Widow as long as they commit to our cause."

Chepi curtsied as Jacob delivered a hefty kick to the moaning Baxter's behind.

"Charmed, I'm sure," said Brina. She turned to Morrigan. "For some reason, I'd assumed you'd work alone."

"Goodness, no. There are so many people I need to help. I can't be everywhere at once. And believe me, I've tried." Morrigan pressed her left eye against her rifle scope. "Mr. Baxter, I've been led to understand that you like explosions?"

"Who the hell do you think you— Ow!" Baxter yelped. Jacob had landed a heavily skirted knee into the small of his back.

"Manners," said Jacob.

Baxter snarled, "Yeah, I like a good explosion. Who doesn't?"

Morrigan smiled demurely. "Then allow me to demonstrate what happens when an incendiary round is fired into a barrel of cheap gin." Morrigan's gloved finger settled onto the trigger.

Brina placed her hand on Morrigan's arm. "But no one will be hurt, correct?"

"Of course not. At least, no one who doesn't deserve exactly what's coming to them for their wicked deeds. Balance must be restored."

Baxter snapped, "Ice-pick Charlie's gonna—"

Morrigan fired, and ten barrels of inexpensive gin detonated into a fireball of impressive proportions. Wood shards blasted into the air. Men ran screaming from the blaze, some diving into the Norwalk River that flowed ever onward into the Long Island Sound.

Baxter howled and spat out a string of colorful expletives that shocked Brina's ears.

Morrigan sat up and expertly disassembled her rifle as the night sky glowed and a distant fire bell began to ring. "Answer me this, Baxter, where is Charlie's main base of operations?"

"I'm not telling you— Oof!" A solid kick from Jacob to Baxter's kidneys punctuated Morrigan's line of questioning. He grunted. "All right, call off your dog. I'll tell ya. Charlie's set up in the old ironworks. He's using the steam hammers to bang out counterfeit gold ingots. Bricks of lead stamped and dipped in real gold plate. He's literally making himself a fortune."

"Now, was that so hard?" asked Morrigan.

Baxter shook his head. He watched, wide-eyed, as Chepi pulled the unconscious Larry's hands behind his back and tied them together with baling wire.

Morrigan said to Brina, "Chepi used to work on her family's farm in Easton, until a couple of greedy real-estate developers decided to poison the crops. Her entire family, gone in one awful weekend. Chepi was fasting at the time, for religious reasons. It seems her gods wanted her to live to avenge her people."

"You poor dear," Brina sympathized. "To lose one's nearest and dearest in such a horrible manner. It's unthinkable."

Morrigan nodded. "Alas, the evil that some men do. Chepi kindly donated the use of her farm to our cause. The developers made excellent fertilizer for our very first apple orchard. Do you like apple pie, Miss Gill?"

"Why, yes, I... Wait, are you saying that—"

"I'm not saying anything. But I do have a second question for Mr. Baxter here." Faster than a scalded puma, Morrigan shot across the tin roof and settled by Baxter's ear. She tilted his double chin up and stared into his face. Brina could almost fancy that her violet eyes were glowing. "Tell me, you villain, how did you kill Mr. Tibbles?"

Brina's heart clenched. Dear, sweet Tibbles. How he used to love to curl on her lap by the fire, purring as she rubbed his velvet ears.

Baxter blinked up at Morrigan. "Who?"

"Miss Gill's kitty? The one you turned into a—"

"Oh, that. I wasn't there. That was Ice-pick Charlie—"

"Then guess. Guess how Charlie ended the ninth of Tibbles's nine lives."

"I dunno. Drowning? Keeps the beggars quiet."

Morrigan released his chin with a snap and stepped back. She nodded at the waiting Widows. "You know what to do."

Baxter whimpered as Jacob dragged him to the fire escape and kicked him over. The farm girl, Chepi, hoisted limp Larry onto her shoulder and followed.

"Make sure that Larry is delivered unharmed to Charlie with a suitable note pinned to his chest," said Morrigan. "Shall we head back home for a nice cuppa, Miss Gill?"

"Larry won't be harmed, you say? What about Baxter?"

"We're not animals, Miss Gill. Larry will be perfectly fine. I'm sure the Widows will take a few moments to enlighten him of better career choices he could make before they send him back to Charlie. They can be most persuasive."

Brina stood and brushed herself down. "And Baxter?"

"Baxter seemed a little quick to suggest drowning a cat was the best way to keep it quiet, don't you think?"

Brina shuddered. "Yes, that was absolutely chilling."

"Who knows how many wee beasts have suffered at his hands?"

A loud splash sounded from below as a large something, or someone, was pushed into the river.

Brina almost cried out, almost ran to the fire escape to check if Baxter still lived.

Almost, but not quite.

Rest in peace my dear, darling Mr. Tibbles.

Rest in peace.

At 1:00 a.m. the following evening, Brina and Morrigan shared a cheese sandwich on a park bench. They munched as Ice-pick Charlie's men scurried to nail boards over grimy windows at the ironworks factory. The thumps of steam hammers echoed from inside as Charlie's soldiers toiled.

"They're preparing for war," observed Morrigan.

"With whom?"

Morrigan's laugh grated like a dagger on a grindstone. "With you, silly. The note pinned to Larry told Charlie that the Tea Ladies were coming for him."

"The Tea Ladies? Who on Earth are—"

"Every club needs a name, don't you think? We're the Tea Ladies, the first Connecticut branch of the Widows and Orphans' Benevolent Fund."

"But I can't possibly—"

Morrigan held up her hand. "Calm yourself, my dear. The club name is merely a tool to frighten the villains. Those who were thinking twice about living a life of crime can make their escape. Those who choose to stay have sealed their fate."

"You do enjoy a rhyme, don't you?"

"It's true, I do. Now that he's been forewarned by our somewhat threatening note, Charlie will assume there's a gang of hardened criminals coming for him, bold enough to blow up his gin shipment and knobble two of his guards. He'll want to make us pay for our audacity. He'll make this a fight worth having."

"I do feel a little guilty about the damage to the dock."

"Why? You didn't do anything."

Brina supposed that was true. "Then what are we, that is, what are the 'Tea Ladies' going to do?"

"We'll serve up a steaming cup of justice, of course."

"Oh dear. I'm not sure...."

The clip-clop of hooves on the cobbled street between the park and the ironworks drew her attention. Four Friesian mares pulled a funeral hearse down the gaslit street. A dozen mourners walked behind the hearse, their veiled hats bowed, their hands held in prayer.

A thirteenth Widow drove the carriage.

Brina's hand flew to her mouth. "Are they with us?"

"It takes an army to beat an army. You'll positively marvel at the things my Widows have tucked beneath their skirts. Rapid-fire bolt guns, incendiary grenades, a couple of steam-powered centrifugal disintegrators. Ice-pick's men will never know what hit them."

The procession drew close, and the sides of the hearse dropped to reveal a large cannon styled as a gaping dragon.

Brina's mouth went dry. "But no one will be harmed?"

"No one who doesn't deserve it. No more cats shall die at their devilish hands. Balance—"

"Must be restored. Yes, you mentioned that. But, should it be restored with a cannon?"

"I don't see why not. An eye for an eye, and all that. Did they think of poor Zimmerman's anguish when her bakery exploded? Did they consider your heartbreak when Mr. Tibbles—"

"Please, don't." Brina clutched at her aching heart. "I'm sure I'll never get over it."

"As well you shouldn't. You're at a crossroads, Miss Gill. Will you cower to monsters, or will you rise to fight the good fight? Isn't it time for the innocent to face the night together? Are we not stronger than our oppressors, armed as we are with love and respect for our fellow Widows?"

"And with a cannon."

Morrigan nodded. "And occasionally, when absolutely necessary, with a cannon."

On a silent cue, the Widows broke formation and sprinted toward Charlie's men. Brina noted that several had produced samurai-style katanas from beneath their petticoats.

Morrigan said, "I once broke up an unpleasant group of

individuals who were selling stolen swords alongside their opium. To children, if you can imagine that."

"And you served them justice?"

"From the great karmic teapot. That is my lot in life. To dispense just desserts to those who deserve them, and to provide a family to the lonely and lost."

"Do you think I'm lonely?"

"Not anymore."

And deep within her heart, Brina knew it to be true.

The ironworks' blazing furnaces lit the brutish face of Ice-pick Charlie as he struggled against the wire that bound him to a slow-rolling conveyor belt. Ten yards beyond his head, a ten-ton steam hammer pounded grading stamps into lead bars. After a trip to the gilder, the bars would look and weigh almost the same as real gold.

Charlie wailed, "I didn't kill your damned cat, Miss Gill. The beast died of old age. It had a bleedin' heart attack in its sleep after consuming half of a particularly large rat. One of my watchmen saw the whole thing go down. I just had the hat made from its skin to scare ya into payin' up."

Brina watched impassively as the conveyor belt inched along. She sat on the gilded throne that Charlie had planted on a raised stage overseeing the factory floor. A handful of his guards lay dead or dying. Most had fled into the night, pursued by the Widows. They would be given the option to join the Widows, leave town, or have their sins determine their method of execution. Brina sincerely hoped they chose their fates wisely.

"How can I believe that, Ice-pick?" she asked, as Morrigan stepped on the throat of a fallen bow-tied brute. So, Hobbes the Hobbler had survived the dockside fire. Never again would he smash a defenseless woman's favorite teapot before her very eyes.

"It's true. I swear on my mother's grave. Well, if she had a grave. You know how it is. A proper burial costs so damned much these days. Much easier to tip her in the river."

Morrigan laughed. "Told you that truth serum was a winner. I picked up the formula from a vile chemist who was using it to drag secrets out of high-court judges, so he could blackmail them. He got paid good money by a lot of bad men to get them off on charges they should have hanged for. Don't worry, though; I handled the situation."

"Quite right," said Brina.

Beads of sweat formed glistening peaks on Charlie's face as the hammer pounded ever closer.

"Miss Gill," Charlie pleaded, "this isn't like you. You're a nice old lady. You'd never say boo to a goose."

"Old?" she bristled. "How dare you, sir. And as for the goose, all I can say is 'boo.' Boo to you and all your rotten kind. I hope you repent your wicked ways. But if you don't, may you all be cast screaming into the eternal hellfire you so richly deserve."

"Spoken like the new head of the Norwalk Branch," said Morrigan, striding toward the throne, her eyes brighter than a newly honed sword.

Brina gazed up at the woman in black. "Me? No, I positively couldn't."

"These Widows are yours to command. You can set this town back on the rails of righteousness. The virtuous will punish the sinners."

Morrigan bent low to Brina and placed an ice-cold hand upon her shoulder. Brina shivered.

"It's what Mr. Tibbles would have wanted," murmured Morrigan.

Charlie screamed, "I didn't kill your cat. I didn't, I tell ya. It's all a big misunderstanding. I'll get you another. A nice, fat kitty from down by the docks. A tabby, a ginger, a black-and-white . . . noooooooooooo!"

The steam hammer smashed down, and Ice-pick Charlie was no more.

"I can't believe he didn't bury his own mother," sniffed Brina. "That's just downright disrespectful."

"So it is." Morrigan seemed to grow a little larger, a little more ethereal. Her eyes burned like the heart of an amethyst volcano. "The donation I would like for you to contribute to the Benevolent Fund is this—"

"My eternal soul?"

Morrigan smirked. "You imagine me to be a monster?"

"I don't think you're fully human."

"What is human, but a tiny piece of the divine? I'm something older than humankind, something younger than those who went before. Rest assured, my dear Brina, your soul is safe—from me, at least."

"Then what do you want?"

Morrigan swung her arm wide. "A shelter for my Widows. A haven for their weary bones to rest and sup the warmth of human kindness. You have always helped the less fortunate, Miss Gill. Open your tearoom's doors now to my black-hatted friends. Every Tuesday and Thursday evening, to be precise. Other than that, we shall bother you no more. Unless of course..."

Brina found her hands had drifted in a prayer position. "Unless?"

"Unless you truly would like to lead our local branch. The Tea Ladies could clean up this town, and the next, and the next. You could help so many of the downtrodden and beleaguered. You could give people like you a sense of purpose, of family. You could be the catalyst for positive change in your community."

"What do you get out of this?"

"Balance. A few eliminations by my human Widows will vastly outweigh the harm caused to countless souls by violent reprobates. Like loose tea heaped on a weighing scale, we return to equilibrium, and our shared world doesn't shatter."

"Shattering would be bad."

"But that said—" Morrigan tilted her head.

"Sometimes you need to stir the pot."

Morrigan beamed. "Then stir away, my dear. This town is yours for the taking."

Brina rose, standing taller than ever before in her sensible boots. "Then let us begin our work. But first, a nice cup of tea?"

"For two, my dear. Tea for two."

Brina strolled into the night, arm in arm with her new best friend.

Mr. Tibbles would surely have approved.

Magic Out of a Hat

BY L. RON HUBBARD

L. Ron Hubbard was one of the most widely acclaimed authors during the days of popular pulp fiction with over 200 short stories, novellas and novels published in numerous genres, including science fiction, fantasy, western, adventure, mystery and detective.

Novice writers who hoped to learn Hubbard's storytelling skills often consulted him for advice. And he was always willing to offer suggestions. In fact, he provided lengthy responses to queries on where a writer should live, how much research one should do, and which type of fiction to write.

He further shared his hard-won experience with creative writing students in speaking engagements at institutions such as Harvard and George Washington University.

He also generated a series of "how-to" articles that appeared in writing magazines of the 1930s and 1940s, offering guidance to help new writers navigate obstacles they were likely to encounter. Many of these articles are a part of the annual Writers of the Future weeklong workshop for Contest winners and the online workshop, which is open to everyone.

The following article provides insight on generating a solid story idea while it also reveals a bit of the effusive spirit that Ron brought to the magic of writing.

Magic Out of a Hat

When Arthur J. Burks told me to put a wastebasket upon my head, I knew that one of us—probably both—was crazy. But Burks has a winning way about him—it's said he uses loaded dice—and so I followed his orders and thereby hangs a story. And what a story!

You know, of course, how all this pleasant lunacy started. Burks bragged that he could give six writers a story apiece if only they would name an article in a hotel room. Considering the way New York furnishes its hotels—and remember Burks lived there—that doesn't sound so remarkable. And so six of us, he tells me, took him up on it and trooped in.

The six were Fred "Par" Painton, George "Sizzling Air" Bruce, Norvell "Spider" Page, Walter "Curly-Top" Marquiss, Paul "Haunted House" Ernst and myself. An idiotic crew if I do say it, wholly in keeping with such a scheme to mulch editors with alleged stories.

So Burks told me to put a wastebasket on my head, told me that it reminded me of a *kubanka* (Ruski lid, if you aren't a Communist) and ordered me to write the story. I won't repeat here the story he told me to write. It was clean, that's about all you can say for it—although that says a great deal coming from an ex-Marine like Art.

This wastebasket didn't even look faintly like a *kubanka*. A *kubanka* is covered with fur, looks like an ice-cream cone minus its point and is very nice if you're a Ruski. I wrote the story and I'll tell you all about the right way to develop it, so don't go wrong and find Art's article (in that issue with the putrid-pink cover and bilge-green head) and see how he did it. I'll show you the *right* way.

Burks told me to write about a Russian lad who wants his title back and so an American starts the wheels rolling, which wheels turn to gun wheels or some such drivel—and there's a lot of flying in the suggestion too. Now I saw right there that Art had headed me for a cheap action story not worth writing at all. He wanted to do some real fighting in it and kill off a lot of guys.

But I corrected the synopsis so I didn't have to save more than the Russian Empire and I only bumped about a dozen men. In fact, my plot was real literature.

The conversation which really took place (Burks fixed it in his article so he said everything) was as follows:

BURKS: I say it looks like a hat. A *kubanka*.

HUBBARD: It doesn't at all. But assuming that it does, what of it?

BURKS: Write a story about it.

HUBBARD: Okay. A lot of guys are sitting around a room playing this game where you throw cards into a hat and gamble on how many you get in. But they're using a fur wastebasket for the hat.

BURKS: A fur wastebasket? Who ever heard of that?

HUBBARD: You did just now. And they want to know about this fur wastebasket, so the soldier of fortune host tells them it's a *kubanka* he picked up and he can't bear to throw it away although it's terrible bad luck on account of maybe a dozen men getting bumped off because of it. So he tells them the story. It's a "frame" yarn, a neat one.

BURKS: But you'll make me out a liar in my article.

HUBBARD: So I'll make you a liar in mine.

So I started to plot the story. This hat is a very valuable thing, obviously, if it's to be the central character in a story. And it is a central character. All focus is upon it. Next I'll be writing a yarn in second person.

Anyway, I was always intrigued as a kid by an illustration in a book of knowledge. Pretty red pictures of a trooper riding, a fight, a dead trooper.

You've heard the old one: For want of a nail the shoe was lost, for want of a shoe the horse was lost, for want of a horse the rider was lost, for want of a rider the message was lost, for want of a message the battle was lost and all for the want of a horseshoe nail.

So, it's not to be a horseshoe nail but a hat that loses a battle or perhaps a nation. I've always wanted to lift that nail plot and here was my chance to make real fiction out of it. A hat. A lost empire.

Pretty far apart, aren't they? Well, I'd sneak up on them and maybe scare them together somehow. I made the hat seem ominous enough and when I got going, perhaps light would dawn.

"That's a funny-looking hat," I remarked.

The others eyed the object and Stuart turned it around in his hands, gazing thoughtfully at it.

"But not a very funny hat," said Stuart, slowly. "I don't know why I keep it around. Every time I pick it up I get a case of the jitters. But it cost too much to throw away."

That was odd, I thought. Stuart was a big chap with a very square face and a pocket full of money. He bought anything he happened to want and money meant nothing to him. But here he was talking about cost.

"Where'd you get it?" I demanded.

Still holding the thing, still looking at it, Stuart sat down in a big chair. "I've had it for a long, long time, but I don't know why. It spilled more blood than a dozen such hats could hold, and you see that this could hold a lot."

Something mournful in his tone made us take seats about him. Stuart usually joked about such things.

Well, there I was. Stuart was telling the story and I had to give him something to tell. So I told how he came across the hat.

114

This was the world war, the date was July 17, 1918, Stuart was a foreign observer trying to help Gajda, the Czech general, get Russia back into fighting shape. Stuart is in a clearing.

... and the rider broke into a clearing.

From the look of him, he was a Cossack. Silver cartridge cases glittered in the sun and the fur on his kubanka rippled in the wind. His horse was lathered, its eyes staring with exertion. The Cossack sent a hasty glance over his shoulder and applied his whip.

Whatever was following him did not break into the clearing. A rifle shot roared. The Cossack sat bolt upright as though he had been a compressed steel spring. His head went back, his hands jerked, and he slid off the horse, rolling when he hit the ground.

I remember his *kubanka* bounced and jumped and shot in under a bush....

Feebly, he motioned for me to come closer. I propped him up and a smile flickered across his ashy face. He had a small, arrogant mustache with waxed points. The blackness of it stood out strangely against the spreading pallor of death.

"The ... *kubanka* ... Gajda ..."

That was all he would ever say.

Fine. The *kubanka* must get to General Gajda. Here I was, still working on the horseshoe nail and the message.

The message, the battle was lost. The message meant the *kubanka*. But how could a *kubanka* carry a message? Paper in the hat? That's too obvious. The hero's still in the dark. But here a man has just given his life to get this hat to the Czechs and the hero at least could carry on, hoping General Gajda would know the answer.

He was picking up the one message he knew the hat must carry. He had killed three men in a rifle battle at long range in an attempt to save the Cossack. There's suspense and danger for you. A white man all alone in the depths of Russia during

115

a war. Obviously somebody else is going to get killed over this hat. The total is now four.

I swore loudly into the whipping wind. I had had no business getting into this fight in the first place. My duty was to get back to the main command and tell them that Ekaterinburg was strongly guarded. Now I had picked up the Cossack's torch. These others had killed the Cossack. What would happen to me?

So my story was moving along after all. The fact that men would die for a hat seems too ridiculous that, when they do die, it's horrible by contrast, seemingly futile.

But I can't have my hero killed, naturally, as this is a first-person story, so I pass the torch to another, one of my hero's friends, an English officer.

This man, as the hero discovers later, is murdered for the *kubanka* and the *kubanka* is recovered by the enemy while the hero sleeps in a hut of a *muzjik* beside the trail.

The suspense up to here and even further is simple. You're worried over the hero, naturally. And you want to know, what's better, why a hat should cause all this trouble. That in itself is plenty of reason for writing a story.

Now while the hero sleeps in the loft, three or four Russian Reds come in and argue over the money they've taken from the dead Englishman, giving the hero this news without the hero being on the scene.

The hat sits in the center of the table. There it is, another death to its name. Why?

So they discover the hero's horse in the barn and come back looking for the hero. Stuart upsets a lamp in the fight, the hut burns, but he cannot rescue the hat. It's gone.

Score nine men for the hat. But this isn't an end in itself. Far from it. If I merely went ahead and said that the hat was worth a couple hundred kopeks, the reader would get mad as hell after reading all this suspense and sudden death. No, something's got to be done about that hat, something startling.

What's the most startling thing I can think of? The empire connected with the fate of the *kubanka*. So the Russian Empire begins to come into it more and more.

The allies want to set the tsar back on the throne, thinking that will give Russia what it needs. Germany is pressing the Western Front and Russia must be made to bear its share.

But I can't save Russia by this hat. Therefore I'll have to destroy Russia by it. And what destroyed it? The tsar, of course. Or rather his death.

The Czech army moves on Ekaterinburg, slowly because they're not interested so much in that town. They could move faster if they wanted. This, for a feeling of studied futility in the end.

They can't find the tsar when they get there. No one knows where the tsar is or even if he's alive.

This must be solved. Stuart finds the hat and solves it.

He sees a Red wearing a *kubanka*. That's strange because Cossacks wear *kubankas* and Reds don't. Of all the hats in Russia this one must stand out, so I make the wrong man wear it.

Stuart recovers the *kubanka* when this man challenges him. He recognizes the fellow as one of the Englishman's murderers. In the scrap, seconded by a sergeant to even up the odds, Stuart kills three men.

Score twelve for one secondhand hat. Now about here the reader's patience is tried and weary. He's had enough of this. He's still curious, but the thing can't go any farther. He won't have it.

That's the same principle used in conversation. You've got to know enough to shut up before you start boring your listeners. Always stop talking while they're still interested.

I could have gone on and killed every man in Russia because of that hat and to hell with history.

History was the thing. It thrust up its ugly head and shook a warning finger at me. People know now about the tsar, when and where he was killed and all the rest. So that's why I impressed dates into the first of the story. It helps the reader believe you when his own knowledge tells him you're right. And if you can't lie convincingly, don't ever write fiction.

Now the hero, for the first time (I stressed his anxiety in the front of the story) has a leisurely chance to examine this hat. He finally decides to take the thing apart, but when he starts to rip the threads he notices that it's poorly sewn.

This is the message in the hat, done in Morse code, around the band:

"Tsar held at Ekaterinburg, house of Ipatiev. Will die July 18. Hurry."

Very simple, say you. Morse code, old stuff. But old or not, the punch of the story is not a mechanical twist.

The eighteenth of July has long past, but the hero found the hat on the seventeenth. Now had he been able to get it to Gajda, the general's staff could have exhausted every possibility and uncovered that message. They could have sent a threat to Ekaterinburg or they could have even taken the town in time. They didn't know, delayed, and lost the Russian tsar and perhaps the nation.

Twelve men, the tsar and his family and an entire country dies because of one hat.

Of course, the yarn needs a second punch, so the hero finds the jewels of the tsar in burned clothing in the woods and knows that the tsar is dead for sure and the Allied cause for Russia is lost.

The double punch is added by the resuming of the game of throwing cards into this hat.

But after a bit we started to pitch the cards again. Stuart sent one sailing down the room. It touched the brim and teetered there. Then, with a flicker of white, it coasted off the side and came to rest some distance away, face up.

We moved uneasily. I put my cards away.

The one Stuart had thrown, the one which had missed, was the king of spades.

Well, that's the "Price of a Hat." It sold to Leo Margulies's *Thrilling Adventures* magazine of the Standard Magazines, Inc., which, by the way, was the magazine that bought my first pulp story. It will appear in the March issue, on sale, I suppose, in February. Leo is pretty much of an adventurer himself and, without boasting on my part, Leo knows a good story when he sees it. In a letter to my agent accepting my story, Leo Margulies wrote: "We are glad to buy Ron Hubbard's splendid story "Price of a Hat." I read the DIGEST article and am glad you carried it through."

Art Burks is so doggoned busy these days with the American Fiction Guild and all, that you hardly see anything of him. But someday I'm going to sneak into his hotel anyway, snatch up the smallest possible particle of dust and make him make me write a story about that. I won't write it, but he will. I bet when he sees this, he'll say:

"By golly, that's a good horror story." And sit right down and make a complete novel out of one speck of dust.

Anyway, thanks for the check, Art. I'll buy you a drink, plenty of pay, at the next luncheon. What? Well, didn't I do all the work?

On "Magic Out of a Hat"
BY ORSON SCOTT CARD

Orson Scott Card is the author of Ender's Game, Ender's Shadow, *and* Speaker for the Dead, *which are widely read by adults and by younger readers, and are often used in schools. His recent series,* Pathfinder *(*Pathfinder, Ruins, Visitors*) and* Mithermages *(*Lost Gate, Gate Thief, Gatefather*) are taking readers in new directions.*

*Card also writes contemporary fantasy (*Magic Street, Enchantment, Lost Boys*), biblical novels (*Sarah, Rebekah, Rachel and Leah*), the American frontier fantasy series* The Tales of Alvin Maker *(beginning with* Seventh Son*), and poetry and drama, including his "freshened" Shakespeare scripts for* Romeo & Juliet, The Taming of the Shrew, *and* The Merchant of Venice.

Card was born in eastern Washington, and grew up in California, Arizona, and Utah. He served a mission for the LDS *Church in Brazil in the early 1970s. Besides his fiction, he is a professor of writing and literature at Southern Virginia University.*

He currently lives in Greensboro, North Carolina, with his wife, Kristine Allen Card, where his primary activities are feeding birds, squirrels, chipmunks, opossums, and raccoons on the patio, and watching reruns of Jeopardy!, Ridiculousness, *and* Beat Bobby Flay, *interrupted occasionally by writing something and trying to get paid for it.*

On "Magic Out of a Hat"

The thing that amazes me is that L. Ron Hubbard was at the top of the field when he wrote this essay. By that I mean that he was one of the few writers who could not just make a living as a writer, but make a very good living. Since a writer's earnings depend on the readers' demand for his work, it would have been clear to novice writers that when he talked about any facet of writing, chances were very good that he knew what he was talking about.

Yet what motive did he have to disclose methods of writing that might help younger writers to learn how to compete with him for precious space in the fiction magazines? Instead of fearing competition, however, he welcomed it. My personal belief is that writers are not competing with each other at all.

When some writers were complaining about J.K. Rowling's domination of the bestseller lists, many of us recognized that every reader of Harry Potter novels would now be looking for more fiction to read, and among their choices might be some works of mine.

Every good story encourages its audience to read more stories, and by encouraging readers, the space in magazines or on the bookshelves will expand to meet the demand. L. Ron Hubbard understood this. The success of new writers does not take a dime out of the pockets of established authors.

So instead of trying to shut out the competition, Hubbard endowed and created the Writers of the Future Contest, which culminates in an annual anthology where every winner is published. Instead of just having a little certificate or a trophy or the ability to tell an editor about it when they're submitting a story or novel, their story is actually published in the best-read anthology, period.

Many writers who were completely unknown, unpublished, or only published once or in obscure places like their own website have, through the *Writers of the Future* anthology, launched a career that brought them to prominence in the field and made them not just influenced by, but also an influence on other writers. I have to regard this as one of the greatest successes in L. Ron Hubbard's extremely successful career. He was a writer who looked out for other writers. I think that's cool.

One of the things I have loved best about the science fiction field is that there are an awful lot of people who are kind to newcomers, take them under their wing, and help them get over the hurdles of life as a writer.

That's what L. Ron Hubbard did even before he founded the Contest. This essay, "Magic Out of a Hat," recounts how a writer friend challenged him to write a story about a certain kind of furry Russian hat, a *kubanka*. From this challenge he wrote an important, meaningful story.

Hubbard describes his own thought processes, how he goes about coming up with a story. What I found most significant was that he didn't instantly go, Oh, yeah, I know how to do this kind of thing, and then start writing.

Instead he thought, Well, the easiest thing to do would be to have a whole bunch of people shooting at each other. We have a situation which is on the Eastern Front of World War I, with a Czech who is interested in trying to defeat Germany, during the time when the Russian Revolution and the Bolshevik coup threatened to make it so the opposition to Germany in the East would just collapse. If that happened, the Germans would be able to take all of their troops, all of their materiel, to the west and fling it at the French and British and the newly arriving Americans. There was a lot at stake, and readers of that time would all have understood exactly what was at stake.

But Hubbard didn't want to write an adventure story where a lot of people get shot. It's not that he was against writing fiction where people get shot. Good heavens, he wouldn't have had a career if he forbade himself to do that, in that era. He simply didn't want to write *just* an action story. He wanted a story where character mattered and where the hat itself mattered; it wasn't just something that would fall off the head of someone who got shot. It had to be an important plot point.

So he thought of the old ironic verse about: For want of the nail, the shoe was lost. For want of the shoe, the horse was lost. The rider was lost, the message he carried went undelivered, so the battle was lost. Hubbard wanted to set up a similar situation.

Now, having said that, we kind of know the broad outline of the story, but not the specifics. One of the gifts that Hubbard had is that he could very quickly—pre-Internet, pre-Google— figure out what he needed to know in the way of facts in order to tell a believable, detailed story. Then he got that necessary information. Some of it came straight out of his head, because there were things that everybody knew who was alive at the end of the Great War.

And there were things that Hubbard simply invented, that might have been possible or true. What mattered was that they happened to *this* character in *this* story. It's true within the story. So while in this essay he doesn't actually give us the story itself, he tells us what the story was going to be, what it became.

Instead of showing part of a draft of the story, where we'd see scenes develop with dialogue and so on, he merely implies those, hints at them. What he actually gives us is the told story, which I believe is the real story, the deep story, the Plain Tale, which is the aspect of the story that is completely translatable into other languages and into other media.

The Plain Tale consists of what happens and why. Not the "plot," because that is a listing of which scenes to write out in detail, including who is present in each scene. The Plain Tale doesn't insist on particular details except those absolutely essential to the motivations and possibilities of the characters. The actions and events in the story, along with enough information for us to know *why* they happen as they do—that's the deep story.

Thus Hubbard describes how he went from what amounts to a prompt—some idea that's a trigger and that makes you start to think—to the process you go through in order to turn that idea into something that will be memorable, where, at the end of reading the story, you go: *That* was a *story*.

The techniques and processes L. Ron Hubbard used in the Golden Age of short fiction still apply, after all these years. They always will.

Hubbard already had the skills of writing for a popular audience, which is relatively rare, because popular fiction has to be so clearly written that an untrained reader, on a cold reading, can understand everything that is said, without the reader having to slow down, back up, and reread in order to figure out what just happened. Once a reader has to stop and struggle to decode the writing, you've proven yourself to be incompetent at writing clear fiction. You never have to do that with Hubbard.

Hubbard wrote his earliest science fiction before all the good ideas had been used up. Now we sci-fi writers have to do a very different thing. We have to create societies that depend on difference in the culture—because of changes in technology, evolution, planetary dynamics, climate, or society. And it's not enough to simply reveal the cool idea at the end; the writer has to lead us to care about the characters and how their lives turn out. So we no longer depend entirely on the science fictional tool set. We have to learn from other genres, broaden our appeal, find ways to make reading our stories a memorable experience.

Hubbard lived in the Golden Age of science fiction. Everything was free. You could do whatever you wanted because it hadn't been done before. The genre was new. The term "science fiction" had only recently been coined. Hugo Gernsback was still trying to get people to use "scientifiction," which doesn't work because you can't place the stress. It's

125

either scienti*fic*-tion, or scien*tif*-iction, and neither one does the job. The language will do what language does, and "science fiction" won out in the end.

It was better than what people *used* to call the nascent genre: "Scientific romances like those of H. G. Wells or Jules Verne."

The name "science fiction" is somewhat misleading. Science does not control even a majority of the stories in the genre. I don't know any science well enough to actually practice it, but because I need the tool kit and subject matters of science fiction, I have to keep up with the relevant sciences well enough to avoid embarrassing myself. But at no point do I even *hint* about how to actually build any of the machines I postulate; to design a spaceship, you're going to need some calculus, and I'm happy to have never needed an intimate relationship with logarithms.

Hubbard didn't write stories in which you could build the cool machines, either. He didn't go into science fiction as somebody who was fanatical about space, requiring him to know everything about it.

No, he was fanatical about writing and telling stories. He knew he was good at that. We all make our stories work the way Hubbard made things work in his story about this Russian hat toward the end of World War I. He didn't have to show every elaborate detail. He showed what was needed for the story to be clear to the reader. That's what we do today.

So while we face the same *kinds* of problems he had to solve, the actual problems have changed. Today, if I was going to set a story at the end of the Great War, I would have to explain the importance of the continued survival of the Tsar as a focal point of resistance to the Bolshevik Revolution, because I can't count on any American high school or college graduate having any idea about that period.

I've studied it, because I love history and read it more than any other genre, so as Hubbard described his story in "Magic Out of a Hat," I recognized the historical situation immediately. There are only about nine of us left who can do that.

I'm exaggerating. There are forty.

But not that many people have studied much about the Great War in order to instantly grasp what the story is about. So if Hubbard had known that he was writing it, not to an audience that had recently read about these events in the newspapers, but to a future audience that had never needed to know the events in detail, he would have devoted considerable time to setting up the situation so that modern readers would grasp it easily as the story unfolded.

If Hubbard had set a story in the court of Charles the Bold of Burgundy, he would have provided enough background for his story to make sense to, and matter to, readers of his time. And *all* science fiction writers who set stories in alternate universes or in remote futures face the same difficulty: carrying the audience into the world of the story and giving them enough of a guided tour to know where they are and what's at stake.

L. Ron Hubbard was not writing for an audience that expected to learn history or science from his stories. He did not want his readers to examine every word, every metaphor, every theme or symbol. Those are fun games to play, but they have nothing to do with the pleasure of experiencing a well-told story. Readers who read that way are like mechanics who can't enjoy driving somewhere in their car, because all they can think about is the workings of the engine, the drive shaft, the axles, the suspension.

It's not that they "can't see the forest for the trees." It's that they can't see the forest for the fungus they're examining in the root system of one particular tree. There *is* no forest for them. Just as, for critical readers who concentrate on the manner of writing, there is no story. Just language.

L. Ron Hubbard wrote for people who wanted to explore the forest, for readers who want to enjoy the drive without thinking of the machinery of the car. Hubbard's readers want to be moved. They want to move through time, experiencing things that will never happen to them in their real life. When the story is well-conceived and clearly written, those memories become part of *their* memory, part of their human experience.

In that way, Hubbard and all of us are trying to write for

127

civilians, for volunteer readers who are not expecting to have to write essays about the fiction they read. Readers who buy fiction, not as gifts, not as requirements, but simply to read it themselves. We are all doing the same job that Hubbard was so good at: creating vicarious memories that people will want to carry around with them. Stories that might actually change them because of what they've seen and heard and experienced while reading.

Now, I don't really think visually. I just don't. All I care about is what happens and why.

But that doesn't change the fact that I have my mental picture of Frodo standing at the Cracks of Doom. I have my own memory about how Bilbo's ring was left behind when he departed, with Gandalf there to guard it, but refusing to touch it or take it himself. He wasn't yet sure what the ring was, but he had his suspicions, and later he comes back and we get the marvelous scene where he tosses the ring into the fire, verifies that it is the One Ring, and then explains the history of the ring to Frodo.

Those memories are imprinted in our memories after reading the first couple of chapters of *Lord of the Rings*. Therefore, I live in a memory world where I have carried the ring, because the author of the story wrote it so well and so clearly that there is nothing standing between me and that memory.

Hubbard was perfectly content to have his writing be accessible. He wants us to care about the characters, to believe in them. That's why his stories hold up, why they're still readable.

Almost all of science fiction is still available to us, still *alive*. That's one of the amazing things about our genre. That is partly because science fiction was never taught in the universities in the early days. Even now, science fiction is rarely taught using the same critical procrustean bed that force-fits everything into the same literary model.

Instead, in those early days, we came up with our own standards of criticism. Defining what makes the difference between "good" and "bad" science fiction, and how to sort out the different subgenres in the field.

By "we," I mean me and my predecessors—mostly them, not me, because I came to the field rather late in the game. The critical standards were not discovered or devised in university English departments, but rather in fanzines, in little mimeographed and dittoed news sheets, in things so horribly reproduced that you could hardly read them, in fanzines that were only mailed out to ten people. Yet if they were the *right* ten people, who believed in what you said, you could influence the whole community of science fiction readers and writers.

That's the world into which L. Ron Hubbard sent his science fiction stories—as did everyone else in those early days. It was a world where the critical standards were being invented according to what the best writers actually did. And the stories that worked, that readers responded to, became the measure by which everything else was judged.

That was so liberating.

People complained because the professors "don't care about what we do, they don't understand, they undervalue our literature." But that was the best environment in which this revolutionary new literary genre could develop. We didn't need professors to define and explain the stories we wrote, the stories we loved to read.

Our stories are designed to be read without the intervention of an interpreter. Only if you write in a language that requires translation into English, is there any need for an interpreter. Our fiction is meant to be read by volunteers, unaided. They can understand what's going on, because we give them, within the story, all the information they need in order to understand it.

Even when Hubbard is writing an essay about the invention of a story, which is what "Magic Out of a Hat" is, he still tells *that* story so clearly that no interpreter is needed. Period. He is speaking directly into the reader's mind, using clarity of language.

In science fiction, we still have all of the writers whose works still live. Asimov is gone, but you can still get his books, and they are still revelatory. You can read L. Ron Hubbard, Ray Bradbury, Arthur C. Clarke. You can read the stories of every period of science fiction you want, after the Golden Age. You want great stories about the Cambrian Era? Blish is still in print. You want to read the beginning of the experimentalists? You can still find Philip K. Dick, Thomas Disch, still in print.

You want to read the "New Wave" of science fiction? Harlan Ellison's "I Have No Mouth and I Must Scream" and "'Repent, Harlequin!' Said the Ticktockman" are still there, waiting to find new readers. Ellison's great early stories are still magical—gloriously overwrought, because that's what he was trying to do. They are still brilliant pieces of fiction.

But then you move right on, and you've got John Varley. You've got Larry Niven, who never stopped writing the clear prose of the Campbellian writers. He's the heir to Heinlein. He's the heir to Clarke. And wonderfully he is still working, still producing. He is the writer who kept that kind of storytelling alive even when the sci-fi community seemed to be in thrall to the New Wave writers.

But that was and is the glory and the frustration of writing science fiction in the English-speaking world. It was free. You could do whatever you thought your readers could bear. You could take them wherever you thought they could understand what you were telling them. And because it was being published on pulp paper, in installments in a magazine with half-clad women and hideous monsters on the cover, everyone would know not to pay attention to it in a serious critical way, science fiction was free to invent itself.

L. Ron Hubbard was part of that invention. When he wrote about writing, as in "Magic Out of a Hat," he wasn't teaching us how to write science fiction. He was teaching us how to tell stories, how to come up with an idea and develop it into something coherent that would give the reader satisfaction upon reaching the end.

As far as I'm concerned, we have had enough cultural changes that much fiction dating from those early days doesn't hold up. Science fiction does better than most, because it was always trying to cut loose from its moorings in time. But the project hasn't changed—you write to the audience of your own time, and then hope that at least some of your stories will have staying power because readers care about them and pass them along to other readers.

When L. Ron Hubbard writes about how to go about thinking of a story, inventing and shaping and structuring, it's still worth paying attention to what he says about it—because the job hasn't changed.

The Dangerous Dimension

written by
L. Ron Hubbard

illustrated by
ANH LE

ABOUT THE AUTHOR

By 1938, L. Ron Hubbard was a well-known adventure writer. Already more than 100 of his short stories, novellas and novels were published in the popular all-fiction magazines (the so-called "pulp magazines") featuring adventure, military, western, detective and romance stories.

He was almost larger than life. Author, editor, critic Damon Knight described him with this: "When Astounding *published a short story called 'The Dangerous Dimension,' few of us had ever heard of L. Ron Hubbard.*

"Hubbard was the typus [sic] of a now-vanishing tribe of pulp writers: like Tom Roan who made occasional appearances in editorial offices wearing a ten-gallon hat and swearing like a mule skinner; Norvell Page, who affected an opera-cloak . . . Hubbard lived what he wrote. Big, swaggering, and red-haired (like many of his heroes); sailor, explorer, adventurer—a man among men . . . he cut a swath across the science-fantasy world the like of which has not been seen before or since."

Ron's initial entrance to the science fiction and fantasy field was made at the request of Street & Smith's management, the publishers of Astounding Science Fiction. *The magazine's editor introduced L. Ron Hubbard's presence to his readers simply saying that it "represents, for* Astounding, *the effort to get the best stories of the science-fiction type by the best authors available."*

Ron Hubbard's first story for Astounding *was published in the July 1938 issue, "The Dangerous Dimension." Ron later described it as "unusual for its philosophy, humor and its emphasis on people and not monsters."*

The letters started streaming into the editor, appearing in Astounding's *"Brass Tacks," including a note from a young Isaac*

Asimov: "I laughed myself sick over it. Some more from L. Ron Hubbard, please."

Ron's second story was serialized September through November in 1938. "The Tramp," was a guy who acquires immense mental powers after a brain operation to save his life.

And then there were more letters to the magazine editor.

In answer, L. Ron Hubbard wrote the following, both as a response and a philosophical inquiry:

In a recent issue, readers were kind enough to treat my story, "The Dangerous Dimension" with more kindness than it probably deserved. And there was an additional gratification about it: no story worth its paper fails to excite damning in one way or another and throughout the kind comments there was still a healthy undercurrent of damnation which had been, of course, expected for a story which lacked "scientific background." One reader in particular was kind enough to say that he wished the author had given some excerpts from philosophic works showing the source of the idea that a man might project himself from one point [to another] mentally. Another very civilly offered to raise the devil if anybody jumped the story from the angle that it had no scientific background.

On the other hand, "The Tramp" had this necessary ingredient because mitogenetic rays are well known, if not intimately. There was then considerable difference between these two stories? Would it be an idle attempt to startle to say that "The Dangerous Dimension" is probably supported far better than "The Tramp"?

Not at first was this difference fully realized. As my realm, if any, is philosophy, I did not question the idea of the story. However this sameness of comment made me wonder. The reader's wish for philosophic background came as a mental catalyst. Was there a background of any validity to this story and if so, what?

The answer led to something also which may prove of interest. Anything is likely to happen when one gets started on a certain chain of thought.

The background of "The Dangerous Dimension" is philosophic.

It is quite authentic. The Veda, Yogism, long, long ago found its first *chela* going into a trance from which he could project himself, the life essence of himself, into far realms and ranges. This Indian basis is quite valid when one considers that all our religions and a great deal of our science has wandered in from India, and that is part of a vast creed.

The next thought comes from Berkeley's *Principles of Human Knowledge* where he gives the impression that all is a divine intelligence. This is only a side play on an ancient idea that everything is a Mind and therefore there exists nothing but Mind and, hence, no space.

We can go to Hume who denies everything on the assumption that we only perceive things through our senses and that the world, therefore, either has no validity or else we can never have any knowledge of it.

Kant actually confirms Hume no matter how hard the "old Chinaman of Königsberg" (as Nietzsche called Kant) fought Hume. Kant says we will never have any true idea of the "thing-as-it-is" because man can only see it, touch it, taste it or smell it, and hear it. This is no guarantee of the actual state of the phenomena and so we can only know it as we sense it, not as it very well might be in actuality. Kant was afraid to allow any space anywhere (because we only perceive this sensorially) as he would then have had to have relegated God to space. If there is no space then and if we cannot ever contact the "thing-as-it-is," we only have to progress a step to fling a man around a Universe where there is actually no space, or, as Kant says, time either because we also perceive that.

Spinoza's works give several leads to such a thing, mainly his assumption that All is Force which is, after all, but a step from the Unity of All of the Veda of many centuries before. In addition there is the modern denial of matter in Christian Science.

There is much more testimony in favor of mental projection of a body through space than there is in favor of mitogenetic eyes and yet the latter will be more readily accepted since it is "science."

But this is almost beside the point as the question led much further. We are all interested in these speculations about matter, space and time than we will care to admit to the professors who sometimes prove "something less than kind." I began to wonder about the validity of this inner circle of "science fiction." Was it science at all? Or was it something else, even greater? Are we children of science or, to be blunt, philosophers? What would be the difference between them?

A treatise followed entitled "Tomorrow's Miracles" exploring philosophy, science and the inherent quality of writers creating new worlds and existences far beyond what is known or possible. That article can be read in Writers of the Future Volume 35.

Here we present the story that incited this thought, "The Dangerous Dimension."

ABOUT THE ILLUSTRATOR

Anh Le was born in Ho Chi Minh City, Vietnam, in 1998. Anh's name is pronounced like the letter N. His family migrated from Vietnam to the United States in 2007 for a chance at a better life.

Ever since Anh can remember, he loved drawing and creating fantastical characters and monsters from his imagination. He didn't even have a concept of what art was—he just drew whatever came to mind. His love eventually evolved into a passion to become a concept artist and illustrator.

Anh started his journey by creating complex colored pencil and marker drawings but was introduced to digital painting several years ago and hasn't been able to stop since. His objective is to immerse viewers in his breathtaking worlds and his own unique view of visual development for films, games, and animations.

Anh was a winner of the L. Ron Hubbard's Illustrators of the Future Contest and was first featured in Volume 36.

The Dangerous Dimension

AUTHOR'S NOTE

For reasons pertinent to the happiness of Mankind, by request from the United States Philosophic Society and the refusal of Dr. Henry Mudge, Ph.D., of Yamouth University, the philosophic equation mentioned herein is presented as only *Equation C* without further expansion.

—L. Ron Hubbard

The room was neither mean nor dingy. It was only cluttered. The great bookcases had gaps in their ranks and the fallen members lay limp-leaved on floor and table. The carpet was a snowdrift of wasted paper. The stuffed owl on the mantel was awry because the lined books there had fallen sideways, knocking the owl around and over to peck dismally at China on the globe of the world. The writing desk was heaped with tottering paper towers.

And still Dr. Mudge worked on.

His spectacles worried him because they kept falling down in front of his eyes; a spot of ink was on his nose and his right hand was stained blue black.

The world could have exploded without in the least disturbing Yamouth's philosophic professor. In his head whirled a maelstrom of philosophy, physics and higher mathematics and, if examined from within, he would have seemed a very brave man.

Examined from without it was a different matter. For one

---

thing Dr. Mudge was thin, for another he was bald. He was a small man and his head was far too big for his body. His nose was long and his eyes were unusually bright. His thin hands gripped book and pen as every atom of his being was concentrated upon his work.

Once he glanced up at the clock with a worried scowl. It was six-thirty and he must be done in half an hour. He had to be done in half an hour. That would give him just time enough to rush down to the university and address the United States Philosophic Society.

He had not counted on this abrupt stab of mental lightning. He had thought to deliver a calm address on the subject, "Was Spinoza Right in Turning Down the Professorship of..." But when he had begun to delve for a key to Spinoza, a truly wonderful idea had struck him and out he had sailed, at two that day, to dwell wholly in thought. He did not even know that he was cramped from sitting so long in one place.

"Henrrreeee!" came the clarion call.

Henry failed to hear it.

"HENrrrry!"

Again he did not look up.

"HENRY MUDGE! Are you going to come in here and eat your dinner or not?!"

He heard that time, but with less than half an ear. He did not come fully back to the world of beefsteak and mashed potatoes until Mrs. Doolin, his housekeeper, stood like a thundercloud in the study door. She was a big woman with what might be described as a forceful personality. She was very righteous, and when she saw the state of that study she drew herself up something on the order of a general about to order an execution.

"Henry! What have you been doing? And look at you! A smudge on your nose—and *an ink spot on your coat!*"

Henry might fight the universe, but Mrs. Doolin was the bogeyman of Henry's life. Ten years before, she had descended upon him and since that time...

"Yes, Lizzie," said Henry, aware for the first time of his stiffness and suddenly very tired.

"Are you coming to dinner or aren't you? I called you a half-hour ago and the beefsteak will be ruined. And you must dress. What on earth's gotten into you, Henry Mudge?"

"Yes, Lizzie," said the doctor placatingly. He came slowly to his feet and his joints cracked loudly.

"What *have* you done to this place?"

Some of the fire of his enthusiasm swept back into Henry. "Lizzie, I think I have it!" And that thought swept even Lizzie Doolin out of the room as far as he was concerned. He took a few excited steps around the table, raised his glasses up on his forehead and gleamed. "I think I've got it!"

"What?" demanded Lizzie Doolin.

"The equation. Oh, this is wonderful. This is marvelous! Lizzie, if I am right, there is a condition without dimension. A negative dimension, Lizzie. Think of it! And all these years they have been trying to find the fourth positive dimension and now by working backwards..."

"Henry Mudge, what *are* you talking about?"

But Henry had dove into the abstract again and the lightning was flashing inside his head. "The negative dimension! Epistemology!"

"What?"

He scarcely knew she was there. "Look, think of it! You know what you can do with your mind. Mentally you can think you are in Paris. *Zip*, your mind has mentally taken you to Paris! You can imagine yourself swimming in a river and *zip*! you are mentally swimming in a river. But the body stays where it is. And why, Lizzie? *Why?*"

"Henry Mudge—!"

"But there is a negative dimension. I am sure there is. I have almost formulated it and if I can succeed—"

"Henry Mudge, your dinner is getting cold. Stop this nonsense...."

But he had not heard her. Suddenly he gripped his pen and wrote. And on that blotted piece of paper was set down Equation C.

He was not even aware of any change in him. But half his brain began to stir like an uneasy beast. And then the other half began to stir and mutter.

And on the sheet before him was Equation C.

"Henry Mudge!" said Lizzie with great asperity. "If you don't come in here and eat your dinner this very minute..." She advanced upon him as the elephant moves upon the dog.

Henry knew in that instant that he had gone too far with her. And half his brain recognized the danger in her. For years he had been in deadly terror of her....

"I wish I was in Paris," Henry shivered to himself, starting to back up.

Whup!

"Cognac, *m'sieu?*" said the waiter.

"Eh?" gaped Henry, glancing up from the sidewalk table. He could not take it in. People were hurrying along the *Rue de la Paix*, going home as the hour was very late. Some of the cafés were already closed.

"*Cognac o vin blanc, m'sieu?*" insisted the waiter.

"Really," said Henry, "I don't drink. I— Is this Paris?"

"Of a certainty, *m'sieu*. Perhaps one has already had a sip too much?"

"No, no! I don't drink," said Henry, frightened to be in such a position.

The waiter began to count the saucers on the table. "Then *m'sieu* has done well for one who does not drink. Forty francs, *m'sieu*."

Henry guiltily reached into his pocket. But his ink-stained jacket was not his street coat. He had carpet slippers on his feet. His glasses fell down over his eyes. And his searching hands told him that he possessed not a dime.

"Please," said Henry, "I am out of funds. If you would let me—"

"SO!" cried the waiter, suavity vanishing. "Then you will pay just the same! *GENDARME! GENDARME!*"

"Oh," shivered Henry and imagined himself in the peaceful security of his study.

Whup!

Lizzie was gaping at him. "Why...why, where...where did you go? Oh, it must be my eyes. I know it must be my eyes. Those fainting spells did mean something then. Yes, I am sure of it." She glanced at the clock. "Look, you haven't eaten dinner yet! You come right into the dining room this instant!"

Meekly, but inwardly aghast, Henry tagged her into the dining room. She set a plate before him. He was not very hungry, but he managed to eat. He was greatly perplexed and upset. The negative dimension had been there after all. And there was certainly no difficulty stepping into it and out of it. Mind was everything, then, and body nothing. Or mind could control body.... Oh, it was very puzzling.

"What are you dreaming about?" challenged Lizzie. "Get upstairs and get dressed. It's seven this very minute!"

Henry plodded out into the hall and up the stairs. He got to his room and saw that all his things were laid out.

Oh, it was very puzzling, he told himself as he sat down on the edge of the bed. He started to remove one carpet slipper and then scowled in deep thought at the floor.

Twenty minutes later Lizzie knocked at his door. "Henry, you're late already!"

He started guiltily. He had not even taken that slipper off. If Lizzie found him in here— She was starting to open the door.

"I ought to be there this very minute," thought Henry, envisioning the lecture hall.

Whup!

It startled him to see them filing in. He stood nervously on the platform, suddenly aware of his carpet slippers and ink-stained working jacket, the spot on his nose and his almost black hand. Nervously, he tried to edge back.

The dean was there. "Why...why, Dr. Mudge. I didn't see you

come in." The dean looked him up and down and frowned. "I hardly think that your present attire..."

Henry visualized the clothes laid out on his bed and started to cough an apology.

"I...er..."

Whup!

"What's that, Henry?" said Lizzie. "My heavens, where are you?"

"In here, Lizzie," said Henry on the edge of his bed.

She bustled into the room. "Why, you're not dressed! Henry Mudge, I don't know what is happening to your wits. You will keep everybody waiting at the university—"

"Ohhh," groaned Henry. But it was too late.

Whup!

"My dear fellow," said the dean, startled. "What...er...what happened to you? I was saying that I scarcely thought it proper—"

"Please, I—" But that was as far as Henry got.

Whup!

"I know it's my eyes," said Lizzie.

"Stop!" wailed Henry. "Don't say anything! Please don't say anything. Please, please, please don't say anything!"

She was suddenly all concern. "Why, you're pale, Henry. Don't you feel well?"

"No— I mean yes. I'm all right. But don't suggest anything. I..." But how could he state it? He was frightened half to death by the sudden possibilities which presented themselves to him. All he had to do was visualize anything and that scene was the scene in which he found himself. All anybody had to do was suggest something and *zip!* there he was.

At first it had been a little difficult, but the gigantic beast Thought had risen into full power.

"You dress," said Lizzie.

But he was afraid to start disrobing. What if he thought—

No, he must learn to control this. Somehow he had missed

something. If he could get the entire equation straight and its solution, he would have the full answer. But Thought was drunk with power and would not be denied.

Henry rushed past Mrs. Doolin and down the steps to his study. He quickly sat in his chair and gripped his pen with determination. There was Equation C. Now if he could solve the rest of it he would be all right. He only had to substitute certain values...

Lizzie had followed him down. "Henry, I think you must be going crazy. Imagine keeping all those men waiting in the lecture hall—"

Whup!

Henry groaned and heard the dean say, "It was to be our pleasure this evening that we hear from Dr. Mudge on the subject—"

Somebody twitched at the dean's sleeve. "He's right beside you."

The dean looked and there was Henry, tweed jacket, ink stains, carpet slippers and all. Beads of perspiration were standing out on Henry's bulging forehead.

"Go right ahead," whispered the dean. "I do not approve of your attire, but it is too late now."

Henry stood up, fiery red and choked with stage fright. He looked down across the amused sea of faces and cleared his throat. The hall quieted slowly.

"Gentlemen," said Henry, "I have made a most alarming discovery. Forgive me for so appearing before you, but it could not be helped. Mankind has long expected the existence of a state of mind wherein it might be possible to follow thought. However—" His lecture presence broke as he recalled his carpet slippers. Voice nervous and key-jumpy, he rushed on. "However, the arrival at actual transposition of person by thought alone was never attained because mankind has been searching forward instead of backward. That is, mankind has been looking for the existence of nothing in the fourth dimension instead of the existence—" He tried to make his mind clear. Stage fright was making him become involved. "I mean to say, the negative dimension is not the fourth dimension but no dimension. The existence of nothing as..."

Some of the staid gentlemen in the front row were not so staid. They were trying not to laugh because the rest of the hall was silent.

"What idiocy is that man babbling?" said the dean to the university president behind his hand.

Dr. Mudge's knees were shaking. Somebody tittered openly in the fourth row.

"I mean," plunged Mudge, desperately, "that when a man imagines himself elsewhere, his mind seems to really be elsewhere for the moment. The yogi takes several means of accomplishing this, evidently long practiced in the negative dimension. Several great thinkers such as Buddha have been able to appear bodily at a distance when they weren't there but..." he swallowed again, "but elsewhere when they were there. The metaphysicist has attributed supernatural qualities to the phenomenon known as an 'apport,' in which people and such appear in one room without going through a door when they were in the other room...."

Dear me, he thought to himself, this is a dreadful muddle. He could feel the truth behind his words, but he was too acutely aware of a stained jacket and carpet slippers and he kept propping up his glasses.

"If a man should wish to be in some other place, it is entirely possible for him to imagine himself in that place, and, diving back through the negative dimension, to emerge out of it in that place with instantaneous rapidity. To imagine oneself—"

He swallowed hard. An awful thought had hit him, big enough to make him forget his clothes and audience. A man could imagine himself anyplace and then be in that place, *zip!* But how could a man exert enough willpower to keep from imagining himself in a position of imminent destruction? If he thought— Mudge gritted his teeth. He must not think any such thing. He must *not!* He knew instinctively that there was one place he could not imagine himself without dying instantly before he could recover and retreat. He did not know the name of that place in the instant, would not allow himself to think of it—

A ribald young associate professor said hoarsely to a friend, loud enough for Dr. Mudge to hear, "He ought to imagine himself on Mars."

Mudge didn't even hear the laugh which started to greet that sally.

Whup!

He examined the sandy wastes which stretched limitlessly to all the clear horizons. Bewildered, he took a few steps and the sand got into his carpet slippers. A cold wind cut through the thin tweed jacket and rustled his tie.

"Oh, dear," thought Mudge. "Now I've done it!"

A high, whining sound filled the sky and he glanced up to see a pear-shaped ship streaking flame across the sky. It was gone almost before it had started.

Dr. Mudge felt very much alone. He had no faith in his mental behavior now. It might fail him. He might never get away. He might imagine himself in an emperor's palace with sentries—

Whup!

The diamond floor was hard on his eyes and lights blazed all around him. A golden throne reared before him and on top of it sat a small man with a very large head, swathed in material which glowed all of itself.

Mudge couldn't understand a word that was being said because no words were being said, and yet they all hit his brain in a bewildering disarray.

Instantly he guessed what was happening. As a man's intention can be telepathed to a dog, these superior beings battered him mentally as he had no brain wave selectivity. He had guessed the human mind would so evolve, and he was pleased for an instant to find he had been right. But not for long.

145

He began to feel sick in the midst of this bombardment. All eyes were upon him in frozen surprise.

The emperor shouted and pointed a small wand. Two guards leaped up and fastened themselves upon Mudge. He knew vaguely that they thought he was an inferior being—something like a chimpanzee, or maybe a gorilla, and, indeed, so he was on their scale of evolution.

The ruler shouted again and the guards breathed hard and looked angrily at Mudge. Another man came sprinting over the diamond floor, a flare-barreled gun gripped in his hand.

Mudge began to struggle. He knocked the guards aside with surprising ease.

Wildly he turned about, seeking a way out, too confused by light, thought waves and sound to think clearly and remember.

The man with the lethal-looking weapon braced his feet and leveled the muzzle at Mudge's chest. He was going to shoot and Mudge knew that he faced a death-dealing ray. He was getting no more consideration than a mad ape, like that one in the Central Park Zoo.... The guard was squeezing the trigger—

Whup!

Weakly Dr. Mudge leaned on the railing of the Central Park Zoo in New York. He took out his handkerchief and dabbed at his forehead. Dully he gazed up, knowing he would see an orangutan in the cage. It was late, and the beast slumbered in his covered hut. Mudge could only see a tuft of fur.

"Thanks," he whispered.

The night air was soothing. He was exhausted with all the crosscurrents which had battered his poor human mind, and the thin air of Mars.

He moved slowly along the rail. There was a sign there which said "Gorilla. Brought from the Mountains of the Moon by Martin—"

Whup!

146

"Ohhh," groaned Mudge pitifully as he sank down on a rock in the freezing night. "This can't keep up. I would no more than start to eat when something would yank me away. I'd starve. And sooner or later I'll think of a very dangerous place and that will be the end of me before I can escape. There's one place in particular—

"NO!" he screamed into the African night.

The thought had not formed. One place he must never, never think about. NEVER!

From this high peak, he could see all Africa spread before him. Glowing far off in the brilliant moonlight was Lake Tanganyika.

Mudge was a little pleased with himself just the same. Back at the lecture—

Whup!

"I am sorry and very puzzled," the dean was saying, watch in hand. "Why Dr. Mudge should see fit to use a magician's tricks, to appear in such strange attire and generally disport himself—"

"I can't help it!" wailed Mudge at his side.

The dean almost jumped out of his shoes. He was annoyed to be startled out of his dignity and he scowled harshly at Mudge. "Doctor, I advise you strongly that such conduct will no longer be tolerated. If you are trying to prove anything by this, an explanation will be most welcome. The subject is philosophy and *not* Houdini's vanishing tricks."

"Ohhh," moaned Mudge, "don't say anything. Please don't say anything more. Just keep quiet. I mean," he said hastily, "I mean, don't say anything else. Please!"

The young man who had suggested Mars was not quite so sure of himself, but the dean's handy explanation of magic without paraphernalia restored his buoyancy.

"I was just..." began Mudge. "No, I can't say where I was or I'll go back, and I won't go back. This is very terrifying to me, gentlemen. There is one certain place I must not think about. The mind is an unruly thing. It seems to have no great love for the material body as it willfully, so it seems, insists in this great emergency on playing me tricks—"

"Dr. Mudge," said the dean, sternly. "I know not what you mean by all this cheap pretension to impossibilities—"

"Oh, no," cried Mudge. "I am pretending nothing. If I could only stop this I would be a very happy man! It is terribly hard on the nerves. Out of Spinoza I wandered into Force equations, and at two today I caught a glimmer of truth in the fact that there was a negative dimension—a dimension which had no dimensions. I know for certain that mind is capable of anything."

"It certainly is," said the dean. "Even chicanery."

"No, no," begged Mudge, pushing his glasses high on his forehead and then fishing in his pockets. "In my notes..." He looked squarely at the dean. "Here! I have proof of where I have been, sir." He stooped over and took off a carpet slipper. He turned it upside down on the lecture table and a peculiar glowing sand streamed out.

"That is Martian sand," said Mudge.

"BOSH!" cried the dean. He turned to the audience. "Gentlemen, I wish you to excuse this display. Dr. Mudge has not been well and his mind seems to be unbalanced. A few hour's rest—"

"I'll show you my notes," said Mudge, pleading. "I'll show you the equation. I left them home in my study—"

Whup!

Lizzie Doolin was muttering to herself as she picked up the papers from the floor and stacked them. The professor was certainly a madman this evening. Poor little man— She was turning and she almost fainted.

Dr. Mudge was sitting in his chair getting his notes together.

"Doctor!" cried Lizzie. "What are you doing there? How did you get in the house? The doors are all locked and...Ohhhhh, it's my eyes. Doctor, you know very well that you should be at that lecture—"

He barely had time to cram the papers in his pocket.

Whup!

The dean was fuming. "Such tricks are known— Oh, there you are! Doctor, I am getting very sick of this. We are too well versed in what can be done by trickery to be at all startled by these comings and goings of yours."

"It's *not* a trick!" stated Mudge. "Look, I have my notes. I—"

"And I suppose you've brought back some vacuum from the moon this—"

Whup!

It was so cold that Mudge was instantly blue all over. He could feel himself starting to blow up as the internal pressure fought for release. His lungs began to collapse, but his mind raced, torn between two thoughts.

Here he was on the moon. Here he was, the first man ever to be on the moon!

And all the great volcanoes reared chilly before him, and an empty Sea of Dreams fell away behind him. Barren rock was harsh beneath his feet and his weight was nothing....

All in an instant he glimpsed it because he knew that he would be dead in another second, exploded like a penny balloon. He visualized the thing best known to him—his study.

Whup!

Lizzie was going out the door when she heard the chair creak. She forgot about the necessity for aspirin as she faced about.

Mudge was in again.

"Doctor," stormed Lizzie, an amazon of fury, "if you don't stop that, I don't know what will happen to me! Here a minute, gone again, here and gone, here and gone! What is the world coming to! It is *not* my eyes. It can't be my eyes. I felt over the whole room for you and not so much as a hair of your head was here. What kind of heathen magic have you been stirring up? You've sold your soul—"

"STOP!" screamed Mudge. He sank back, panting. That had been close. But then, that had not been as close as that other THING which he dared *not* envision. He chopped the thought off and started back on another.

"Maybe," said Mudge, thoughtfully, "maybe there isn't... Oh, I've got the test right here. Can I throw myself back and forth between life and death?"

He had said the word.

"Death," he said again, more distinctly.

And still nothing occurred. He breathed easier. He could not go back and forth through time, as he had no disconnection with the time stream. He could whisk himself about the universe at will— or against his will—but he was still carrying on in the same hours and minutes. It had been dark in Africa, almost morning in P—

"NO!" he yelled.

Lizzie jumped a foot and stared to see if Mudge was still in his chair.

"Whatever are you up to?" demanded Lizzie, angrily. "You frighten a body out of her wits!"

"Something awful is going on," said Mudge, darkly. "I tried to tell you before dinner, but you wouldn't listen. I can imagine I am someplace and then be in that someplace. This very instant I could imagine something and *zip!* I'd be someplace else without walking through doors or anything."

Lizzie almost broke forth anew. But it awed her, a little. She had seen Mudge appear and disappear so often this evening that this was the only explanation which she could fit.

Mudge looked tired. "But I'm afraid, Lizzie. I'm terribly afraid. If I don't watch myself, I might imagine I was in some horrible place such as—

"NO!" shouted Mudge.

"I might imagine I was someplace where I—

"NO!" he yelled again.

Those shouts were like bullets to Lizzie Doolin. But she was still awed—a little.

Mudge held his head in his hands. "And I'm in trouble. The dean will not believe what is happening to me. He calls me a cheat—

"NO!" he cried.

"What do you keep yelling for?" complained Lizzie.

"So I won't go sailing off. If I can catch a thought before it forms I can stay put." He groaned and lowered his head into his hands. "But I am not believed. They think me a cheat. Oh, Lizzie, I'll lose my professorship. We'll starve!"

She was touched and advanced slowly to touch his shoulder. "Never you mind what they say about you. I'll beat their heads in, Henry, that I will."

He glanced up in astonishment at her. She had never shown any feeling for him in all these ten years. She had bullied him and driven him and terrified him....

She was conscious of her tenderness and brushed it away on the instant. "But don't go jumping off like that again! Drive over to the university in your car like a decent man should."

"Yes, Lizzie."

He got up and walked toward the door. Her jaw was set again.

"Mind what I tell you," she snapped. "Your car, now! And nothing fancy!"

"Yes, Lizzie. They're waiting...." He didn't, couldn't stop that thought and the hall was clearly envisioned and there he was—

Whup!

The dean had his hands on both hips as he saw that Mudge was here again. The dean wagged his head from side to side and was very angry, almost speechless. The audience tittered.

"Have you no respect?" cried the dean. "How dare you do such things when I am talking to you. I was saying that the next time you'll probably—"

"SHUT UP!" shouted Mudge in desperation. He was still cold from his trip to the moon.

The dean recoiled. Mudge was a very mild little fellow, with never anything but groveling respect for everybody. And these words from him...

"I'm sorry," said Mudge. "You mustn't say things or you'll send me off somewhere again. Now don't speak."

"Mudge, you can be assured that this performance this evening will terminate—"

Mudge was desperate. "Don't. You might say something."

The audience was delighted and laughter rolled through the hall. Mudge had not realized how his remark would sound.

The dean had never been anything but overbearing and now with his dignity flouted he turned white. He stepped stiffly to the president of the university and said a few words in a low voice. Grimly the president nodded.

"Here and now," said the dean, stepping back, "I am requesting your resignation, Mudge. This buffoonery—"

"Wait," pleaded Mudge, hauling his notes from his pocket. "First look at these and maybe you will see—"

"I care to look at nothing," stated the dean frostily. "You are a disgrace."

"Look," pleaded Mudge, putting the papers on the lecture stand. "Just give me one minute. I am beside myself. I don't mean what I say. But there is one thing I must not think about—one thing I can't think to think about but which I— Look. Here, see?"

The dean scowled at the sheets of scribbled figures and symbols. Mudge talked to him in a low voice, growing more and more excited.

The dean was still austere.

"And there," said Mudge, "right there is Equation C. Read it."

The dean thought Mudge might as well be humored as long as he would be leaving in the morning for good. He adjusted his glasses and looked at Mudge's reports. His glance fastened on Equation C.

The dean was startled. He stood up straight, his logical mind turning over at an amazing pace. "That's very strange," said the dean, bewildered. "My head feels..."

"Oh, what have I done?" cried Mudge, too late.

The assistant professor in the front row, a man of little wit but many jokes, chortled, "I suppose *he* will go to Mars now."

Whup!

Whup!

Mudge was almost in control by now. He knew that a part of Equation C was missing which would make it completely workable and usable at all times without any danger. And he also knew that being here on this sandy plain was not very dangerous unless one happened to think—

"NO!" he screamed into the Martian night.

It was easy. All he had to do was visualize the classroom—

Whup!

Mudge took off his glasses and wiped them. Then he bent over and emptied the sand from his slippers. The hall before him was silent as death and men were staring in disbelief at the little man on the platform.

Mudge replaced the slipper. He took up a pencil and bent eagerly over his notes. He had to work this thing out before he imagined—

"NO!" he roared.

It would be awful if he dreamed it. Dreaming, he would have no real control and things would happen to him.

The president rose cautiously and tapped Mudge's shoulder. "W-w-where is the dean?"

Mudge glanced around. True enough, the dean was not there. Mudge chewed at the end of his pencil in amazed contemplation.

"Do you mean," ventured the president, "that that statement about—"

"SHUT UP!" cried Mudge. "The dean may find out how to get back unless he thinks of something he..." He swallowed hard.

"Dr. Mudge, I resent such a tone," began the president.

"I am sorry," said Mudge, "but you might have said it, and the next time I might fall in a Martian canal—"

Whup!

He was strangling as he fought through the depths. He broke the surface like a porpoise and swam as hard as he could, terror surging within him as these dark waters lapped over him.

Ahead he could see a houseboat with a beautiful lady sitting at the rail. He swam breaststroke, raising himself up to shout for help. The cold suddenness of the accident had dulled his brain and he could not know what monsters lurked in these Martian depths.

The woman was strangely like an Earthwoman for all that. Perhaps there were colonies of these people much as there were colonies of chimpanzees on Earth. But the houseboat was silvery and the woman dressed in luminous cloth.

Strong hands yanked Mudge from the water and he stood blowing upon the deck, water forming about his feet in a pool. The woman was staring at him. She was a beautiful thing and Mudge's heart beat swiftly. She spoke in sibilant tones.

He bowed to her. "No, I haven't time for a visit or tea or anything," said Mudge. "I am sorry, but I am busy at a lect—— NO! I am busy on Ea—— NO! I am busy."

Oddly enough he knew that he could not speak her language, and yet he understood her perfectly as she placed her hand on his arm. It must be more telepathy, he thought.

"Yes, it is telepathy," said her mind. "Of course. But I am astonished to see you. For years—ever since the great purge— no humans of our breed have been here. Alone with these yellow men as servants I am safe enough. My parole was given because of certain favors—"

"Please," said Mudge. "I have an appointment. Don't be alarmed if I vanish. I'll be back someday." He looked around to fix the spot in his mind, feeling devilish for an instant.

He bowed to her. "I must leave—"

"But you'll take cold," she said, picking up a shawl of glowing material and throwing it about his shoulders.

"Thank you," said Mudge, "and now I really must go."

Again he bowed, and envisioned the classroom this time. *Whup!*

The water dripped to the lecture platform and Mudge was really getting cold by now. He hauled the shawl more tightly about his arms and was aware of protruding eyes all through the hall.

ANH LE

The water dripped and dripped, and Mudge shivered again. He sneezed. It would be good—

"NO!" he shouted and everybody in the hall jumped almost out of their chairs.

Mudge turned to the president. "You see what you did?"

The president was cowed. But he picked up in a moment. "Did...did you see the dean?"

"No," said Mudge. The warm room was drying his clothes rapidly, and he rolled up his sleeve so that he wouldn't blot the paper. Feverishly, he began to evolve Equation D.

He almost knew why he was working so fast. He was wholly oblivious of the audience. Very well he knew that his life depended upon his solving Equation D and thus putting the negative dimension wholly in his control. His pencil flew.

The thought began to seep into his mind in spite of all he could do.

"NO!" he yelled.

Again people jumped.

There was a grunt at his elbow and there stood the dean. He had sand in his gray hair and he looked mussed up.

"So you got back," said Mudge.

"It...it was terrible," moaned the dean in a broken voice. "The—"

"Don't say it," said Mudge.

"Doctor," said the dean, "I apologize for all I said to you." He faced the crowd. "I can verify amply everything that has happened here tonight. Dr. Mudge is absolutely correct"—he paused to swab his face and spit sand out of his teeth—"about the negative dimension. I have the uneasy feeling, however, that it is a very dangerous dimension. A man might—"

"Stop!" said Mudge, loudly.

He was working at a terrific pace now, and the paper shot off the stand to the floor as he swept it aside. He grabbed a new sheet.

He knew he was working against death. Knew it with all his heart. That thought would not long be stayed. At any minute he might find out where he was that he dared never go—

Equation D was suddenly before him. He copied it with a

weary sigh and handed it to the dean. "Read that before you get any ideas," said Mudge.

The dean read it.

"Mars," said Mudge.

Nothing happened.

The dean began to breathe more easily.

"Moon," said Mudge.

And still nothing happened.

Mudge faced the audience. "Gentlemen, I regret the excitement here tonight. It has quite exhausted me. I can either give you Equation C and D or—"

"No," said the dean.

"NO!" chorused the crowd.

"I'm frightened of it," said the dean. "I could never, never, never prevail upon myself to use it under any circumstances less than a falling building. Destroy it."

Mudge looked around and everybody nodded.

"I know this," said Mudge, "but I will never write it again." And so saying, he tore it up into little bits, his wet coat making it possible for him to wad the scraps to nothingness, never again to be read by mortal man.

"Gentlemen," said Mudge, "I am chilly. And so if you will excuse me, I will envision my study and—"

Whup!

Lizzie was crying. Her big shoulders shook as she hunched over in the doctor's chair. "Oh, I just know something will happen to him. Something awful," said Lizzie. "Poor little man."

"I am not a poor little man," said Mudge.

She gasped as she stared up at him.

"My chair, please," said Mudge.

She started to her feet. "Why, Henry Mudge, you are soaking wet! What do you mean—?"

He cut her short. "I don't mean anything by it except that I fell in a Martian canal, Lizzie. Now be quick and get me some dry clothes and a drink of something."

She hesitated. "You know you don't drink," she snapped—for a test.

"I don't drink because I knew you didn't like it. Bring me some of that medicinal whiskey, Lizzie. Tomorrow I'll make it a point to get some good scotch."

"HENRY!"

"Don't talk like that," said Henry Mudge commandingly. "I am warning you that you had better be pretty good from now on."

"Henry," said Lizzie.

"Stop that," he said. "I won't have it. I refuse to be bullied in my own home, I tell you. And unless you are very, very good I am liable to vanish like that—"

"Don't," she begged. "Don't do that, Henry. Please don't do that. Anything you say, Henry. Anything. But don't pop off like that anymore."

Henry beamed upon her. "That's better. Now go get me some clothes and a drink. And be quick about it."

"Yes, Henry," she said meekly. But even so she did not feel badly about it. In fact, she felt very good. She whisked herself upstairs and trotted down again in a moment.

She placed the whiskey and water beside his hand.

Henry dug up a forbidden cigar. She did not protest.

"Get me a light," said Henry.

She got him a light. "If you want anything, dear, just call."

"That I will, Lizzie," said Henry Mudge.

He put his feet upon the desk, feeling wicked about it but enjoying it just the same. His clothes were almost dry.

He sank back puffing his cigar, and then took a sip of the drink. He chuckled to himself.

His mind had quieted down. He grinned at the upset owl. The thought which had almost hit him before came to him now. It jarred him for an instant, even made him sweat. But he shook it off and was very brave.

"Sun," said Henry Mudge, coolly taking another drink.

How to Steal the Plot Armor

written by
Luke Wildman

illustrated by
DAN WATSON

ABOUT THE AUTHOR

Luke Wildman may be a figment of your imagination—or you may be one of his. Either way, he was born and raised in West Africa, came to the US for college at nineteen, and has lived with his wife in Indianapolis ever since. If you ever find yourself wandering the Indiana woods and notice a rambling weirdo muttering about books, that's probably Luke. Say hi! He's awkward at conversations, but no longer gives a damn.

When not terrorizing the countryside, Luke reads copiously, devotes unhealthy amounts of time to working on his novels, and dreams of making his living through fiction. His work has appeared in Havok *magazine and* Parnassus, *Taylor University's literary journal.*

If you happen to be an agent, please know that he is capable of acting professionally.

ABOUT THE ILLUSTRATOR

Dan Watson was born in 1994 in Reading, UK. An only child, he spent lots of time drawing monsters, knights, and animals.

He has always been inspired by the world around him and curious about how it worked.

He attended the last GenCon in the UK in 2008. It was there he was truly introduced to sci-fi and fantasy, and his lifelong love of the genres was cemented.

After school he started an apprenticeship as a mechanical design engineer. However, creatively unsatisfied, he started to learn drawing from books and attended figure-drawing sessions at night, while he attempted to illustrate his favourite novels. After completing his apprenticeship in 2017, he continued his artistic development by visiting museums, travelling, and learning online.

Dan now enjoys spending his time painting and drawing dreams and nightmares. And he still attempts to illustrate his favourite books.

How to Steal the Plot Armor

The day before it started, I had to chase off three more heroes with a stick. I swear, winter is the worst season for them. You get a few enterprising farm boys during the spring and summer, and fall's the time for disinherited princes looking to reclaim kingdoms that their uncles stole from their murdered fathers, but winter is when the big ones arrive. There's nothing worse than sitting down in front of the hearth, a tome on your knee and a tankard of ale at your elbow, all cozy while the blizzard howls outside—and hearing a knock at the door.

You'll have no peace till you open it. When you do, you're greeted by the sight of a hulking, smelly barbarian, snow clinging to his fur cloak, sword bigger than your leg strapped over his back, with a story of an omen-prompted journey into the mountains to seek one who will tutor him in magic, or guide him to hidden paths, or interpret runes on an ancient map, and might you be that one? And, of course, you are. Try to deny it and he'll point out that the prophecy specified the man he sought would be holding a tome and a tankard, and would be venerable of years, knobby of knees, bearded of chin, and dark-skinned as the night. Really, they might leave out the knobby knees part, just once. Do they think I have no feelings?

Over my lifetimes, I've developed quite the repertoire of tricks for sending heroes away. They never catch on that a person living in a shabby cottage at the highest pass of the most remote mountain in the farthest corner of the world might not want to be bothered, the insensitive jackanapes. So I always had to use other strategies.

DAN WATSON

The beginner's mistake is thinking rigor alone will deter your average hero, but it only encourages most of them. Their eyes light up when you swear to only take them on as a 'prentice if they descend into the Tomb of the Necromancer and steal the ruby eye from the idol of Ang'Vel'Nazsh. If they survive this perilous deed, then you really can't put them off.

No; the secret is to give them dishonorable, icky chores, like cleaning your chamber pot or mucking out your pigsty. That usually works.

Unfortunately, there's a breed of hero that revels in humiliation, and might, I shudder to add, even be a bit turned on by it. Such a one was the young gallant who galloped into my life that winter day.

It was one of those bright, cold mornings when life in the mountains feels almost a treat, the pines resplendent with icicles and the snow an unbroken field of dazzling white. He arrived while I was hobbling on my staff from the barn to the cottage, having just fed the old nag. I focused on my footing, and so didn't immediately notice the rider dismounting outside my door.

"Hail, honored wizard!" the man called, startling me half out of my wits. "Lo, I have ridden many weeks and endured many perils to seek you."

I sighed as I looked him over. He had the usual shaggy golden hair and storm-blue eyes, the usual disregard for animals (his poor horse was half dead), and the usual lack of sense when it came to dressing for the weather, clad as he was in silver armor that glittered with frost, and a thin cape of purple silk.

"What can I do you for?" I asked irritably. "Enchanted sword? Vague riddle that will come in handy at some future date? Bit of relationship advice?"

"Wizard, I seek a guide for a quest most perilous into the heart of the Ash Lands, where I shall forge a blade from star-metal and challenge the Master of Shadows for supremacy, along with the right to woo his daughter."

My hopes for an easy resolution sank dead away. The most

bothersome heroes of all are those who want me to accompany them on their quests. Not only is it an imposition on my reading time, but such journeys invariably lead to a crucible where the hero loses their mentor and must carry on alone. Hard luck, if you happen to be the mentor. Even if you're lucky enough to get resurrected, as I've done thrice, there's always a backlog of other adventurers waiting to meet you when you get back, and a surprising amount of paperwork, to boot. A body gets no rest.

"Why don't you come inside," I told the golden-haired cretin. "We'll talk it over, see if we can't work something out."

He bowed and followed me in.

I found myself observing the old ritual, hanging a kettle of tea over the fire and offering a repast of bread and cheese to my travel-weary guest, as hermits are wont to do. It was all muscle memory. "So," I said as I bustled around the kitchen, "the Ash Lands, eh? Treacherous country."

"Verily. Yet that is where my path lies."

Aromatic steam frothed from two mugs as I poured the tea, and my hand hovered for an instant above the tin of powdered hemlock. But of course, disposing of my problem in *that* manner would only switch my role to one of villain, an even more dubious position in any quest. There'd be no end of distant relations and bosom friends seeking vengeance. With a sigh, I spooned sugar into the mugs instead and set them on the coffee table.

"And so," my guest was saying, finishing a story I hadn't listened to, "it is destiny that brings me to your door this day, and destiny that shall lead us hence."

"Yes, yes," I said, waving a hand, "destiny certainly has it out for me. But tell me, are you quite certain you don't need some other sage? Old Copperhand usually deals with star-metal enterprises—he lives at Storm Mountain Pass. As for wooing a Shadow Lord's daughter, Argula of the Vale might be more help, as she can provide a woman's intuition. Between you and me, I'm awfully dense when it comes to flirtations."

"The omens led me here, Good Master. When I was but a babe, a centaur uttered words of portent over my crib, that run thus—"

"No recitations, please. Look, I'll be square with you. I know what the ancient self-help texts say about finding someone with experience to show you the ropes, but being asked is no honor, believe me. Why, I'd wager that my chances of mortality increased twenty percent just from you speaking to me. For the love of life, I beg you to find someone else."

The golden-haired fop scowled. Sir Barm, I think he said his name was.

"Good Sage, there *is* no one else. We are, both of us, as twigs caught in the stream of destiny. We cannot choose our fates, only how we comport ourselves in the midst of them."

"You're reading from my script, whippersnapper," I mumbled. I cleared my throat. "Well, if you're set on this, there's only one thing to do. I must test your worthiness. At the foot of this mountain lies a field of auroch dung. For reasons arcane and mysterious, I need you to—"

"Already accomplished," Sir Barm said.

I raised my eyebrows. "Really? You mean, without my asking, you just...the whole field?"

"A most formidable task, but one that taught me the value of humility among the chivalric virtues."

His raiment wasn't soiled, and no manure-stink clung to him, but it wouldn't make sense for him to lie, knowing I would check the field in a few hours. He must've really done it. *Freak.*

"Well," I said, nonplussed, "that saves us some time, I guess. For your next task, you must make a three-week journey to a small town situated by a lake. On a midden heap, you'll find a beggar woman of scabrous appearance, left that way by certain venereal indelicacies. Only a salve of rare pink snowflower blossoms can bring her relief, and it must be applied by hand so that—"

"Truly, the lady of whom you speak was most grateful for assistance," Sir Goody-goody told me gravely. "I met her by chance on my way hence. The ointment restored to her the great beauty she possessed in her youth."

I spluttered on my tea. "You *cured* Abominable Alice? But...but I didn't even..."

"For my part, I learned that no corruption is so great it cannot be reversed."

I blew out of my cheeks. The immensity of this trouble was starting to dawn on me. The only thing worse than a hypocritical knight of the Lancelot persuasion is an aspiring Galahad. But even the puritanical Galahads of the world can usually be put off by asking them to help someone who's not as virtuous as they. Abominable Alice was my fail-safe.

Something wasn't right about this.

"All right, Sir Barmy, or whatever you call yourself, here's the deal: you've worn me down. At great personal risk, I'm going to accompany you on this journey. We can haggle over my commission later. But first I need you to swear that you're going to do *whatever* I say, *whenever* I say it, even if it may seem ridiculous. Even if, from your perspective, it seems like I'm hindering your quest rather than helping it. Do we have an agreement?"

"I swear on my honor as a chaste-yet-passionate lover to do all you ask, striving with my every word and deed to be a hero worthy of your tutelage."

"Terrific," I said. And I actually meant it. Because, as the implications of this man's fanaticism settled over me, I glimpsed an opportunity. Not just to deal with him, but to dissuade every would-be hero in the future from seeking me out. A way to ensure that I lived a long, peaceful life after this adventure, enjoying my books by the fireside without interruption. A way to put myself beyond danger.

No more dead mentors.

"Right, then," I said, as we sauntered down the cobbled streets of fair Omlath, "I've told you my Rules Three. Just this once, I'll allow a recitation. Repeat the rules for me."

Sir Barm cleared his throat and held up a finger. "Rule the First: Without express permission of the Great Sage, there are to be no recitations. Not of ballads, nor of heroic verse, nor of any form of prophecy."

"Damn right," I said, nodding. "Can't abide recitations. Now, what's the second rule?"

"Rule the Second," Sir Barm recited, adding to his finger count. "The Great Sage brooks no disobedience. Insofar as our quest endures, his command is as iron law unto me."

"And the last?"

Sir Barm completed his finger count, then made a gauntleted fist. "Rule the Third: Under no circumstance will the Great Sage ever, *ever* enter a crypt, tomb, tunnel, or any other form of subterranean space. So saith the Sage."

"Underground spaces are death to my people," I said, shuddering. "Abide by those rules, and I swear by my wizardly power and my love of books that you'll be wooing that poor girl in no time."

Sir Barm nodded solemnly. "Your oaths are to me an unassailable truth."

"That's the spirit. You're really coming along with Rule the Second. Now...let's go over the plan."

We stopped and gazed up at Omlath Castle, which dominated the town like a wart on a witch's face, except prettier. The pale masonry and graceful curves of the buttresses resembled a castle of cloud, capped by a bright spring sun. I mean that literally: a tower rose from the center of the castle, its capstone engraved with luminous spells that filled the sky with eternal noon and ensured that the surrounding lands always flourished, even in dead winter. Omlath was a wonder of the world; just the sight of it was worth every step of our three-month trek. We only halted once during that journey, at a royal outpost, where I sent off a few letters by Pegasus Express. Living on a remote mountaintop doesn't provide much chance for personal correspondence, and I sometimes miss it.

"Now," I said, "though Omlath seems like a fair settlement, its beauty only endures through hideous powers. That capstone is wrought of dark enchantments, by none other than the Shadow Lord himself. For lo! This is his summer home."

"That fiend!" Sir Barm smacked his gauntleted fist against

his breastplate. "We will bring his fortress crumbling down around him."

"That's the idea. Once we remove that capstone from the tower, not only will the landscape revert to its natural climate, but the entire structure will fall. Publicly humiliating your enemy will give you bargaining power, which could go a long way toward wooing his daughter."

Sir Barm must have been even more illiterate in the ways of women than I, because he didn't question this assertion.

"For myself, bringing the castle down will make me famous enough that I won't have to accept any more blasted hero 'prentices," I said. "That's the whole reason we came south rather than journeying north toward the Ash Lands. What's the point of triumphing over absolute evil if there's no one around to impress, eh?"

The knight frowned. He was the crusader sort, who probably thought that vanquishing evil was its own reward. But he was too obedient to contradict me.

"So," I said, "the difficult part is getting inside the castle. Security's tight. You see those guards in crystal armor on the causeway? Their armor lights up like solstice holiday trees in the presence of magic. I can't glamour us up any disguises. There are tons of posterns and secret entrances to the castle, but opening one from outside would trigger the arcane alarms. Besides which, some of them go underground. Really, our only entrance is the front gate."

Sir Barm nodded, but his frown deepened. "If you will permit a question, Great Master..."

"If I must."

"You say removing the capstone will cause the fortress to crumble. Will we survive this calamity? Or"—feverish excitement kindled in his eyes—"perhaps we shall sacrifice ourselves for the greater good?"

Yikes. "Slow down with the martyr talk. I certainly don't intend to die over this; no Shadow Lord is worth that. The castle will start crumbling the instant the capstone is removed, but

I've arranged some alternate transport. Transport with wings."
I smiled my most mysterious arcane-old-man smile. "In fact, it's
time you met the rest of our team. This way."

The ale at The Rusty Ploughshare was only okay, subpar as far
as touristy taverns go. But the place had proper atmosphere,
and that was the important thing: woodsmoke and pipe-fumes
mingled, swamping the common room with a veritable stinking
fog. Convenient shadows pooled in the corners where rangy
adventurers could sit and brood, and a raucous drinking song
rattled the mugs and plates, even back in the private room
I'd rented. A perfect setting for the hatching of plots and the
contemplation of dire schemes, preferably with a rogue at either
hand. In that regard, I was pleased.

I leaned away from Bacchus the Bard as he belched theatrically,
then took another long pull from his tankard. "An exquisite ether
to accompany such ingenious elocution," he said, raising the
mug to me. "Bacchus the Bard is profuse in praise."

I grinned. "That's one for the plan, I take it. Garsteaodeafix?
Your vote?"

The rogue on my left ruffled her tail feathers. "It is a fearsome
scheme, worthy of such a bold company. I do not believe it will
succeed. Therefore I, too, approve of it."

"Glad to hear it," I said. "I think. So, Bacchus, you and Sir Barmy
and I will slip inside as courtly entertainers, while Garsteaodeafix
waits on the western cliffs to swoop in and carry us away once
we remove the capstone. The stone itself can't be transported
via magical beast, but that's okay: castles on this scale take a
stupidly long time to build. Even if the capstone wasn't going to
be buried in rubble, it would take several years before Tom—I
mean, the Master of Shadows—could raise his summer home
again." I glanced at Sir Barm. "Good enough?"

"Verily. Yet, if I may question..."

I nodded.

"What shall befall us if the Shadow Lord is in residence? Will he
not pick apart our guise as a farmwife picks apart a work of wool?"

169

"Firstly," I said, "I'm confused about your metaphor. Have you known many farmwives? They're a thrifty bunch. Why would one pick apart a perfectly good work of wool? Secondly, the Shadow Lord won't be home. He spends this time of year terrifying villages in the southern cantrefs. No worries on that account."

Sir Barm pounded a fist on the table in a pleased sort of way. "A daring venture! We shall comport ourselves with courage and aplomb!"

"Uh-huh. Personally, I just hope not to get killed. I guess there's no sense wasting time, though. Let's settle up and head out."

Bacchus and the knight left in search of the publican, but Garsteaodeafix tapped me on the shoulder with her beak. "You have not told the fool knight of the capstone's curse?" she asked.

I grimaced. "It doesn't seem like something he needs to know."

The gryphon cocked her head in parrot-like fashion. Her golden mane ruffled, then smoothed against her neck like a bird settling its feathers. "This scheme grows more savage with each passing moment," she said. "You did not lie when you wrote that I would have a wonderful bedtime story of brutality for my hatchlings."

"Oh, how are the kids, by the way?"

"They fare well. Little Iggistifigix devoured her first dwarf the other day. Her father and I were greatly pleased."

"I can imagine," I said, nodding. "They grow up fast, don't they?"

We spent the rest of that day renting our equipment, then got a good sleep. Midmorning of the day after, we were ready. We strapped on full troubadour kits, cymbals and snare drums that clanked and banged as our ankles tugged at the pulleys, accordions that wheezed faintly with each movement of our chests and arms, bagpipes that wailed their reedy torment when we exhaled too sharply. Of the three of us, only Bacchus bore the honor of a harp. He wouldn't hear of Sir Barm or myself carrying one, not even as a disguise.

Tension coiled in my chest as we strode over the causeway. The crystal guards stood dead ahead, guises impassive.

"Greetings, great garrison!" Bacchus boomed as we drew close. "Myself and my cadre of companions have come to conquer your court with choral cantrips. Lyrical lays, robust ballads, artful arias, and vivacious verse...all these and more will we endeavor to unfold! Might we pass?"

"Papers?" the captain said, unimpressed.

I handed over our forged bards' licenses. They were good forgeries, though not infallible. Red light flickered in the captain's crystal plate at my proximity, making my breath hitch. The captain didn't notice as she skimmed the parchments with a bored eye. "In order," she said. "On with you."

We stepped beneath the hanging spears of the portcullis— and we were in.

Something was obviously wrong from the moment we entered the great hall. Too many folk milled about, too many by far. Logs crackled in the fire pit. The tables groaned under a weight of food and drink too profuse for the number of retainers who abided here while the Lord of Omlath was absent, and something was wrong with their eyes...a sort of dull light. They moved in a jerky, mechanical way, as if someone had wound them up and set them to clanking from task to task. Disconcerting, to say the least.

The explanation soon became apparent. In a flower-carved throne at the head of the hall, the Lord of Shadows presided.

The Master of Darkness swung his gaze to us when we entered, and his obsidian eyes seemed to pierce all hopes and disguises. "Ah," he said, "entertainers. Come! Play a song for your great lord."

Sir Barm stiffened beside me. I followed his gaze and beheld a willowy slip of a teenage girl lounging on the steps at the Shadow Lord's feet. She wore a fetching red gown, a gold circlet over brown curls, and she possessed the same delicate pasty features as her dad, though they looked better on her. From how Sir Barm was gaping, I knew at once that his love for her was no fickle impulse. There was a story behind it, though I hadn't listened when he told it to me. This could spell trouble.

"Lords and landed gentry!" Bacchus said, bowing. "Behold— we trifling troubadours shall traipse through twittering tunes, endeavoring to entertain for the honor of your encores!" And with that, he began to play.

I'd hired the man for a reason. Neither Sir Barm nor myself had the faintest idea what to do with the musical paraphernalia strapped to us, so we banged our drums and blew our pipes at random... and somehow, Bacchus made a song of it. He wound our cacophony into a greater melody, sweeping discordant notes along as if they were intentional. The song reared to the vaulted roof, reverberated among the ceiling beams, sank low and mournful into the souls of our listeners. In this song, wrought partially of my own ineptitude, I recalled every grief of my life, relived each failed and faithless moment, remembered all my bitter choices, until I longed to weep. And still it continued.

Bacchus was rearing the song toward a triumphant crescendo when jeers interrupted him. His accordion squawked in protest, and the music fell apart. All heads turned toward the source of the desecration.

"You call *that* music?" the Shadow Lord's daughter asked. "There weren't even lyrics! When I hear music, I want poetry. I want to hear about ancient deeds of valor. In short... I want *recitations*."

A cruel smile played on her rosebud lips as she rose and sauntered toward us.

"Play a *good* song, a song with *words*," she said. "Make them play one, Daddy... or chop off their heads!"

The Shadow Lord looked bemused. He raised his eyebrows at us. "Well, boys? You heard my daughter."

I clenched my jaw.

Bacchus was shooting me worried glances, but he should've

been more concerned about Sir Barm. The knight was trembling from head to heels, his accordion emitting tiny squeaks as he took shuddering breaths, his gaze fixed on the teenager. When she halted a foot away from him, I feared he would go into cardiac arrest.

"Oh lovely Lady," Bacchus said, "while your request reveals rarefied refinement, we troubled troubadours are poor players of proper parts, being best at instrumental anthems and—"

"Don't sell yourself short," she said, smirking. "You're professionals, right? At least *one* of you must have a decent voice. You, knees?" she asked, looking me up and down pointedly. "Or how about you, goldilocks?" Her eyes drank in Sir Barm's impressive physique.

The knight blinked several times. He glanced at me, and I nodded. I'd allow a recitation just this once, for the sake of not getting my head chopped off. Of the Rules Three, this was the least important; it's just that I've heard more than enough damned songs and poems and prophecies over the years. Why does every company of dwarves or party of adventurers seem to think music is a good way of explaining their quest's backstory?

"If my lady wishes, I will sing," Sir Barm said in a hoarse voice.

"My lady-self wishes."

Bacchus and I braced for disaster as the knight cleared his throat. After trilling through a few warm-up exercises, he began.

"Oh, once there was a lady,
Lovelier than the stars.
Her eyes made strong hearts shudder,
Her voice made weak men's arms.
To glimpse her a brave man journeyed,
Through heaven and earth and hell.
But if this lady loved him,
The brave man could not tell.
He asked, "How may I win your favor?"
She laughed in a scornful way.

She said, "First you must sway my father,
To let you ask me out today."
Now this lovely lady's father,
Was renowned as a wicked lord.
The brave man knew that to beat him,
He would need a star-forged sword.
He sought the aid of a wizard,
A most Sagacious Sage.
Who suggested to him a different plan,
To win his lady fey.
They journeyed to a castle, and—"

I burst into a fit of coughing that made my accordion and bagpipes wheeze hideously. Sir Barm cut off not a moment too soon; he'd been on the verge of spilling all our secrets.

"Is it over already?" the girl asked mockingly. "Thank the gods. I was having *awful* flashbacks to all the men who seem to think the most romantic way of winning my heart is to murder my beloved father. A new dunce comes along every other week. I can't even remember them all anymore."

Sir Barm's eyes bulged. He looked a bit purple in the cheeks, so I decided this was an opportune moment to slip away.

"Liege," I rasped to the Shadow Lord, "is there a place where an old man can get some air? My lungs aren't what they once were." I made sure to give a full blast of the bagpipes with my next cough.

"Yes, yes," the Lord of Darkness said hastily, "there's a balcony right up those stairs. When you come back, perhaps you can stick to the percussion instruments rather than the woodwinds. You go with him," he said, pointing at Sir Barm. "Just leave your third friend behind. The one who can actually play."

We bowed our way from the hall.

We lingered on the balcony just long enough to discard our kits, then hammered up the spiral staircase, Sir Barm taking the steps three at a time. I huffed and puffed behind him as we wound toward the castle's uppermost tower.

"So," I said, desperate to distract myself from a stitch in my ribs, "you and the lady. That song. Autobiographical, I take it?"

Sir Barm glanced back at me, hardly seeming winded. "Many a tale reached my ears and heart concerning her beauty, but when I sought her out in her enchanted tower—as instructed by the centaur's crib-prophecy, you recall—she said she dares not wed for fear of her father. Doubtless, his presence is the reason she pretended not to know me. She *does* love me."

"Oh, *doubtless*," I said, though the real story was obvious. Here was an unhinged, pampered young man who couldn't imagine anyone not being into him. He didn't know how to handle straight rejection or take a hint. My disgust for him was rivaled only by my irritation that the girl had called me "knees" and forced me to endure a recitation. Maybe they deserved each other.

I might've pushed the issue, but I had to save my breath until we reached the top. A couple of crystal guards stood on duty, but Sir Barm dispatched them with frightening ease.

As we burst into the unnatural summer daylight, a scent of wildflowers and fresh grass hit us. The source was a glowing, rune-engraved stone on a pedestal in the center of the round tower. I've seen miracles aplenty in my life, but even I paused and gasped at the sheer magicalness of it.

Sir Barm approached the capstone as if in a trance. His hands hovered over it—then he wrenched them away and glanced at me. "Master, it would be wrong for me to steal the honor of unseating our foe. Yours should be the hands that enact his defeat."

"Oh, unseat away," I said. "This quest is all you. Just wait a few minutes, till our gryphon friend arrives. We wouldn't want the castle to collapse with us trapped up here."

We didn't have long to wait. I gazed for a couple minutes into the distance, admiring the spell of summer-magic that kept all the lands of this cantref green to the distant horizon, where I just caught the glitter of winter ice. Soon enough, the *whump-whump-whump* of wings beat the air, and a yellow speck circled down, becoming Garsteaodeafix the Gryphon. She landed with unlikely grace, her lion's claws grasping the parapet.

"Where is the bard?" she asked.

"The Shadow Lord wanted him to stay and play awhile," I said. "By this time, he should be following our alternate plan and making excuses to leave by the gate."

Garsteaodeafix bobbed her head regally. "Then let us proceed."

Sir Barm approached the capstone again. It throbbed gently as his hands hovered over it. His fingertips brushed the surface . . . then he blinked at me again.

"My ladylove is below," he said. "What shall become of her?"

"Are you forgetting everything I told you in the tavern? Even before we knew that the Shadow Lord and his daughter were here, I wasn't about to let all the innocents in this castle perish. The collapse won't be instantaneous. The walls will *start* to rumble as soon as you pull the capstone out, but it will take time for the foundations to split apart and the roof to cave in. The people below will realize what's happening and flee."

Sir Barm nodded but continued to look hesitant. Fear seized me—*He knows!*—and I was contemplating backup plans when the knight finally reached out, seized the edges of the capstone, and wrenched it from its iron brackets. All three of us held our breaths.

Nothing happened.

A moment passed. Stretched longer. Turned into a full minute . . . and still no rumbling. Sir Barm shook the stone, turned it around in his hands, and held it up to his ear, as if it might whisper to him like a conch shell. Then he looked at me.

"Sage?"

I scratched my chin. "Well, that's . . . huh. That should've worked."

I took the capstone from Sir Barm, ran a finger over the runes, mumbled inaudibly. Then I slapped my forehead. "*Gah!* I must've gotten a bad translation of the rune writing in those secondary texts I studied. This clearly says that one must actually remove the stone from the castle's premises to break the magic."

Garsteaodeafix's golden eyes narrowed to slits as I spoke, but Sir Barm looked utterly aghast. He leaned over the parapet, clearly considering hurling the stone off the tower. But there was no chance it would clear the rooftops below.

"Oh, dire fate!" the knight wailed. "Our enemies will triumph! What shall we do, Wizard?"

I gritted my teeth. "There's only one thing *to* do. As I told you in the tavern, the stone can't be transported via magical beast—which means one of us must carry it out through a doorway. And since *I'm* the one who made this mistake..." I sighed. "You're a young man, with your life ahead of you. Just promise you'll use your years well. Live life to the fullest. And—pardon a piece of unsolicited relationship advice from an old fogy—when young ladies tell you they don't want to be courted, try to respect their wishes."

What's an adventure without a moral, right?

Sir Barm was staring at me in dazed amazement. I'd already half-shoved him onto Garsteaodeafix's back before his brain seemed to catch up with events. "Master, no!" he cried, dismounting and tottering dangerously close to the edge. "I cannot let you sacrifice your life for mine. I will descend back with you into the castle, and we shall cut our way out together or die in the attempt."

"You fanatical whelp," I snarled. "Have you *completely* forgotten Rule the Second?"

In Sir Barm's expression, I read a war between his desire for heroic martyrdom and his slavish zealotry to rules. I doubt concern for my life came into it. Sir Barm stepped toward Garsteaodeafix again...then shook his head, as if to clear it of cobwebs, and planted himself. "No, Master," he said. "I will not abandon you."

Uh-oh.

"Listen," I said, trying to look mysterious, "there's something you should know about me. It's my duty to deal with the Shadow Lord because...because I *created* him. I haven't always done a good job of mentoring my pupils."

Sir Barm gasped, then frowned. "Wait...our enemy did not appear to recognize you, down below."

"He has amnesia."

"But the story of his life is recorded in many histories," Sir Barm said. "The devil sired and raised him, and he came straight from the depths of hell to begin his conquests. At no time did he study under a mortal teacher."

"Um...all the historians have amnesia, too?"

"Why are you trying to deceive me, Master?"

I flung up my hands. "Just let me do this, all right? I feel as if my entire life's journey has prepared me for this sacrifice, yada-yada-yada, etcetera."

Sir Barm rested a hand on my shoulder and looked down at me, his blue eyes somber. It made me feel shrimpy. "No matter our pasts, we can choose to be braver men in the future," he said. "We will fight them together, Master. You will cast off your cowardice, and I...I will sever the compulsion that the witch must've laid on me."

"Hold on. *Cowardice?*"

"Come, Master! Come...to a glorious end!"

Seizing one of the fallen guardsmen's swords, he brandished the blade aloft and, tucking the capstone under his other arm, rushed back down the stairs.

Garsteaodeafix fixed her gaze on me, and I shrugged. "Well, now he's broken Rule the First *and* Rule the Second. Gods spare us any more infractions."

The gryphon raised a brow and said, "Indeed. How unfortunate that you did not properly understand the capstone's magic."

"A real bummer."

"And you still have not told the knight—"

"About the curse, yes. I know. He'll learn in good time."

Garsteaodeafix chuckled as if this was all a very fine joke, then sprang away to drift on the hot air currents, her tawny fur and feathers magnificent against the sky.

Grumbling imprecations, I followed my imbecilic mentee back down the stairs.

The castle shuddered when we were halfway down, making Sir Barm yelp and throw out his arms for balance, though I'd already braced myself.

"What devilry is this!" he cried. "Did you not say that the stone must be bodily removed from the fortress?"

"You know, some translations are a bit ambiguous. I always forget if the ancient runes are meant to be read top to bottom or in a widdershins spiral."

"Master Sage, I begin to doubt your sagaciousness."

On some of the flights along the stairwell, we glimpsed servants and crystal guards scurrying back and forth, but with the same jerky movements as before, as if they were windup toys with their springs coiled almost to the breaking point. Still, most seemed to be heading for the exits, which reassured me.

Pebbles plopped from the ceiling, and a couple steps cracked right before we put weight on them. It was with enormous relief that we both spilled from the stairwell onto the bottom floor. Short-lived relief.

Chaos filled the great hall. An oak beam had tumbled from the center of the roof into the fire pit, scattering embers. Half the courtiers jigged madly to stomp out tiny blazes while their fortress collapsed around them. The other half fainted dead away or scrambled for the exits. I saw no sign of the Shadow Lord or his daughter.

A couple of men glimpsed the capstone under Sir Barm's arm and tried to stop us, but he knocked them aside and rushed to the door.

"Ah-*ha*!" he cried, standing framed against the daylight. "Behold your fate, evildoers! Be buried under your sins!"

He turned to rush out...and we both saw the entire garrison of crystal guards congregating before the gates. From the snarls on their faces, they'd heard Sir Barm's speech.

We sprinted back through the great hall and into a corridor. War cries and thumping boots echoed behind us as we took the turns at random, praying we wouldn't strike a dead end. Hanging tapestries and suits of armor flashed past, and a thick scent of dust scratched at our nostrils as we tangled deeper into the warren of passages. We became thoroughly lost.

The air grew chilly, and realization crept over me that we were descending below the earth...which meant Rule the Third was in serious peril. Of all my rules, it was the deadliest.

I skidded to a halt in front of a low-arched doorway of brick. A sign stood next to the archway, with a helpful arrow pointing at the entrance and runes underneath it that proclaimed: "Ye Olde Family Crypt."

"Oh no," I said. "I am *not* going in there. Nuh-uh, no chance. Not this side of the underworld. *No crypts!*"

"Master, the tunnels are our last hope. Listen...our pursuers gain."

The tromp of footsteps *was* growing louder, but I backed away. "I'll take my chances with the guards," I said. "This is the part where a mentor always gets killed."

"Have you lived all your life on a mountaintop because you feared the world below, Master? You have spoken words of courage to many heroes...but have you kept no courage for yourself? You are strong enough for this! We shall risk this danger together!"

"Easy for you to say," I grumbled. "Your destiny will lead you right out the other side of this tunnel. That's some nice plot armor you've got."

"Master, please." He said nothing more. Just looked at me with those ridiculously piercing hero eyes.

I shuddered—then took a step toward him. "When did you grow so wise?" I asked. "Truly, I have nothing left to teach you. It seems that I'm the 'prentice now, you the master. You know, if I'd ever had a son, I would've wanted him to be exactly like—"

The crystal guards burst into the hallway behind us.

We both froze.

"Go, go, go!" I yelled, pushing Sir Barm into the crypt-tunnel ahead of me. "For all this to mean something, we must keep the capstone away from them!"

"Master, we can both make it. We—"

"No," I said. I clasped my pupil's hand. "It's not cowardice this time. You've shown me the meaning of courage. Fare thee well, Sir Barm."

I strode back toward the guards, spread my arms, and began to chant nonsense words. They pulled up short.

A rumble shuddered the earth, as if we stood in the throat of some great beast. I pointed at the guards. "You fools dare challenge me? You would challenge one who has survived a thousand quests, destroyed a thousand evils, seen a thousand prophecies fulfilled? Come and get me, curs!"

The very foundations of the castle cracked and heaved. Bricks showered the crypt's entrance. A curtain of dust descended, through which I glimpsed the knight, staring back at me, arms outstretched... and then an avalanche of masonry collapsed the tunnel between us.

I let my arms drop to my sides.

"He's a hard fellow to get rid of," one of the guards observed. He lifted his helmet's visor, revealing delicate, pasty features.

"Tom," I said, nodding to him. "Glad you got my letter."

We grinned and embraced. Always a pleasure to see old friends.

The second guard doffed her helmet. Coffee-brown hair tumbled free. "Oh my gods, that knight was *so* annoying. And he was too old for me! I'm *so* glad he's gone."

"You, young lady, were not very nice today," I said, shaking a finger at her. "You know how much I hate recitations. And calling me 'knees'? Really?"

She shrugged, packing the gesture with insecure scorn as only a teenager can. "What was all that stuff you said at the end? Something about, if you'd ever had a son..."

"I had to stall him somehow until you two arrived. You took your sweet time getting down here."

"My apologies," Tom said. "We did not expect to need the backup plan. I had to trigger the spells manually to get that bit of tunnel to collapse on time. Also, a stone conked me on the head in the great room. I nearly lost control of the hex I've been using to enslave the minds of the castle staff."

"Any trouble kidnapping the real lord?" I asked.

"None whatsoever. My dragon, Smoggy, thought he was delicious."

The corridor trembled again, dust dribbled onto our heads, and we beat a hasty retreat, aware once more that this fortress was disintegrating. If Sir Barm had flown off on Garsteaodeafix, as I'd intended, I would've had ample time to escape before the process started.

"You're certain that everyone will hear of the knight's shame?" Tom asked me. "He must be punished for his disrespect toward my daughter and myself."

"Oh, people will hear," I said. "That bard who I told you to set free is excruciatingly good at what he does. He won't be able to resist composing a ballad of these exploits—especially when he learns that the castle Sir Barm destroyed was a fortress of goodness and light, not the summer home of some scummy evil lord. Er, no offense, Tom."

Tom grinned wickedly at me. "None taken."

The next time I beheld Sir Barm, his head and arms were trapped in a wooden stockade. Egg yolk dripped down his clean-shaven cheeks. Rotten, by the color and smell.

"You addlebrained dunce!" a peasant woman shrieked at him, pelting his rear with a tomato. "You destroyed our lord's castle! Lucky we don't chop off your head, you are."

"Good damsel, you must believe me! I have been betrayed. My mentor—"

"Rubbish! Seems to me that a real knight, an honorable knight, would take the blame for what he's done, and the punishment, too."

"You impugn my honor!"

"I'll show *you* impugnment, I will!"

A volley of rotten produce plastered him with fetid juices.

It took a few hours for the crowds to grow bored and drift away. I waited across the courtyard, nursing ales at a table

☐ YES! Sign me up to receive a FREE *L. Ron Hubbard Presents Writers of the Future Volume 37* eBook and Galaxy Press catalog **plus** newsletters, special offers and updates on new releases.

To receive your free eBook and catalog, fill out and mail in this card to Galaxy Press or email your request to info@GalaxyPress.com with **Code: WOTF37**

FREE eBook and catalog!

PLEASE PRINT IN ALL CAPS

FIRST NAME: _____ MI: _____ LAST: _____

ADDRESS: _____

CITY: _____ STATE: _____ ZIP: _____

PHONE #: _____

EMAIL: _____

CALL TOLL-FREE: 1-877-842-5299 (For Non-US 1-323-466-7815)
OR VISIT US ONLINE AT:

GalaxyPress.com

Fill out and return this card today to get a FREE *Writers of the Future* eBook and FREE catalog!

7051 Hollywood Blvd. • Hollywood, CA 90028

CALL TOLL-FREE: 1-877-842-5299 (For Non-US 1-323-466-7815)
OR VISIT US ONLINE AT:

GalaxyPress.com

WOTF 37

outside The Rusty Ploughshare. When Sir Barm was alone, I stood, yawned, and ambled into his line of sight.

His eyes widened when he saw me. "You scoundrel! You fiend! You are the architect of my downfall."

"Harsh words," I said. "But not untrue ones, I guess. What can I say? Having you destroy this castle was an honest mistake, and I'm terribly remorseful."

"A *mistake*? You caused me to tear down an innocent wonder of the world! You have heaped disgrace upon my name."

"Oh, it's not that bad. Tell you what. I'll get you out of these stocks, we'll buy some supplies, and we'll journey up to the Ash Lands for a *real* adventure, like you wanted in the first place. We'll pay that Lord of Shadows back for tricking us, I tell you."

I could actually *hear* Sir Barm's teeth grinding. "Do not touch me," he growled. "I swear on my honor as a knight, you will *never* mentor another hero. You think *my* name is shamed, now? By the time I am finished, there will not be a person in the world who won't have heard of your ineptitude. Adventurers will mock your name! You will become a tavern jest, a byword for duncery...and then you will be forgotten! No hero will come within a thousand leagues of your wretched mountain!"

I hung my head and whimpered. "Please," I said, "mentoring is all I've ever known. What do you expect me to do with my time...read *books*? Live a life of boredom in my cozy cottage, drinking endless tankards of ale and mugs of tea? I beg you, give me another chance!"

"You should have died in that crypt," Sir Barm said. "Then, at least, you would be remembered as a martyr, and knights might foolishly venture to your cottage, hoping to find you resurrected. Leave me, now. The next time I behold your face, I will strike you down."

I blinked fake tears from my eyes and shuffled away from the stockade. A chilly breeze made me shiver. Glancing up, I saw gray clouds mounding above us, threatening snow. The summer-spell had been broken.

At the very edge of Sir Barm's vision, I paused and glanced back. "Good knight," I said, "I should give you a warning. I've pondered the runes on the capstone—the ones that I misinterpreted before. I've made one last translation of them, and this time I'm sure it's correct. Be warned, Sir Barm: A curse lies on the stone! Its power is not that of turning winter to summer, but of revealing hidden natures. Just as it pulled back winter's veil from this town, showing the land beneath, so will it strip away the pretenses from anyone who possesses it for any length of time. For a truly good person, that's not a problem. But for a hypocrite—say, someone who withheld healing from a scabrous beggar woman until she cleaned up a field of auroch dung for him—well, for a person like that, I can only imagine the punishment would fit the crime."

I smiled at him. "You have a little something on your cheek, just there."

Sir Barm stared at me, then rubbed at his cheek with his shoulder, smearing the egg yolk more thoroughly. The skin beneath was already scabbing over.

I chuckled to myself and took the main road out of Omlath, stopping briefly to purchase a couple books. I'd arranged to meet Garsteaodeafix on the town's outskirts. The gryphon didn't know the extent of my deception, but she'd volunteered to fly me back to my mountaintop. Judging by the weather, that was a good thing.

It was starting to snow.

The Redemption of Brother Adalum

written by
K. D. Julicher

illustrated by
ISABEL GIBNEY

ABOUT THE AUTHOR

K. D. Julicher has been writing for as long as she can remember. She has a master's in computer science, which leaves her with an unfortunate fondness for semicolons. Since college, she has lived in every time zone in the contiguous United States. These days she lives in Nevada, where she collaborates with her husband on stories and children. Turns out all the best brainstorming happens while off-road.

She is proud to have been a published finalist in Writers of the Future Volume 32. *She made it her goal to return as a winner and now has. She also won the Baen Fantasy Adventure Award and had stories published in* InterGalactic Medicine Show, Abyss & Apex Magazine, *and* Deep Magic.

Her next goal is to publish a novel series featuring the bear warriors that have graced her most popular stories.

ABOUT THE ILLUSTRATOR

Isabel Gibney was born in 1998 in Washington, DC. She began creating stories at a young age. That passion led her to pick up the crayon, and later the stylus, to share her worlds with others through art. Their responses inspired Isabel to continue and refine her work and push her skills in engaging emotion through color and light.

Isabel is finishing her degree in history of art and architecture from Harvard University. She hopes to combine a love of narrative, history, culture—everything from food to archaeology—to encompass more diverse perspectives and expand the realm of storytelling through art.

The Redemption of Brother Adalum

I rose as the fourth bell tolled, my bare feet ice-cold on the stone floor, and reached for my robes. My tiny cell was just big enough for me to stand beside my cot and dress. Fifteen years of habit meant I didn't need light to prepare for the day.

Good morning, the bear spirit whispered plaintively in my mind. *Will you speak to me today?*

Its voice was as bleak as my cell. I refused to allow myself to feel anything the bear might read. Every day for the past fifteen years it had asked. Every day I kept my heart stony. It knew as deeply as I did why we could never again be one. The bear's pleas echoed my own deepest wish, but I had to be strong for us both.

Taking my long mountain ash staff from its place in the corner, I stepped into the hall and joined the line of my brethren as we filed down the corridor toward the sanctum at the heart of our mandra house.

Our sanctum lacked any ornate touches. A white linen cloth draped the altar. Rushes mixed with pennyroyal and lavender covered the floor where we knelt to begin our day with contemplation, laying our staves beside us.

The cold floor made my aging knees ache only a few minutes into our morning devotion. I tried to keep my mind on my litany. I'd grown old in the Order of Saint Hubrik, and my bones felt it.

I can ease that, the bear whispered.

I redoubled my litany, reciting from the first chapters of the *Book of Wayspeaker Relorn*, trying to keep my mind on the verses of self-control, even as the cold floor pressed against my knees. "I am a man. My mind is my own. Neither fear nor desire can take my soul from me. I am a man, and I choose to be no more, no less."

Won't you let me in? Why won't you talk to me? Just a word, and I can be with you.

That last plea nearly always threatened to break me. The bear spirit had been my companion since thirteen years of age, some thirty years ago now. We had become warriors together, we had struggled and fought for our liege lord, gaining glory, winning conquests. Together we had been invincible. The bear's strength had even won me Maris, daughter of my liege lord, as wife, and his son as my dearest friend. Even now, I could feel the bear's strength ready to aid me. All I had to do was break my vow and I could again be the man I had once been.

I fingered the amulet around my neck and vowed again not to give in to temptation, drawing strength from my brothers around me. The bear spirit was not one of the demons condemned by our scriptures, whose whispers would lead a man to madness and corrupt his soul. The High Prelate and the Temple made that clear. A warrior blessed with a bear spirit could keep his soul free. Our cousins and fathers and sons went about their daily lives in communion with their bears, seeking their aid in battle or labor. But we brothers of Saint Hubrik had learned that for us the bear was a stumbling block. And so we came here and shut ourselves away, each with our own sad history, each with a beloved voice in our head that we could not answer for fear of our immortal souls. The harsh life of duty and abstinence was no hardship. Keeping myself away from my dearest companion, the other half of my very being, that was the sacrifice that I made every day, so that no innocent would ever again die by my hand.

We finished our devotions together, facing the eastern wall where a narrow slit let in birdsong and the first pale light of day. Together we chanted the oath that forged us into brothers. "I shall not take up arms against man or beast, even at the cost of my own life, from this day until the day I die."

187

Morning rituals completed, we broke fast on hard brown bread, apricots, and pale-yellow sheep's-milk cheese. I waited for my assignment from Brother Ansel and found myself tasked to the fields.

I marched out with half a dozen of my brothers, strapping my staff to my back and taking up my scythe. We left the mandra through the wide-open gate, passing through the thick, curved stone walls into the fertile fields beyond. The day was cool, the mist not yet burned off the face of the river as it passed beside our walls, but the clear blue of the sky promised heat later. Three red deer nibbled ferns under the edge of a stand of birch along the road. They watched us warily and bolted before we'd gotten within a hundred paces. If I'd had a bow and arrow, I could have taken at least one of them before they bounded out of reach.

But no. My hands had wielded no weapon for many years. The stave and the amulet are the marks of Saint Hubrik. No brother is ever unarmed. Wielding it against a human, even in defense, means breaking our vows. Saint Hubrik intended that we keep our vows from devotion, not because we lacked the means to break them.

Then why are women forbidden in this place, when you've taken vows of celibacy? the bear asked. Its voice had grown too loud lately, too knowing. I wondered whether the barriers were growing thin. I would have to make an appointment with the Confessor. Yet I yearned to reply, to banter with my bear once more, the truest comrade of my soul who knew me as I didn't even know myself.

We reached the field. I took my place in the line, wielding my scythe as once I'd wielded a sword, slicing through the shoulder-tall stalks. Every slash laid a mound of wheat at my feet. Another brother followed along ten paces behind me, gathering the corpses of my slain into sheaves with their heads pointed skyward.

It felt good to push my muscles until they burned. In honest labor there is forgetting. I could lose myself in this work. I have never feared toil. I welcomed the calluses it brought, trading my sword-marked hands for the scrapes, burns, and rough patches of a common laborer.

I reached the end of the field and glanced behind; my companion lagged back. I'd outpaced him by a good bit, the comforting rhythm of the scythe speeding my work. I could be halfway down the field again before he finished this. The golden wheat beckoned me.

Instead I set down my scythe and started gathering sheaves at this end of the field. I stood each on end and tied them around the middle with a few loose stalks. When I reached Brother Randolf, he straightened up, acknowledging me with a brief nod, and we started back across the field again.

I swung my scythe and the wheat fell before me. My heart raced as I moved along, swinging my blade. Blood rushed to my ears. I was back on a battlefield, feet planted firmly on the ground, the haft of my weapon in my hands. My blood sang with the joy of combat, of proving my worth the only way that truly matters as a warrior.

My bear roared and leaped in me, the barrier between us no more than a hair's breadth. All I had to do was reach out and the veil between us would part and we would be whole once more.

No!

I shoved my bear away, hard. It retreated, reproach and pain radiating like heat off a fire. *I won't hurt you*, it cried. *I just need you.*

I dropped my scythe mid-swing and fell on my knees in the dirt. I plunged my hands into the soil, seeking to fill my senses with common things. The feel of dirt crumbling over my fingers. The smell of the new-mown wheat and the moist earth. There was a bitter taste of shame in my mouth.

"Brother Adalum?"

I looked up as Brother Randolf set his hand on my shoulder. His lips were pressed together in a worried frown. "Are you all right?"

"I will be," I told him. "I am struggling. But I will be fine."

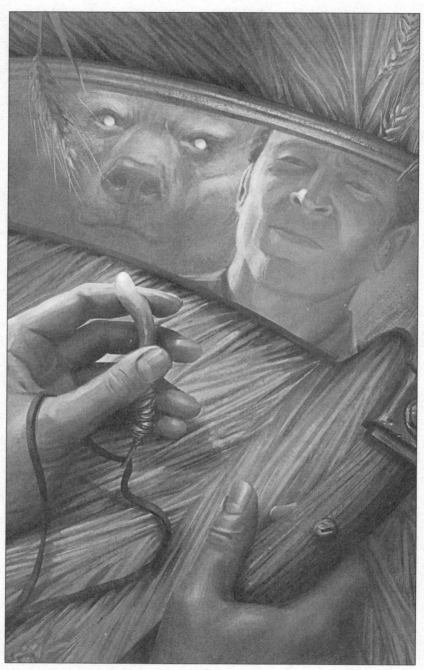

ISABEL GIBNEY

"You must speak with Brother Confessor," Brother Randolf said. There was understanding, not judgment, in his voice. We all fought the same battle here in Saint Hubrik's fields.

"I will. After lunch. Right now, I need labor." I stood. "Will you switch with me? I think I should not have a scythe in my hand today."

He nodded and I took his place with the fallen stalks of wheat. He moved on ahead of me, his body catching the easy rhythm.

I bound the sheaves and wondered why today was so hard. It was like the walls I had spent fifteen years building were made of smoke.

Then I remembered. Today was the fourth day past the solstice, and fifteen years ago I had stood in a field like this, where bodies had been the only harvest.

That was the day I had my illusions ripped from me and realized that what I had told myself was glory and honor was no more than defilement. The day I went past a warrior's bounds and became just a murderer, destroying those I had sworn to protect. The day I had killed the man whose name I now bore.

My hands slipped as I tied the sheaf and the stalks scattered on the ground. An oath leapt to my lips. I stifled it. All my old habits were coming back today. I bent to pick up the fallen wheat, and as I did, I caught the scent of smoke and heard distant screams.

I straightened up and looked around. My brothers did the same, searching. Brother Bjorn cried out and pointed westward. A thin plume of gray smoke rose over the trees from the village, two miles distant, but I wouldn't have heard the screams from that far. Not without the bear sharpening my ears. I worried that my walls were falling. I double-checked them and, with the other dozen brothers, headed toward the road.

We reached the road just as the first fleeing villagers came around the bend—two women carrying babies and dragging older children behind them, a boy hurrying a milk cow along, and a pair of young girls with bare feet and terrified expressions.

Brother Randolf reached them first. "What? What happened?"

"Raiders." One woman pointed behind. "Help the others!"

"You and you, get them back to the mandra," Brother Randolf said, pointing at two brothers. "Hurry, we must help the rest." He ran down the road. I followed, one hand checking that my stave was secure on my back still. I felt the tug of desire to take a weapon in hand. To defend these people, of course, from whoever was threatening them. That was a noble use of my strength, and the desire of my heart since boyhood.

But still against my vow. Taking up arms in the defense of the innocent is a good thing, as long as you can put the weapon down again and are sure who the innocent are. I had proven that I could do neither.

We passed more fleeing villagers on the dusty, tree-shaded road, and some of our number peeled off to escort them to safety, but I kept pace with Brother Randolf. We flew over the bridge crossing the reed-filled river and neared the town.

Most of the low thatched huts were on fire, the communal cattle barn and sheep pen a roaring inferno. No screams from within; at this time of day the animals would be in the field and I prayed no villagers had tried to take refuge there. The last few stragglers hurried past us. "They rode off to the west, chasing the ones who fled that way!" one woman shouted at me as she dragged a braying donkey along by its halter. Our liege lord's keep lay west, but four miles off; the refugees would never make it. "Go east!" I urged them. "The mandra's walls will shelter you."

We hurried farther into town, passing bodies of slain and dying men with pitchforks and clubs. These people didn't have many weapons. This was a peaceful land, and we hadn't seen bandit raids or war in many years.

A ring-mail-clad body lay facedown in the dirt, head bashed in, a leather cap with a spike in the middle lying in the dirt beside the corpse. I found myself studying the wound, imagining the blow that dealt it. One of the peasants had got in a good hit with a club. I rolled the body over and stared down into blank green eyes. The dead man had no beard and a thin greasy dark mustache running down past his mouth. "Kethmari!" I exclaimed, and jumped back. The spiked helmet should have told me as much, but it had been years since I'd seen one of the nomadic raiders from the east. My bear stirred. *They make good sport*, it remarked. We'd hunted Kethmari outlaws together, in our old life.

I knew their tactics. They'd hit a village, scatter the people, then hunt them down at leisure as they fled.

"Let's get the villagers to safety," Brother Bjorn said, "and tell our archimandrite what we've found."

We didn't dare take time to tend to the dead. I raged inside— or was it the bear raging?—at leaving them lying in the dirt, but we had a duty to the living. Many of the hovels were engulfed in flame, the smoke too thick to approach. I stepped inside one hut whose thatch had just begun to smolder, looking for any survivors. I saw none and started back out. My ear caught a tiny noise, like a mouse squeaking.

My heart raced. I dropped to the floor and peered under the single bed. The mattress sagged against its ropes, not quite concealing a little girl. Her wide eyes stared at me. "It's safe now," I told her. "Hurry!"

She didn't move, but she didn't resist as I pulled her out and carried her from the house. My brothers had finished checking the other huts. Together we hurried back up the road, catching the fleeing villagers and reassuring them that the Kethmari hadn't come back yet.

Our procession trudged back toward the mandra house. My neck prickled as we went. I longed to ask the bear's power to strengthen my senses. I wondered if it already had, in the hut, letting me hear the little girl's terrified gasp. The Kethmari were still out there. They weren't done with us yet.

I strode along behind the villagers. Their eyes begged me to protect them. It felt good to stand guard over the helpless once more.

Brother Randolf questioned the village mayor, who held a cloth to his slashed arm. "How many were they?"

"Dozens, all mounted." The mayor described their gear and faces—their pale eyes and darker beards—and I nodded.

Kethmari, yes, but why here? They didn't usually raid this far into civilization.

We reached the mandra's walls without incident. The archimandrite waited for us, his thin shoulders stooped inward under his deep crimson robes, thin halo of wispy hair glinting in the sunlight. He ordered our gates shut and barred and our guests made safe inside our strong round walls, twice the height of a man. The mandra had only ever barred our gates twice in all my time here. That's when I knew this was serious.

I studied the throng of refugees settling in the courtyard before turning back to the archimandrite. "Eldest brother? I don't think we've seen the last of the raiders. Once they've hunted down the stragglers, they'll come for the townsfolk."

He nodded, tiredness apparent in his small frame. His few remaining hairs were white. When I'd first arrived he'd still had a good crop of gray. Like all of us, he had been a warrior once. I could see thoughts of strategy and tactics flashing behind his fading blue eyes. "I had a message last week, warning of roving bands of raiders. They're mercenaries, hired by the satrap of Conselou."

We share a long border and an uneasy peace with the satrapy next door. "Is it war, then?"

"I don't think so." The archimandrite shook his head. "Our duke and the satrap are negotiating trade deals, alliances, possibly a marriage between their children."

So, the satrap was sending us a little reminder that it was better to have him as a friend than an enemy. And our townsfolk were paying the price. Fury rose in me. My bear growled.

The archimandrite studied me. "Brother Adalum, I think you should report to the Confessor."

"There's too much to do," I said roughly, starting for the courtyard where there would be crowds of women and children to feed and tend.

"As your superior, I order you to go." The archimandrite softened his voice. "Markus, I can't risk losing you now."

I started. I must have shown more of my struggle on my face

than I'd thought. For the archimandrite to scold me and to use my old name that only he and the Confessor now remembered...I bowed. "Of course, Eldest Brother."

The Confessor dwelt in the chamber below our sanctum. Even now, with the mandra in turmoil, our duty templar stood watch on the door to the Confessor's chamber. I greeted the templar politely. He pointed up the stairs. "What's going on?"

I summarized for him. He touched his sword hilt. Our trio of templars, who take their meals alone and speak to us only as necessary, were the only men armed with blades in the mandra, sent by the High Temple to guard us not from our enemies but from ourselves. "If you have need, my men and I will come."

"The archimandrite knows," I assured him.

He took the key from around his neck and unlocked the Confessor's chamber. "Ring my bell when you want to leave," he said, "and if you don't ring it by noon, I will call my brothers and come in after you."

He'd said the same words every time, but today he met my eyes while he did so, and his hand gripped the hilt of his sword. Did he feel the turmoil inside me?

I was resolved not to break. There would be no need for the templar's blade. "I understand," I told him. A shiver went up my spine as I stepped over the threshold. The templar closed the door behind me. I heard him drop the heavy wooden bar into place. He knew the lock would do nothing to stop me, if I lost myself here, but the thick iron-strapped oak door, barred with a three-inch-thick slab of hard wood, might hold long enough for him to call for help.

The Confessor's chamber was perfectly round, ten paces across. The floors and wall were undressed stone, cool even in the height of summer. A low wooden rail surrounded a hole in the center of the room where a glowing golden orb sat atop a pillar.

I knelt at the rail. The stones pressed the homespun cloth of my robes against my legs. I knew what would come next: my soul laid bare before me and my confessor. It was as uncomfortable as the stone and rough woolen robes beneath my knees and yet I yearned for the peace that I knew would follow. I raised my hands, took a breath, and plunged them into the orb. As the gentle resistance gave way, my hands felt like they were plunged into ice-cold water.

The room spun around me, bursting into a riot of colors like a rainbow ripped from the sky and flung around me. Music—birdsong trailing into distant piping—filled my ears. I smelled honeysuckle, then roasted pork, then fresh cream.

I blinked, and the room was all white. A shape stood before me, not a man's but a huge dark-red bear with a golden patch on its chest, taller than me, even on four legs. The Confessor. I didn't have to look around to know my own bear was manifest, too, sitting silent on its haunches beside me. It would not speak here. It never did.

"What troubles you, Markus?"

"My vow chafes," I said. I recounted the day's events. "Several times now I have longed to break my vow and summon my bear. The thought of fighting excites me."

"No surprise for a born protector's heart to beat faster when there are innocents in danger," the Confessor said. His voice hit my ears strangely, almost as if I wasn't really hearing him. "There is no shame in temptation, only in giving in." He lifted a paw, and the room spun again. "Your walls are thin," he said. "Is that your doing?"

"I think perhaps," I admitted. "Confessor, today is fifteen years since my failing."

"Ah." The Confessor wagged his shaggy head from side to side. "Will you permit?"

I bowed my head. "As you feel is right."

He leaned toward me. His muzzle brushed my head, but all I felt was a cool breeze. "Ah," he said again, and the world shifted around me.

I stood on the field of battle, my bloody sword in my hand, exuberant as the last of the enemy fled. The edges of my vision were tinged red. My head rang. My bear raged in me, demanding more blood. We had fought well, we had been victorious. Our flank had been more than successful; we'd broken through enemy lines and then routed them, chasing them down into this wheat field.

My liege lord approached, his own sword still drawn, his personal guard at his back. His lined and worried face peered over his raised round shield. His brass-studded leather armor was splattered with blood. His bloody sword was raised, ready for enemies, yet he was staring at me. "Markus!" he shouted. "Lower your weapon!"

I shook my head, trying to focus. "Hurry, we can catch the rest before they escape!" I pointed at the fleeing men.

"Markus! Take a look around you! Look what you've done," my liege lord bellowed. "Drop your weapon or God help me, we'll end you."

I turned. What did he mean? I stood atop a pile of my foes. My men had gone, chasing the rest. I should have followed them, but had been distracted, mowing down the last few survivors.

One corpse at my feet moved. I stepped back, ready to deliver the finishing blow, but the dying man turned his face toward me. "Markus," he groaned. "Why?"

I knew that voice. The face was unfamiliar, but I knew that voice, my liege lord's son, my wife's brother, my dearest friend. I stared down as my bear urged me to strike.

This is a trick, it said. *Finish him!*

But as I stared, my eyes cleared. I looked down into Adalum's face, the bright green eyes, bronzed skin and close-cropped brown beard of my dearest friend. The bear's paw pin on his chest matched the one I wore, that his father had given me the day I married Adalum's sister. The men at my feet wore the same leather armor as me. I saw the blood on my own hand and sword, and I knew what I had done.

I flung my sword away and knelt, howling in rage and sorrow and guilt, as my liege lord and his men came for me.

Blood-rage, they call it, when a bear warrior so loses himself in battle that he cannot tell friend from foe. It is not the bear's fault. The warrior is supposed to give the bear spirit context for what is going on. I'd let myself be lost to the rage of battle. I'd clouded my vision, not the bear.

But it did mean that I must never, ever call the bear again. Not now that I had lost the ability to use a sword without killing those dearest to me as readily as my enemies.

My vision blurred and I was back in the Confessor's chamber. The glowing orb hung over me, not judging, just being.

"Do you remember, now, why you took your vow?" the Confessor asked.

I nodded. "Yes." *I shall not take up arms against man or beast, even at the cost of my own life, from this day until the day I die.*

"And do you still choose to keep them?" There was no reproach or scorn in the Confessor's voice. He was not here to punish me, but to help me find my path. Who or what the Confessor truly was I did not know, but every time I met with him my soul was laid bare to me.

I didn't feel entirely sure that I wanted to honor my vows. They were no longer the armor that protected me, but chains keeping me from aiding others. "I must," I said. I rose. "I am ready to return to my duties."

I emerged back into the courtyard and found chaos, smoke rising outside our walls, and the sound of angry shouts. I found the archimandrite standing atop the gate watching along with Brother Randolf and a handful of other brethren. I climbed up to stand beside them, looking down fifteen feet to the cleared space outside the walls.

The Kethmari had arrived, four-dozen mounted warriors with cruel hooked swords and long spears. They barked profanities up at us, harsh words that needed no translation. I had shouted such taunts at foes beyond my reach, once. They mocked us and dared us to come down and face them.

"What do we do?" I asked. "Can we get word to the duke?"

"Some of the ones who fled west may reach Medenville, then word will be sent. It may be days before the duke can react." The archimandrite's shoulders slumped. "Brothers, our walls will not keep them out."

I fingered the amulet at my throat, the anchor which held my walls in place. Mere twisted bronze wire around a polished rib of bone, as easy to break as any vow and as impossible to repair.

"Prayer is our only weapon now," Brother Randolf said. "We must plead with heaven that they will leave us alone."

"These savages are not here by accident," I said, looking down at the Kethmari. They rode about in front of our gates on their small war-horses, whooping and shouting mockery at us. Their oily locks streamed out behind them from under their close-fitted leather caps. A metal spike protruded from the center of each cap. The spikes sported hanks of hair, some long, some short; the scalps they had taken. I saw fresh blood on some of the scalps and rage filled me for my slaughtered neighbors. "They've been sent to kill and burn and destroy. They won't leave until we are dead." A mandra full of dead peasants and monks would be a fine message for our duke, better than just a burned village. The satrap was reminding our liege lord that his strength and our faith were no match for the satrap's will. The villagers had come to us for protection, and we offered none.

The archimandrite fingered the amulet around his neck. I felt my own, like a lead weight dragging me down. He mused sadly, "We are sworn not to take up arms against any man." He looked at his withered hands. "I am past the temptation myself. My bear has grown weak in the decades we have spent apart."

I felt an itching sensation in the small of my back. My bear was in my head again. My walls were up, but it whispered, *Let me out. I can protect them.*

I knew it could, but it would destroy us both. Even at the cost of my own life, we could not take up arms. That was what the vow said. But there was more to the vow than that, wasn't there? "Until the day I die..."

199

I'd spent long midnight hours reflecting on that clause.

Once, long ago, I had taken another vow. At my liege lord's feet, I had sworn to protect the helpless. I'd broken that vow fifteen years ago and replaced it with another, the idealistic boy I'd been swept away by the broken man I had become.

They will kill us all, peasant and monk alike, the bear whispered. *We can kneel as our throat is slit, or we can die together atop a pile of bodies.*

I'd been atop that pile once before. Never again, I had sworn it.

But there was a wall between the Kethmari and the innocent. Not enough to protect them from the raiders. Just enough to keep me from making a terrible mistake in a blood-haze.

I turned to the archimandrite, and begged, "My elder brother, forgive me."

I saw the acceptance in his face. He knew what I was going to do. "I cannot relieve you of your vow," he said softly. "I can only pray for your soul. Both your souls," he added, looking deep into my eyes.

"Send for the templars," I said. The archimandrite nodded. The templars would protect the innocent, if it came to that.

I raised a hand and felt the amulet beneath my robes. My bear was close, trembling. I felt as though my heartbeats stretched out for an eternity, each beat pulsing in my ears.

If I did this, there was no going back. To break my vow meant no place for me in the brotherhood, whatever my reason. If I allowed my bear to gain control of me, I was a danger to those around me. I would be better off dead to the templars' blades.

Not that there was much chance of living that long.

But a hundred scared villagers, and my three-dozen brothers, stood behind the gates, and below me were only enemies.

I ripped the amulet from my neck and snapped wire and bone between two fingers. *Come, brother,* I called, and the bear leapt up gladly. For the first time in fifteen years I felt it slide inside my blood and veins, its power humming like my own heartbeat.

I leapt from the wall like a bolt of lightning.

The Kethmari shouted a warning as I fell. Two horsemen

charged me. I slammed my staff left, then right, knocking them out of the saddle. I stooped and seized a curved sword from one man's hand. Staff in one hand, sword in the other, I advanced.

My bear sang in my mind, a chant with words I could not understand. My enemies charged in on all sides. I bent and turned, blocked and slashed, my body finding the moves perfectly. One man could destroy an army, if he was a bear.

A spear pierced my shoulder. I hacked the shaft short and fought on, the wound leaking blood down my robes, but the bear kept me from feeling it. My enemies screamed as I cut them down. A dozen fell, and my bear and I were eager for more.

Blood dripped from my stolen sword into the dust of the road, staining it darker brown. Bodies clad in ring mail littered the ground like fallen sheaves, their pale eyes staring sightlessly at the sky. Twice as many circled just outside the reach of my sword. I remembered a day fifteen years ago when I had covered the ground in the corpses of fine warriors. The shouts and cries and clash of swords was the same. The iron scent of blood, so strong in my nostrils that I could smell nothing else, setting my own veins on fire with its intoxicating scent. I adjusted my torn palms on the grip of the sword. My hands remembered the sword calluses long lost by the years of scythe and shovel.

Everyone around me was an enemy. A distant part of me knew that I'd never be able to tell friend from foe. But my friends were safe on the other side of the wall. All I had to do was destroy my enemies.

A mounted Kethmari warrior charged at me, curved sword raised, his face a grinning rictus of hate, his horse's hooves kicking up a froth of dirt. I lunged to meet him. His eyes went wide as I stabbed my sword up through his gut, parting the ring mail beneath the tip of the blade. His blood ran down my arm as I withdrew my sword. He toppled sideways, foot catching in his stirrup. His horse plunged on, dragging its master's corpse behind. They were all too slow. My bear and I were one. We were a match for any of them, for all of them.

Another spear caught me in the side. The Kethmari were thin

201

now. They had me trapped, but still they circled me, hesitant. Their horses' nostrils flared, haunches dripping sweat. Men and mounts were exhausted. I felt my reserves burning. This ended now.

Don't hold anything back, I told the bear.

As if I ever did, the bear said as the Kethmari charged en masse. Now we were a whirlwind, sword and staff streaking through the air, knocking men from saddles and cutting them down in the dust as they fell.

The last Kethmari spurred his horse past me and fled. My heart pounded in my chest. Blood gushed from two spear wounds and more deep sword cuts I hadn't even felt. I took a step to follow, and my head swam. I caught myself on my staff with both hands, the stolen sword falling to the dirt beside me. All around us lay the bodies of the slain.

My bear's power abruptly vanished. *I'm sorry, brother,* it said. *I have nothing left to give. I have failed you.*

No, I said as I sagged toward the ground, one more body among the fallen. *It was always my fault. I severed our bond. You never left me. And we did not fail. We protected the villagers. They're safe now. We can rest.*

The bear didn't answer with words, just a feeling of acceptance that filled me as its power had, as the world dimmed around us.

I dropped backward to the ground and lay staring up at the sky, blinking. Someone leaned over me. Was that Adalum, who I had killed in my blindness and whose name I had worn all these years to remind me of my crime? I could almost make out his quick smile, the laughing green eyes that danced when he spoke. I longed to hear his lilting voice once more, though I feared what he would say.

I tried to speak, to beg forgiveness, but only a croak came out. My eyes blurred. My limbs were heavy and cold. I could rest now.

I didn't know if the voice was Adalum's or the archimandrite's or my confessor's, it was too distant. "Well fought, Brother."

The Argentum

written by
Anj Dockrey

illustrated by
RUPAM GRIMOEUVRE

ABOUT THE AUTHOR

Anj Dockrey is a Filipina-American author, artist, and educator. She writes sci-fi and fantasy, or whatever the muses choose to channel through her. Like most of her stories, "Argentum" started with a dream that demanded to be told. Anj has published short fiction and poetry on the semipro scene for years, including on Aphelion Webzine, NewMyths.com, and the indie anthology Wings of Change. *This is her first professional sale.*

Anj currently lives in Texas with a beagle and a fellow human, where she peddles Shakespeare to Philistines (aka high school students). However, she has lived in four countries and eight states and hopes her wandering days aren't completely over.

ABOUT THE ILLUSTRATOR

Rupam Grimoeuvre was born in 1985 in New Delhi, India. He has always been fascinated by the shapes around him. As an introverted kid, he spent most of his childhood in practice, drawing those shapes, although it was a confused dichotomy between getting attention for his artwork while avoiding interaction with other children.

As a student of science, Rupam always wanted to be an astrophysicist, but his dread of mathematics was too much to overcome. However, his love for science is still strong and has helped to shape his illustration skills. Well, that and his unsettling attraction toward darkness. He has never seen a horror movie, yet his work always leans toward the dark side.

These days, when not working on a personal project or writing his dark sci-fi shorts, Rupam works as a freelance artist.

The Argentum

I unlatch my helm, the vacuum seal popping free with a sigh. My limbs feel heavy in my suit, all the aches and chills I've ignored all shift coming to call.

The window glass feels cool against my forehead. I look out onto a Stygian night, holding still long enough that the interior lights flick off to conserve energy. When we pass Ares Canyon, the dome of Nadeyus Station will shine like a beacon in the darkness, but not yet.

Not yet.

A jolt bumps me awake. The lights flicker back on.

A man sits on the bench across from me, dressed in a silver uniform with spare, crisp lines. He is so handsome it hurts: hair of gold, straight nose, firm jaw. Plato's ideal.

Our eyes meet, and he smiles. Adrenaline thuds in my ears. I'm sure I was alone when the train left Temerity Station.

"I'm Argent," he says, offering his hand over the aisle.

"Merope."

"I know."

He's not a stranger then, though I don't remember meeting. As I take his hand, I note another oddity.

His hands are clean.

No one's hands are clean. The dirt of Canis is fine as diamond dust, black as midnight. And though we filter it from the air that comes into our domes and sift the soil to a nontoxic index and wear vacuum-sealed suits exo-dome, the black grit still gets everywhere. It's permanently ingrained in my nail beds, in the lines in my palms and the soles of my feet, and when I'm older, it will stick in the creases of age as if the planet wishes to leave its mark alongside the years.

"You're named for the train?" I ask.

"Yes."

"What do you do?"

"This." He indicates the train. I take in his uniform.

"You're the engineer?" I laugh.

"What amuses you?"

"Your name is Argent, and you work on the Argentum—but I'm not making fun of your name. I have a friend named Temerity, after the station. Do you hate your name?"

"No, I'm fond of it."

I worry I've offended him. I'm not the best at conversations. I spend over half my life in the Svart, clambering up its steep surfaces or delving down toward its heart, with radio silence maintained for safety. Most of the other miners are equally bereft of words, except Temerity. Someone is always snapping at Tem for cluttering up the channel with chatter.

We ride in silence for a while. The lights flicker on and off, the train thrums and jolts on the tracks in a familiar cadence. Finally, I find a question.

"How do you know me?"

"From here. You're always alone on this last leg, and I've been wanting to talk to you for some time."

The lights flick off as I process this. There must be vid feeds, and he must be very bored if he's using them to watch me.

"What about?"

"I wonder what you think about while you ride."

"Rocks," I say, too off guard to think of a polite lie.

"Any particular kind of rock?"

"Gold, today."

"Gold?"

"*Mohaya*, specifically." We'd found a large vein of gold today, glistening like lost sunshine in the halo of our lamps, and for an instant I'd understood why our ancestors had been so bewitched by its aureous luster they committed great evil to possess it.

"To be led into error through the folly of infatuation," Argent finishes the definition.

"You study Sanskrit?"

"I know many languages."

I purse my lips at this offhand boast, but my pleasure at having found common ground outweighs the annoyance.

"Is it good or bad to have found gold?" he asks.

"Neither, really. We've got a surplus of it in our stockpiles. We're looking for rare earths like promethium, which naturally occurs here, and uranium of course, and lithium to refine tritium for fusion…" I stop, for this is usually the place where people's eyes glaze over.

But Argent's eyes shine with interest. "Go on."

I need no other encouragement. "We thought we were close to a uranium deposit. We drilled for the whole night, but we found gold in a large wall of chert—that's a type of microcrystalline quartz. Beautiful but useless. My supervisor has decided to leave it and prospect elsewhere. But I…I've got a feeling we should go deeper."

"Then why don't you?"

"Not my call. I'm the youngest on my team. The others say I haven't grown my nose yet, so my hunches are worthless."

The conversation lulls. I make myself look at him and see something I don't expect.

Loneliness.

"The Founding Festival…would you like to go together?" I ask. Then, realizing how it sounds, "With my friends too."

He lights up so suddenly, for a second I imagine he's floated off the seat. But then gravity reasserts itself.

"It may be difficult, but I'll try."

The lights flick off again. The train must have passed over the canyon without my noticing because now Nadeyus Dome appears as if floating in the darkness. I stare at it as I always do, an ethereal lodestar that, even though I've lived my whole life there, still seems unreal.

When I look back again, Argent is gone.

Day on Canis is the gray, concave inner surface of a dome. I visit my friend Terra in the fields, pleasantly warm under the UV lights, but instead of attending to her chatter about the new citrus hybrid she's developing, I stare up at the dome. It's not visible, but I mined the gadolinium that coats it, shielding us from radioactivity.

"Mer," she says, waving a hand before my face. I inhale the perfume of orange blossoms as she brushes one of the saplings. A bee, its predecessors carefully, cryogenically transplanted, buries its fuzzy body in the trembling flower. "Where've you been wandering?"

"Have you ever met someone named Argent? About our age?"

"Like the train? Is he from Temerity Station?"

"I don't know."

This prompts a slew of questions I don't feel equipped to answer. I don't tell her I invited Argent to join us at the festival because at this point I'm not sure I didn't hallucinate him. I'm reluctant to explain how I blinked, and he was gone. Or how the memory of our conversation glows in my mind, brighter than its surroundings, like Argent himself. She would take it the wrong way.

We ride the Argentum to the festival on Temerity Station. It's packed with people dressed in their finest, and Terra's long, blond hair gives admirers whiplash.

She reaches up and brushes my dark bangs to lay slanted across my forehead.

"Do I look like a boy?" I ask, because I've given in and cut it so that it doesn't bunch in my helm. The draft on the back of my neck is a constant reminder of its absence.

"Not a bit," she said. "You look tall and elegant."

I preen a bit and surreptitiously look for Argent.

Tem is waiting for us at the station under string lights hung for the occasion. He waves, face scrunching to a grin when he catches sight of us. I tower over him, but Terra fits into the crook of his arm. I let them get ahead of me and smile at the way his eyes flit after her.

Then the crowd shifts, and I see a glimmer of silver. Argent, leaning against a pillar at the outside edge of the station. Our eyes meet, and he straightens, smiles. I make my way to him, and we face each other, awkwardly silent.

"Who's your friend?" Terra asks.

"This is Argent. Argent, Temerity and Terra."

Tem is fighting back a grin as he holds out his hand. They shake, and I feel a foolish relief because this is proof that I haven't dreamt Argent up after all.

"Well, let's go, guys!" Tem says. "That beer isn't going to drink itself!" He pushes Argent and me forward, he and Terra giggling behind us. My face goes hot.

The main avenue running from the station to the recycling plant is lined with booths built from materials recycled or waiting to be utilized. Each department has contributed. Terra leads us eagerly to the agricultural booth, where we wait in line for samples of beer made from the first generation of hops. We take our cups behind the tent. None of us has ever tasted it, though our parents have waxed nostalgic about it in the days leading up to this festival. Argent holds his up to the light, inspecting the golden brew.

"Ready?" Tem asks, sniffing his.

"Bottoms up," Terra says, tapping her cup against mine.

I take a sip of mine, the foam tickling my nose.

"It's..."

"Yeah."

"Pretty gross," Tem says, earning a smack from Terra.

I take another sip, hiding my grimace at the bitterness. But there's a pleasant aftertaste that reminds me of my parents' stories of summers on Earth.

"It grows on you," I say.

We finish our glasses and move on. Most of our food is protein processed from algae, supplemented by tubers and hydroponic vegetables. The fields are finally beginning to produce luxuries like fruit and the hops, and we sample tisanes and jams made from fresh basil and mint, chili and strawberries. We play games of chance and skill, fighting for elbow room with children who are only slightly more excited than we are. The beer is limited to a glass per person, so we switch to vodka, the first and, for many years, the only liquor distilled on Canis. I enjoy watching Argent. He seems to savor every experience with his entire being.

Bands play in the square before the hydroplant, and we make our way into the thick of the crowd. Argent stands awkwardly until I take him in hand. He picks up the steps quickly, and soon we're whirling and laughing. Tem produces a bottle, and we pass it around and sway and yell in one another's ears until the night seems clothed in a golden nimbus.

As the band packs up, we make our way back to the station. Argent and I have been drifting closer all night, and now I've had enough liquid courage to hold his hand. He's still humming the last tune, twirling me in a clumsy dance down the alley we take to avoid the crowds. Tem and Terra disappear into a shadowed doorway. Argent stops to watch, and I pull him away to give them privacy, snickering at him.

"What, jealous?" I ask.

"Yes."

I stop. He pulls me closer, presses his lips to mine. I close my eyes.

The sensation of the kiss is as ethereal as a soap bubble and pops just as quickly. I open my eyes.

Argent is gone. I turn in place, disoriented, but there is nowhere for him to hide, nowhere he could've gone.

"Hey, where'd Argent go?" asks Tem as he and Terra catch up with me.

"He was here, wasn't he?" I ask. "You saw him too."

Tem laughs. "I think you're drunk."

209

I have one more day off, and I spend it with my mother, sisters, and niece, Taygete—Ty for short. Together, we form the Pleiades. My parents wanted to have all seven of us, but my father passed away from an aggressive cancer when Celaeno, my youngest sister, was three.

Dad was an engineer by trade, a mythologist at heart. On the transport from Earth, he used two-point-six pounds of weight allotment for an antique copy of the *Bhagavad Gita*. I take it from its airtight storage and pull on the white cloth gloves Dad always made us wear so we wouldn't leave black fingerprints. We have every book ever written in our data banks, but there is something holy about this gold-gilt book. I turn to my favorite passage, the one I recite whenever I miss Dad. *"You speak sincerely, but your sorrow has no cause. The wise grieve neither for the living nor for the dead. There has never been a time when you and I... have not existed, nor will there be a time when we will cease to exist."*

My thoughts turn to the mystery of Argent. I'm sure he exists, but I am less sure that he is human. He came to me like Krishna to Sanjaya, riding on a cloud.

"Who's the engineer of the Argentum?" I ask my sister Maia.

"Well, Dad was primary," she says, escaping the kitchen, which has reached max capacity.

"I know that. I mean, who maintains it now?"

"No one in particular. It never breaks down."

"So there's no conductor?"

She gives me an odd look.

I think back to my first conversation with Argent. He'd implied he ran the train. "It's run by an AI?"

"Nothing so sophisticated. It's more a series of programmed automations."

"But could it have developed an AI?"

"Can an automatic door develop intelligence? Because it's the same concept. It runs on a loop, Mer. What's wrong, has someone been charging you for tickets? Because we don't use money either."

210

Back in the Svart, we mark the gold deposit and move on with our survey. I'm with the away team, and we bump and rattle along in the rotorcraft. We're only halfway through the Canis day, a forty-six-hour cycle, so it should still be light when we return to base. The sky is an orange haze, the horizon to the west black and flat. To our east, the Svart occludes the sky.

We fly for six hours. Stein falls asleep and snores over the comm until Lopez shakes him awake and makes him mute his mic.

We've reached the coordinates where we have to leave our vehicle. The Svart is a hotbed of seismic activity, and we've got a limited supply of fusion engines that power the rotorcraft. Easy enough to fuel and maintain them, but it will be some time before we have the means to manufacture new ones, so they get more consideration than we do. We get out and stretch, check suit integrity, load the "dumbwaiter," a drone-lifted platform that we use to haul gear up the mountain, and begin the climb.

I'm not sure how to describe the scale of the Svart to someone who's never seen it. On Earth, Everest is the highest peak at approximately nine kilometers. The highest parts of the Svart are closer to twenty, and dozens of Everests form its foothills. When you look upward, the black rock seems to reach forever, the uppermost peaks invisible behind the haze.

We reach a dune of loose, glittering black sand. Analysis finds a high concentration of magnesium; we flag it and move on.

As we climb higher, our feet find solid stone. The uniform blackness shifts to the dark green of chert, accents of ocher, sudden sparkling patches of peacock ore.

I bring up the rear, taking time to measure elevations, note surface minerals, snap pictures. Lopez scouts ahead, delineating our increasingly steep path. Jameson walks with half his attention on the drone in the sky, Stein steadying him whenever he stumbles.

I find a shining silver patch of beryllium, and Lopez calls a halt.

"We'll stop here," she decides. "Rookie, Stein, take a core sample. Jameson, land that drone."

I've been "Rookie" for two years and will continue to be until someone younger joins our team.

I sip nutrient pap from the stem inside my helm as I take measurements of the elements in the surrounding area, making sure there's nothing dangerous before I set up the wurtzite-crystal coring drill. Back on Earth, a steady flow of water would have been used to cool the bit as it drilled, but Canis has high concentrations of magnesium, which explodes when it contacts water, and though the air isn't breathable, sulfuric acid suffices as oxidant for flame. We use a flame-retardant coolant instead, and its tanks constitute the primary load on our drone.

Distance, protocol, neatness is the key to safety. After assembling the drill, Stein and I withdraw twenty meters, and he braces up a shield made of dome material.

I begin to drill. The beryllium deposit is disappointingly shallow. The computer populates my screen with atomic readouts, giving me eyes as the drill pierces a tough layer of flint. My optimism rises as I read a mixture of rare earths in the hard mineral—lanthanum and cerium and neodymium. I check the twin Geiger counters, one connected to a sensor on the drill, the other here with us. Still well within suit parameters.

The drill Geiger count jumps.

"We've got radioactivity."

The reading goes red. Beyond the shield, the drill lurches and screams.

"What happened?" Stein demands.

My brain translates the readings. "We hit an air pocket."

"Pressurized?"

"We're still standing here, so no."

I withdraw the drill bit and unpack a surveying bot. It's about the size and shape of a tarantula. I send it down the hole. It reaches the air pocket and drops, but it's basically unkillable, and when it hits the bottom, it uses echolocation to map the space. A 3-D rendering appears on my screen.

"There's a cave. A big one."

"Then let's find the entrance," says Lopez.

Stein finds it first, a fist-sized fragment of absolute black. We expand the entrance and I get to crawl in first after my bot. A three-meter squeeze, then the space opens into a cave of wonders. We spend hallowed hours delving where no human feet have ever tread. Our headlamps glint off a wall of amethysts, more ribbons of beryllium, a waterfall of mercury dripping down to a pool of liquid silver.

When I change my visor filter to the ultraviolet, the cavern glows with light. Uranyl galore. Lopez taps the Geiger counter, reminding us to swallow our iodine. Though our suits offer protection, there are protocols in place. Regretfully, we pack up early. We've found what we came for.

I'm riding the Argentum at the end of my weeklong shift, alone again after Temerity Station. It feels good to feel the air on my skin. I've barely slept all shift, and I flutter in and out of consciousness as the lights flicker on the train.

At some point, Argent appears beside me.

"What are you?" I ask.

"This," he says, gesturing around him.

"You're the train?"

He smiles, a crinkling at the corners of his eyes. A human gesture. "Not quite."

"You're not human," I say. It's not a question.

"Well, yes and no."

"How can you be human and not human?"

"I'm what you call the Argentum, the energy that powered first your ship and now this train. But this body I've created is within the genetic parameters of 'human.'"

I reach out my hand, tentatively, and he presses his palm against mine. He's solid. I'm not sure why I'm surprised; he held my hand at the festival. We danced. We...

"Why did you disappear?"

"It takes concentration to focus part of my energy into a specific physical form. I'm still getting the hang of it."

"You fooled me," I say, half compliment, half accusation.

"I told you that I was the Argentum, but I could see you didn't understand. I'm sorry."

He's right. He never lied; I just didn't see the truth.

"You even understand lies by omission and how to apologize," I say. "You translate Sanskrit and use colloquial expression. You've been studying us a long time."

"I've assimilated all the information in your database. Your languages, genetic patterns, history. I observe my passengers. Before humans made contact, I was alone. I'd never conceived of the concept of society, so you fascinated me. I couldn't help but go with you, to learn more about you."

I flashback to history class—the mysterious orb of scintillating light discovered on the outskirts of Neptune. The vids of triumphant politicians claiming to have harnessed the energy that would bring us to a new earth. The skeleton of the colony ship being built around it. The orb ship transported my parents safely across unfathomable distances to Canis, and when they arrived, they dismantled the ship and used its materials for the domed cities. The orb originally powered Nadeyus.Dome, but as the solar and fusion generators came online, it was relegated to running the train.

"You let them use you like a battery."

"I helped them," he corrects me. "I was afraid you'd die out if I didn't. Your lifestyle on Earth wasn't sustainable."

"Why didn't you ever try to communicate?"

His fingers lace with mine. "Isn't that what I'm doing now?"

My heart trips, and I blush, embarrassed by my reaction to him, that I'm still responding to him as if he were a man, when no doubt he has no concept of romantic attraction.

"Why did you kiss me?" I steel myself for his answer.

"I wanted to."

Not what I expected. I try to pull away, but he doesn't release my hand.

"Please don't say things like that."

"Why not?"

"You're just…experimenting, right? Observing the mating rituals of the natives. But humans, we have emotions involved with things like kissing and holding hands." I look away.

"Merope." He tilts my chin back so that I must meet his eyes. "This is a human body. When I'm in it, a part of my consciousness is separate from the whole—still connected but separate. And I can feel. I feel your hand right now. I feel…I'm not sure of the word." He draws my hand toward him, presses my palm against his beating heart.

"Everything is all so much more vivid in this body, especially when I'm near you. I should be able to maintain this form for longer intervals if I practice."

"To what purpose, Argent?"

"To experience what it's like to be human. Could I try that? With you?"

Logical arguments are born and die in the space of an eye blink. It's not rational, but I accept this situation the way I reconcile science and faith.

Due to protocols following a survey, I have a mandatory forty hours off. Argent and I walk through the older part of Nadeyus, where the first apartments were built out of shipping containers, green stacked upon blue stacked upon red. Most are overgrown with devil's ivy, a vine that survives off water and air, their roots in the condenser vats. I grew up in three maroon containers on the top level, arranged in an "L" and welded together, plus a shared roof garden.

I point it out to Argent as we walk past, explain the corporate sponsor logos on the container exteriors, only of historical significance now.

There's a small market in the old town where people barter

handicrafts and roof-garden vegetables. Someone has made strawberry-flavored ice pops, and I use some of my free ration points to buy some. As we're complimenting each other on the redness of our lips, we run into Maia and Ty.

Maia grins widely. I'm caught and have no choice but to make introductions.

"Nani's making samosas," Ty says. "You should come."

This is directed to Argent, who defeats me with a look.

Dad used his personal weight allotment for books; Mum used hers to pack a lifetime of spices. Cardamom and curry and turmeric and delicate red strands of saffron and star-shaped anise. She's a surgeon and pragmatic in her vices. Words, she said, could be transported in digital form; flavor could not.

I lead Argent up to my parents' apartment, Ty bounding up ahead of us. Inside, Electra is working the dough, and the rooms smell like hot oil and spices. Argent takes in the braided rag carpet that covers the living room floor, the packed bookshelf, the patchwork lamp I made in basic metallurgy.

Maia ducks into the kitchen, and a moment later Mum comes out and shakes Argent's hand.

"It is always a pleasure to meet one of Merope's friends," she says with a smile that makes up for the others' grins.

Argent hovers over Mum's shoulder while she mixes the filling, smells each spice and listens to her explanation of how it's grown on Earth. He picks up our digital photo cube and inquires about the grainy scanned photographs of our great-grandparents. He seems genuinely delighted while Ty gives him a lecture on the history project she's doing at school.

Mum sets down the first batch of golden-brown triangles.

"Eat them quick before the neighbors smell them and 'happen' to stop by," she tells Argent with a wink.

In what little spare time I have, I try to unravel the science behind Argent's ability to physically manifest. I don't ask him to explain. I want to understand at my own pace. The quantum physics text I download from the database seems to go hand in hand with Dad's beloved mythology, powered more by belief than math. Matter is just another aspect of energy, convertible from one state to the other. It sounds like the relationship between body and soul, life and afterlife.

Theoretically, a being made of energy, with the ability to manipulate that energy at will, could absolutely convert some of that energy to matter. Could, with enough study and patience and time, replicate the intricacies of the human body. We are our DNA, and what is DNA but a string of code? Apply the right code to raw material, and one could print infinite complexities.

The uranium deposit eludes us. Trace deposits in every core sample, but never in the concentrations we theorize should be there. Tem, Lopez, Stein, Jameson, Eun-ji, and I are all off-shift and riding the Argentum home, and it's the topic of the hour. Tem ropes everyone into going to "happy hour," an Earth tradition that Jameson and Stein have kept alive in our crew. We get off at Temerity Station, and Argent materializes beside me, attaching himself naturally to the end of our train. We go to our usual place, a pub that Jameson maintains isn't entitled to the name until they get beer on tap, order a bottle of vodka and one of soda, plates of potato latkes and fries, which never put too large a dent in one's ration quotient. During the second round, Eun-ji pulls out her notebook and projects the geological map of the cave over the table, and we resume our ever-ongoing argument of where to dig next.

"I think here," I say, marking a spot with a half-eaten fry. "There's a discrepancy in age between this rhodochrosite deposit and the flint next to it. I think it's an indication of an unconformity."

"Nope," Stein argues, countering with a quarter latke. "Outside the cave, where we found that sandstone."

"There were only micrometers of that sandstone!" Eun-ji scoffs. And so it goes.

Throughout this, Argent sits quietly, a vacant expression on his face. The others assume they've lost his interest.

"Sorry, man." Tem notices first and slaps Argent on the back. "Terra would have thrown down a red flag by now. Come on, guys, ix-nay on the mining talk in mixed company."

"You should dig where Merope says," Argent says, coming out of his funk.

"Oy, lover boy, look at you racking up the points," cries Jameson. "If that's the case, I say we dig where Stein wants."

The conversation devolves. Only Lopez stays aloof, her eyes glued to the holo-display still superimposed over the latkes and glasses.

Argent's hand finds mine on the bench.

Argent and I are in my apartment. I feel shy as he inspects my rock collection. He doesn't glow like he used to, though his skin is still too clean. This is because he rebuilds his body from scratch every time he manifests.

He sits next to me on the bed, and I note the depression from his weight. I feel like I'm always looking for evidence of his physicality. He touches my cheek, kisses me. It feels real. There's a twisting pain in my heart. I know, logically, that as closely as Argent can mimic, he isn't human. I have no idea how his mind works, whether he even has emotions, whether he sees me as anything more than an experiment. It's foolish to fall in love with a ball of energy that can power a starship, traverse time and space, and print matter at will.

Argent breaks the kiss, and we look into each other's eyes. His eyes still glow, yet they seem the most human part of him, and I know that I've already fallen off the edge. All I can do now is enjoy the trip down.

His lips trace the line of my pulse, his fingers wander. I feel his weight atop me, but it's my own anticipation that is crushing me, making it hard to breathe.

And then, he's gone. I punch my pillow in frustration.

My hunch is substantiated by Lopez's nose, and we hit uranium. Accordingly, we're all working doubles, catching sleep in the lead-lined, pressurized bivouac we've erected on the plains near the dig site and living off iodine-laced mush. We take two-hour naps in the bivouac; otherwise, we're in our suits, and we feel like sardines stewing in cans.

When I finish decontamination and walk into the bivouac for my nap, Argent is sitting on my bunk, no protective suit, looking perfectly clean and untouched and so different from my tired, sweaty self, that something Dad used to say flashes through my mind. He used to say that if people truly wanted grace, they should look not to the gods but to their fellow man. A god, by definition, is perfect. A perfect being doesn't feel pain, doesn't make mistakes or have regrets. And if one doesn't know regret, how can one forgive? If one doesn't know pain or want or need, how can one feel compassion or love?

"Why are you here?" I ask waspishly.

"I wanted to talk to you," Argent says, smiling.

"You don't even have a suit. There's radiation."

"The radiation doesn't bother me. And this body is actually relatively easy to adjust to different atmospheres. I might have to grow something like gills to filter out toxins."

"Argent, if you want to experience being human, you can't just grow gills when it suits you. Being human means being vulnerable. It means you need breath masks and radiation suits. It means you get sick and old and one day die, and it means..."

He reaches for me, but I shy away.

"Are you angry with me?" he asks.

"No, I just need some time alone. Please?"

Our eyes meet, and there is an expression I've never seen in them before. He nods, mute, and dematerializes.

I lie red-eyed for an hour, trying to pinpoint the source of my anger. I realize, as I pull my suit back on, that I'm a self-fulfilling prophecy. I'm afraid of Argent hurting me, so I hurt him first.

And then, I realize, *I hurt him*. I've rendered my own argument invalid.

I'm inside the cave, operating the drill. Tem and Lopez are down in the shaft, digging out what the drill has loosened and loading the ore into a cart for the drone to lift out. Eun-ji is arguing with Czerny over preservation of cave integrity.

"You two, fight on a private channel," Lopez snaps.

I smile as, instead of switching off, they draw Lopez into the fray. Belatedly, I focus on what the bots are telling me.

"Tem, stop drilling," I say over the chatter, noticing something that I don't have time to register because there is only the briefest of rumbles before the earth rushes toward my faceplate.

A great, suffocating weight. Hot, yellow darkness like sulfur. I think of hell and believe I'm there.

Then the weight lifts. I see Argent peering down at me. He is different. Human in form and yet not human at all. His skin glows. He picks me up and lays me upon a slope of rubble that didn't exist before. I watch him dig, wrenching up boulders that fill the circumference of his arms and setting them gently aside as if they weigh nothing. Then I fall back into darkness.

In the small hospital on Temerity Station, I regain consciousness. My mother sits at my bedside, professional and comforting in her crisp white coat, and tells me that Tem and Lopez didn't make it. Later, Chief Singh comes by and explains that we hit a pressurized pocket of hydrogen. It blew the shaft and caused a cave-in.

"I was the spotter, I should have caught it," I say.

"Some things are out of our control, Merope. Sometimes fate takes a hand." Singh's the same age Dad would be if he'd lived. They were friends from the colony ship, and I hear Dad's words in his. Permission to forgive myself someday. Maybe.

Several of my ribs are fractured, and my left leg is shattered from the knee down. Mum thinks my spine will be fine, but they are keeping me in traction to be safe. Jameson, Czerny, and Eun-ji are all here too, nursing varying degrees of injury.

Lopez and Tem both suffocated. The weight of the rock above them crushed the air from their lungs.

No one mentions Argent, except indirectly as they go on and on about the miracle of how they found all six of us aboveground, laid out in a row, survivors and corpses side by side.

Terra comes by. Singh visited her, too. She sits at my bedside and tells me she's glad I survived, that she couldn't have lost both of us. I start to apologize, but the words choke in my mouth. She holds my hand, unspeaking, and we cry together. I go back and forth, a pendulum swinging between self-loathing and blame, sadness and acceptance. My sisters visit in a constant stream. They ask about Argent at first, but it gets around that he hasn't visited, so they stop.

I'm fitted with an exoskeleton that allows me to walk while my body is adjusting to the artificial patella Mum installed. My first solo excursion is to ride the Argentum.

I ride from Nadeyus to Temerity, from Temerity to the Svart, but he doesn't appear.

When the doors close again at Svart Station, I say, "Argent, please come out. I need to speak with you."

A breath, then two, then he appears. He glows at first then, as if with great effort, the glow fades.

"I've been looking for them," he says. "But I can't find them anywhere."

"Looking for whom?"

"Lopez and Tem."

"You did find them, Argent. Thank you, by the way, for saving us, for recovering their bodies."

"No, I mean I looked for *them*. What I found under the rock was inanimate matter, but you all have an energy that powers you. Energy can't just disappear."

"Argent, you've studied us. Surely you know we die."

"Yes, I know about the state of death, but almost all your

literature says at that point your energy transforms into the soul. That is the true part of you, a higher energy state."

I realize that the tales of the afterlife must sound to Argent like his own existence. "You thought of it as evolution?"

"Isn't it? Your books say it is. Even the *Bhagavad Gita* says, 'The body is mortal, but he who dwells in the body is immortal and immeasurable.'" He looks at me like a child, desperate to understand.

Tears sting my eyes. I'm still in grief's grip, but Argent... Argent bleeds. I was wrong when I thought he couldn't be hurt, couldn't want or need or love. He just never had the opportunity. And now he is overwhelmed by the finality of a truth for which his experience has given him no context.

I step outside my own sorrow, my own disbelief in a future where my leg has healed, and I go back to the mines where there is no Tem joking over the comms, no Lopez going silent to listen to her legendary "nose." I take his hands in mine and quote lines of scripture that I only half believed before. But I believe them as I say them, with all my heart.

"'O mighty Arjuna, even if you believe the Self to be subject to birth and death, you should not grieve. Death is inevitable for the living; birth is inevitable for the dead. Since these are unavoidable, you should not sorrow.' 'All goes onward and outward, nothing collapses, and to die is different from what any one supposed, and luckier.'"

"That last part isn't from the book," he says.

"No, it's Walt Whitman. Argent, Tem and Lopez as we know them are gone. Each person, each life is a ... an accumulation of miraculous coincidence. Beautiful because there has never been anything like them before and will never be again. But I don't believe their energy is gone just because you can't find it; it's just converted into something you can't recognize. Maybe into a new life. Maybe as part of the cosmic energy that binds the universe together. What you're feeling now, this pain, it's you finally experiencing what it is to be human. Because to be human means living and falling in love and working hard and dreaming of the future, knowing all the while that at any moment you might have to say goodbye."

Tears glisten in his gray eyes. I wipe them with my thumbs, leaving dark streaks on his pale cheeks. The dust of Canis touching him at last.

"I didn't know it would be like this," he whispers. "And you, someday you'll die as well."

"Yes."

Hope lights his face. "I could study, experiment. Perhaps I can change your matter, teach you how to regenerate...."

He trails off, reading the revulsion in my face.

"No, Argent," I say. "You mustn't do that."

"But why?"

"It would make me into something not human, and I don't think I'd like that. And you shouldn't feel like you need to be different either. I'm sorry I pressured you to act more human."

Argent is disturbed, and it's affecting his concentration. He's starting to fade, and there's a distance in his eyes as his hold on his physical form loosens.

"It was better before. I was alone, but I didn't feel lonely. I didn't hurt." He puts a hand to his chest and rubs. His fingers meld with the fabric.

My grip on his other hand slips; no, slips through. He looks at me. "I don't want to say goodbye to you."

"Then don't," I say.

But still he disappears.

When I graduate from the exoskeleton to a brace, I'm cleared for work, though I'm housebound to Svart Station until Mum clears me for climbing mountains. Mostly, I'm glued to a console, monitoring the heap-leaching process. After a long shift, instead of catching a flight home, I climb the maintenance ladder to one of the rooftops, my leg aching in a way it never did before.

RUPAM GRIMOEUVRE

If I face north, I can watch the great smokestacks belching into the sky. But I sit facing westward and watch the Canis sunset, which has been going on for the last three hours. Not that I can actually see the sun. Sunset is only apparent by the color of the haze. Usually, it's a deep, bloody red, shading to violet. Sometimes it's orange and green. But today it's a pale, yellowish silver with bright rays illuminating the hidden features of the Svart like the radiance of God.

The Argentum, the tireless train, runs no more. The mysterious energy that powered it has gone. And though I know it will puzzle our engineers for generations to come, I don't share what I know.

If I could see Argent one more time, I would tell him I understand. I think love must be the most terrifying thing in existence. When I view things from Argent's perspective, I marvel that we can all go around day after day, loving spouses and parents, siblings and children, without reserve, all the while knowing that each goodbye could be the last. But humans have developed an evolutionary capacity to survive—the ability to forget, to believe in our delusions of hope. I don't blame Argent for running. How impossible it must be to be human without that ability. Argent, with his perfect memory, would never be able to forget, to deceive himself.

If he'd stayed, maybe I could've helped him develop that ability. Maybe it's something that can be learned.

But though there is no indication he'll return, I'll continue to look for him out of the corner of my eye. Will think of him before I sleep and whenever I have too much time. I'll keep the light on in the window. Because that's what we do.

The Phoenixes' War

written by
Jody Lynn Nye

inspired by
ECHO CHERNIK'S *PHOENIX PASSAGE*

ABOUT THE AUTHOR

A native Chicagoan, Jody Lynn Nye is a New York Times *bestselling author of more than fifty books and 170 short stories. As a part of Bill Fawcett & Associates (she is the "& Associates"), she has helped to edit more than two hundred books, including forty anthologies, with a few under her own name. Her work tends toward the humorous side of* SF *and fantasy.*

Along with her individual work, Jody has collaborated with several notable professionals in the field, including Anne McCaffrey, Robert Asprin, John Ringo, and Piers Anthony. She collaborated with Robert Asprin on a number of his famous Myth-Adventures series, and has continued both that and his Dragons Wild series since his death in 2008.

Jody runs the two-day intensive writers' workshop at Dragon Con in Atlanta, Georgia, over Labor Day weekend.

About "The Phoenixes' War," she said, "After my splendid experience last year writing a story to complement the cover painting by Echo Chernik, the Illustrators of the Future Contest Coordinating Judge, I learned that she was going to paint a companion piece for Volume 37, and that I would have the opportunity to write a story to accompany that one. I love her work, with the curving lines, lush figures, and rich colors inspired by art nouveau. It was fun to bring my characters up to date and incorporate the new elements Echo imagined into their world.

"The new painting has an entirely different feel from the first. My main character is Melana, a young priestess of the Temple of Peace. I am familiar with the legend of the Phoenix. At the end of her long life, the mystical bird settles into her nest and bursts into flames. Nothing remains afterward but ashes—and one shining egg. From that egg, the

Phoenix rises, reincarnated as a young chick to begin her life again. In Volume 36, Echo took the legend in a different direction: what if, instead of one egg, the dying Phoenix left two? I found the concept intriguing and inspiring. How would the world change from the moment they hatched? Now, the two Phoenixes have changed the world. They have come into their power, and Melana must come into her own. Tough decisions await her. She wants to prove herself worthy of her magical charges.

"I started publishing professionally too early to participate in the Writers of the Future Contest, but I am very glad to be part of it now as a judge. I offer the kind of story I would enjoy reading, that starts off with a bang and races breathtakingly to a satisfying conclusion. I wanted to show the growth of compelling characters like my priestess Melana and her sacred Phoenixes facing dangerous challenges, not only for herself, but for people that she loves and respects. It was a treat to revisit this world, and explore new facets of it, thanks to Echo's beautiful artwork."

ABOUT THE ILLUSTRATOR

Unlike all of the other stories in this anthology, where the illustrations were commissioned after the story was written, here Jody Lynn Nye conceived her story based on Echo Chernik's illustration, which graces the cover of this Writers of the Future volume.

About her painting, Echo said, "While creating the cover art for Volume 36, I wanted to reflect the hope and anticipation of the Contests. And then the pandemic hit and the big awards event for the winners in Volume 36 was postponed. So it occurred to me that if I did a follow-up cover for Volume 37, we could link the two anthologies and the award ceremonies to celebrate all the amazing new talent we've discovered over the last two years."

For more information on Echo, see page 4.

For more information on Echo, see page 4.

For more information on Echo, see page 4.

For more information on Echo, see page 4.

228

The Phoenixes' War

Atop the mountain crag, Melana, Priestess of the Temple of Peace, surveyed the sweep of the plains of Jraga. Winds whistled across empty grasslands, with only a stunted tree or so clinging to the ground here and there. The noonday sun beat down upon her, burning her shoulders like molten fire. The heavy golden regalia she wore, sweeping golden wings, a diadem covering her thick black hair, and jeweled breastplate arrayed over her bare brown skin, seemed to anchor her in place.

Helplessly, she watched as warriors of Dembia, her beloved nation, fell and died by the thousands. The Phoenixes of War and Peace, black-and-silver Solingwa and golden Coletwa, clung to the shoulder joints of her armor. They did not move or fly. The calming sensation they normally exuded had fled, leaving Melana bereft and frightened.

"Save them!" she begged the Phoenixes. "Stop this battle. Use your magic!"

Solingwa, the smaller of the two by half, bowed her black-and-silver head.

We cannot, she said.

Our power is swallowed up by that evil force, Coletwa added.

Melana looked from one of the sacred birds to the other.

"Then if you cannot, I will!"

With a cry, she wrapped herself in a dark cloud of magic and flung herself down toward the two armies two thousand feet below. Thousands of lightning bolts pierced her body, but she carried on moving forward toward her beloved warriors until

229

she fell to the ground in agony. Her last view was of the paired Phoenixes rising high into the sky, their flight intertwining in a column of red light, leaving her behind. She was only eighteen years old.

"Priestess, come back to us!"

High Priestess Aduna's voice came as if from very far away. Melana shook herself. The golden regalia rattled, bringing her fully to waking. No longer upon the battlefield, she was in the grand hall of the royal palace of Dembia, where she had been when the terrifying vision had overtaken her. She sat upright and planted her hands upon the armrests of the Phoenix Throne, and discovered that everyone stared at her in concern.

Not the least of them were the two small worried bird-faces, one perched on either of her wrists.

The glorious Phoenixes walked up her arms until they could nestle beside her like a couple of cats. Clinging to the shoulders of her elaborate gold-feathered pectoral, they rubbed their beaks against her ears and cheeks. Automatically, her hands rose to stroke them and scratch among the tiny feathers of their necks.

"I had never dreamed before you came," Melana said, fondling them with all the love in her heart. "Now I almost wish that I could not."

"Did you see where the king has gone, Melana?" asked Aduna. The elderly priestess's dark, wrinkled skin was gray with worry. She clasped the head of her sturdy staff of office with both hands to steady herself. "Where did that beast carry him off to?"

"I didn't see that," Melana said, her voice trembling. She knew her own deep brown skin had paled. It felt as though all of her blood had retreated into her belly. "I saw war."

The grand lords and ladies in the great hall of the palace in the capital city of Luros murmured, frightened, frozen in shock. As accustomed to small workings of magic as they were, a dark spell of such power almost never intruded into their peaceful lives. The floor-to-ceiling glass doors stood open to the tropical sun, but the breeze flowing through them scarcely dispelled the terror they had just suffered.

Only a moment before, their king had stood before them. He was a handsome man, not quite thirty, with deep brown skin and liquid sable-brown eyes. His crown, which bore a golden phoenix surmounting a flame-orange gem the size of a plum, nestled into his thick, curly black hair. He looked delighted to enjoy a gift from his affianced bride as he swung into the saddle of the magnificent black stallion. In the next moment, he and the great horse had been swept away, and the flood of power had thrown Melana into a vision.

"What do you think it means?" Melana asked the senior priestesses. "Does Jraga really intend to declare war upon us?"

"You know dreams can be a warning, not necessarily a foretelling," Olinke said. The serene priestess came to lay a calming hand on her arm.

Melana chided herself. She knew that. The senior priestesses had taught her the same lesson again and again. Nor was she the same callow youngster who had stood in the Nest Room of the Temple of Peace over two years before when the twin Phoenixes had begun to hatch from their golden eggs and she had become their keeper.

The yoke of service to the Temple had been one she had shouldered willingly. With that came responsibilities she had never dreamed of in the small town where she had grown up. She had known love and anger, war and redemption, peace and triumph. With the advent of the Phoenixes, she had had to learn to control magic more powerful than anyone else in Dembia—with a keen knowledge that it was not necessarily the most powerful in the rest of the world. Power must be guided by wisdom and experience. So, what did she know about what had just occurred?

King Alimbi had chosen as his intended bride the Demigoddess of Jraga, the nation that lay beyond the great mountain ridge bordering Dembia to the north. Jraga was known for its devotion to the Horse Goddess, proud of the herds of stallions and mares that galloped its nearly endless plains. Gifts had been exchanged over the course of a couple of years between Alimbi and Eona's father, the God-Ruler, and with Eona, the lady herself. She had exchanged letters with Alimbi that indicated she regarded his suit with approval. Once her father gave his consent to allow her to form a strategic alliance by marriage, her correspondence became warmer and friendlier in nature. A female warrior on a destrier more magnificent than any that lived in Dembia delivered to Alimbi a portrait of Eona. Melana had seen it herself on visits to the palace. Nearly life-sized, the oval image depicted a woman whose heart-shaped face was as golden as a sunset, with eyes the same amber color as Coletwa's and flowing hair like rivers of syrup. If Alimbi's interest had not been growing for the lady through their correspondence, Melana thought surely that the portrait had cemented his interest in her. Their exchanges grew more frequent.

Alimbi had made several visits to the Temple of Peace to make offerings to the Phoenixes, to ensure good relations between the two countries and success in his marriage. Those gifts included not only gold and gems to support the Temple complex but treats of rare berries and nuts for Coletwa and Solingwa.

A few days ago, the Demigoddess Eona had sent a very important present to the king: a tall stallion, shining black, with eyes as green as the grass of the Jraga plains. Alimbi understood it to mean that the Jragans were trusting him with one of their most prized possessions. In joy, he threw open all the doors of the palace for a festival to celebrate his coming engagement and for everyone in the capital to see the horse. He sent a special invitation to the priestesses of the Temple to attend. Musicians and singers clad in brightly colored flowing festival robes filled the air with sweet sound. Savory smells proved that the king had called for the finest food to be served, and the Mistress of the Wine Cellar ordered her minions to and fro with pitchers of rich red wine. The four grooms around the beast, clad in sober, self-effacing brown livery, who had accompanied the stallion from Jraga, seemed embarrassed by the fuss being made over them. They accepted food and drink and allowed the visitors to admire the horse, but did not let them close enough to touch the rearing and snorting animal.

"He has such spirit!" Alimbi told the priestesses with delight. "I will make an official visit to Jraga soon with precious gifts for Eona, too. May the Phoenixes bless our union."

We do, Coletwa assured Melana, who passed along the message. Solingwa ate fruit from a golden bowl. Human marriages meant little to her. Coletwa, gently amused by her sister-self's disdain, pulled a long scarlet-and-gold feather from her own tail and dropped it into Alimbi's palm.

"It...it tingles on my skin," he said wonderingly, stroking the long pinion. "I can feel it suffuse through my entire body!"

"Its magic will bless you both," Melana assured him.

He beamed and bowed deeply to the Phoenix of Peace.

"The Demigoddess will be thrilled with this," he said, holding the treasure in both hands, like a child instead of the ruler of a great nation. He smiled, and tucked the feather into the sleeve of his flowing amber-colored robe. He turned to the crowd. "Drink and feast, my people! Share in my joy!"

Melana had taken her place on the golden seat beside the thrones, reserved for the Keeper of the Phoenix. Her twin charges flew about the black steed, peering at it with curiosity. Solingwa made as if to land on its head. The great stallion tossed its head and snorted. The black-and-silver bird flitted back to Melana.

I do not trust this creature, said the Phoenix of War.

"Why not?" Melana had sat up straight in alarm.

Solingwa cocked her small head. *It is of two spirits, much like my sister-self and I.*

"He must be special, or the Demigoddess would not have sent it to our king," Shala said. The slender priestess, of Melana's own age, had begun in the Temple at the same time and was Melana's very good friend.

233

He is special, Coletwa confirmed. *He thinks two thoughts, one of grassy hills and running, and the other...*

"Attention!" called Oded Milihido, the king's chief minister. The portly man, whose cropped, grizzled hair spoke of long years' service to the throne, pounded the staff of office on the stone floor. "Behold His Majesty!"

Alimbi couldn't wait another minute. He strode toward the great horse. The four grooms had risen from their table to assist Dembia's lord to the deep blue painted saddle. Alimbi was an experienced horseman, having ridden to the country's defense more than once. At his weight, the stallion began to dance, then reared up on its hind legs. Alimbi laughed, and the hall of visitors and courtiers cheered.

The noise alarmed the horse. He bucked, trying to unseat the king. Alimbi held on tightly with pressed thighs. He looked as though he was enjoying himself. With practiced hands, he gathered the reins and tried to control the horse by pulling his nose down to his chest.

The black stallion shook his head. Once more, the great horse rose to his hind legs. He pawed at the air with his shining hooves... and exploded.

Or that was how it seemed to the onlookers. With one deafening noise like a clap of thunder, horse and royal rider vanished, leaving a cloud of black smoke. The noise and the haze threw Melana into her dream.

It had withdrawn into memory now, as everyone in the great chamber cast about in horror for the king and his mount. Not a trace remained.

"What happened?" Lord Milihido pleaded. He turned to the priestesses and wrung his hands. "The Jragans have betrayed us! Our lord has been murdered!"

He has not, Coletwa insisted. The voice inside Melana's mind dragged her away from the horrifying vision and brought her back to the present. Not reliant upon pure sound alone, it also overpowered the shouting in the hall. The noise died away as everyone turned to the glorious golden bird, desperate for reassurance. *He has been carried away. The beast's second spirit caused it to happen.*

Melana's heart was still beating like a drum. It wasn't the first time she had pictured her own death; those other times it had not come true either.

"They carried him off?" Lord Milihido echoed. Though not audible to the ordinary ear, the Phoenixes' speech could be heard in the minds of everyone present. "Why? Where?"

It is a test, Solingwa said.

"A test? Testing who? Testing what?" Melana asked.

"Our wit and intelligence," Aduna said shrewdly. She looked at Milihido. "Pull yourself together, man. The Phoenix has spoken. The king is not dead, yet I have no doubt his life is still at stake."

"We will ride to battle!" Lady Vora boomed. The Dembian army general's imposing frame gave her voice extra carrying power. Her black eyes burned like coals in her broad, strong face. "His Majesty offered honorable marriage and alliance to the Demigoddess. They have insulted us by sweeping him away in such a fashion! I will assemble the troops to ride to Jraga and bring him home. The Horselands will be left in rubble." She strode toward the hall, calling for her aide-de-camp and her officers. Men and women wearing Dembian uniform left their places in the crowd and flowed into her wake like a skein of birds.

Melana jumped up from her golden chair and rushed to intercept her, the golden wings rattling on her back. The Phoenixes swirled around her head like storm clouds caught in a whirlwind.

"No, General!" she said, halting the big woman before she could reach the door. "If we fight, we will lose. I have foreseen..."

She didn't know how to begin to describe what she had seen. The sensations of the magic raining down on her was still too vivid. She felt every lightning bolt that had pierced her in the dream. Vora glared down at her.

"Then what? Wait for them to return him at their leisure? We must go to him!"

"Where?" Mihilido demanded. "The Jragan plains are vast! The so-called God-Ruler of the Horse Plains occupies one of a hundred tents as the fancy takes him." He rounded on the Jragan grooms, who fell to their knees with their hands outstretched. Their expressions told Melana they expected to die. "You! Where has that beast gone with our king?" At their puzzled expressions, he switched to the Jragan tongue and barked his questions.

They gabbled at him, pointing to the north. It was no use. Even though she didn't speak Jragan, Melana could tell they knew nothing.

"Magic took him away! How do we find him?" Lord Mihilido asked.

He holds my feather, Coletwa said. *I can take you to him.*

"Do it at once!" Vora demanded. "Defenders of Dembia, to me!"

"How many can you take?" Melana asked the Phoenixes. Her heart swelled with hope.

Enough of you to pass the test, Solingwa said. Her mental voice sounded peevish. *Don't waste time. The second spirit is still here.*

"Spying on us!" Mihilido barked. He looked around as though he would be able to see a ghostly presence. "We cannot trust the Jragans."

Solingwa cocked her head, listening. *The spirit laughs at you. Take action now!*

"Take us to the king!" Lady Vora demanded.

"No," Melana said, as a thought struck her. "If they swept him away once, they can do it again. Take us to the source of the second voice."

Solingwa's silver eyes glinted with wry humor. *It did not expect that answer*, she said. She and Coletwa landed on the wing joints of Melana's golden armor. *Those who would join us, come to us now! Make haste!*

The priestesses of the Temple of Peace came forward; even Aduna, her ancient body creaking with arthritis.

"Should you come with us?" Melana asked her. "You might come to harm."

She halted at the resolute expression on the old woman's face.

"The mission of the Temple is to protect Dembia, and what represented Dembia more than the person of its ruler?" Melana was abashed. Coletwa walked down her arm and up onto Aduna's. With an indulgent smile, the old woman stroked the golden bird. "Child, we have prepared all the years before you were born. I will defend my beloved country every day of my life. If I die, it will be in her defense."

Every one of the military officers and not a few of the courtiers, both male and female, flocked close. As this had been a celebration, only a few wore weapons, and those mostly of a ceremonial nature. Some of the men tore ornamental swords and spears from displays on the walls. The rest took carving knives and cutlery from the tables. Melana almost wanted to laugh, but she feared there was no time to locate proper arms. Solingwa fidgeted from one foot to the other.

Are you ready? the kindly Phoenix of Peace asked her.

"No," Melana admitted, "but we have to go anyhow."

They appeared in the midst of a huge flat plain lined with thin grass no higher than the first knuckle of Melana's finger. It was the same place that she had seen in her vision, only from a different perspective. She imagined this roughly circular stretch of land to be the palm in the middle of a hand whose massive digits were the mountains she could see in the distance. Nothing was defensible. If they were attacked here, they had to stand at bay. The weather was far colder than Dembia. She shivered in her formal attire, which had no sleeves or covering over her torso under the gold pectoral to the waist. Her companions, equally uncomfortable, surveyed their surroundings with unease. The sun that had seemed so hot in her dream hung veiled in ominous clouds.

"Horses could not live here," Vora observed. "There's no forage."

"No," Olinke said, peering around her. "This is not a home or a haven. It's a playing field. A chessboard."

"What is the game?"

"Like any chess game: war."

Mihilido jumped. "What is touching me?"

"It's horrible!" said a lady of the court, brushing at her body.

A sensation like cold slime enveloped Melana. The others felt it too, jumping and batting at their bodies. She felt the invisible touch slide over her skin, almost snakelike, chilling her through and through. It left her with the overwhelming desire to run away, anywhere! Automatically, she threw her arms up to dispel the feeling. It kept pushing back, sneaking in through her personal wards, until she drew upon the protective force radiating from Coletwa to seal it out. She felt dread, but not as crippling as from that slimy touch.

Molding the air with her hands, she covered each of the men and women with a similar shell. The rest of the priestesses were doing the same. In moments, Melana was warm and dry again, but wary.

An opening salvo, Solingwa said, with a nod that almost indicated approval.

That is the second spirit, Coletwa said. *It assesses us.*

"To determine what?" Melana asked, in concern.

What force we can withstand.

"What force?" Mihilido echoed, turning his broad face to see. "There is nothing for miles around us!"

As if in answer, the ground began to rumble. Ocher dust shimmered up from the plains in a vast ring of cloud. The thundering grew louder, until it sounded like the world would shake apart under their feet. When the dust clouds settled, they saw armored cavalry by the thousand, men and women wearing bronze-colored leather armor and smooth silver helms topped with flowing tails of horsehair. Above each company fluttered a banner featuring a running horse on a field of bronze. The mounted warriors leveled spears at the knot of Dembian defenders and clapped spurs against the sides of their steeds. The horses leaped forward.

"We will die!" the chief minister shouted. He fumbled with the staff in his hand.

"Ready arms!" Vora shouted. With one smooth motion, she drew the ceremonial sword that hung at her side. Melana observed that it was just as sharp as a battle weapon. "Guard us, Phoenixes!"

Melana felt the power flowing into her from the twin birds. She concentrated, shutting out the hammering of hooves on the plain.

From Coletwa came golden force that protected and nurtured. The young priestess spun in a circle with both palms turned outward. She felt the magic radiating outward from her hands, her eyes, and her open mouth. She and the other priestesses recited an incantation as old as humankind itself, adding intention to the shell to make it impenetrable against all attack. The golden energy spread out around them and formed a glistening bubble that she could see in her mind's eye. The bubble broke into smaller spheres, surrounding each person and forming around them like a translucent suit of armor. Within their boundaries, the Dembians were safe. Two years ago, Melana couldn't have created such a bubble of protection, but she had learned to wield the mystic force since then. In fact, she had had too much practice on the border between Dembia and Jumheuri. This was different, she chided herself. She put aside her memories of that war and concentrated on being where she was.

Now Solingwa sprang off her shoulder and flew around her head, calling. The Phoenix of War drew living power from both the sky and the ground. The burst of silver energy, surprising from such a small creature, almost knocked Melana off her feet, but she braced herself and opened herself to it. The power filled her to the tips of her fingers and toes, to the very ends of her hair. She knew herself to be mighty, even invincible! With the magic of the Phoenix of War, she could flatten companies of horsemen, or make every weapon in Dembian hands many times as deadly as wood and steel. She could fling every horse and rider back to the underground realm that had brought them forth.

"Well?" Vora demanded, staring at the blade she wielded. "I

don't sense the power in my sword! They are coming, Priestess. Enchant it!"

Another spell that she knew by heart, Melana started automatically chanting the words to transfer the blazing silver energy to the others. To her astonishment, Solingwa landed on her shoulder and bit her lips with her sharp little beak.

Do not! the Phoenix commanded. *The second spirit is watching! Hold back the silver fire!*

Melana stopped, as did the other priestesses. It was a strange command, but they trusted Solingwa. She, Aduna, and Olinke looked at one another. Melana wasn't sure what to do. Their battles against the Jumheuri were straightforward, meant to repel the invaders on the border with as little bloodshed as possible. But not to fight at all? She sent a desperate look toward Aduna. The old woman smiled and nodded. *Trust the Phoenixes,* her look said. Melana bit her lip, tasting the drop of blood that Solingwa had drawn.

"What are you doing?" Vora asked, who clearly did not have the same faith in the Phoenix. "The enemy is almost upon us! Thousands of cavalry! They will kill us!"

They can't come through the shell of power of my sister-self, Solingwa said, turning a baleful silver eye on the general. *Stand firm! Do not react. It will be fatal.*

The thunder of hoofbeats grew until it was almost deafening. Melana could smell the odor of horse, leather, metal, and sweat carried by the sweeping winds. She was terrified for herself and her companions, and feared for Alimbi's life, wherever he was. Vora looked from the Phoenixes to the oncoming army. Her eyes were wild with anger.

"Why? Why will you not arm us! *That* will be fatal if we cannot defend ourselves."

Because this is not the battle we need to win! Solingwa insisted.

"I do not wish to die because you pose us riddles!" Vora said. Her face glowed red. "Your job is to protect us! We are outnumbered many hundreds to one!" She glared at Melana.

"Make them arm us! If not, we die here, and our king remains a prisoner in this land."

Solingwa hopped up on Melana's arm and stared at the general. *Do you question me?*

"I am a general of a great nation, trusted by her king and protector of her borders!" Vora said. "I have led troops on the ground and bled beside them. I'm not a bird who can fly away from danger when it threatens. Or a girl who doesn't understand the meaning of war!"

The others gasped. Coletwa leaped to Melana's wrist and interposed her golden body between her sister-self and Vora.

We do not flee. We are here with you.

Melana drew herself up to her full height, which still put her a head shorter than the angry general.

"I have seen a few battles," she said, keeping her voice as calm as that of the Phoenix of Peace, although she trembled inwardly. "But the Phoenixes are born and born again! They have been in every war to protect Dembia since our nation began. I've never led an army. But I do my best to defend the country as much as you do. If I am wrong, if the Phoenixes are wrong, you may call for my punishment if we survive this. But never them. They have seen thousands of battles."

Vora had the grace to look ashamed.

"This is not our first war," Aduna reminded the general. "We have had to meet unfamiliar strategy before. If the Phoenixes demand caution, then exercise it!"

"Is that it?" Melana asked Solingwa. "Is that the key to this game? What do we face here, if not a deadly army?"

The Phoenix raised her beak high as if listening. *We face ourselves. We are observed.*

We told you it is a test, Coletwa added.

"I don't like to be tested or toyed with!" Vora snapped.

The spirit laughs at you, Solingwa said. *Observe and do not react!*

"Then pray for us, Priestess," Vora replied, glaring at Melana. "Say the prayer for the dead, because our doom is upon us!"

The riders were only minutes away now. Armored in well-worn battle gear of black and brown leather with jointed pauldrons on their shoulders, they seemed as much like animals as their steeds. The first rank propped long painted lances on one foot, ready to couch when they came close enough. The others drew sabers with a clash loud enough to be heard over the pounding hooves. Melana could see the riders' eyes through the slits in their tall silver helms and the grim set of their jaws. Closer. Closer...

Spear couched, the first of the Jragan warriors charged the circle of Dembian defenders. Lord Mihilido clutched his staff with both hands and closed his eyes so he didn't have to see the death blow as the silver point penetrated his chest.

WHANNING! The lance struck, and a golden flash burst forth. Mihilido fell backward, but the rider fell too. The spear went flying, its head bent at the tip. The horse charged off with an empty saddle.

Some of the courtiers stooped to help the minister to his feet. He goggled as if astonished to find himself alive. More riders thundered in. They had seen the fate of their leader, but were moving too fast to react before they, too, struck and were unseated.

They scrambled to their feet and drew swords, signaling to the riders behind to dismount and attack on foot.

"Those with arms, form around those who have no weapons!" Vora ordered.

"Don't...!" Melana began, but Coletwa stropped her head against the young woman's cheek.

"Give the soldier something to do," Olinke murmured. "Just do not let her hurt anyone!"

Vora continued to deploy her troops. The priestesses and the unarmed nobles drew close to the Phoenixes and away from the endless stream of charging horses. By now, the Jragan troops had discovered they couldn't break through the Dembians' shields, but they continued to strike at them nonetheless.

"A test, you say? A test of what?"

"The thing no one has said," Aduna replied. "We are not at war with Jraga! If the God-Ruler didn't want to ally with us or encourage his daughter to marry our king, he wouldn't have." The old woman shook her head. "This is to become a sister nation to us, not an enemy. Alimbi wants to marry this woman...."

"*If* he still does," Lord Mihilido interjected, looking miffed.

"And she him. Yes? Then something else is afoot here."

"The second presence," Melana said, with sudden enlightenment.

"Yes, child, yes! It may be that someone here believes that King Alimbi is not worthy of the Daughter of the Horse."

"Ridiculous!" Mihilido snorted. "He is the finest man and the finest ruler in the world!"

"So, if it is looking for an excuse to make Eona call off the match, we must not give them one."

"But we must bring back our king and go home," Mihilido said, his light-brown complexion suffused with red. "We can't stay here forever!"

"No, we can't," Melana replied, thoughtfully. "Coletwa, is the second spirit the horse himself?"

Of course not! It is as mortal as you. But beware: everything you say and do is being observed.

A wild cry came from the perimeter. The priestesses spun. One of the Dembian courtiers had fallen, and a Jragan attacker's horse reared above the man's prone body. Vora pushed forward to place herself where the hooves would fall.

Olinke threw out her arms, then pulled her closed fists toward her chest. Melana felt the outrushing of power from the older priestess. The fallen man and Vora herself were dragged over the brown clay. When the horse's feet touched the ground, its chosen victims were not there. The horsewoman shook her fist. She laid reins on her steed's neck to turn it away.

Others rushed to help the man to his feet as another troop of riders plunged toward them. And after them, another and another. The Jragans could not penetrate the shields, but they continued to ram into them, sending them flying like skittles.

243

"Help us!" one of the women cried to the priestesses. "By the Phoenix, do something! Defend us!"

"You must defeat this spirit," the minister pleaded. "Hurry! Or we must surrender to save our lives!"

"No. I think..." Melana reached out with her mind, sensing the mood as she would the actions of an enemy general. "I don't feel malice within it. I think it means us no real harm. I believe this spirit...wants to know how devoted our king is to his new queen."

Aduna's eyes lit up. "And how would that be demonstrated?" she encouraged Melana.

"By...showing he trusts us to treat our new allies with respect." She smiled slowly. "But if this is to be a union of equals, we do not gain their respect by showing weakness."

"Then how will you stop the onslaught without harming them?" Olinke asked, clearly pleased with her old pupil.

Melana hesitated. The dream she had had in the great hall flooded her mind.

Melana looked at the twin Phoenixes, who waited, gold eyes and silver eyes fixed on hers. Their love for her gave her the courage to go on.

"Power can harm or heal. It can repel, but also embrace. We serve the Temple of Peace. Solingwa, can we *impose* peace on this battlefield?"

The black-and-white Phoenix took to the air again. Her raucous call sounded like human laughter. Coletwa followed her sister-self into the air. They rose high into the sky. The power they exuded was the same force that would be used to inhabit weapons and make them stronger than any forged by human hands, and to form barriers impenetrable by wood, steel, or stone.

In her mind's eye, Melana watched the cloud of silver and gold energy grow and grow until it was a circular cloud hovering over the field. To her, the force was palpable, tangible. She started to gather strands of it in her hands. The first handful she wove into a net. Her fellow Dembians huddled together, besieged, their gorgeous court gear and elegantly coiffed hair soiled and torn from being battered by their attackers. As the net settled, the Jragans bounced off its filmy weave as if it was solid stone. At last, the Dembians were able to rise to their feet, away from the plunging hooves. Many of them rubbed at bruises, but no one was badly hurt.

Melana took only a moment to notice that, then sent the rest of the silver-gilt strands shooting out across the plain.

The moment the power left her hands, she felt a wave of panic. It was so strong that it flooded her lungs and filled her mouth, preventing her from breathing. Jraga did not want peace! The terror from her dream was back in full force. The Phoenixes were far up, nearly to the clouds, which were turning red like blood. She could not call them back. The force that surrounded her dragged her down into a mire of dread. She would die here, and all of the king's trusted allies with her.

No! She was the Chosen of the Phoenixes! She served the King of Dembia and the cause of peace. If she died, it would be because she wanted her nation to be strong and safe.

With every morsel of magic, with every strand of strength that remained to her, she pictured a benevolent cloud of blue suffusing the nation of Jraga. It was her gift to them, in the name of the king. Then, everything went black.

"Priestess? Priestess?" Lady Vora's voice came from far away. "Are you all right? The battle is over."

Melana found that she was sitting on the ground. Olinke and Shala held her hands. The Phoenixes had returned and sat on Olinke's shoulders, regarding Melana with concern.

Beyond them, thousands of riders on dancing Jragan horses waited, but their faces were no longer full of hatred. Lord Mihilido spoke with the most elaborately armored rider, a muscular man with shining black hair and bronze-gold skin.

"Is the second spirit still here?" Shala asked timidly.

Melana felt the air, then studied the terrain around them. She looked up and recognized the rocky ridge. The jutting lip of stone was familiar to her and raised a sensation of dread that made ice form in her belly.

"No. It is up there," she said, pointing. "Where I stood in my dream. Where...something tried to make me fearful. Where I..." She swallowed, then deliberately made her voice stronger. "Where I died in battle."

"Well, you did not die," Aduna said, pounding the end of her staff on the ground. "Nor did anyone else. You succeeded. The captain of this army offers us the hand of friendship. No one won. No one lost. No one had to surrender. It is a draw."

It was chess, Coletwa said. *But we are not pawns. We are queens.*

It was nothing to defeat horses. They shy at anything, Solingwa said, with perhaps understandable smugness. *We are not horses. We are the Phoenix.*

Melana laughed. Her natural confidence rebounded.

"And it is time to retrieve our king," she said. "He is up there, isn't he?"

He is, Coletwa said. *But he has given my feather away.*

Alimbi was indeed atop the ridge. When Melana and the others appeared there by means of the Phoenixes' magic, he rattled the barred window of an elegant, gold-painted carriage and shouted for help. Lord Mihilido rushed past a cadre of armed and helmed Jragan guards to let him out.

"I apologize," said a tall and lithe woman with lustrous golden skin and wide brown eyes. Coletwa's feather was woven into the braids of bronze hair bound up at the back of her head. Melana recognized her at once from the portrait in Alimbi's great hall. This was the Demigoddess Eona. She was just as beautiful as the artist had pictured her, but very angry. She snorted, horse-like, at a tall man wearing long black and brown robes. What was left of the hair clinging in a ring around his head just above his ears was the same bronze as Eona's. "Targon, the Hierophant of the Horse God, is my uncle, and he insisted on knowing just what we were allying ourselves with. I am pleased that you acquitted yourselves in a manner that even *he* considers befitting me. You showed wisdom and strength. Even I might have blanched at ten thousand war horses charging me, but you—you held firm! It was most impressive. Oh, Alimbi!"

The king bustled toward them, with Mihilido brushing stray horsehairs from his royal festival robes, which were now wrinkled and torn at the hem. He accepted Eona's embrace, and glared over her head at the Hierophant.

"He is *not* coming to our wedding."

"But he must! He will perform the ceremony," Eona protested.

Alimbi held his intended away from him with gentle hands so he could look into her eyes.

"He will not, my dear love. It will be held in the Temple of Peace, conducted by the priestesses of the Phoenix and blessed by the sacred birds who succeeded so well in a test that *none* of us should have had to undertake." He gestured toward Melana and the two Phoenixes, who had taken up their usual posts on her shoulders. "We have bested your Horse cult, and I will not be married by an inferior god." Alimbi's statement bore the stamp of finality.

Eona looked, well, mulish for a moment, then smiled, showing dimples in each rounded cheek. "I would learn their wisdom. Now, please make me known to these people, as I am to be theirs very soon."

The king went through the crowd of relieved courtiers, introducing his chief minister first, his general, courtiers, and then the priestesses. Melana, he left for last. He beamed at her, and chucked Solingwa under her beak with a cocked finger.

"Melana is the Chosen of the Phoenixes," King Alimbi explained. "She is a most important person and, it would seem, the architect of our success on the playing field."

"Then she must have a gift befitting her station," the Demigoddess Eona said. She signed to the guards near the carriage. They brought the black stallion forward. "Melana, please accept him as a gift and an apology from me—and from my uncle."

The Hierophant snorted like one of their own horses and turned away.

"He's magnificent," Melana said. "I...don't know if I can accept him. He bears a portion of your uncle's spirit."

"What?" Eona demanded, taken aback.

Not so, Coletwa said. *He has only one spirit now. The other intellect is gone. An ordinary horse.*

Take him, Solingwa insisted. *We will rule him well.*

Melana was thrilled as the reins of the glorious horse were put in her hand. For all that he was an entire male, he was gentle and affectionate. He lowered his soft lips and nuzzled Melana's hand. He didn't shy as the Phoenixes landed on his back.

Spoils of war, Solingwa said, with satisfaction.

And peace, Coletwa added.

"And for a new and bright future for our nations," Melana said.

It was the right thing to say. Eona wrapped her arms around her intended husband and embraced him. Over his broad shoulder, she gave Melana a wink.

ECHO CHERNIK

Soul Paper

written by
Trent Walters

illustrated by
MARIAH SALINAS

ABOUT THE AUTHOR

Trent Walters has lived all over the United States and Honduras. Aside from inching up steep snow-covered roofs to fix satellite dishes with winds biting at forty miles per hour, pulling cable through sauna attics, and decorating his hair with the cobwebs and spiders in crawl spaces, Trent has taught science and creative writing, washed dishes, delivered liquor throughout New Orleans, volunteered as a first responder, worked in ship engine rooms with temperatures rivaling Hades, and stacked sixty-pound bags of potatoes.

His father warped his brain with L. Frank Baum Oz books, and it all went downhill from there. His first twenty-page novel was handwritten in shaky letters, illustrated, and side-stapled with jagged edges, all by himself. It tells the tale of a Martian who lands on Earth to rescue children whose bus gets stuck in a pothole. Dear Hollywood producers: this novel is still available for optioning.

He got serious about writing after high school. His stories have been award finalists—in Amazing Stories' Gernsback Writing Contest*—and appeared in* Fantasy Magazine *and* Pindeldyboz. *He is now working on a novel series and revising poetry manuscripts.*

Barring COVID *complications, rapture, and strange cloud formations, he will have completed his* MFA *in poetry by the time this story appears. It marks his second professional publication.*

ABOUT THE ILLUSTRATOR

Mariah Salinas was born in 2001 in Orlando, Florida, the home of Walt Disney World.

She has been drawing as long as she can remember—possibly even longer. Either doodling on the wall with crayons or scribbling in her

251

notebook in the middle of algebra class, Mariah was always creating. She tried her hand at many different methods and mediums of creation: sewing, marker, watercolor, acrylic, clay, 3-D animation, and her favorite, digital art.

Mariah has won many accolades, including the title of Senior Representative of 2-D Art during her 2020 senior year award night, the Senior Art Legacy award from her high school, the Presidential Scholarship from Ringling College of Art and Design's precollege program (which happens to be the college she is currently attending), and now the Illustrators of the Future Contest!

She is working toward a degree in illustration and hopes to create her own comics with her best friend, who is joining her on her journey at Ringling. She can't wait to see where this road takes her!

Soul Paper

Do you want to know why I never became famous?

That's a joke. Songwriters seldom become famous—at least not with the cutthroat kind of fame that leeches the soul. I wanted to hold on to my soul. Instead, this is the story of how I found souls, forged them, and borrowed one before shaping my own.

It all started when I was supposed to fetch Uncle Clif from the basement to come up for dinner. He was hard of hearing, and I had to shout, since he couldn't hear me over the Lawrence Welk show he'd been blasting. He was sleeping through it anyhow.

He opened his eyes, looked into mine as if trying to speak. After waiting, shrugging, and figuring he'd gotten the message, I sprinted upstairs and smelled the caramel early-apple pie coming out of the oven. Mom ignored my pleas to taste it. Not even a sliver. After rejecting my fifth "please," she asked where my uncle was and said I should help him upstairs for dinner.

I groaned and dragged myself to the stairs, holding the railing. "Uncle Clif," I shouted from the top stair, leaning toward the stairwell. I clopped down a few steps, shouted, descended a few more, and repeated this until I stood beside his plush, aquamarine easy chair. I shook his warm shoulder twice. I folded my arms as if with the matronly disapproval of a recalcitrant boy. For a second he looked dead until his chest rose and fell. "Come on, Uncle Clif. Ain't you hungry? We got pressure-cooked roast, carrots, taters, brown gravy, and a hot apple pie."

His eyes flicked open, searching mine—not that he didn't know me, but was trying to know-me know me. Trying to see past the physical into the beyond. I remembered that old saying—"The eyes are the window to the soul"—and a chill shivered through me: a presentiment of what that might mean.

And then the light in Uncle Clif's eyes went out—as if someone or something had been behind the eyes but now they'd gone. Did I see a vapor exit his body—a mist that dispelled into a million fluttering... wings? I'm not sure. What I do know is that whatever was in his body had left, and Uncle Clif stopped breathing.

The family apparently called me, and I didn't hear. Later, they said I was just staring, swaying slightly, breathing shallowly, catatonic.

Some in the family say this is what drove my grandpa crazy— that he and Uncle Clif used to play in the same band together, toured the big-city clubs from the time jazz hit it big until it hit its peak. The days when if you were Black, you had to use the back door. Some argued that wasn't true. Grandpa had been crazy long before. Perhaps from the day he was born.

I was in Vacation Bible School when I first heard about the soul. We were playing Red Rover on the spongy green grass behind the trailer-home church when the girl I was standing beside, Suzy, asked if I had colored blood in me. We'd been best friends for five days straight.

"Everybody's blood is colored," I said, exasperated, "red mainly— although I saw a movie once where they skewered a guy and his blood was green! Or maybe blue. Super gross."

We were both strong and held on tight when a boy tried to break our bond. We taunted the boy as he ran to get in line. She sighed dramatically. "No, silly, I mean African. Do you have any Africa in you?"

"Aren't we all from Africa? Going back to Adam and Eve?"

That shut her up for a bit. Part of it was because the boy she was sweet on was going to try to break our bond, and she squealed in anticipation, closing her eyes. Surprisingly, she held on. "No, I mean Black people."

I winced, sensing something—a bad premonition about how she'd respond to what I was about to say—but Mama taught me to be honest. Besides, the people who came over in the bellies of ships like Jonahs spat out on the new continent were legends, superheroes, saints, which didn't mean they didn't suffer but were built out of tougher stuff. Not meaning to boast, I whispered, "My grandpa's ancestors came over on a slave ship."

"That's what I thought when I saw your curly hair. My mama thought you must be slaves, and because of that you ain't got souls and cain't get to heaven. I told Mama that you had light skin, but she said you can't always tell by that. Turns out she was right, so we cain't be friends no more."

When a weak boy tried to run between us, she let go.

I had liked my curls up until then.

In a church pew, swinging my legs 'cause my feet couldn't touch the floor, I had on a white, lacy dress, white knee-highs and shiny black shoes. If I swung hard, since I was on the edge of the pew cushion, I could slide the cushion around on the slick wood varnish. It made a small farting sound, so I covered my mouth to keep from giggling. Daddy winked at me, but Mama frowned. This was back when men wore suits to church and women wore dresses, although some women wore fancy colored suits and heavy perfume.

The preacher said something about saving souls, and I kept wondering about where you'd find the souls and where you'd keep them after you found them. Was it like fireflies, where you put them in a jar with holes poked in the lid?

After church, when it was our turn to shake Pastor Joe's hand, I asked him what a soul was. I flushed with embarrassment at his loud laugh, glad his laugh interrupted my question where he kept his saved souls because I had the feeling his laugh would have been louder.

He kept a hand on his prodigious belly, as if it might get away in the laughing. "Well, well, little lady. Good to know someone was paying attention."

Mama beamed. "She is a good girl."

I gave Mama a funny look since during every service she would shush and pinch me.

He leaned down to talk, face-to-face, his tie dangling. My eyes couldn't help but fall from his face to the shiny thing with a stripe of every awful color creation ever made. "Every man has a body," he said, "a soul and a spirit."

"Men only?" I considered painting his tie lemon or chartreuse. I still had extra Easter-egg dye if he wanted to try it out.

"Women are men, too. Wo-man, a man with a womb, or maybe a woman is a man who needs to be wooed." I pulled my eyes away from the ugly tie to catch his wink.

That left me a thousand questions. "Okay, I have a body. I get that. It dies and I'm left with a ghost and a soul. Which has the personality—I mean which one is me? Or is the ghost the soul? Which goes to heaven and where does the other one go? Hell?"

The preacher laughed and said we'd need to set up a meeting to talk about this further. He took a ballpoint pen and business card out of his inside coat pocket, scribbled a time after lunch.

All during the church social over grape-flavored drinks, creme-filled chocolate sandwich cookies, and homemade peanut butter cookies, Mama told any woman who would listen about how her special daughter had a meeting with the pastor about the soul. All the women with big hair cooed about that, and they asked me what I was going to ask, and they all nodded their towering beehives that they wanted to know the answer to that, too.

When Mama and I met the pastor in his office, she was busting her buttons, perhaps dreaming I had a destiny in the church—except the preacher talked in circles, so I never did understand him. He made it sound like I was too young to comprehend. Too young! People always said that. Drove me batty. I was suspicious of talkers who acted smart but said nothing. I figured they were as hollow as their words.

When I asked Mama and Daddy, they deferred to the preacher. "We agree with Pastor Joe."

At family reunions or adult parties, I'd ask, but no one knew squat about the spirit world, although they all agreed we lived in it, and a few said they'd heard tell of those who saw spirits depart from their bodies—some going up, some down like on invisible escalators. They patted me on the head and went on to argue about the best football teams or the most delightful sewing patterns they'd found.

After a year or two, I gave up on finding someone who knew about the soul.

Now and then, on the oldie radio station, they'd play a song about a "Soul Man." I got the notion that maybe singers knew. The only singer I knew about was Grandpa, who was a singer *and* songwriter.

The only problem was that he lived in an insane asylum. I think that was around the time they were trying to take out the stigma, but most people back then saw living in the asylum as a shame. No one talked about Grandpa except Grandma—the only one who didn't talk about him in the past tense, as if he'd passed away.

She romanticized their marriage as if on an "Errol Flynn adventure" (that Technicolor Robin-Hood guy). Grandpa was a colored man so light-skinned that he passed for white on first glance. Grandpa had gotten away with being married to a white woman in the north, but when they moved south they had to claim being kissing cousins to take care of his parents who weren't so light. Their marriage was like Abraham and Sarah's, deceiving others of its true nature. It wasn't a lie, they figured, since they were cousins if you went back to Noah.

Somehow they were found out, yet Grandpa always knew the magic words to escape lynching. The way Grandma described it, he was like Jesus when the Pharisees tried to seize him: Grandpa just up and walked through the crowd, going on his merry way.

They had to move to a nearby town, and she returned to caring for his parents while he worked at a mill in a town farther away, but folks would follow her and stir up trouble in the new town. After much coaxing, they moved his parents up north.

Their Errol-Flynn adventure didn't sound romantic to me. Grandma admitted all their cloak-and-dagger stuff must have been what drove Grandpa nutso.

I kept asking to meet him, but Mama would put it off. . . .

Until the summer I stayed with Grandma by myself. She visited him every day and, unlike Mama, had no qualms about hauling me along.

The asylum exterior was hidden by a tall, red-brick wall, a canopy of trees, and well-maintained labyrinthine hedges. The building itself was two-story brick with small, barred windows that hadn't been cleaned in forty years. I shuddered to think of Grandpa or anyone who wasn't criminally insane in there.

The inside turned out to be worse. Except for the dark walnut doors and their brass knobs, everything was white tiled or painted white. Though you could smell it was lemon clean, all the white had aged a faded daffodil yellow. Even the nurses and orderlies wore starchy whites. I expected to find Grandpa in a padded room, strapped in a strait jacket, but he was in striped pajamas, in bed, reading Madeline L. Engle's *A Wind in the Door*. Grandpa said he knew all there was to know about the soul, but first we needed to get to know one another.

He said much of what Grandma said except crazier. He'd stop, though, hold his forehead, and say, "What was I just saying?" Grandma would remind him, and he'd carry on.

After his repeating that a third time, I asked how he didn't know. He looked into a cobwebbed corner, then at me, then at Grandma. She nodded. He said, "They give me what they call *electroshock therapy*."

I gasped, covering my mouth, remembering the time I stood in the wet grass and tried to plug two extension cords together, one plugged into an outlet. I was frozen in place for a minute solid as the electricity coursed through me. Or so it felt.

"It doesn't hurt. I just get a headache and sore muscles, later.

After a day, I can walk, more or less. At least I don't remember the shock hurting. I don't remember it at all, actually. It's for my brain. It resets me to normal. But sometimes I forget stuff, especially recent things. People have to tell me."

While we were talking, Grandma snapped photos as if she were paparazzi and we royalty. I held up my hand to Grandma's flashing bulb. "But what about the soul?"

What he told came in dribs and drabs. I'd sigh as he retold the same stories. I kept expecting that tomorrow I'd know everything about souls, but it dawned on me by week two that this was a put-on.

"Grandpa, is this like a soap opera, designed to keep me tuning in daily with the sole purpose of getting me to buy your soap?"

He laughed. "You got me. I have the perfect jiggling lure to make you come visit. But you need to come at the soul slow, because it is a film negative of what we think the world should be. People without soul will never get it. You heard the story of the blind men and the elephant?"

"Yes, but they could have put their stories together, couldn't they?"

He nodded. "That's the soul. The more fractured, the more it sees. A broken, flexible, glued-together mirror can see around corners."

I countered, "You can put a straight mirror at an angle and see around corners."

"You *are* my granddaughter, aren't you? Well, if you ever figure out the soul, straight gives just one view, and the reassembled shines in all directions. That's 'cause the broken, if they've got soul, speak straight to the soul. That's art. But you're still too young to know what I'm talking about."

"Too young?" I told him about Suzy.

He whistled. "Oh, yeah. That's soul building, right there. Yes, sir, you're on your way."

"On my way where?"

"To the soul, and maybe to paradise."

Since an hour a day with Grandpa wasn't all the hours in a day, Grandma and I picked lemons from the stone-fenced grove in her backyard. We chucked the rotten ones into the backwoods. The good ones we took to make iced lemonade with water beading off the glass, and lemon bars dusted with powdered sugar, and a lemon meringue that won a blue ribbon at the county fair.

Since Grandma did grandma things all day, I found playmates. Suzy had turned me off of girls, so I'd found three boys, picking whom I played with depending on my mood. They were all a little dull. One I went downtown to play the arcades with. He always played the pinball machine with the motorcycle and the bikini-clad lady. He was really good, so I'd play thirty seconds to his five minutes. He also liked to build things, like ramps for cars. He wasn't much for talk.

Another played soldiers and cowboys and Indians. One side had to die, which was usually mine. I may have yawned. "Where do they go home for supper?"

"Soldiers don't go home."

"Sooner or later, everybody has to go home, eat, get some rest, and talk to their kids. Does your dad talk to you?"

So I managed to make his wars a little more interesting, the bad guys a little less bad.

And the last guy collected action figures and invented elaborate stories—often superheroes or space invaders—and we ran around the woods shooting at each other with sticks and had to make woo-woo sounds. He was always trying to run the narrative. The stories often lacked women. I pointed out that either the boys had to self-replicate or they needed women. So the stories started to get more women, but a few featured self-replicating boy armies.

It went well enough until each boy wanted me to "go steady" with him. I didn't say they were too boring, but I did hatch a plan to help them get interesting: to grow souls and have one soul—the shiniest—emerge the victor for my affections.

I had them all meet at the swimming pool. Each was to wait for me at a different area—by the lockers and kiddie pool, the high dive, and the concessions. I didn't know how to kiss back then, but I'd seen plenty of movies. I visited the high dive, kissed like a movie star, one leg lifted, told the guy to wait and watch, and I went on to the next kissing booth. I only managed to get halfway to the concessions. The first two got in a fistfight by the high board. And the imaginative one with the action figures ran away—the one with the big talk about boys being tough and having to fight in wars, the one who'd been leaning against the concessions.

Most disappointing was their mothers banning me from ever seeing the boys again. I apologized and wheedled because I wanted to meet them once they gained their souls. Their mothers were such party poopers.

When I told Grandpa about it, he laughed until tears welled up. "Child, you bring life to this old man." He dabbed at his eyes with tissue paper.

I let my jaw drop, hand pressed to my chest. "Why are you laughing? This is my trauma."

He nodded, sniffing. "We have to see the funny side. We laugh at the things that hurt us to keep ourselves in balance, to keep the world from making us cuckoo."

He folded up the tissue paper and stuffed it into his striped pajama top's pocket. "But I'm afraid I hadn't told you the difference between soul *makers* and soul *breakers*. A soul maker makes art, coaxes the soul from the cocoons of others. A soul breaker is like what you just did and Suzy did to you. While you forged souls, it came at the expense of your own. You choked your own soul to pave the way for those boys to grow. You ever hear a preacher say, it's easier for a camel to squeeze through the eye of a needle than for a rich man to enter the kingdom of heaven?"

I nodded. "I never did get that."

"That's because the rich—not all of them, mind you, but a number—break their own souls by paying employees too little, not feeding the hungry, not clothing the naked, etcetera. They're pounding their own souls to death."

My eyes went wide. "You mean I just killed my soul?"

He blew his nose and chuckled. "Naw, you just keep making soul."

"How was I supposed to stop those boys from being in love with me?"

"You don't. You give succor to souls. Speak soul to soul. Only grow hard if they don't respond to kindness. If you can't be kind, you just lost ninety percent of your power and one hundred percent of your soul."

I stood, hands on hips. "How in the world can you be nice when you have to do something mean?"

"There are a million ways to say 'thank you, but no thank you,' and sometimes all you have to say is 'thank you' in the right way. Learn that and learn true power, power that wields souls." He must have studied the doubt on my face, for he pulled the extra pillow from under his back and lay down, scooting over. He patted the empty pillow. "Here. Lie beside me."

I plopped down with a humph and crossed my arms.

He gestured at the ceiling as a barker presenting his circus. "Have you ever looked into the ceiling and wondered how many stars are up there? Look at that one." He pointed at the spackling, and for a minute I thought he really was crazy, rather than acting that way for the adults of the world. "See that cluster of stars? It laughs like my grandpa used to, squinty eyed. Back when I was a kid, he used to say 'You're too young' too much and I didn't believe a word he said. Now I think he held the keys to the universe."

I sat up and excused myself, angry, unable to say why. I clacked down the hall to the bathroom. Using the mirror, I brushed away anything that looked like tears and blew my nose on a rough brown paper towel. My nose was red, eyes bloodshot.

Outside the door, the floor squeaked as if a bunch of boys shot hoops in a gym. I opened the door a crack to watch four orderlies wrestle a man down the hall. Nobody was saying anything, just grunting. I felt bad for the guy they ganged up on and hoped he'd break free, find something to bust the window and escape. I followed them out, on tiptoe. Nobody noticed.

A nurse left her station to open doors as they struggled to push him into a room and on to a table. The struggling man said, "Before you do that, I need a crown."

They managed to strap him down and rub something on his temples with a tongue depressor.

The man shouted, "A crown of thorns!"

When his mouth opened again, the nurse inserted a plastic bit. "This is for your safety, so you don't bite your tongue." She turned to a corner of the room that I couldn't see. "We're ready for you, doctor."

The white-coated doctor crossed the room, engrossed in a file, and absently depressed a button. The body of the man strapped to the table spasmed, flopping like a fish out of water.

Maybe it was my imagination or flawed memory, but electricity sizzled through flesh, and a faint whiff of singed hairs and gamy meat lingered in the air. My mind was frozen as it seemed his jerking body was mine. I tried to scream. Nothing. I opened my mouth wide and tried again. I squeaked. The third time I succeeded.

The nurse glared at me. "Mr. Kesey, would you please escort this young woman off the property."

I wept that night believing that Grandpa was killing himself and that I'd killed my soul, because Grandpa had been too slow to tell me what it really was. I shouted at the ceiling, "It's not fair. He deserves to lose his soul over this, not me."

When Grandma dropped into my room early in the morning for me to go with her to the hospital, I said I was too sick. After she left, I wandered around the town to all the houses and arcades and candy stores I used to visit. The boys' faces had bruises and black eyes and they ignored me. One mother stopped her gardening to shake her hedge shears and scream, "Haven't you done enough damage, little hussy? They should lock you away like your crazy Grandpa."

I cried my way to the swimming pool, but they wouldn't let me in for a week, because I'd incited violence. The lifeguard behind the desk winked. "Come here." She handed me a lemon lollipop shaped as a life preserver. "Enjoy what's left of your summer."

I was still sucking on that candy when I called Mama and told her everything, and she started cussing like a sailor. "I told you not to visit him. There's a reason why he's in an insane asylum. He's crazy. He'll make you crazy if you listen to him. Don't go near him ever again. If he hands you anything, don't take it. You hear me? Don't take it."

I told Mama I heard her. I promised I wouldn't see him ever again and that I'd have Grandma call Mama when she got back.

The instant Grandma brought in groceries, I told her everything. The set of her jaw and lips said she was just as livid as Mama. I realized all the lies I'd been believing had caused everyone a lot of pain. It really was Grandpa's fault all the boys and their mothers got hurt. I'd probably never be able to set foot in this town again, which was fine by me.

In the morning Grandma came in to say, "You've only got five more chances to see your grandpa before you leave for the summer." I said I had a tummy ache like something was eating at my insides, which was true, and wandered around town for the day, avoiding all the places I used to enjoy.

And then it was "You've only got four more chances" and "You've only got three" and "two." And then it was the last morning.

Grandma had in her arms a box, a photo album, and a kiddie piano. I was sitting up in bed and had just confirmed that, no, I wouldn't be going. Her lips were tight pressed. Her nostrils flared. She moved the items in her arms to her left. She turned as if to leave, but her right arm shot out and grabbed me by the ear. "You're coming with me, young lady."

"Ow, ow, ow! Grandma. You're hurting."

"What do you think you're doing, you little snot?" she asked, hauling me to the foyer door. "Open the storm door."

"No. Ow! Okay. Jeez."

We moved to her Oldsmobile, and she told me to open the back door and sit. I did. She crouched before me so we faced each other. "You don't have to go, but I'm going to tell what I promised your grandfather I wouldn't tell. He's dying. Your deciding not to visit is killing him faster. If you don't go today, you will regret it the rest of your life."

"Whatever. I'll go. Just let me get out of my jammies."

"No. You go in your pajamas. He'll be in *his* pajamas."

Grandma had me wait outside Grandpa's room while she carried in her armload of stuff. The nurse behind the nurse's station narrowed her eyes at me. I tried to clear my throat of the cloying disinfectant in the air.

Grandma spoke to Grandpa, alone. I couldn't hear her, but his voice rang out a little too loudly: "I have a granddaughter? Wonderful! This is her? My, isn't she pretty. Who's this strange old man beside her? That can't be me. I don't look like that. What did I tell her? Oh, yeah, I remember that. I thought that was a dream. I remember that, too, I think. Yes, it's trickling back to me now."

When she let me in, Grandpa opened the box, withdrew a sheet of smooth and shiny paper, drew five lines and a treble clef, and plunked at the kiddie piano. He'd sing the notes out loud, play a sequence, and write the notes down. "I hope you're here of your own accord, and your grandma didn't force you."

Grandma made a face, which I didn't understand, so I mouthed "What?" She motioned that I unfold my arms.

I unfolded my arms and sighed. "I'm here of my own accord," I said unconvincingly.

He plunked a few notes. "Good, because I'm going to give you something. I call it 'soul paper' because you can write down your soul on it."

My jaw dropped. Mama had told me not to take anything. That meant she knew something could be given—something that would lead me to the soul. Maybe it wasn't Grandpa who'd lied, but Mama. Mama believed everything Grandpa said and

265

that's why she was afraid I'd listen and believe. It wasn't just what he said, but the notes he was playing on the piano. Tears leaked from my eyes like the drip of a faucet. And like the drip of a faucet that you try to twist shut, I couldn't stop it. I could feel something rising from my belly into my throat that I kept having to swallow.

He sang a few bars. "You'll meet people who carry sledgehammers and love to take them to your mirrors. They are camels trying to squeeze through the eyes of needles. But sometimes *we* carry the sledges, and it broke my heart that I broke yours. This is that song. I'm gathering that broken mirror, and I'm gluing it back together on paper. People have been doing that for centuries. Think of 'Clementine.' Silly old song, right? But why do you know it? Why do people try to steal its bars for their own songs? It's got a piece of someone's soul fluttering there. If you don't feel it, you haven't heard it played with the right feeling or you haven't got soul yet."

He plunked a few notes and scribbled them on the soul paper. "That was what I was trying to do in the sheet-music era: write my 'Clementine.' Up until the depression, I made a bundle, and it warmed my heart to enter a bar and hear my song played like they meant it. And if you're in tune to it, you can sometimes catch the soul fluttering nearby.

"But one day you'll come too close to using up your soul and some people will call you crazy, and that's okay because pieces of your soul are still fluttering all over the world. What hurts are the copies, the songwriters trying to steal your soul because they haven't got one."

He handed me his song. Now that he'd stopped, I could finally dry my eyes, although a flicker of the melody would rise from my belly into my throat and a fit of crying would hit me again. I was weeping for everything: for the boys and their mothers, for Grandma who believed but was about to lose everyone whoever mattered to her and Mama who believed but didn't want to, for myself and my own confusion, for Grandpa and his certainty and certain end, and for the man in the asylum who wanted a crown but was getting shocked instead and for the end of summer.

Then Grandpa played and sang "Clementine" on a kiddie piano in a broken voice, and oh, how I missed her, my darling Clementine. I'd never heard it sung that way.

Grandpa patted me on the back, then lifted my chin. "You write your dreams and your brokennesses in a notebook. It doesn't matter if they're songs or poems or paintings. Wait until you're eighteen, and then go through those notebooks looking for soul and write those down on the soul paper. You hear, my darling Clementine?" Grandpa wiped my wet cheek and showed me his damp fingers. "Evidence of a newborn soul."

Mama searched my bags when I got home and found the box of soul paper and the kiddie piano. She lectured me about keeping my promises and threw them in the trash and had me clean my room. I sneaked out the window and pulled the box of soul paper and the piano out and hid them in the toy chest. Later, I moved them into the attic.

School had started when Grandpa passed away. Mama wouldn't let me attend the funeral since I had school, but I skipped anyway, while Mama flew back to visit her mama. I called Grandma to tell her that I had wanted to come. She said I should celebrate Grandpa's life the best way I knew how, and that I didn't understand the heartbreak Mama and Grandpa had caused one another, and would probably never know. Then she had a catch in her throat and couldn't talk. She said she'd talk later.

I climbed into the attic and got down the piano and soul paper. I set them on my bed in front of the floor-length mirror. My bedroom was on a corner, so I had two windows on both sides open, letting in air and light. I pulled Grandpa's song out and put it aside. On the first sheet, I wrote "I love you, Grandpa!" Nothing happened. I didn't know what to expect. I drew a butterfly in a riot of colors and maybe it looked three-dimensional, or maybe it shimmered with colors I didn't use, but it was hard to tell what was happening from what I wanted to believe. Maybe I'd just wasted a part of my soul, or a sheet of rare paper, or maybe I was delusional.

I put Grandpa's song on my lap and was about to file it away when I decided to play the song to celebrate his life. I'd only had a year of lessons, so I wasn't very good, but I had a notion of how it should be played since he'd played it. I played until it sounded pretty good. I was about to put the piano away when I noticed an iridescent blue butterfly resting on the outside window screen to my left. *Morpho peleides*, I'd learn later. I played the song again and another butterfly was on the right. A Monarch, but too vividly golden.

I recalled Grandpa saying, "Play it like you mean it." So I closed my eyes, and lyrics popped into my head, and I sang of the loss of love. I banged on the keyboard until the music and words sounded right. When I opened my eyes, the window screens of both windows were packed with butterflies—all kinds, all sizes, all colors: *Nymphalidae, Swallowtail, Pearl crescent, Vanessa atalanta*.

I couldn't breathe. Something in my belly rose, and it wanted out, and I wanted it out. And I sang again, playing for the person in the mirror. At the high point, a butterfly in riotous colors emerged from my throat. It rested on my outthrust tongue, testing its wings. It flew down to the paper and looked uncannily similar to the butterfly I'd just drawn except the color in its wings shimmered.

Grandpa's song was my first hit, updated a bit. Almost no one pays attention to songwriters, so you won't recognize my name. I don't mind not being famous, but I do want a paycheck.

My songs were largely earworms, so if I've written ones you hate, it may be that the song wasn't played right or maybe our souls weren't connecting. Death metal bands redo my songs—sometimes as a joke, but other times with real heart.

MARIAH SALINAS

I finally know why Grandpa lived in an asylum. It's like you set your soul out there, and you know how easy it is to break others and be broken, so you hide in the strongest fortress you can find—to protect yourself and others.

I still have the airline ticket stubs from when I visited my grandparents. I also have Grandpa's death certificate. He'd died the day I left. Grandma somehow put off the funeral, perhaps to keep me from knowing.

I've had children and grandchildren but haven't told any of them about the soul. Mostly because I don't want them to experience a lifetime of torment, of sensing everything wrong behind every human interaction. But I suspect I will, if any of them ever asks about the soul. What will I do if my kids try to put me in an asylum? I'll probably let them. No electrodes, though. Just a warm bed and striped pajamas surrounded by grandkids whose hair will tickle my chin as I tell them:

"If you look into the spackled ceiling stars, you can see your great, great Grandpa smiling down."

The Skin of My Mother

written by
Erik Lynd

illustrated by
SHIYI YU

ABOUT THE AUTHOR

Erik Lynd writes novels and short stories primarily in the horror, dark fantasy, and urban fantasy genres, with the occasional science fiction story thrown in. He lives in the Pacific Northwest with his wife and kids where, yes, it does rain a lot and, no, he does not mind it. When not writing prose, he can be found writing songs and producing music.

ABOUT THE ILLUSTRATOR

Shiyi Yu was born in Ningbo, China. At the age of eleven she and her family moved to America. As a child, she often found chances to analyze all kinds of species of living creatures. Thus, being an illustrator/painter/ jewelry designer, she has been greatly influenced by nature.

Shiyi is currently pursuing a degree in illustration at the Fashion Institute of Technology in New York City.

The Skin of My Mother

The best part of that first cigarette in the quiet of morning was that sizzling sound. The sound of tobacco and paper flaring and crackling in the stillness. It was like you were the only one alive in the world, the only one that mattered, and that sound, fizzing through the silence, was the proof. Then a little piece of ash, paper or tobacco or both, would break off and flutter back against your lips. Then you do this half sputtering sound with your lips to blow it off, like a fart in the silence. Then the moment would be over. You are no longer special in the world, nothing is sacred. It's all just a fart sound.

This is how most mornings started for Elise and that was how this morning started. Only she hadn't been alone, her world was not empty. She watched the woman across the street.

The corner of Wilburn and Main was a barren and weedy patch of land surrounded by buildings of peeling paint and shacks of tenuous structural integrity. There was a gas station near where she parked. Small and not a name brand, at least not a name she recognized.

It hadn't changed. The peeling paint, the rundown buildings, the nondescript gas station. The same town Elise had left fifteen years ago.

She sat in her car, a miracle of duct tape, filler, and rust, near the gas station. There were a handful of cars along the street. Early comers to the farmers' market. Booths were still opening, customers flittered about.

The customers squeezed the fruit, inspected the vegetables,

laughed along with the owners. Craft booths were off to the side, second-class citizens in a farming community.

Elise didn't care about that. She cared about the woman. Just the one. The woman whose hair started as silver at the scalp and ended as a dirty gray mop just past her waist. The woman in a billowing brown dress light enough for summer, but long and covering most of her sagging and sallow skin.

Elise knew the portions of her skin not covered were slathered with sunscreen. Homemade and smelling like roses and slightly rancid grease. She knew that smell well.

The woman strode from booth to booth with purpose, grabbing up produce, inspecting it with a "Hrmph" that Elise was sure she could hear from her car seat. She sorted through the veggies, the fruit, the herbs, selecting just the right ones.

Picky bitch.

Elise saw her talking to the vendors. Whatever words the woman was saying, they were never kind, never thoughtful. Elise didn't have to hear, didn't have to see the slowly fading smiles. She knew the woman's words too well. They were curt, to the point, at best. Hurtful and mean at worst.

And still, the people of this town trusted her. Needed her. It pissed Elise off. The great con. It had always been a con between the woman and the town. Between the woman and Elise.

Her mother was the problem, had always been the problem. Elise felt pretty sure she would be able to kill her.

Again in the car, again with the cigarette. This time she sat outside the house. The one she had grown up in, but it would never be home. The garden, if that controlled chaos of nature could be called a garden, had grown up around the porch. It stretched its leafy green tentacles up the sides and across the latticework along the bottom. It grew onto the porch itself. Vegetation gripping it like the hand of a jolly green giant.

But that was the way her mother liked it. This overgrown mess had a shape to it, one her mother guided.

Elise could name every plant in the garden, every plant in the back garden—that one made this small front yard look like a container garden on a city balcony—even the trees and weeds. It had been drilled into her head from an early age. Mercilessly.

She should go in. Her mother knew she was here. The old woman knew everything that invaded her property, and her property extended far beyond the lines the plot maps tried to contain her in.

As Elise walked from the car to the porch, she could feel the garden. It reached out to brush against her. Common herbs and flowers, ferns, cursed crowfoot, jewelweed, and such all seemed to vie for her attention. But she knew plants did not move, did not think. It was all an illusion and brainwashing delivered by the loving mother. The con artist of redneck idiots and backwoods fools.

And the killer of children.

On the porch, Elise lifted her hand to knock against the wood side of the screen door. But then she saw her mother through the wire mesh, tightly knitted, making anything beyond dark, shadowed. Her mother stared back at her. Coldness in the deep-set eyes, sunken. Her whole face writhed with wrinkles. She had aged much since Elise had last seen her. Less like her mother and more like her grandmother, even great grandmother.

That gave Elise some satisfaction.

Her mother's lips pursed for a moment like she was thinking. It made her look even older.

"Well," her mother said. "Come on in. I'll make tea."

She turned and walked to the back of the house, not waiting for a response. Elise's mother moved slowly, with a small limp. A knee that acted up perhaps?

Good. Maybe she would fall, break a hip, suffer.

Elise went inside, letting the creaking screen door slam shut behind her. She gripped her purse, a small one, just big enough to hold the gun.

The inside was almost unchanged since her childhood. The same barely used furniture, a couch, two chairs, a coffee table, a lamp. The walls covered in shelves that stored books, knickknacks of some indiscernible uses—but Elise knew their uses, that too had been drilled into her—and jars and vials full of dried herbs, plants, and other more fleshy ingredients.

It smelled of dryness and earth, like dust and powdered plants. The scents of many different dried flowers combined, blurring together into an olfactory offense.

Her mother continued through the living room and into the hall beyond, and beyond that the kitchen. Her real domain, her mad-scientist laboratory. Elise had grown to hate that room more than any other in the house. In her own home, thousands of miles away, she rarely spent time in the kitchen. Just to grab food, then flee to the couch and TV.

In the kitchen you measured, you cut, you poured, you boiled—*No, no. All wrong*—you ground, mixed, blended just the right—*No, no, you are a fool, child. You will never learn*—you learn to hate.

Elise sucked in hard, then followed. She didn't glance into any of the rooms she passed. She wondered if her mother had any "patients" here today. It didn't matter. She didn't care if there were any witnesses.

The kitchen was clean, neat. No experiments or concoctions.

"Sit. I've had a kettle ready since I saw you at the market this morning," her mother said. "You took your own sweet time making it out here. Sun's low, almost time for dinner."

Elise sat without thinking and she felt ashamed, following her mother's command without question. Automatic. Just like when she was a child. The old habits die hard.

The kitchen was filled with jars, vials, and drying plants hanging from rough twine. But nothing boiled on the stove. The laboratory was silent. Elise didn't think she had ever been in here when her mother wasn't mixing up some new ointment or potion.

Her mother set a cup and saucer down in front of her. Elise just stared at it, watching the liquid slowly stop spinning. Her mother sighed and took a sip.

"If I had wanted to dose you girl, I wouldn't be so obvious about it."

Then she sat across from Elise, drinking from her own cup. Elise made no move to drink.

"Her name was Elizabeth," Elise said. Her voice was rough, as though she hadn't spoken in a long time. And she hadn't. It had been a long time since she had someone to talk to. Her mother said nothing. "And you killed her."

"No girl. I did not, you did."

Elise slammed her hand down on the table. "I tried to save her," she yelled. Elise *had* tried. The beautiful little girl who made life perfect. "You killed her with the lies you told, that you still tell. When it came, when the cancer was on her, I took her to the doctors and did everything they said. But then when that didn't seem like it was working, I was desperate. I turned to what you had taught me, I turned to the old magics."

Her mother nodded as though she knew the story and just needed confirmation. And maybe, somehow, she did know something, though Elise had no idea how. Sometimes her mother just knew.

"None of it worked. I knew all the tricks, all the ways that you had taught me. The hours, the years following your instructions. Nothing. None of it worked, none of it mattered."

At some point the tears had come, anger slipping away, replaced by the empty.

"But that's not true," Elise continued. "Time mattered. Time that could have been used on more treatments, scientific treatments. Time that could have been used to find a real way to treat it. But I pissed it away on...on..." Elise gestured at the room around them. "This. All this nonsense. All these lies. The lies you taught me."

"It was destiny, fate," her mother said. "You were never meant to have a child."

Elise winced. Those words hurt. She lifted her purse and set it on the table. It made a clunk sound, the gun heavy inside.

"Fate, destiny. More magic words from the crazy old witch. Tell me, do they still believe? Your patients? The people of this screwed-up community?"

"They do," her mother said. "Some anyway, but every year there are less and less. I practice a dying art. Less and less take this path. They all want to run off to the shiny cities."

Elise laughed, loud, hard, no mirth. "That's a much better adventure than staying here."

"How was your adventure, Elise? Was it worth it?"

"Yes," Elise rasped, sounding more desperate than she meant to. "To have those five years with Elizabeth, no matter how horrible the last one was. That would be worth anything."

Suddenly her mother seemed to deflate a little, and was that softness that crept into her hardened eyes? "I might have been a little harsh when I said you killed your daughter. I do not doubt you tried the right things, and I don't doubt your skill. After all, I taught you. No, no matter what you did, she would never have survived. As I said, it was destined. You were not meant to be the mother of that child."

Elise smiled slightly. She felt stupid. What had she thought she could gain from telling her mother all this? Tell her it was all a lie she told herself? Her mother was no witch. Just a crazy old woman who was so lost in her own delusions she could not be pulled back. She was too far down the path of crazy, and she pulled those in the community willing to follow down with her. Her delusion had killed her own granddaughter. How many others had died because of her false hopes, her con?

It was time to end this.

She put her hand in her purse. Her fingers wrapped around the cold steel. The fear hit her hard, the metal of the gun seemed to grow colder. But she could do it, had to do it.

Then her mother's hand was on top of the purse, making Elise hesitate.

"Just one night. Have dinner, sleep here in your old room. In the morning if you still wish to, you can kill me."

Elise froze, her fingers numb against the gunmetal.

Sometimes she just knew.

Elise nodded slowly. She needed more time. Time to stoke the hate, work up the nerve. Killing was an event, a happening.

It changed everything. There was nothing wrong with being cautious. "Yes, I haven't eaten, really eaten, in days."

"I can see, girl. You are weak, your eyes sunken. You need a home-cooked meal."

Elise sat numb at the table as her mother started dinner. Her mother was right, she needed food. She shook, she felt dizzy. She had been running on caffeine and cigarettes, boosted by an undercurrent of adrenaline. Now she was crashing.

The smell of food soon woke her from her stupor. Her mother was a sometimes witch, full-time crazy, but all-around amazing cook. She was a master with herbs, vegetables, and a hunk of meat.

Her mother roasted a chicken, which should have taken an hour or more, but seemed like only minutes. Elise must have dozed. She shook her head to clear the haze when the plate was put in front of her. But she didn't need to. Her gut took over and she started eating. Shoveling food in.

Her mother spoke, Elise listened, but only half aware, she was focused on staying awake and eating. Her mother talked of the plants and how they prospered a little less this season. Each season they seemed to grow weaker, dying quicker, their potency less. It might have been her, her mother said, she was old and it was harder to nurture the ground, to give the toil, the sacrifice necessary. As she had said before, new blood was needed.

Elise nodded as she ate, mumbled comments when she could. Then her mother was standing over her.

"You're tired, girl. Your head almost in your food. Let me take you to your room. I haven't aired it out, but it should be clean. And just as you left it."

Elise allowed herself to be guided up from the seat, but she snatched her purse off the table and clutched it close. She was tired, not stupid.

Her mother hadn't lied about her room. It looked exactly the same. Elise walked in, stunned. So many memories came back, a three-dimensional picture of her life years ago. She ran her finger along the many books on the shelves. Mostly on herbs and their properties, gardening, and a few books on the occult that her mother had said held some semblance of truth.

There were also fiction books, her escape, her first love. They more than anything gave her the courage to leave, to try and find her own path. As she learned, they were fiction for a reason.

The desk still had a stack of notebooks. These contained the secrets, the scribbled notes, and diagrams her mother had made her learn. Treatises on the old magics.

Now they were a symbol of years wasted.

The room was clean, dusted, the window open, letting in fresh air. It occurred to Elise that her mother had been keeping it ready for her return. Had she known Elise would? Or had she merely hoped?

Her bed with the same simple pale-pink striped comforter sat against one wall. As soon as Elise saw it, the weight of exhaustion pressed down on her. It was early, just seven, but at that moment, the only thing she wanted was to sink into that familiar bed and not wake up for a year.

It was warm, she fell onto the bed fully clothed. No need for the comforter. Before she let sleep take her, she pulled her purse close, her fingers brushed against the barrel of the gun.

Tomorrow. Tomorrow she would end this nonsense.

Something woke her, pulling her from blurred dreams of plants and dead children. Elise's eyes opened abruptly. The echo of a harsh noise remained in her head. She had no idea if it had been part of the dreams or something here in the house, something real.

Then she heard it again. A screech that went on forever before deteriorating into a moan. The sound had come from outside.

It was dark, still the middle of the night. Her mother had no neighbors, no large towns close by so the night was black here in the valley. It was a clear night and the moon almost full, shining a spotlight down on the backyard and large pond at the edge of the garden. The shadows were thick in the surrounding forest. The contrast made the trees look like a wall of blackness.

The pond reflected back the moon, making it appear like a slick, shiny pool of black ink. And there, just beyond the garden and on the edge of the pond stood her mother. She was naked, her face turned up toward the night sky. She wailed once again.

A cold bolt of fear shot through Elise, though she wasn't sure if she was suddenly afraid *for* her mother or *of* her. She ran out of the room, snatching her purse from the bed. Somehow between the time she left her room and arrived on the back porch, she had lost the bag and held the gun. No more trying to hide now.

From the back porch she could still see her mother. She shook and swayed at the edge of the water. And the screeching, the screeching had grown louder and like an ice pick, it drove through Elise's brain. Even at this distance, it caused physical pain.

She walked half the distance toward her mother before raising the gun. The woman was obviously in pain. Death would be a mercy. She was consumed by madness.

Her mother brought her hands up above her face, to where scalp met forehead. It took a moment for Elise to understand what she was seeing. Her mother had dug her nails under the skin at the top of her head.

Elise watch horrified, stomach turning, as the mad woman pulled at the skin, peeling it, hair and all, from her head. The gun was still raised, it shook as Elise looked beyond it, as her still-wailing mother pulled the skin away from her body.

It was unnatural, how it split behind her in a seam down her back, separating in a straight line. It peeled away with a wet ripping sound, like peeling back the rind of an orange. But it pulled away orderly, muscle underneath, like an article of clothing rather than the fabric of flesh.

When she had pulled it down to her shoulders, Elise's mother pulled her arms from the . . . the sleeves—it was the only way to describe it—and gloves of skin that covered her arms.

What was underneath was gleaming wet, black in the dark and moonlight's gleam. A splatter of blood, also black in the moonlight, covered the plants near where she stood. When she had reached her waist, the skin of her head, torso, and arms hanging limply at her side, she pulled the skin at her hips as if she were removing tight leggings.

Still she screamed, still Elise stood, gun raised, heavy and shaking in her hand. Should she kill this thing? Was it her mother? Was it a monster? Sickening fascination held her, paralyzed.

When her mother had removed her feet from the skin boots, she stepped lightly away, leaving flesh crumpled on the ground like a discarded jumpsuit. The wailing had stopped. Now it was just sobs, but not the husky, rough sobs of an old lady. It sounded higher, younger. Her mother, or the thing she had become, walked into the pond. Slowly wading in. Step by step, the shiny black thing sank into the still water. Then it was gone.

Elise gasped. The gun dropped to her side, still hanging loosely in limp fingers. The water had stilled as soon as her mother's head had disappeared beneath its surface. Now Elise approached the shore.

The skin was there, a heap of clothing. The water stirred and her mother began to emerge, washed, the water running off her long hair. She had hair now. As she came closer to shore Elise could see it wasn't her mother anymore. It was a girl, perhaps four or five. But even in the dark, she could see the familiarity.

Hair, dark but probably brown in the sunlight. For a moment, Elise's breath caught again. The eyes, the shape of the nose, the cheekbones. The child was her daughter, she was Elizabeth. Elise's eyes blurred, tears coming. The girl came closer, moonlight water dripping from her naked form.

And Elise could see it wasn't her daughter. But they shared the same features. This girl was so close, she could have been Elizabeth's sister. She *could* have been Elise's child. Elise could see the shadow of herself in the girl's face.

As she came closer, the stoic face of the girl slipped away, confusion and fear quickly taking its place. The girl scanned the shore quickly, tears coming.

"Momma," she said and then again a little louder, "Momma."

"Hello?" Elise said, unsure who, what this was. The girl didn't seem to hear or even notice her.

The girl continued to look up and down the shore. She stood on dry ground peering around quickly, panic in her movements.

"Momma! I need you!"

"I can help you," Elise tried again but knew it would be of no use. The girl could not see her. Elise felt a new fear. The panic in the girl was spreading. Elise's heart was thumping in her chest. She had to do something, she was supposed to do something.

Then Elise's gaze fell on the skin. What had she thought? It looked like a pile of discarded clothes. It became clear with a chill. She knew what to do with certainty so strong she might have known it her whole life. She started taking off her clothes.

She knelt and picked up the skin. It was soft and thin in her hand. She should have been revolted by its touch. But she wasn't. It was like holding an outfit. It should have been fragile, but when she lowered it, when she pushed her foot and leg into it, there was no tearing.

It slid on like wet leather. It was tight, but she got her leg in, then the other. Once she was dressed to the waist, she slipped her arms in and through to the gloves. The seams in the front and back joined as they came together. Sealing up as if they had never split.

She felt a slight tingling in her legs and the skin that had moved against them stilled and the sensation of having something on her legs disappeared. She pulled it past her shoulders. She paused because she thought this was going to be the hard part, covering her face, putting on the mask, hiding.

It turned out it wasn't.

She looked down at herself. It was no longer a skin suit, it was just skin. Her skin. It was a little older than it had been but not as old as her...her...who?

"Momma?" the girl asked. Her eyes were wide. Relief brightened them as she leaped up.

SHIYI YU

Elise nodded. The girl looked so much like someone she once knew, someone important. But she was here, this girl, her daughter, and she was important. Elise opened her arms and the girl rushed into them.

"Momma," she said, sobs of relief shaking through her.

"Hush girl." Elise turned her toward the house and started walking her back. "Everything is good now. It's right, the way it should be. Let's go inside. We have much to do, and I have much to teach you."

Elise picked up the gun and tossed it into the pond. It sank to the bottom, next to the other pistol, the two older rifles, the knives of steel and the knives of stone.

Death of a Time Traveler

written by
Sara Fox

illustrated by
JENNIFER BRUCE

ABOUT THE AUTHOR

Sara Fox, an information specialist and a ne'er-do-well, can often be found wandering in airports both local and abroad. A fan of continuously recreating themselves, they've been a researcher, elementary through college teacher, and a techie. Their stories have been found online on The Book Smugglers ("When the Letter Comes") and in the book Schoolbooks & Sorcery *("Honest Tea").*

ABOUT THE ILLUSTRATOR

Jennifer Bruce was born in 1991 near Detroit, Michigan. As a child she had an avid interest in drawing but didn't have access to art classes until high school, so she was largely self-taught. After high school, forced to choose a career in college, she struggled to settle into a major that felt fulfilling, but avoided an art major because it felt daunting and impossible.

She eventually regained her confidence and attended the College for Creative Studies in downtown Detroit, graduating with honors and a bachelor's in illustration (and a minor in concept art). She is now pursuing a career as a freelance artist, with a focus on young adult and children's literature book covers.

Her style of illustration mixes her foundation of traditional media with the ease and flexibility of digital media. Her digital paintings combine semirealistic figures with graphic elements, texture, and patterns, infused with dramatic emotion and narrative. She draws inspiration from nature, beloved works of fiction, and her favorite cinematic and electronic/indie-pop music.

She currently resides near Detroit with her husband Steven and their pets Misa (adorable cat) and Benji (murderous rabbit, "Bun" to his friends/enemies).

Death of a Time Traveler

You get the call on a gray Sunday, still plastered in bed with last holiday's pajamas and a dozen chance-based app games keeping you company. It's not a hangover, you tell yourself, because you haven't touched a glass in over two weeks and you're more than proud of that.

"You need to come home," Mom says. "Dad's in the hospital."

"Which dad?" you ask, slow and unthinking. You pick your way out of the blankets, rummage for underwear, a dress. There's no hurry, yet. The only way Dad's-in-the-hospital is bad is if he's older than eighty-eight. He was only seventy yesterday.

I'm not traveling this year, he'd promised. So it's bad. It's not dire. The light coming from the window is bleak with fog, but you know everything will be okay.

"*Your* dad." Her voice burns the haze and you stop between the bed and the doorway. "Does it matter?"

"Maybe." Your hands twitch over the storm of clothes and old coffee cups strewn across the room. You've been meaning to get this all cleaned up soon, today, tomorrow, next week. The cups have to wait even longer now, grow whole ecologies in your absence. You wonder when they will overtake the porcelain and conquer the carpet.

"Maybe," you say again, but the silence, the slow tilt of words in between the static and your ear, means you are already throwing half your dirty laundry from floor to suitcase. "Okay, whatever, I'm coming. What happened?"

286

It doesn't matter what happened. It's bad enough that you cry the entire three-hour drive back to the hometown you swore you would only ever return to in triumph. When you swan into the ICU, it's been four hours and you arrive with your family's cache of phone chargers, ketchup on your hip, and grief already cold under your collar.

"You would have loved the drive," you tell your dad, who is pinned down by tubes and pillows. They are insensible words to you, to him. His eyes are open, a clueless blue that still manages to search and meet yours. Hands touch, squeeze, release. His right side has drifted into the void; his left leg will join it before long.

He's still here. Hope still pumps through your veins as the doctor says, "The damage to his brain is catastrophic, but we won't know all the details for a few days because of post-trauma swelling."

Your brother has been standing in the corner behind the bed since before you arrived. He turns now, away from the window overlooking another empty room and toward reality. "So we won't know for—?"

"It will be months until we have the full picture," the doctor says and then adds, "but the damage is severe. He will not go home from here."

There are conversations in that statement you have missed, but you gather the threads when your mom starts to cry and your brother turns back to the empty room. You look for someone else to take your mom's hand or wrap an arm around her but there's only you, so you do it and think: *The P value is a significance level for a given hypothesis. Who decided* P, *why not* K? Later you'll wonder why your brain settled there, swirling along the eddy of the inconsequential. P has always stood for probability.

You do not want to cry.

Across from the hospital bed, there is a window and you can see the ICU nurses swapping out for their lunch breaks. The doctor leaves.

"He's too young," your brother says. No one argues. This dad is over a decade from the *age of last sighting*. Your mom swears she met him for the first time at eighty-five and loved him then as nothing more than a sweet old man.

It's not until that night, curled up in your childhood bed, that the question buried in your brother's statement unearths itself, already rotting in your stomach: *What if Dad time travels like this?*

You and Mom visit the hospital every day. You drive in together. You force breakfasts and lunches into her hands; remind her to drink, eat, leave. Dad loses movement in his left leg. When they take the tube from his throat he reaches for ice. His face is sweetest as the water melts into his lips, but he cannot swallow and he gags. You cover your ears that night, hearing over and over the sounds of the nurse plumbing his throat so he doesn't drown.

The doctor explains that much of his brain is simply gone. Words, pictures, voice—all understanding has disintegrated, even if his eyes still dance when you say, "Well, this is a bunch of crap, isn't it?" on the third day.

He does not time travel and no one comes to tell you what this all means. *He visited us older than this, didn't he?*

Sometimes you can't take the white walls, the constant handwashing, the multitude of quiet sounds in the hospital room. In those moments, your eyes fill with tears and your chest catches between breaths. It's quiet, barely started grief, but between one moment and the next your mom looks up, fixes you with a glance, and says, "Oh, don't."

So, you don't. You swallow the hitch, blink away the burning of your eyes, and smother both in an onslaught of meaningless thoughts: *Twelve times thirty-two is three hundred eighty-four* and *How was tax code even formed?* Back on campus, your fellow grad students are discussing the allegory of objectivity. Questioning the nature and structure of research is beyond you now, although isn't this a place with the perfect question: What happens if a time traveler dies when they're not supposed to?

You do not know.

You write: *looking methodically at the here and now you avoid the trap of attempted transcendence* . . . into your work notebook and then scratch it out.

Every day feels like a month.

This is not an easy death where there is nothing to do but wait against the backbeat of an indifferent universe. This is a death with choices. Except it's not really your choice, is it? He chose again and again.

The question is simple: Will you honor his decision or dismiss it?

It's as easy and as terrible as that.

You think you see your father outside his own hospital room. He's young, maybe twenty, with a seventies-style light-blue suit and sweep of thick brown hair. He's smiling at the nurse, who laughs as you stumble from the chair at your older father's bedside. The older body shudders between sighs. He's been sleeping most of the day.

"Wait." You're not sure it's even audible. You want to scream, *Tell them what you want.* You want to cry, *Dad, please.*

When you finally breach the door, the man is already gone. Typical. "Wait," you say, before you start to cry. Mom stepped out ten minutes ago, so this is just you and one more moment when the *man out of time* has seemingly made the choice to step away.

The nurse props you up in a chair and hands you a bottle of water.

"I'm sorry. I know this is hard," she says. You wonder if she knows. You wonder if she's one of *us*. There's no support network for the children of the temporally challenged.

You don't ask.

You do not search the internet for what happens when a time traveler dies before their time. You're not sure anyone knows and you don't want to invite the curious through thoughtless keystrokes on hospital Wi-Fi.

After you put your mom to bed, you sit in your childhood room feted with frills that barely fit you then and now feel like a farce. You had pink walls once, then dark blue; now they are *acceptable gray*. You want to spit on them, cover them with all the rancid paint left in your closets from a long-forgotten artistic phase. Instead, you sit on the edge of your bed and breathe.

The question is not what do we do next, the doctor said. *There is always a* next. *The question is what would your father want? Given all the factors: 24–7 care, loss of communication, swallowing . . . the fact that this will happen again . . .*

The answer is something everyone knows, from Dad's children, to cousins, to friends. He told you every holiday since you were twelve. He told your mom. He told your brother, who hasn't been able to stand the hospital since the day your mom woke up to find Dad staring insensibly at the ceiling.

"I don't want to go to a nursing home. Give me a whiskey, take me out back and shoot me," he said for the hundredth time just that fall. He was younger then, maybe fifty. There were fewer lines on his face, less salt in his hair. There's a softness to the older versions of your father that did not exist yet, even though if he were a linear man he would have stayed a stable seventy to your thirty. "Do not keep me alive for that, no matter how old I am."

"Dad," you said, kicking leaves with amused frustration, "you've told me and told me and it doesn't matter; we've seen you older than this. A lot older."

He took a breath, held it, and then let it go. Whatever annoyance had been on his tongue mellowed into a smile better suited for a much-younger version of you both. "Aren't you supposed to be doing some bigwig research?"

"I'm researching people, not timelines."

"Isn't that the same thing?"

You puzzle through that, weighing how your research on temporally impacted families feeds into timelines. It's hard to say.

"Not the way I'm researching it." It's hard to find research participants. It's hard to analyze quantum physics with sociological and psychological impacts to a family unit. "Time is a loop, anyway."

"Says who?"

"You."

Your father smiles again and it's almost childlike, bright and guileless. "But did I?"

When he leaves, it is dark and you're still in the woods. He hugs you hard enough to bruise and returns to the conversation that began at the beginning of the day with a whispered, "No peg tube, no feeding tubes. Remember."

On the fourth day, you call your brother home to talk. He passed you in the hall saying, "You're so calm. I don't understand how you can be so calm." But now he burns in the corner, head canted to the side, not making eye contact.

"We can order pizza after," Mom offers. "But first we have to talk about your dad."

It's the same story you have lived since you drove pell-mell through the gray on Sunday. The doctor said then it would be bad, that he wouldn't go home. Your brother scrambles over scraps of hope dropped between facts. *He will never go home* dismissed for *Of course we can't be sure what recovery he may achieve for three months*. He parrots them now, and if the vape were a cigarette he'd have already lit himself on fire with the way it dips against his pant leg. "We can't be sure. Plus, we've seen him alive, right?"

"Not since this happened." You do not mention the young face in the hall. Your nose burns with the scent of juniper berries and cheap wine, the flavors of the conversation poured into a glass with ice. You think of how the funeral will smell: potpourri, candles, gifted flowers.

JENNIFER BRUCE

"It's only been four days." The goalpost has moved and you can feel those days shift and sink in your bones.

"Yeah."

Mom is silent. Time is bedridden recovery bleeding into a bedridden forever. Time is a confused mind being sent back and forth along a timeline unable to comprehend or explain what it needs. There is no voice left to cry *help*, no strong hands to pull out a feeding tube or reach for a hug. Time is not recovery, not really, it is just sending pain backward to...

What?

You don't know, but you do know that any future he might travel to is pain.

"If Dad knew this...this was coming for him and he couldn't stop it, what would he have done?" It crawls out of your mouth in a growl, germinated in hospital soap and the calm your brother dismissed upon entry. He won't meet your eyes, just shakes his head. "Say it," you insist.

It's a cruel thing, but there isn't space for fantasy. Reality needs to root itself here, in this den where the wood paneling has been painted white and the sofa has begun to fray.

You wish there was a knock at the door. You wish your father's smile would flash upon you all and voice the answer everyone knows but refuses to voice: *Let me go.* He asked it too often.

But you were never going to be rescued by your father appearing out of time. You never have been before, why would this be any different?

"I know what he would have done," your brother admits, finally, and the vape clouds him until, for just a moment, you wonder if he will step out of time, too. The skill follows families, after all. It doesn't matter that you both were adopted. "But it's Dad—we've known him...older. What happens if we...?"

There is no accomplishment, no pride. The air in your lungs is lead and you don't know if the tears are gone because you've cried too much or if it's just simple dehydration. "What are you going to do if we don't? Are you going to visit him every day?

293

Every weekend? We have never been able to ground him here, how will now be any different?"

You want to say more, to keep exploding this bile onto your brother's work boots and avoidance but Mom cuts you both off. "Everything has changed. I want— I want your father back but here is the truth: What we remember is over. It can never happen."

And that is the reality of it. Your brother turns his head from the floor to the window where the sun is setting into empty trees. He never looked like Dad except in this moment when his face softens into grief.

There is no peg tube, no feeding tube. Comfort measures only. Your father smiles at you. You remind yourself: He doesn't know. He can't know. It hurts anyway because all the timelines spin out before you in *what if... what if... what if...*

You look at your notes about looking methodically at the here and now and think *I want transcendence, I want that circle to infinity.*

But that does not happen. A time traveler dies.

Two months later your dad walks out of the woods with the face of a thirty-year-old.

The Battle of Donasi

written by
Elaine Midcoh

illustrated by
BEN HILL

ABOUT THE AUTHOR

Elaine Midcoh lives in Pembroke Pines, Florida. At age eight, she wrote to NASA *asking to be an astronaut, but was rejected. Undeterred, she penned her first book, which featured a young girl as* NASA's *first child astronaut. Yes, the kid's name was Elaine. To seal the deal, she bought herself a junior astronaut medal, which she still wears on special occasions. Later, when adulthood loomed, she diverted to law school, became an attorney, and spent many happy years teaching college students about criminal justice and the Bill of Rights, while still writing an occasional tale.*

These days, Elaine spends time at her kitchen table thinking up short stories and poetry. In 2019, she was spotted dancing in front of her living room window after learning one of her stories earned an Honorable Mention in the Writers of the Future Contest. And we won't discuss what celebratory acts the neighbors saw when Elaine received word that "The Battle of Donasi," was selected as a published finalist for this WotF anthology. Police were called, but one was a science fiction fan and she was let go with a warning.

Finally, she must offer a shout-out to her older brother for reading her stories. ("David, just read this one more time, okay?")

ABOUT THE ILLUSTRATOR

Born in 1996, Ben Hill did not start pursuing art seriously until he was eighteen. Without any local schools or classes, he chose to be a self-taught digital and traditional artist.

Now living in rural Florida on the space coast, over the last four years he has focused on studying with online resources and taking SmArt School mentorships.

Inspired by artists like Alphonse Mucha and Arthur Rackham, he draws creativity from old fairy tales and art nouveau.

In his work, he has a love for experimenting with movement, texture, and pattern, and he tries to learn something new with every piece.

Ben was a winner of the L. Ron Hubbard's Illustrators of the Future Contest and was first featured in Volume 36.

The Battle of Donasi

Captain Linae Tower walked through the entrance of Earth Space Command HQ, grateful the security team manning the detectors pretended not to recognize her. She tried to ignore the people in the crowded lobby. Some stared, others glanced away, a few nodded at her, but one young Marine private stopped and came to full attention, blocking those around him. She resisted the urge to slug him. "Move on, Private."

She went to the elevators. The people waiting there parted, allowing her to board first. No one else got on. Linae thought about promising not to infect them, but the elevator doors closed before she could say anything. She was startled by the image reflected on the metal doors. Though only thirty-two, her eyes, red-rimmed and worn, belonged to someone ninety-five. And she spotted new gray hairs mixed in with her auburn strands. As the elevator rose, she patted her inside pocket and felt a sharp prick from the corner of the envelope holding her resignation letter.

Linae emerged on the top floor at the end of a long hallway. Directly across from the elevator doors, shimmering bright on the maroon walls, were large gold letters: "Earth Space Command—Chief of Staff." And right beneath them, sitting on a gold-colored textile padded bench, was Ash, complete with his trademark smirk.

Lieutenant Commander Asher Betowan, Medical Corps, rose to his feet, managed a legitimate, yet sloppy, salute and said,

"Commander Destructo, I presume." Then he pointed at the red stripe across her shoulder. "Oops. I mean Captain Destructo."

Linae smiled, an expression so long unused that it felt foreign. Ash appeared rested; his dark brown skin had a glow to it. The three months home with his family in Nairobi certainly had helped his recovery. The scar on the left side of his face had faded to a barely visible crescent moon. She hugged him. "Looking good, Ash."

"This isn't proper military protocol."

She stepped back. "As if you would know. What are you doing here?"

"Like you, I have been summoned."

"Why? To make sure I don't commit suicide when they fire me?"

Ash's eyebrows shot up.

"I was joking," she said.

"Uh-huh." He gestured toward the padded bench. "Let's sit."

"But we have been summoned."

Ash checked his watch. "We have five minutes, thirty-six seconds." He sat down. Sighing, she sat next to him.

"You did what had to be done," he said.

"Which part? Genocide or bringing biological warfare to space?"

Ash frowned. "That article got it wrong."

She didn't answer, but Ash knew her too well. "Earth's Gift to the Universe: Biological Weapons!" the headline had read and beneath it a photo of her at the World Parliament building receiving the Medal of Valor from President Sagun. That damned editorial went viral. On vid they discussed it endlessly and always, always, the morality question. Then one of the talking heads labeled her "Captain Destructo." That's when her stomach began launching acid up her throat, that's when sleep wouldn't come without a pill or two, and that's when she couldn't stand people anymore, like the Marine private in the lobby.

"You can talk to me," Ash said. Of course, she could; Academy classmate, friend for a dozen years and shipmate for the past three. She'd been 'best man' at his wedding and was 'official auntie' to his toddler son. She could talk to him. She knew it...but...

Ash waited, then shrugged. He peered at his watch. "We have four minutes and twenty-seven seconds. Quiz. How many Earth ships were lost in the battle at Cerium 3?"

Linae laughed. Ash was back in Academy cadet mode, when they'd relentlessly drilled each other before exams.

"378," she said.

"And how many people did we lose?"

"174,452."

"And if we hadn't beaten the Hiturans at Cerium 3, what would have happened?"

"They'd have continued into our system. Europa, Mars, the Moon, Earth."

"And what would they have done?"

She stared at him. "They would have killed us, Ash."

He nodded. "And who started the war?"

She hesitated. "They did—we think."

"Incorrect. They did—definitely. The idiots who say we somehow provoked them, that we must have unknowingly violated a 'sacred Hituran cultural norm,' ignore that they attacked first. We tried to contact them. We asked other planets to intercede. Do you remember when President Sagun broadcasted that, 'Don't know what we did, but we're sorry, please forgive us' speech? She sounded like a confused lover. But the Hiturans didn't care. They ignored every attempt at dialogue."

Ash rubbed the scar on his face, the place where a piece of their ship's buckling hull had sliced into him. "And we were losing, our pulse weapons slightly more than useless. What would our military history instructor have said? 'Throwing rocks against tanks.' That was us." He pointed his finger at her.

"Then you, Commander Tower—oops, I mean Captain, saved us."

She remembered her excitement when she'd come up with the idea. With their ship damaged, weapons offline, and Captain

Arayas dead, Linae had taken command. Through grit and luck they managed to bring the *David Roy* to the fallback rendezvous point, only to find they were the only battle cruiser to get there. It was supposed to be a place for a regrouping of forces, a place to organize a second stand, but the devastation at Cerium 3 had eliminated that possibility. Then Linae had seen the eight robotic supply ships standing by and got an idea.

The Hiturans would never board an occupied human ship without carefully eliminating biohazards, but automated supply ships were designed to be bioclean. That was how the worlds conducted trade with each other. The Hiturans would be happy to steal the supply ships and their cargo. All she had to do was plant a surprise for them. And then she saw the medical ships and got another idea.

Ash checked his watch again. "Final question: Was it your goal to commit genocide?"

Linae stiffened. "No. But who cares? I'm 'Captain Destructo.'"

"No, you're Captain Tower. The Hiturans going extinct didn't happen because of you. You know our protocol in such circumstances?"

She had reviewed it several times since Cerium 3, always wondering about the Hiturans. "If a space crew gets infected with an unknown disease, we send in a medical ship. Hopefully, they can help. If not, then both ships and crews get quarantined in their own private mini space station until such time as a cure is found, or forever, if no cure is found."

Ash nodded. "That's the only smart course of action. There was no reason to think the sick Hiturans would go back to their planet. We still don't know why they did. Maybe it was a 'sacred cultural norm,' maybe dying Hiturans have to go home. But they made that choice. All you did was come up with a defense strategy designed to defeat enemy forces in the middle of a battle." He tapped her on the knee. "You know that, right?"

"Sure, absolutely." Linae tried to smile, but her face just couldn't get there.

He stood up. "Thanks for saving us, by the way. I like being alive. We have forty-five seconds."

When they entered the conference room Linae saw two officers already sitting at one end of the long antique oak table. Her heart skipped when she realized that the gray-haired man at the head of the table was the Chief of Staff himself, Admiral Ideema.

She and Ash both came to attention and saluted. This time Ash's salute wasn't sloppy at all. "Captain Tower, reporting," she said.

"Lieutenant Commander Betowan, reporting," Ash said.

Admiral Ideema stood up, as did the other officer, which was strange because they both outranked Linae and Ash. Then she realized it was her Medal of Valor pin. Tradition required that all officers present, regardless of rank, stand when a Medal of Valor recipient walked into a room. Damn.

"Captain, Commander," Admiral Ideema said. "Sit down."

Linae wondered if the fancy chair was designed to be deliberately uncomfortable or if the erupting muscle spasm in her back was her body's response to this meeting.

Admiral Ideema introduced the other officer as Vice-Admiral Coyman, a sharp-looking woman in her fifties. She was Earth Space Command's Chief Medical Officer.

Admiral Ideema said, "Before we begin, I want to thank you personally, Captain Tower. Without your innovative strategy employed at Cerium 3, I doubt any of us would be sitting here today. Or anywhere."

Innovative strategy, nice phrase for *genocide*. She nodded in acknowledgment.

He said. "What do you know of the planet Donasi?"

Donasi? Linae had to think for a moment. "Of the thirty-two worlds known to have intelligent life, Donasi—"

"Thirty-one," Admiral Coyman interrupted. "There are now just thirty-one planets known to have intelligent life."

Linae saw Ash's hands clench into fists. Admiral Ideema

regarded her without expression. *Screw them*, she thought. *If they want to fire me, fine, but I'm not going to punch out a superior officer and give them the satisfaction of a court-martial.*

"Thank you, Admiral Coyman. Of the thirty-one planets known to have intelligent life, only thirteen have developed interstellar travel."—*Thought I'd say fourteen, didn't you?*—"The remaining eighteen, including Donasi, have not developed space flight and are at different stages of cultural and technological development. Donasi is considered a 'D' planet, at a technological stage roughly the equivalent of Earth in the early twentieth century, about where we were 200 years ago. They've just begun to develop electricity as a power source. They have multiple nation-states across the planet, ranging from dictatorships to democracies. They are located in an isolated part of space, away from the interstellar trade routes and shipping lanes. Their planet is not known to hold any unusual natural resources that would make it a target for exploitation."

Admiral Ideema grinned. "I see you still remember your Academy textbooks. But do you know when that textbook entry was written?"

"Sir?"

"Your information is nineteen years out of date. That's the last time an Earth Space Command ship surveyed Donasi. We want you to go back. Do a new survey."

"Why?" It made no sense. Donasi was a nothing planet. No special location, no special resources.

"Why not?" asked Admiral Coyman. "It's not as if there's another war to fight."

Ah, so that was it. She wasn't being fired. She was being sent away. Give the war hero a medal, then hide her in isolated space.

Admiral Ideema gave Coyman a hard look. "There's more to it," he said. "It's important for us to show the other worlds that we're not interested in war. Going back to routine missions is a start. Having you lead such a mission emphasizes that point." He smiled. "Also, I'm sure you won't mind, we're giving you the *David Roy*."

Linae and Ash glanced at each other and Linae felt a surge of joy. As for Ash, he could barely contain himself. "The *DR*'s been fixed?" she asked.

Admiral Ideema said, "We're repairing all the ships we can, even those we might normally scrap. It's not as if we have a lot left. We prioritized the *David Roy*. It's the first one off the line and is ready for a shakedown. That's another reason for this mission."

"What about our crew, Admiral?" Linae said. "We lost about a third at Cerium 3, but I'm sure the rest will be pleased to return to the *David Roy*."

"We've already assigned you a crew, Captain. Admiral Coyman, if you please?"

Coyman nodded to Ideema, then turned to Linae. "About half the crew will be your own, but the other half, and all the officers except for you and Dr. Betowan here, will be from other ships, ships that fought at Cerium 3."

"Ah, survivors," Ash said.

For the first time Coyman smiled. "I see you haven't forgotten your psychology studies, Doctor."

"No, ma'am," Ash responded.

Ash clearly understood what was going on, but Linae did not. She said, "I haven't had psychology studies."

Coyman folded her arms and gazed at Ash.

Ash turned to Linae. "We lost a lot of ships at Cerium 3, and people too, but there are always survivors."

Linae flinched. *Not for the Hiturans*. If Ash saw it, he pretended not to notice.

"Many of the survivors of Cerium 3 are traumatized. There've been multiple medical conferences over the past months. We've been trying to figure out effective treatments. It's clear that some crewmen and officers will end up leaving the service, perhaps never returning to space. Others will need to gently ease back. But some should return to space duty now, immediately. For them, the sooner, the better."

Admiral Ideema said, "They've fallen off a horse, Captain,

and if they don't get back on right away, they might never ride again."

Is that why they picked her for this, as part of some psychological treatment? Then it hit her. "I'm commanding a therapy ship?" That's all she needed, a weak, whiny crew. She felt her face reddening.

Admiral Coyman glared at her and leaned forward, but whatever she was going to say was cut off with a quick hand gesture from Admiral Ideema.

"Captain Tower, no Earth Space Command crew needs coddling. If this mission is . . . somewhat therapeutic, then your crew's therapy is that they're not in therapy. They are all Space Command personnel, and you should hold them to the same high standards as any crew." He smiled again. "They'll expect nothing less from the hero of Cerium 3."

The journey to Donasi was uneventful, even boring, the prime definition of a milk run. Linae ran a series of drills to test the *David Roy* and her crew, including battle scenarios. She half expected Ash to protest. Maybe battle drills were too stressful "therapy" for this damaged crew. But Ash laughed when she set up the exercises. "Y'know the war's over, right?" he asked.

The renovated bridge was just as crowded as the old one, with the captain's chair smack in the middle of its long rectangular shape, surrounded by the various stations. Ash spent a lot of time on the bridge, sitting in the observer's chair that was to the right and slightly behind her own. He complained that the crew was too healthy to keep him busy and that the refurbished sick bay smelled funny. Linae didn't mind his presence. Though she made a point to meet and chat with all of the officers, Ash was the only one she knew well. Of course, there was an advantage to being on a ship with Cerium 3 survivors, even if they were strangers. Not one gave her a funny look or called her "Captain Destructo."

Only when they reached the outer edge of the Donasi system did they get a surprise.

Ensign Irena Terry, working the forward helm, made the discovery. "Captain, we're scanning an unmanned craft up ahead, either a probe or a satellite."

Terry was one of the Cerium 3 survivors on board. Unlike other survivors, she did not consider herself lucky. Her husband and sister had both died in the battle with the Hiturans. She rarely talked about her loss and she performed her duties with an intensity that Linae admired. "Main screen on, Ensign."

Terry had to magnify the screen five times before the object's features became clear: a simple metallic box with solar panels on all sides.

"Not very stylish," Lieutenant Batak said. Batak was the ship's navigator and another survivor, but to Linae he didn't seem troubled at all. He was jovial and happy, a cheeriness that went well with his short roly-poly body.

Terry looked up from her instruments. "Captain, even though the object has solar paneling, its primary power source is nuclear. It's leaking radiation, though there's no danger to us. I've heard of stuff like this, but only in museums."

"Captain Tower, we're receiving a signal from the object," Ensign Flare's booming voice echoed across the bridge.

"Audio on."

Flare stood close to seven feet, tall for a human, but which Flare swore was small for a Texan. He loved hand-to-hand combat and continually challenged other crewmen to meet him in the ship's gym. Linae felt tempted to match him, but wondered if that was appropriate for a ship's captain. Still, she appreciated Flare's aggressiveness. He would have been a great crewmate at Cerium 3, but Flare had been on leave when the Hiturans attacked. He missed the entire battle. His old ship, the *Venture*, was lost with the entire crew. Flare didn't talk about them— ever—but he often said that he would never take leave again. Flare hunched over the station at tactical. "Ma'am, it's not an audio signal, it's visual."

"Then visual on," Linae said, drumming her fingers.

The main screen filled with an image of a male. He had the

distinguishing characteristics of the Donasi: blue, hairless, short, barrel-chested, powerful arms, and long elegant fingers that seemed incongruous with the rest of the body.

Within seconds the Donasi began to wave his arms in front of his body.

"It looks like he's waving us off," Terry said.

"We don't know that, Ensign," Ash replied. He had entered the bridge just as the signal came through. "We don't know their customs or body language. Maybe this is the Donasi way of saying hello." He took his observer's seat.

Linae nodded a greeting. "We do know it's crazy for the Donasi to have this technology. Less than twenty years ago they barely had electric power. How likely is it that they developed space flight in so short a time?"

"Maybe they're intelligent," Batak said.

Linae frowned. "Maybe. Or perhaps they had help."

"Another world? Why?" Ash asked.

"Captain, look." Terry said.

On the screen appeared an animated image of the planet. The Donasi stood in front of it and began to swing his arms, first to the right and then to the left.

"Go around, maybe," Ash said.

Then the Donasi crossed his arms across his huge chest, with his long fingers resting lightly on his powerful arms. His face took on an angry look as he planted his feet firmly in place. His body shielded the animation of Donasi, completely blocking it as it disappeared behind his defiant stance.

"You're right, Ensign Terry. He's not saying hello," Ash said.

Linae stared at the Donasi's image. *So they don't want visitors. Okay, but that didn't answer the question of how they got to space so fast.* She said, "Ensign Flare, of the known inhabited worlds, how many planets developed space flight within twenty years of developing electricity?"

Flare responded immediately without having to check with the computer. "None."

"How about thirty years?"

"None."

"That doesn't mean they didn't do it on their own," Ash warned.

"No," Linae said, "but it's unlikely. One of the other worlds is here or came here. I want to know why." *Was it the Hiturans? Could some have survived? Had they come to Donasi to make a new home? A lonely planet off the grid would be a good place to regroup.*

Ash leaned forward. He whispered, "I know what you're thinking. Forget it. They're all dead."

"Someone's here, Ash. We're going to find out who."

Linae folded her arms and her face took on an expression eerily similar to that of the Donasi on the screen. "Ensign Terry, take us to Donasi."

Exactly three minutes and forty-two seconds after the *David Roy* entered orbit around the planet, the first Donasi ship approached.

"They knew we were coming," Ash said.

"That welcome wagon probe sent a signal," Batak replied.

Linae turned to Flare. "Will we be able to communicate with them?"

"Yes, ma'am. We've been monitoring their broadcasts since we entered the system. The computer's translation matrix has us at ninety-seven percent clarity."

"Excellent. Establish commlink. Put it on the main screen."

"Commlink open."

Linae faced the screen. "My name is Linae Tower. I'm the captain of the Earth Space Command vessel *David R——*"

"I am Ben Ami," a gravelly voice cut Linae off as the image of the Donasi filled the screen. He was clearly old, yet strength emanated from him. There were wrinkles around his green-blue eyes, but the eyes themselves were bright and alert. Ben Ami reminded Linae of an old half-dingo/half-husky dog she had watched over one summer, all folded up and contained within itself, ready to uncoil and strike at the first sign of danger or prey. "I am the commander of the Donasi Defense Force. You have invaded our space. Surrender your ship immediately."

Linae felt her eyebrows shoot up and forced them down. "Commander Ami—"

"Ben Ami," he said, again cutting Linae off.

Linae reminded herself that so far there was no cause for hostility. "Commander Ben Ami, we mean you no harm. Our mission is peaceful—"

The channel shut off. Linae turned to Ensign Flare.

"It wasn't me," Flare said.

"Then get him—"

"Ma'am, there's a power surge in the Donasi ship," Terry said.

This was the fourth time that Linae had been stopped mid-sentence, but at that moment she didn't care. "Engage shielding, Battle Alert."

A microsecond later the *David Roy* was bathed in a sparkling bluish-green light. Linae squinted her eyes until Terry filtered out the brightness.

"Analysis," Linae said.

"It's an energy pulse," Batak responded. "They meant to disrupt the ship's structural integrity. Their weaponry seems similar to the first experimental pulse weapons we developed years ago. It's too weak to hurt us. Our shielding dispersed the energy before it could do any damage."

"A warning shot?" Ash asked.

"I don't know," Linae said. "Ben Ami doesn't strike me as a warning-shot kind of guy. Mr. Flare, damage report?"

"Reports coming in. No damage, no casualties. A few inquiries asking about the pretty light. Some of the crew don't even know we've been attacked. Shall I return fire?"

Linae saw Ash watching her, not with his usual smirk, but with a seriousness that made her stomach contract. Another battle. Damn.

"No. Resume commlink," she said.

"Captain, two more Donasi ships approaching," Terry said.

"Mr. Flare?"

"I'm trying to reestablish comm, but they're refusing to respond."

The two Donasi vessels immediately flanked the first ship. Linae noted that they positioned themselves in such a way as to provide for maximum defense, while still enabling them to initiate an attack.

"Mr. Flare," she repeated.

Flare's hands flew rapidly across his board. "Captain, they won't answer, but their comm system is pretty simple. Got it. They may not respond, but they'll hear you."

Linae nodded. She leaned toward the main screen. "Commander Ben Ami, I know you hear me. We are not here to fight. I only want to talk with—"

Ben Ami's image filled the viewscreen. "There is no reason to talk. You trespassed in our space. Surrender or be destroyed."

And then Ben Ami waited. He did not break off communication, he did not make more demands, and he did not order his ships to fire. He simply gazed at Linae. Though Ben Ami's gaze was calm, there was something else there... something Linae could see, almost recognize. *What is it? What am I missing?*

Ben Ami was waiting for Linae's response... but what response? *I'm not a damned diplomat, just a dumb captain.* She glanced at Ash, hoping he might have an idea, but he just stared back at her. Great.

"Ben Ami," she began, "it was not our intention to trespass. We came in response to your probe. We were surprised to find a spacefaring people in this region—"

"No doubt," Ben Ami said. His image disappeared from the screen. Seconds later it was replaced by the luminous bluish-green light of the Donasi energy pulse weapon.

"All three Donasi ships fired simultaneously," Batak reported. "No damage to us. If this is the best they've got, they can shoot at us for months. It won't even dim the lights."

"That went well," she said to Ash.

"At least this time we're the tank and they're throwing the rocks," he replied. "I wonder why."

"That's the question, isn't it?"

"Captain, shall I return fire?" Ensign Flare asked.

Linae rubbed her forehead. "Fire a warning shot across the bow of Ben Ami's ship."

"Aye."

The pulse blast flew across space.

Linae sighed.

Ash whispered, "This isn't your fault. They started it." She wondered if he knew he had said the same thing about the Hiturans.

"Ash, it's pretty clear Ben Ami won't talk with me. Monitor their communications. See if you can learn something."

"Aye, Captain." Ash turned to his seat's screen.

Twenty minutes later Linae shook her head. Now there were five Donasi ships and four more on the way, expected within the next fifteen minutes. Once again the five ships fired, this time aiming at the propulsion systems. Once again the *David Roy*'s shielding easily absorbed the energy pulses. By now the Donasi had to know that their weapons were useless. Earlier they had fired simultaneously. When that failed, their ships fired one after the other, creating a continual flow of energy that still couldn't penetrate the *David Roy*. One time they concentrated their energy pulse on just one section, oddly enough the area where the kitchen mess was located, and later they dispersed their fire so that the whole of the *David Roy* was bathed in the bluish glow from their weapon. It didn't matter; the Donasi energy pulse was too primitive a weapon to break through.

The *David Roy* vibrated slightly as the Donasi attacked yet again. Ensign Flare checked his board, then looked up at Linae. "Still no damage. Shall I fire another warning shot? Again?" His lips formed a thin line.

Linae understood. She wouldn't mind giving the Donasi a thorough lesson in modern weapon technology. Still, she knew she hadn't a clue as to why this was happening. Just like with the Hiturans, a fight and not knowing why.

"No, don't fire another warning shot. Ash, have you found out anything?"

Ash looked up. "Not in terms of helpful information, but there is something of interest. Our 'battle' is being broadcast across the entire planet. They have an extensive mass-communication network and right now it's focused on us. I know you want to keep your eyes on them"—he gestured toward the Donasi ships on the main screen—"but listen to this."

Within seconds an excited voice filled the bridge, "And so Commander Ben Ami and the five defender ships have stopped the invader. This is the first time the enemy has not returned fire—"

Linae turned in her captain's chair. "Ensign Flare, prepare to fire on all five ships."

"Aye, Captain."

"Hey, wait a sec," Ash said.

"I can't have them think we're weak. Don't worry, I won't rip them apart, but they need to know they can't win. They need to understand that their only option is to talk to us. Mr. Flare, set weapons to minimum strength. Do not damage their ships. I repeat, do not damage them, but make sure they feel it. Fire when ready."

"Aye, Captain. Firing now."

The five Donasi ships lit up with the impact of the pulse beams.

Terry said, "Good God, they have no shielding."

"I know that," Flare said. He bit his lip as he examined the info coming across his board. "I made adjustments. They shouldn't suffer damage, at least not much."

"Captain, you'll want to hear this," Ash said.

Again the Donasi announcer's voice played across the bridge. His words came out in huffing breaths. "By the Divine, all five defender ships have been hit. For so long we have prepared and now the invaders are here and, by the Divine, we don't know if we can defend—"

Ash shut it off. "They don't think we're weak now, do they, Captain?"

Linae ignored his icy tone. "He said they had 'prepared for so long,' as if they knew we were coming—or someone was. At some point someone must have come to their planet. Ash, keep monitoring their communications. We need more info."

She turned to Flare. "Did we damage them?"

Flare reviewed his board. "One ship lost about half their engine output. The other ships haven't suffered much damage."

"Open the commlink." At Flare's signal, Linae began, "Commander Ben Ami, there is no need for continued hostility. We mean you no harm—"

Once more the *David Roy* screens glowed as the Donasi fired their energy pulse weapons. Linae didn't bother to ask for a damage report. She knew there wasn't any.

"Captain, the other four Donasi ships have arrived," Batak reported.

Linae watched the four new Donasi ships as they positioned themselves. Ben Ami was no fool. Now with nine ships at his disposal, Ben Ami arranged his ships so that they completely surrounded the *David Roy*. Apparently, it didn't matter to Ben Ami that there was no chance of winning. He had to know that. Still the Donasi ships kept firing and Linae sat in the captain's chair, wondering how this mission was going to end.

"Oh no," Ash said.

Linae turned to him. Ash stared at his screen. "What?" she asked.

Ash looked up, eyes wide. "I was monitoring one of their broadcasts. They were doing a review, a history of events. I found out who their alien visitors were." He rubbed his scar. "It was us."

The entire bridge crew stared at Ash. Linae said, "We just got here."

"Not us, the *David Roy*; us, Earth Space Command. Nineteen years ago when Captain Zared and the *Pueblo* came here, they were seen."

"But that's not possible," Batak said. "The Donasi didn't have scanners back then. They barely have scanners now."

"No," Ash said, "but they did have telescopes, and some good ones. Apparently, the Donasi have a strong interest in astronomy."

BEN HILL

He turned to Linae. "I checked the *Pueblo* logs. Captain Zared had a hobby. He liked planetary geography."

Now Linae's eyes widened. "Are you telling me he did low sweeps?" That was in direct violation of Space Command rules when surveying an inhabited world.

Ash said, "Not exactly. The sweeps weren't low enough to be spotted with the naked eye, so he thought he was okay. But while the *Pueblo* was here, one of the Donasi moons, the largest one, was full in the night sky. Initially, the *Pueblo* was spotted by a young astronomer. At first he thought the *Pueblo* was a comet, streaking between Donasi and the moon, but then the *Pueblo* changed course."

"And comets don't change course," Linae said.

"Right. The Donasi knew that it was a ship. For the next three nights, they had dozens of telescopes searching the sky and four different course changes were noted. Captain Zared was mapping the planet. It was us, Earth Space Command. We were the ones who showed the Donasi that they weren't alone."

"So they were surprised," Linae said. "But that still doesn't explain their hostility. The *Pueblo* didn't attack them."

"No, but they didn't introduce themselves, either. The Donasi are afraid. They couldn't understand why the *Pueblo* would visit their world and not stop to say hi. Eventually they decided that the *Pueblo* must be a scout ship for an invasion. Everything in their society is based on that. All of the Donasi resources were turned to planetary defense. They developed flight, then space flight. They went from electricity to nuclear power in just a few years." Ash shook his head.

"They're remarkable. They set aside their differences, created a world government—mostly based on democratic principles, though with a strong military—and they made astounding technological advances in a very short time. All of it done in anticipation of this moment. They spent years and years waiting and planning, until today, Invasion Day. That's what they call it. And we're it, we're the invaders."

There was silence on the bridge. Terry's face went pale. Linae studied her bridge crew, hoping someone would have an idea. Instead, she saw that they all looked to her. *How wonderful to be captain*. She turned to Ash.

"I don't know," he said. "I don't know how we make this right."

Linae didn't know either. She had ignored the Donasi "stay away" message determined to find out what alien species had come here and why, only to learn that Earth Space Command was at fault. And now the situation had become hostile.

Captain Destructo at work. So she gave the only order she could think of. "Let's go home."

The nine Donasi ships completely encircled the *David Roy*, blocking all avenues of exit. Linae would have to get one of the ships to move. Of course, the *David Roy* could attack the Donasi vessels to clear a path. Linae refused to consider that option. No, Linae would have to get through to Ben Ami. Linae told Flare to open the commlink. "Commander Ben Ami, we acknowledge that we trespassed into your space. We respectfully request permission to leave."

Immediately the nine Donasi ships responded with a unified blast of their energy pulse weapons. It barely shook the bridge.

"Why are they so stupid?" Flare's fist banged against the console.

"What do you mean, Ensign?" Ash asked.

"They know they aren't hurting us. They know we can hurt them, yet still they keep at it. They can't win. It's stupid."

"No, it isn't," Terry said. "It's courage. It's Cerium 3 all over again. An invader, impossible odds, yet a refusal to give in. It's my husband and my sister and all the other Earth officers who died." She flushed and her voice shook. "The only difference is that this time we are the Hiturans."

No one answered her. Now Linae knew what she had recognized in Ben Ami: the face of all warriors who willingly enter into hopeless battle. She had seen it on her own captain and crewmates just a few months ago. *Terry is right, this is Cerium 3. But she's wrong, too.*

Linae stood up. She glared at each member of the bridge crew. "We are not the Hiturans."

Flare actually seemed to grow taller under Linae's gaze. Terry nodded her head and so did Batak. Ash gazed at Linae and gave her a small smile.

Linae addressed the bridge. "I want each of you to think. We want to create a path through the Donasi ships, but we don't want to damage them or cause casualties. Suggestions?"

"What if we grazed them with our pulse weapons, kind of pushed them instead of doing direct hits?" Ash asked. "Could we clear a path?"

"No way, Doctor," Flare said. "You saw what happened when we hit them with a blast at minimum power, and we weren't trying to push them then. Also, we'd probably have to hit them multiple times to push them. I doubt their ships could take that."

"Couldn't we modify the pulse beams to make them weaker— much weaker, enough so we could push the Donasi ships, but not damage them?" Terry asked.

"Maybe," answered Flare. "I've never tried to weaken one of our weapons. We'd have to hit their propulsion systems first, knock them offline and then push. We could try." He looked at Linae.

"How long?" she asked.

"I'm not sure, ma'am. At least twelve hours I think."

"Captain," Batak said. "Six more Donasi ships are on their way. They should be here in about seven minutes."

"I don't think we have twelve hours," Ash said.

Flare said, "Sure we do. Those six ships won't matter. They can fire on us for twelve years and our shielding would hold."

Ash said, "According to their broadcasts, this is the last of their fleet. They have no more ships. I'm not worried about their weapons. I'm worried what they'll do once they realize that six more ships don't matter. I think they may already realize that."

Linae nodded. "I think you're right. I'm surprised Ben Ami waited this long."

316

"Waited for what?" Batak asked.

"They're going to ram us," said Terry. "That's what we were going to do at Cerium 3. Captain Milton gave the order. But then the Hiturans withdrew. It was this ship that did it, that saved us." She laughed. "That's why I was so happy to get this assignment, to be on the *David Roy*, the ship that stopped the Hiturans. Now look at us, the evil invaders."

"Ensign Terry," Ash said.

"It's okay, Doc. I'm fine," she answered.

Linae sighed. "Mr. Flare, if they ram us, will our shielding hold?"

"We would have damage. Of course, the Donasi would not survive."

Batak said, "Captain, their ships are nuclear-powered. If any of their ships rammed us, depending on what debris falls into the atmosphere, parts of the planet may be contaminated. Thousands of the Donasi could become sick or die."

Linae felt her heart thudding. *No. I can't infect another world.*

Flare said, "Maybe we should blast one or two of their ships now and clear a path. Yes, it would destroy those two ships, but we could hit the debris before it enters the planet's atmosphere. If they ram us and we're damaged, we might not be able to contain the debris. Taking out two of their ships now is better than letting their atmosphere get poisoned."

Ash leaned over. "Linae, once these last ships arrive, eventually Ben Ami will reach the same conclusion we have, if he hasn't already. They will ram us. There's no other choice for them."

Linae stood in silence. The rest of the bridge crew waited quietly for her decision.

She asked, "How long until the other six ships arrive?"

"Approximately two minutes," Batak answered.

Flare said, "I've targeted two of their ships. Respectfully, Captain, if we wait for the other ships, then we may have to target three or four of them."

"It's all right, Linae," Ash whispered. "It's not like you have a choice."

Ash always seemed to be saying that. We have no choice. We do what we have to.

Linae looked at each member of her bridge crew. Flare's hands were poised above his board, waiting for the order. Batak checked his screen.

"Captain, the ships will be here in one minute."

Linae gazed toward the main screen. She knew she should give the order, but a thought floated in her brain and wouldn't leave. *Why isn't there a choice?* She wondered if, when the Hiturans started the war with Earth, they also thought there was no choice. *Maybe we did do something to them. Maybe we just didn't understand.*

Now no one would ever know.

"Thirty seconds," Batak said.

Linae knew what to do. It was, she realized, the only act that would have made the Earth Space Command ships pause in their suicidal efforts against the Hiturans. Linae sat down in the captain's chair. "Open the commlink, Mr. Flare."

Flare's hands still hovered over the weapons board. "Ma'am?"

"Commlink, Mr. Flare. Now."

"Yes, ma'am." Flare hit the switch and nodded to Linae.

"Commander Ben Ami, this is Captain Tower of the Earth Space Command vessel *David Roy*." Linae took a deep breath. "We surrender."

Linae ignored the surprised reaction from her crew and waited for Ben Ami. For several seconds, the Donasi did not respond.

Ben Ami's image filled the main screen. "Repeat yourself, *David Roy*."

Linae stood. "We trespassed in your space. It was wrong. We wish to surrender. What are your terms?"

Around Ben Ami chaos erupted. Several Donasi, some in uniform, some not, were hurrying behind him, while others manned what appeared to be a communications network. One small Donasi kept trying to hand Ben Ami something, an earpiece perhaps, then shoved a tablet at him, but Ben Ami ignored them all. He stared at Linae. She stared back.

Batak said, "The six other Donasi ships have arrived."

Linae did not acknowledge Batak. She kept her eyes locked with Ben Ami. Slowly the chaos behind Ben Ami quieted. The *David Roy*'s bridge crew barely moved. It was just Linae and Ben Ami.

Finally, Ben Ami began to sway his head side to side. His blue-green eyes closed slightly and the wrinkles deepened in his face. And then he barked what could only be a Donasi laugh.

"Captain Tower, our terms are simple. We want you to leave and not come back."

Linae nodded. "Ben Ami, you lead a brave people and a generous one. We accept your terms."

Ben Ami gestured to two of his aides.

Batak said, "Three of their ships have moved away. We're clear to leave."

Ben Ami raised both his hands even with his head. "Goodbye, *David Roy*. You are not the invaders we expected. We may need to rethink this 'victory' of ours. Perhaps one day, we'll meet again."

"I welcome that day," Linae said. She nodded to Flare and the commlink was broken.

"Ensign Terry, get us out of here," she said.

"Yes, ma'am!"

Linae sank back in her chair.

"That was magnificent," Ash said. "What would you have done if his surrender terms had been unreasonable?"

She shrugged. "I don't know. Negotiate, I guess."

Ash laughed. "Well, so long Captain Destructo. What will it be now? Captain Peace? Captain Surrender?"

Linae smiled. For the first time in months, her stomach felt fine. She was even hungry. "Captain Tower will do."

The Rewards of Imagination

BY CRAIG ELLIOTT

Craig Elliott is an artist based in Los Angeles, California. He received his education at the famed ArtCenter College of Design in Pasadena, California, and studied under artists such as Harry Carmean and Burne Hogarth. Craig's carefully crafted and arresting images of nature and the human form have captivated audiences with their visual and intellectual celebration of the beauty in this world and beyond.

A multifaceted artist, he is also an accomplished landscape architect, sculptor, and most recently, jewelry designer. Especially known for his exceptional ability with the human figure and creative composition, Craig's work has evolved into a unique vision informing and influencing fine art, print, animation, and commercial worlds.

In addition to his fine-art work, Craig has had a hand in designing many of today's most popular animated films from studios such as Disney and Dreamworks including Hercules, Mulan, The Emperor's New Groove, Treasure Planet, Shark Tale, Flushed Away, Bee Movie, Enchanted, Monsters vs. Aliens, *and* The Princess and the Frog *as well as other upcoming features. Craig has also created fully painted comic book and cover artwork for Dark Horse Comics, World of Warcraft trading cards, editorial illustration for* Realms of Fantasy *magazine, and more. His work can currently be seen in the books* Treasure Planet: A Voyage of Discovery, The Art of The Princess and the Frog, *fifteen years of* Spectrum: The Best in Contemporary Fantastic Art, The World's Greatest Erotic Art of Today *volume 2,* Erotic Fantasy Art, Fantasy Art Now *volume 2,* Aphrodisia I, *and another twenty, too many to list here.*

The Rewards of Imagination

Imagination takes skill, hard work, and courage to release. We visual artists need years of training in perspective, anatomy, light and shadow, color and composition. One can dream up upside-down worlds made of drinking-straw people living on snake mountains that writhe through a slimy dark sea, but without these hard-won art skills, we can't communicate our ideas in powerful and convincing ways.

The world around us also wants to fight us and stop us from being imaginative. Teachers and parents accuse us of daydreaming, or tell us that what we are doing doesn't make sense or a difference to the world or to them. As we grow older, we are told that the only things that matter are good grades, fitting into society, and gathering skills for a pre-prescribed job type. Even when we do gather our skills and are able to express ourselves, our art can be limited by others who lack imagination.

I was once told that a dragon I painted didn't look like a dragon, and I needed to repaint it. Think about that for a second. Nobody has ever *seen* a dragon, so how can one idea of a dragon ever be incorrect? And you might say, well, maybe they wanted to see a traditional dragon? What does that mean? What culture, what part of the world, and when should that traditional dragon come from?

Imagination is one of the greatest gifts we can give the world. Imaginative stories, images, and ideas give us a place to occupy in which we can be free, relax, and experience the thrill of new and novel ideas. When reading a book like *Lord of the Rings*, we can forget our own cares and difficulties and actually balance our psychological state with a space to go into, far from daily life and its worries.

As I write this, the world is exceptionally full of stressors that need balancing. A global pandemic, terrible fires in my native state of California and across the western United States, economic disasters, joblessness, and much more. Without artists and imagination, we would all be so much worse off, and have far fewer tools with which to cope, and no place to escape to in order to feel normal, even for an hour or two. Imagine if there were no movies, TV shows, books, or video games for escape. I think you can see how important this is to the people of our planet.

Yes, there are a world of skills to learn to be able to express our ideas, but the benefit for all people is clear, and worth the effort it takes. You can reach others, heal them, thrill them, make them cry with joy, and lift their hearts with your imagination and ideas. You can make new worlds that have never existed before, and your audience can feel calm and relaxed as they stroll through your landscapes and worlds in their minds.

Many people ask me how they too can dream up worlds like the ones I have created, such as the underworld in Disney's *Hercules* or the Victorian high-tech alien landscapes, language, and symbols of Disney's *Treasure Planet*. I always try to explain that there is not just one kind of imaginative artwork, and that the process is fairly simple when you understand the procedure.

Imaginative art lies on a spectrum ranging from fully borrowed to reinvented to completely novel. A film such as *Avatar* clearly borrowed many of its imaginative visual ideas from the artwork of Roger Dean, and so much so that there is a legal battle around it!

Most imaginative works fall somewhere in the middle of the spectrum, in the reinvented range. A company such as Disney reinvents its films intentionally, most often borrowing from elements of previous films to merge with new ideas. This is done so that the look and feel of Disney films are maintained more or less throughout their catalog, and their audience knows what to expect when they see something associated with the Disney brand.

At the extreme novel end of the spectrum lies artistic ideas that are either inspired by completely unrelated ideas or are created with no inspiration point. The former is a far more common and easy way to arrive at a novel idea. Combining things that are not normally associated with one another to create novel ideas takes advantage of how the human mind actually works. It is thought that the mind organizes any new stimulus in relation to previous stimuli. The mind is a relational database of sorts. The smell of burnt toast might have associations with things like a toaster, breakfast, or your grandfather who liked his toast well done. A carrot could be associated with salads, gardening, chicken pot pie, and more. These associations help us navigate the world. If we hear screeching tires and smell burning rubber behind us, our previous associations help us quickly realize that it might be a car about to hit us and we had better get out of the way—even if we do not actually see the car yet.

These associations cause a hindrance when we are trying to think of a novel idea. Our minds can become trapped, only associating carrots with salad and dogs with pets. But what about a dog made of carrots? We have no previous reason to associate these things to one another. This is a novel idea.

One or more ideas, objects, smells, sounds, etc., that in most people's minds are not normally associated with one another create a novel idea when combined. It is often even better for something like illustrating a story or a script for a film if those associations are not just randomly unassociated things but also have meaning to the story in some way.

An example of this from my career is the language and symbology that I designed into the alien technology for Disney's *Treasure Planet*. The directors asked me to design many alien buildings and the planet itself as a machine. There were possible needs in the script to show words in a foreign tongue. And I thought it would work well to extend that design into a decoration or a language so complex to us that the language looked more like alien decoration. I could have pulled ideas from several sources that were not normally associated with language, but I wanted to derive my symbols from something that had meaning or a connection to the story itself. The inspiration for *Treasure Planet*'s story came from the Scottish novelist Robert Lewis Stevenson's book *Treasure Island*. In prehistoric Scotland and England, stones were carved with concentric circular motifs and lines. Later, in the 1990s, a number of late-night artists repurposed these symbols to create the famous English crop circles. This seemed like a perfect symbology that was not associated with any type of language yet and had a wonderful connection to the origin of the *Treasure Planet* story. This is the kind of ideal and novel imaginative concept that I strive for. One cannot expect to always be able to join these things together, but it can happen if you try!

Even with the rewards of striving to be imaginative, the path of an artist can be a bumpy one at times. Because of the very way our minds work, and as I explained above, people can find imagination jarring. Something out of the ordinary or unexpected is a way that horror filmmakers and writers scare us! Some people will be wary of your art at first or even put off by it. Film studios and publishers will usually reject imaginative ideas in favor of concepts they know and understand or that have made money before. As a result, the imaginative approach has always been an uphill battle in some way.

The creative world is filled with stories of creators butting heads with studios, publishers, or patrons. George Lucas had Twentieth Century Fox shaking in their boots, and they even fired the executive in charge of *Star Wars* in the process, most likely due to fear and anger over something they didn't associate with something they already understood. I tell you this so you know that it happens to everyone, even the greats.

The rewards of being creative are so wonderful and long lasting that the bumps in the road are truly minuscule in comparison. Works such as *Star Wars* and *Lord of the Rings*, and the work of artists such as Hieronymus Bosch or Moebius are creations that have lasted and will likely last forever.

In the end, the pleasure given and the endless fascination created for people are some of humanity's most precious treasures; they bring calm happiness and momentary escape through which we can all rebuild our strength and psyche. L. Ron Hubbard himself clearly understood and summarized what I have said when he wrote that "A culture is as rich and capable of surviving as it has imaginative artists." You are vital, and you are needed. Without artists to hold a mirror to it, society cannot see its weaknesses and failings and overcome them. Artists can see what the average person cannot. Heed the call and give strength and wisdom to us all. This is your birthright and function as artists!

The Museum of Modern Warfare

written by
Kristine Kathryn Rusch

illustrated by
ISABEL GIBNEY

ABOUT THE AUTHOR

International bestselling writer Kristine Kathryn Rusch has won awards in almost every fiction genre. She writes romance as Kristine Grayson and mystery under the name Kris Nelscott (as well as under the Rusch name). She's the first female editor of The Magazine of Fantasy & Science Fiction. *She retired from that job at the age of thirty-seven, although she still edits anthologies in her spare time. She owns a number of businesses, including a publishing company. She's the only person to ever win a Hugo for both editing and writing. She also writes a popular publishing blog. The latest installment appears on her website, every Thursday. Every Monday, on the same website, she puts up a short story for free for one week only.*

A few years ago, Kris published "The Museum of Modern Warfare" as the free short story on her website for Memorial Day. That became the most popular story she'd ever put on the website. The story hits a chord, so she figured WotF readers would like it as well.

ABOUT THE ILLUSTRATOR

Isabel Gibney is also the illustrator for "The Redemption of Brother Adalum" in this volume. For more information about her, please see page 185.

The Museum of Modern Warfare

Flew into Craznaust on an orbit-to-ground vehicle. I don't plan my own schedule, so I had no idea we'd be traveling in an upgraded C-73. I would have protested more, if I knew.

The guts of the C-73 are completely different nowadays, and—they say—so's the interior. But the advance team used the C-73 because of its innate stability, something any vehicle needs around Craznaust.

Craznaust, the central island in the largest chain on Gephherd, has its own microclimate. Daily winds of eighty kilometers per hour, sustained.

Drove us crazy when we deployed there forty years ago. I still remember the grit in my hair, on my tongue, in my nose. The wind left my skin chapped and my ears raw. Hats didn't help, nothing helped, and the goggles we had to wear over our eyes, they left their marks too.

I still have a tiny white scar from those goggles beneath my right lid, puckering the skin slightly. Doctors always touch their right eye, and nod toward me silently to tell me they can repair that scar with the brush of some magical medical device. I always walk away from docs like that. They're younger than me now, and they don't understand badges of honor.

I got that scar before the Battle of Craznaust, and consider the scar my badge because living on Craznaust day to day was harder than that battle, and in its own way, more devastating.

I've lived through dozens of battles, lost hundreds of friends to combat, but none of it haunts me like that year before the Battle of Craznaust broke out, when we were training the locals, coping with the wind, and pretending that nothing was going to happen to us.

I told my husband (the first one) when I finally left active duty (the first time) that the waiting was the hardest. He was career military too, but admin mostly, and he just looked at me like I'd grown a third head.

"You were lucky you weren't in combat the entire time," he said. "Some units fought for their full eighteen months."

I suppose he didn't mean to be dismissive. At the time, I even knew he was right. We had lost a quarter of our people that year because they were sent to other units, to replace folks who died.

Even back then we tried to fight our wars remotely, but some things can't be done by drones or bots or whatever form of fighting machine we come up with. Sometimes, when you're fighting an enemy as technologically talented as the Dylft, you don't send in unmanned equipment at all, for fear that equipment will get repurposed within the hour and deployed against you.

Yeah, we learned that the hard way, and yeah, it was ugly. Read the accounts of the war if you don't believe me. Because I'm not rehashing it here.

In fact, the only reason I'm reporting this now is because I'm required to. I waited until the last minute to compose this, partly out of a habit I learned in the Dylft Wars and partly because I needed to get away from Gephherd so that I could think clearly.

I know I'll touch this thing up, take out half the personal crap—hell, take out *all* of the personal crap—but I learned when I took this job almost a decade ago that I had to do a primary draft, because the personal always creeps in.

And there's a lot more personal than the official record shows.

For starters, I lied at my confirmation hearing for my nomination as Ambassador to the Dylft System. I didn't lie about the "important" stuff, like my politics or my inability to be influenced by money, or fame. I lied about the war's impact on me.

The Members of Parliament's questions—CYA questions—echo in my mind as I dictate this draft:

—*Ma'am, do you have any lingering emotional scars from your experiences in the Dylft Wars?*

—*Mr. Minister, according to the reports which you received in my nomination packet from the doctors in the various institutes of health, I have no lingering emotional scars from any war in which I served.*

—*Yes, Ma'am. We're familiar with your documentation. But we're asking you now, under oath, if you believe you have any lingering emotional scars.*

—*No, sir, Mr. Minister. I do not believe I have any lingering emotional scars, and it would be improper to offer to show you the physical ones I've opted to keep as reminders of my service.*

[general laughter]

I do not *believe* I have any lingering emotional scars. I *know* I have lingering emotional scars. In my defense, I also believed at the time of the hearing that I could conquer those emotions. Ambassador to the Dylft System mostly meant dealing with protocols and fussy meetings with members of my own species. I could—and did—designate underlings to handle negotiations with the various aliens of the system, holding meetings with the representatives of those alien groups only after the topics had been vetted, the discussions preapproved right down to the handshake (or tentacle rub).

Once appointed, I got to design my position, so I didn't have to worry about the nitty-gritty of cultural investigation, the tiny moments of introduction before a topic was broached in which anything could go wrong, the inevitability of bad translations or communications errors.

My staff dealt with those things, and I appeared for the document approvals, the live-on-camera record of a preplanned event, the state dinners (in which half the diners sat in a different room with completely different atmosphere), the balls, the formal speeches, the ceremonies—the things that needed a figurehead, and I was the figurehead that would do.

My actual work consisted of meetings with my staff, listening to arguments, approving things—things that I could handle, even with my emotional scars.

I was appointed, and ultimately sent to the Dylft System because I understood it, because I spoke five of its languages fluently (and understood fifteen more without an in-person or automated translator), and because I did ceremony well.

I did not expect (nor had I experienced) a meeting that wasn't vetted, approved, and rehearsed. For that reason, I tried to get someone else to handle the crisis on Craznaust.

I failed.

Which was why I was heading to Craznaust with an entourage of five, a security detail of ten, and a mountain of lingering emotional scars clawing at my heart.

The thing about Craznaust:

It's beautiful. Golden-white sand beaches, emerald-fronded trees with golden bark, the bluest lagoons I've ever seen, and rich, powerful sunlight that bathes everything in a bright but forgiving light.

On my first approach decades ago, I thought I had received the best posting anyone possibly could, particularly in a time of war. An island paradise with warm temperatures, Earth-like vistas, and naturally grown food that I could actually eat.

Then I stepped outside the arrival vehicle into the dry air and felt the water leach from my skin. The wind buffeted my body and I staggered sideways, thinking the gust was part of a storm, not part of a normal day.

I later learned that the storms were something else entirely, with winds that could literally shred anything in their path. We barely had shelter that stood up to storms, and finally learned how the locals survived.

They burrowed.

They had gorgeous cities belowground, reforming water-made caverns into well-lit, well-apportioned rooms that seemed to go on forever.

But for our first few months we didn't know that and the Cranks, as we call the locals, didn't tell us.

They didn't tell us most things.

The Cranks were humanoid bipeds with two arms and four hands. The second pair of hands could emerge from a slit in their arms, almost as if someone had given them all automated limbs. Those second pair of hands allowed the Cranks to carry large items on one side of their bodies without raising one arm and allowed them to hold weapons while moving machinery or rocks or whatever we needed.

The Cranks also had a second set of eyes, but we didn't learn that for months either. The eyes were literally on the back of their heads, and their hair—or that straw-like stuff that passed for hair—separated like curtains being pulled apart when the Cranks needed to look at something behind them. The elbows on their regular arms bent in either direction, although when the Cranks were near us, they rarely used the arms in that backward way.

The extra arms swiveled from that arm slit, so if the Cranks needed to hold something behind their backs, they could.

There were other differences in their anatomy that we didn't learn until a few Cranks died in maneuvers and our resident doctor decided to act like a coroner—causing one of the most disturbing incidents at the base.

The Cranks hated having someone unsanctioned touch their dead.

We had a mutiny on our hands, and I had been the one to quell it—only because I was the only one who had attempted to learn Naust, the Cranks's language. I talked to them as best I could, told them (as best I could) that we hadn't meant harm, and convinced them that we had simply made a logical error based on our own customs.

And then we went back to our not-quite-harmonious existence.

The Cranks weren't that interested in fighting the Dylft. The Cranks just wanted everyone off their island chain and we had gotten there first, with a promise of aide, personnel, and equipment.

Until this past week, I thought that if the Dylft had arrived first, the Cranks would've fought with them.

No matter.

What matters is this: we arrived first, we trained the Cranks, and together we fought—and won—one of the turning-point battles of the war, if not *the* turning-point battle.

Once Craznaust was secure, we parted as allies who had gone through something harrowing and escaped to the other side with our lives more or less intact.

I'd like to say I never thought of the Cranks and Craznaust again, but I still dream in Naust, mostly in long, pleading conversations as I try to get the Cranks to use weaponry designed for two-handed bipeds or to line up in proper military formation or learn how to run any piece of our unmanned equipment.

The Cranks brought bodies to that major battle—thousands of them—and a fierce fighting style that startled even us. In that first blood-filled day we lost 5,000 Cranks, 1,000 humans, and sixteen large enemy vessels that we later discovered carried crew of more than 10,000 apiece.

Crank casualties went up the next day as they invaded the vessels approaching their island, but the Cranks (not us) destroyed another twenty-five vessels.

It was only when the untrained Cranks were all that remained that the humans stepped up. We were the ones who designed the last day's battle, and we didn't take out the attack vessels: we took out the command ship, an action which—to our surprise—also took out command ships all over the sector.

The Dylft didn't have a hive mind, but they had designed command ships based on that principle, and when a command ship got hit, another command ship took over. Only we hit so hard and in such a creative way that the attack went through the hive communication and into the operating systems, destroying hundreds of command ships and hundreds of less-important vessels.

We won the sector because the Cranks's fierceness held the island chain long enough for us to plan that final attack—which, if I'm truly honest with myself, we screwed up. We never meant to put so much power into that first strike on the command ship. If that accident hadn't happened, our base on Craznaust would've been overrun or destroyed, taking out the Cranks as well.

Because the Cranks had no habitat anywhere else on Gephherd. The Cranks stuck to their island chain and generally refused to interact with others in the universe.

Of course, we hadn't known that when we approached them with an alliance in mind.

But we learned it later. And I had already decided to remind them that we'd saved them from genocide as our C-73 landed on the newly cleaned off airstrip that we had built forty years before.

The wind buffers were back in place, and almost-clear sand was piled behind them in a familiar way. I had taught the Cranks how to put tarps on top of the sand so that it wouldn't get blown back onto the strip—and I had watched, when we flew out soon after the battle ended, as the Cranks pulled off the tarps, took down the wind barriers, and let the landing strip revert to its natural state.

The buildings near the strip looked neglected. The sand had eaten away the surface, and the normal nano-rebuilders had either failed long ago or simply weren't enough to put up with decades of sandblasting. One side of the old hanger had caved in, sand emerging from it as if the dune grew from fertile soil.

Behind the buildings that we'd built and the Cranks had abandoned were other structures, golden and solid, reflecting in the powerful sunlight. In fact, an entire community that hadn't existed forty years ago stretched along the bay, glimmering like a lost city from the worst kind of adventure stories.

The Cranks had taken our help and our technology and brought their architecture skills aboveground. The island no longer looked primitive and wild. Now it seemed like a wealthy community just waiting for tourists to arrive.

The C-73 landed with the usual bump and slide. The slide lasted just a bit longer than it should have. Apparently no one had cleared off every last bit of the sand.

Six members of the security team exited first. The remaining four protected me and my people. I took nothing, but my staff carried the required recording and uploading devices, the cameras, the tablets, and all of the little things that most diplomatic visits required. My personal assistant handled my clothing, in case I needed to change for some sort of state event.

The Cranks did not show up to greet us. In fact, no one led us to our quarters. Instead, we had received directions before we arrived, and as we approached a door swung open, revealing a beautiful but empty foyer in a house designed in the human style.

I was relieved to get inside. Even though I'd worn a thin skin-shield to protect me from the blowing sand, I could still feel the pellets as they bounced off my body. I shuddered the whole way there, that feeling even more intense than it was in my nightmares.

That was the moment—or series of moments—when I thought I might contact the PM and beg off, no matter how long it took. Or let my assistant take over while I hid inside the building.

But, as I walked into the cool windless shade of the interior, I realized I couldn't stay indoors long either. The constant susurration of the sand on the building's exterior was almost as bad as the sand hitting my skin.

I had forgotten that sound, and yet as I heard it I realized it haunted my dreams as surely as those arguments had. I just hadn't realized what that susurration was. The hackles were actually up on the back of my neck, and my entire body was on edge. My heart was beating so hard I thought maybe it was trying to pound its way out of my chest.

I must have had an odd expression on my face because Tempestad, my assistant, looked at me sideways.

"You all right, Ambassador?" she asked me.

"Yes," I said a little more curtly than I probably should have. "Let's just get over to the museum and get this thing done."

The Museum of Modern Warfare had become the centerpiece of Craznaust, commemorating the battle and condemning it at the same time. The Cranks had planned this thing for three decades, and the exhibits were in Naust, Dylft, English, and Arabic, as well as dozens of other human languages and all the languages of Gephherd.

Everything probably would have been all right if the Cranks had kept the museum to themselves. But when it was completed the Cranks sent a notification to all species in the sector, inviting them to virtually visit the museum.

Actual in-person visitors needed to go through rounds of applications and approvals. Veterans of the Battle of Craznaust received free admission, as well as overnight room and board if they agreed to a recorded interview about the battle for the museum's archives.

Oddly, the museum had sent me that very offer privately as we set up the diplomatic meeting, as if the museum's administrators didn't understand that such an offer violated diplomatic protocol. I sent a cordial response, telling them that as Ambassador arriving on an official visit, I did not have time for an interview.

I had seen the virtual museum on all the different Dylft War sites, along with the advertising that Craznaust was doing to promote their new (if inept) tourist economy. I had known that the virtual museum showed all of the displays mostly because of the responses I'd had from other vets who'd visited, so I was braced for the differences in the interior.

I was not braced for differences in the exterior.

The Museum of Modern Warfare rose from the center of Craznaust like a mountain out of the sea. The museum dominated the landscape. I had actually seen it when I emerged from the C-73, but I hadn't registered it as a building.

The museum's architects had done what the Cranks did best—they had used an existing rock structure to build the museum, only they had done it aboveground. Apparently they had hollowed out one of the major rock formations to place the museum inside.

The images that composed the exterior of the virtual museum were from the entrance only, a building that attached itself to the front of the mountain like a barnacle on the side of a boat.

The real entrance was gold, like everything else here, but unlike the new community built along the water's edge, the entrance sat in the shade of the mountain, so that the gold did not reflect the brilliant sunlight.

There was very little wind here because the entrance was tucked into a hollow on the side of the mountain, so the sand blew across the road in front of the entrance, but not across the entrance itself.

When I stepped into the mountain's shadow, the temperature went down dramatically, and the constant bombardment of fine grains of sand ceased. A level of tension left my body, and I stumbled.

Two different assistants grabbed my arm, and one asked if I needed a moment.

I didn't need a moment. I needed to get the hell out of here.

"No," I said. "I'm fine."

I also needed to keep moving, so I did.

I sent Tempestad to meet with the museum administrators, ostensibly to make certain that the proper protocols were being met. Not that there were proper protocols for this: I wouldn't set up a meeting with the Crank officials if I thought my contacts (and the PM) were overreacting.

Besides, if the museum officials wanted to see me, they should have greeted me when I got off the C-73.

Instead of talking to anyone in authority, I followed a map

that almost forty-five veterans had sent, taking me to the most offensive parts of the museum.

The information I had was fragmented, and mostly existed in a series of words:

    ...horrifying...

    ...disgusting...

    ...insulting...

Which wouldn't make this rise to a diplomatic incident if the Cranks had designed a standard museum display. But here's a quote from the first missive that caught all of our attention.

These are not images. And every single human figure on display is of someone whose body we never found.

The vets had their own theories for all of this, most believing that the Cranks were working off imagery of the war that we had never seen. Several, though, accused the Cranks of keeping the remains of soldiers and using them as the models for the replicas in the museum.

We had received other theories, but they were too fantastic to be believed, especially since they had come from vets who had never recovered mentally from their experiences on Craznaust.

We had sent one team ahead to investigate, and because of language (and diplomatic) issues, they were unable to get the Cranks to cooperate. The team wasn't even able to see the displays, because there were no Dylft War veterans among them. Only DW vets were allowed inside the combat displays of the museum itself.

I had brought Roberta Cantare, the only Dylft War vet left on my security staff, to accompany me to the displays. We walked past the public viewing areas, heads down.

I didn't need to see Dylft armor or the sandblasted laser rifles found after the battle ended. I didn't need to view the short holographic histories of the war. I didn't need to hear how the war started or how dramatically it ended.

I certainly didn't need to see the recreation of the human bases half-covered in sand. I was having troubles enough.

The floor sloped downward, and the air got cooler the deeper we went. The displays we were going to see were deep inside the mountain, and very hard to access.

I'd read the instructions for the museum before leaving. The only way Cantare and I could access these displays was to bring our war tags. These tags were actual artifacts, designed for creatures that we didn't want to scan us. The tags, no larger than my thumbnail, attached to the wrist and hung down like a bracelet. I kept mine framed in my office—the tags were useful for some diplomatic meetings—but Cantare had lost hers and had had to send away for a replacement.

We held up our tags as we hurried down the corridor. Section after section appeared before us, all of them labeled in Naust. All pretense of labeling in hundreds of languages had disappeared the deeper we got. A soft genderless voice did give us an interpretation in English of any sign we passed; I assumed the language was chosen because of the language on our tags.

Our presence brought up the labels, but the tags highlighted the doors to each room in a flaring blue that I remembered from forty years before. Cranks used that flaring blue as a welcoming beacon, something that encouraged movement forward.

We ignored the doors, though, and continued to follow the map. We rounded a corner, and the genderless voice said, "Room of Privilege."

"Crap," Cantare said, skidding to a halt. "Nothing's lighting up for me here."

I frowned. She couldn't see the blue-flaring door?

"It's lit up for me. You want to try going together?" I asked.

She threaded her arm through mine. Now I saw the door in flaring blue and flint-gray at the same time. The flint-gray was a Crank warning color, which they used the way we used red.

We walked forward and some kind of barrier sprang up in front of Cantare. A warning appeared in all of the languages. Then some fine print appeared in Naust.

"What does it say?" Cantare asked. Like so many who served here, she had never learned to read Naust. By the end of the tour, every soldier had acquired a smattering of Naust, but it was all verbal, never written.

Back then, most of the written Naust was belowground.

"It says that the age of your tags does not match the information on them," I said.

She looked at me. This was the turning point: either I went forward alone to see the display before I met with the administrators, or I went back and worked from a disadvantage.

My heart was still pounding, but not from the exertion. From simply being here.

I knew what I had to do.

I unthreaded my arm from Cantare's. "We've had no reports of deaths or injuries from that display," I said to her.

"But there's emotional distress," she said.

I smiled. It was a rueful smile. "Warriors always feel distress at the memorials established for their wars."

She tilted her head slightly. "You might come to harm. I'm supposed to protect you—"

"File half of your report now. Tell those bastards in those government watchdog offices that I'm intransigent. You couldn't stop me from going inside. Because you literally *can't* stop me."

I slipped past her, around that sign which explained why she couldn't move forward. The moment I stopped touching her, the blue-flaring door became brighter and a Naust sign leapt to life.

I read the words and immediately translated them in my head: *Honor Room.*

I frowned slightly and wiped my sweaty palms on my pants. I took the remaining steps to the door, then touched its edges.

Like any good door designed by the Cranks, it slid open silently. I glanced over my shoulder at Cantare. She still appeared to be looking at the sign and I realized that, from her perspective, I was probably inside that gray haze. If she saw me at all, I probably appeared as an outline or a moving shape.

I squared my shoulders and fixed my posture. For the first

time since I got here, I felt like the soldier I had been all those years ago. I shuttled my emotions to one side and focused on the task at hand.

I needed to see this horrifying, disgusting, insulting display with clear eyes—not to condemn, but to understand.

I stepped inside.

Initially, the room was dark, and for that brief second I worried that I too lacked the proper identification.

Then, in the distance, bright red light flared from above, illuminating a holographic image of soldiers heading into a dust cloud caused by the Dylft ships.

My breath caught: I remembered seeing that. We all remembered it, those of us who survived. It was the last moment before the insanity descended, the last moment before total war engulfed us for days.

Back then, the thwap-thwap-thwap of the approaching ships had nearly deafened us. The wind from their engines mingled with the wind that constantly blew over Craznaust and caused eddies of sand to rise up like long-dead warriors.

After that one moment of clarity—the one commemorated here—the chaos enveloped us: sand, sand devils, Cranks, humans, machinery, and the Dylft, wearing their beautiful white technologically advanced armor. The sand stopped up the joints, and locked half of the invading army in position, but didn't stop their weapons from working.

The Cranks had gone first—of course—using their noncomputerized weaponry, so much more sophisticated than any nontech weapons that humans had. We had fought wars with noncomputerized equipment, but centuries and centuries ago. The Cranks still used those weapons every day; they were adept at them. They had tried to train us, but we were like children in comparison to the Cranks's expertise.

It had been their idea to surround the Dylft, not ours; their idea to attack with noncomputerized weaponry, not ours;

their idea to cut their enemy to shreds with weapons we would have called swords, knives, and bayonets if those words didn't already have slightly different meanings for us.

The Cranks did manage to sever the Dylft body armor, but at great cost. All of those Crank lives, exploding in boiling purple blood. All of those screams—literally inhuman and just as terrifying as one of our own.

I ran a shaking hand over my face as the image vanished. My heart was pounding harder than it had at the actual battle. Then, I'd been filled with adrenaline, and all of that confidence that boredom brings. I *wanted* a battle; I *wanted* something different.

I just hadn't realized how ridiculous that wanting had been.

More lights. I let my hand fall. The lights, filled with images, didn't last as long this time.

Light
Cranks surrounding a Dylft ship.
Darkness
[Pause]
Light
Cranks overrunning Dylft warriors, frozen in the sand.
Darkness
[Pause]
Light
A single Crank chopping a Dylft warrior in half.
Darkness
[Pause]
Light
Humans trying to rescue wounded Cranks.
Darkness
[Pause]
Light
A single human fighter holding back the second Dylft incursion, using only a single repeating laser rifle.
Darkness
[Pause]

"Go back," I said in Naust. My voice sounded foreign, even

to my ears. Some of that was the shaking. Some of it was the echoey quality. I realized that these images weren't occurring in complete silence. The rush of two winds slapping against each other sounded as loud as it had that day.

I had just tuned it out.

Light

The single human fighter, a starburst on the back of his uniform, holding back the second Dylft invasion with only a laser rifle.

Darkness

[Pause]

"Again," I said in Naust, voice no longer shaking. "And hold on that image."

Light

The single human fighter, a starburst on the back of his uniform, standing alone in front of dozens of Dylft pouring out of ships. Something in his stance, the way his shoulders rounded, the angle of arms—

My eyes knew it before my brain did, because tears were streaming down my face.

"Jorge," I whispered as I stepped forward. "Jorge."

Jorge Domingos Cantos. Six feet tall and bronzed from the Craznaust sun. Worked shirtless half the time, regulations be damned. No one wrote him up. No one even complained.

Somehow those bronzed muscles enveloped me, held me in the nighttime, gave me comfort against that susurrating sound, helped me forget the numbing slice of the continual wind.

I never told anyone about him. Not my husband. Not my old friends and not my colleagues in later battles. Jorge was mine. And somehow, he and I, even in the middle of that wind-blown hell, believed in a future. We could almost see it, like a cloudless day on the horizon, waiting for us—after we had fixed our home lives for the better.

But we didn't speak of it much. Instead, we moved forward, each and every day. Doing our duty and tending to each other.

343

ISABEL GIBNEY

I bandaged his wind burns, mentally catalogued the white scarring along the surface of his pecs as the sand dug grooves into his skin. Mentally catalogued because I couldn't actually catalogue them: Jorge wouldn't let me.

They'll make me repair the scars, he said, *and I want them to know how difficult the day-to-day is at this posting, how devastating the constant wind can be.*

He ministered to half the squad, especially those who contracted wind madness. We didn't know what else to call it, but that unceasing noise, the slap of the sand, the way that nothing rested here, made some of our squad unable to function.

He was the one who negotiated with the Cranks to allow us our own cavern underground. He set up the rotating schedule so no one spent more than six hours in the wind. He made certain that the wind-mad got three full days of rest before ever returning to duty—and that duty never occurred aboveground.

And he hadn't been our commanding officer. Our commanding officer, the first to fall to the wind madness, later took credit for the changes, but the surviving members of the unit knew he hadn't done it.

Jorge had.

Jorge, who had set out on the third day of battle, with two rifles slung over his shoulder and one more in his hands. Jorge, who felt he was wind-toughened enough to survive anything.

Jorge—who had not come back.

The image freeze I had asked the museum for caught that moment between light and darkness, almost like the latter stages of dawn. Enough light to see by, but not enough to fully illuminate anything.

Jorge had painted that starburst on his uniform—against regulations—only as the battle progressed, figuring we needed a way to distinguish each other without using our computer systems. If we could distinguish with tech, he said, the Dylft could too.

He had been wrong about that: the Dylft hadn't had that

kind of tech. But his theory sounded good, and the commander approved it, and ultimately that idea did lead to rescues, rescues that happened days after Jorge had disappeared.

I let out a breath. I hadn't allowed myself to think about Jorge, to talk about him, or to remember him. I hadn't dared. I had needed to move forward.

But he shadowed my nightmares. Often I bandaged his skin. I never ever saw his face.

I made myself walk toward the display. I could see shadow displays on either side of me. From this angle, away from the door, I could see parts of the other displays as well.

Thin light reflected off Crank uniforms (and as I realized that, I remembered it was Jorge who nicknamed them Cranks, because the early negotiations he attempted for that underground space had ended so badly. That was why I decided to immerse myself in Naust. Not because I was bored or tired or even curious but because I too wanted out of the wind and assisting Jorge's negotiations seemed the best way to do it). The light marinated the Dylft figures in a semblance of reality—I hadn't realized they were almost as small as the Cranks—and cast shadows on the human fighters deeper in the display.

I didn't look at the other humans. Instead, I stumbled toward Jorge, who had been caught in that moment when everything looked possible, when he seemed like the conquering hero about to single-handedly vanquish the enemy.

He had vanquished the enemy, but not this enemy. The enemy he had vanquished had been that wind, the land, Craznaust itself. This last stand commemorated here, it meant little in the scheme of the battle. He had been one more soldier, attempting one more impossible task, with aplomb.

But he had gotten us to this battle. He had made it possible. His ingenuity, his strength, his creativity.

He had helped us survive so that we could figure out a way to defeat the Dylft once and for all.

I have no idea how long I stood there, staring at the display. Minutes maybe. Hours. I never asked my staff. Time seemed to have stopped.

I couldn't go around it. I couldn't look at the face. I didn't want to see the details that would be slightly off as they always were in replicas. I didn't want to see his fake eyes.

But I couldn't stand forever. So, finally, I reached up, and touched the arm of the Jorge replica—and screamed.

I had fallen to my knees. I forced myself to get up and touch the arm again.

The *skin* again.

I remembered that skin. It showed up in my dreams. When we'd arrived on Craznaust, Jorge's skin had been almost unnaturally smooth and had an odd softness that I'd never felt on a man's skin before.

By the last days before the battle his skin was chapped, pitted, and scarred, but beneath that the odd softness remained, as if part of him were made of butter.

And this model, this replica—it had that oddly soft texture beneath the pitted and scarred surface.

As I peered closer I saw the map of white scars, the ones I had bandaged myself. I traced my fingers over them, felt the pits, felt the raised skin, saw the small hairs.

No replica was this accurate.

No replica *could* be this accurate.

The Cranks didn't have that kind of tech—did they?

My heart was pounding. I would get my answer when I walked around him, when I looked at that face.

But I might have had my answer even before I moved, because of those contacts, those reports from the vets about this room.

It was

...*horrifying*...

...*disgusting*...

...*insulting*...

But somehow, not.

347

I was calmer than I had been since I arrived, maybe calmer than I'd been in forty years. The shaking had left my body. The shock had either numbed me or left me, I wasn't certain which.

I let out a small breath, realizing that if this was Jorge, if his body stood here in this defiant pose, then I would finally know what had happened to him.

He had clearly died shortly after this, outnumbered and alone, defending all of us.

The Cranks weren't recording images of the battle. They were recording those moments just before the end—those last hopeful moments, as the future loomed on the horizon.

Each display told a story, and each story was of impossible odds, and unimaginable courage.

And, unlike our human memorials, this display did not tell a story of loss.

The story of loss was private, and only in the eye of the beholder.

I swallowed hard, and took a deep breath, remembering (because I had forgotten for a brief moment) that I too was a soldier, and I too had faced things that seemed impossible at the time.

Facing the front of this display seemed impossible right now. So I did it.

I walked around the display and peered up and saw—

Jorge's long-lost well-loved face, grooved and pitted and chapped by the sand, his eyes not quite empty but not quite his, looking forward at the last few moments of his life, his mouth open ever so slightly in anticipation of the fight to come, and the determination in the tilt of his head, the rise of his chin.

He hadn't been thinking about his death. He hadn't been thinking about the impossibility of what he was about to do.

He had simply been about to do it.

That was his face and that had probably been his expression in that last hopeful moment just before the end. The Cranks had captured it, and they revealed it here, in what they called the Honor Room.

It was not a room of privilege. Someone, a Crank probably, had chosen the wrong translation of the word "honor." The room was not reserved for the privileged few. It was there to honor those who had died for us—human and Crank alike.

And it was open only to those who would truly understand what these sacrifices meant.

I reached up, touched the hand gripping the rifle, remembering the feel of those fingers on my skin.

And then I walked away, unable to look at the rest of the display, all the others being honored, because I was too overwhelmed by what I had seen already.

When I finally emerged, I found Cantare still standing near that sign that had blocked her entry. Only now she was surrounded by Crank security and three Cranks who, by their blue outfits, had to be some of the administrators.

I felt wrung out, emotionally exhausted. My eyes ached from unshed tears. But I straightened my spine and nodded at every single one of them.

"Are you all right?" Cantare asked.

"Yes," I said without looking at her. My focus was entirely on the Cranks around me. I spoke in Naust. "That is an incredibly moving display."

Their bodies relaxed even though their expressions did not change.

"But," I said, "it highlights the difference between the way humans treat their dead and the way that Cranks treat theirs."

One of the Cranks let out a small "ah." A sound our two species shared. That sound made at the moment of recognition.

"Let's go talk," I said to them. "We need to figure out how to make both sides of our alliance understand what you have created here."

We walked down the corridor, past other displays that lit up, displays I did not want to see. I wasn't emotionally prepared for them.

I hadn't been emotionally prepared for this one.

But that didn't matter. The display had grabbed me and held me, and I knew that some nights, when I dreamed of that never-ending wind, that display would comfort me.

I had seen Jorge's face again.

I had to acknowledge how deeply he had touched my life and how traumatic his loss had been.

How ironic that the first thing I had to do after I saw him again was my job. Not my old job, but my new one.

I had to be a diplomat—a real diplomat.

I had to earn the title Ambassador.

I had never done that before.

But it mattered for both sides that I do it then.

Because I understood what so many had missed: This place, this carefully designed place, could heal us all—the way it had started to heal me.

A Demon Hunter's Guide
to Passover Seder

written by
Ryan Cole

illustrated by
JEFF WEINER

ABOUT THE AUTHOR

Ryan Cole is a lucky husband and father to one very spoiled pug child named Wally. After six years of living and working in contract negotiation in San Francisco, California, he has recently moved back home to Virginia to pursue his dream of writing full time. When not writing, Ryan likes to read epic fantasy, hike, and bake vegan treats that are quickly devoured. This is Ryan's first professional fiction sale.

ABOUT THE ILLUSTRATOR

Jeff Weiner is a serial entrepreneur, executive, and innovator. Jeff began his business career over forty years ago and has garnered many accolades during his tenure in a variety of businesses.

He received numerous honors from the software industry, including six Best of Show Awards for technological innovation and application. He has created and developed a wide range of products for companies such as AT&T, BMG Music, Sprint, McDonald's, Lucent, Dialogic, and many others.

As CEO of RocketTalk, Jeff teamed up with Paramount to bring the legendary Star Trek Communicator to the internet—an application promoted by Paramount immediately following each episode of Star Trek: Voyager.

Jeff was recognized as a Star of the Industry by Computer Telephony Magazine *and named one of the top twelve technologists to watch by the* Silicon Valley Reporter. *He has also been in numerous publications, including* Wired *and* Forbes. *He wrote, produced, and hosted* The Venture Catalyst, *a* PBS *television show that brought start-up companies together with a billion-dollar panel of venture capitalists. He has served on numerous boards and consulted for* NASA. *Recently he released a business book entitled* 71 Seconds to Funding.

Jeff decided to pursue his passion for art by entering the Illustrators of the Future Contest and won in the third quarter of 2020.

A Demon Hunter's Guide to Passover Seder

Rule number one: Don't drink uncovered water on the Sabbath.

Bubbe and my parents already know this rule well, after years of me and Zayde forcing them to remember, but David, for some reason, still pretends it's a joke. Scratch that—I think I know *exactly* the reason. Her name is Abigail Rollins (or Avigayil, as Bubbe calls her), and she has a long black ponytail in a polka-dot scrunchie, with a pale face of freckles that makes her look like a white giraffe. She is tall for a sixteen-year-old, but David says that's just me. He says everyone looks tall when you're only eleven years old.

Abigail and David are closer than ever, even after what she did to our family, and the sight of them holding their hands behind their backs and nuzzling the bridges of their freckle-covered noses makes me want to cast her into a pit where all of our demons can have her. She isn't even Jewish—well, maybe by birth, since her mother is Jewish—but that shouldn't count. Being Jewish by technicality is like winning a game of dominoes by stacking the tiles. It isn't the real thing.

Bubbe and my parents don't seem to mind though. They don't seem to mind much about anything anymore, not since we lost Zayde in the blur of last summer. Eight months isn't long enough to forget a family's anchor.

But tonight will be different. It is the end of the Sabbath on the week before Pesach, or Passover, as we say around Abigail, and with all of us gathered to partake in havdalah—Bubbe and

353

my parents, David and Abigail, myself and little Aaron—we reinstate the tradition that Zayde once led. It is the first that we have celebrated in a very long time.

"Here," says Bubbe, handing me a candle, its thick braids of wax like a blue-and-white scepter. "Place this on the mantle."

We surround the havdalah candle as Bubbe strikes a match, the flame casting ripples across our somber, watching faces. My mother reaches over and grabs the besamim, the small wooden box filled with spices that burn our noses. She takes one sniff and passes it to my father, who passes it to Aaron, who shimmies away in disgust.

"We light this candle to usher in the week, to remember who we have lost and find the strength to move forward." Bubbe then nods at me to approach the candle, the wrinkles in her cheeks soaking in its fleeing shadows.

We watch the reflection of the flame in our fingertips, and before I begin the blessing, I clear my throat.

"Barukh atah Adonai Eloheinu melekh ha'olam—"

Abigail giggles from the semicircle behind me, and I turn my head to see David tickle her ear, whisper something unheard that makes her giggle even more. My mother and father and Bubbe try their best to ignore them.

"Bo're m'orei ha'esh." I finish the prayer in a heated rush and glare at my older brother, who doesn't notice.

Bubbe walks up and pats me on the shoulder. "Well done, Noam. Zayde would be proud."

My throat feels tight at the mention of my grandfather. Bubbe, whose pale-green eyes and curly dark hair mirror my own, looks at me with one of her all-knowing expressions, silently acknowledging that she knows how much I miss him. She misses him too. "This will be a Passover to remember, I promise."

I hope that she's right, for all of our sakes. Zayde was the best demon hunter in the family, and with him gone and David entangled in Abigail's web, I am the Yesowitz family's only defense.

"Shavua tov," says my mother without a hint of expression, not a smile or a nod or the playful wink she used to give me, as if her muscles have forgotten how to work these last eight months.

"Shavua tov," says my father, but with more concern than passion. He is worried about my mother's impenetrable sadness.

"Shuva tuv," says Abigail, swimming in David's arms.

David doesn't reply. He chases her outside through the mesh screen door, to the tree in the backyard where they always go to kiss. But before they reach the lawn, Abigail picks up a glass, the one that she left uncovered on the porch's wooden banister. The one filled with water that she poured before havdalah.

I watch through the kitchen window as she takes a long, indulgent sip, oblivious to the evil that she so blatantly tempts.

"Shavua tov," I say to Bubbe, then follow the two of them outside.

David and Abigail sink into the darkness of the magnolia tree's bough, its branches drowning out the porch's two dim light bulbs.

There isn't much time. I need to act fast.

Abigail's water cup stares at me from the banister, empty yet menacing, biding its silence until the darkness between the porch and the tree coalesces, forms into a deep, yawning pit of endless black. And out from that abyss comes a snouted hog's face, covered in whiskers sharp as knives and strong as steel.

Shabriri, the demon of blindness, approaches me.

I turn up the porch light, but it doesn't dissuade her. Her empty eyes seek me through rheumy lenses, her bestial body slinking like a predator up the steps. Each of her six legs holds a fistful of claws, laced with poison from her gullet, and I know that if they touch me, I will be dead within a moment.

So, I do what Zayde taught me.

"Shabriri," I hiss so that my parents don't hear. They have enough to worry about with Pesach on the horizon. "Shabriri, briri, riri, iri . . ."

Each word lashes at Shabriri's skulking form, repelling her step by step into the eternally blind night, where she can wallow in the emptiness that she casts on all of her victims. The key to this demon is her very own name.

"Shabriri, briri, riri, iri..."

I repeat Shabriri's name until the demon herself is gone. Then I'm alone on the porch, victorious. Unbeaten.

Bubbe calls my name, and I shout for David and Abigail. A few more stolen kisses, then they eventually come inside, skipping by the empty glass that could have meant their doom. They don't even realize how close Shabriri had come.

I receive no thanks, nothing for my effort. And while Abigail finally leaves to go home, I am reminded of a very important rule number two: Don't associate with people that will summon your demons.

Rule number three: Prepare the mezuzahs and lock all the doors.

Well, all doors except the *front* door, that is. Elijah can't come if we don't allow him to enter, which, when I think about it, is strange. If a ghostly eternal prophet could endure through the millennia and act as the hand of Yahweh in all of his divine endeavors, it would follow that a wooden door shouldn't bar his passage. But sadly, I don't make the rules. I just follow them.

The night is finally here. The first night of Pesach, at the end of the week in which Abigail cursed havdalah. My mother and father are downstairs with Bubbe, preparing all the pieces of our intricate meal, and I am with Aaron inspecting our wards. It wouldn't be wise to leave ourselves vulnerable to Lilith and Ashmedai and their filthy, demon spawn. The succubus queen and her hell-crowned prince would never be welcome at a Yesowitz Seder.

Aaron and I start with the front door of the house. The mezuzah rests above the tip of my head on the door's right post, the glazed ceramic exterior tilted on its axis. This one doesn't worry me, but I check the klaf anyway. The thin, rolled scroll of parchment hidden within the casing slides out into my hand. My mother hired a sofer soon after Zayde died, and I hope that the scribe did his duty with diligence. I tap at the scroll to verify its integrity. Everything is intact—no tears, rips, or smudges—and I check two more times to make sure that I am right.

This step is critical. The mezuzah is our shield against rogue, hostile spirits, the barrier to anything that would seek to cause us harm. Which is especially important when the door is kept unlocked.

Unfortunately for me, it doesn't keep out girlfriends.

"Hi Noam," says Abigail from behind me on the driveway. Her muddy purple mountain bike lies abandoned on the curb.

"Hi Abby," says Aaron from the ground at my side. She tousles the curly brown hair on his head, then strolls through the door, unwanted and uninvited. Or so I would have thought.

"What's *she* doing here?" I say to Bubbe. "This is supposed to be a night for just us, just our family."

Bubbe grabs my hand. "Just let her be. She makes David happy, and I think we can all agree some happiness would be welcome. Don't be jealous of your brother."

"Jealous?" I say. "I'm not jealous at all. She keeps ruining our traditions. She's the only reason that Ketev Meriri came here."

The mention of the demon lowers Bubbe's eyes, makes her shoulders slump deeper than they were. "Go finish the mezuzahs." Then she waves me away and walks into the kitchen with the burden I gave her.

David and Abigail sit at the bottom of the staircase. They barely move aside as Aaron and I pass, clawing through a tangle of interwoven limbs. It's impossible to tell where David starts and Abigail ends.

"Can you help me with the mezuzahs?"

"Don't worry," says David, "looks like you've got it covered. I'm sure we can leave a few doors unguarded for one night." He says this into the space between Abigail's lips.

Aaron and I stomp past them up the stairs, and we stop at each room to lock its door. For each one, Aaron hands me a separate mezuzah that is filled with a sofer-inspected, tightly rolled klaf. One on David's door, one for our parents, one for Bubbe; but when we reach the door to my and Aaron's shared room, with its twin-size bunk beds shaped like race cars, the mezuzah doesn't stick. The grip of the doorframe won't hold up the casing.

"Noam!" calls my mother. "It's time for us to start!"

I panic, thoughts aflutter. There *has* to be a ward on every single door—I even put one on the closet and the bathroom and the attic. I won't take any chances with Abigail here, won't let her harm us with her ignorance. I close our bedroom door and slide the klaf underneath, making sure the parchment is buffered by the carpet.

I drag Aaron downstairs past David and Abigail, who like Zayde's demons, must have a weakness. There must be a way for me to expel her from our lives.

She doesn't care about Pesach, doesn't care about the destruction that her presence has already caused. Ever since she first came to the Yesowitz household, when she plucked David up from his most recent breakup, she has poisoned his mind and diluted his passion. He allowed her disbelief to become his own, and in doing so, she pulled him away from my demon-hunting side.

She is what summoned Ketev Meriri last summer, and *she* is the reason that Zayde is dead.

Rule number four: Avoid the outdoors between the fourth and ninth hours from the seventeenth day of Tammuz to the ninth day of Av. Those are the hours in which Ketev Meriri prowls, and that is when David and Zayde had their fight.

We are seated in the dining room around our humble table, Bubbe's famous melamine plates out on full display. Each of us is provided with a tray of assorted food, which we aren't allowed to eat yet, not for quite some time. But Abigail doesn't care. She pokes a hard-boiled egg and plops it into her mouth. David, by her side, picks at his tray and does the same.

"David," says my mother, "not until the prayer." She rests her chin in two grief-ravaged hands, the skin as thin as the klafs that hide within my warded mezuzahs.

David pretends to listen but only stops when Abigail does. She smiles at my mother through a papier-mâché facade. My mother smiles back at her with empty, robotic lips.

Abigail is a virus that feeds off its host. If I don't stop her soon, don't find her weakness, she will overcome each member of my slowly shrinking family.

I imagine what she said to David to convince him to drop out of Hebrew school. I picture the look on Zayde's face when David told him that he wasn't going back.

I remember listening from my bedroom on that nineteenth day of Tammuz, hearing the front door slam as Zayde stormed out onto the driveway. I remember watching him strut onto the black asphalt cul-de-sac, fuming with disappointment for his eldest, most precious grandson. I remember trying to yell through the glass cage of my window, to tell him to turn around and come back into the house.

Instead, he kept walking into the treacherous morning sunlight, toward the shade of the twin palm trees that our neighbors forced to grow, even though Connecticut is nowhere near tropical. That is when she came, the shadow-spawned demon. Ketev Meriri waited for the shade to touch Zayde, and as he was blinded by anger and sadness, she struck.

Her sole cyclopean eye trapped him in her gaze, and in one heart-stopping look she struck Zayde down. The doctors at the hospital all assured us it was a stroke, which my mother and father believed. But Bubbe knew the truth, and she believed me when I told her. David, on the other hand, scoffed and called me a child.

Something had attracted the attention of Ketev Meriri, some*thing* or some*one*, and Zayde paid the price. So, while David and Abigail can pretend what they want, that our demons don't exist, they are unknowingly relying on someone else to keep them safe.

But I can't protect them all by myself forever.

359

Rule number five: Pour each guest an odd number of wineglasses.

Or, I should say, an odd number for each *adult*. My father stands up and goes into the kitchen, opens the holiday cabinet to grab the Manischewitz. Bubbe always tells me that this is her favorite drink, but I don't really like it. Too sharp and sweet, like grape-flavored vinegar.

Lilith and Ashmedai and the rest of their brood don't care what type we pour, don't care how awful it tastes. Especially Agrath bat Mahaloth, the roof-dancing demon, the succubus who lusts for nothing more than things in pairs, be they wine cups or brothers or unwanted guests.

Bubbe recites the kiddush once the adults all have their cups filled, including the one that waits for Elijah at his empty seat at the end of the table. The prophet's place is set the same as ours—with food and drink and even a Haggadah—just in case he decides to come and grace us with his presence. Bubbe promises that he'll come this year. She assures me that Elijah knows when we need him most.

Bubbe concludes the blessing with a solemn bow of her head. "Now," she says, "it's time for Urchatz, the ritual washing of hands."

We all rise from our seats except for David and Abigail. "We already washed our hands before we sat at the table." David casts defiant eyes at my mother and father and Bubbe, but I don't let him win.

"It's a required part of the Seder, *David*. We all have to do it."

David's chest expands in an attempt to look brutish, but Abigail pats his arm. "It's all right, let's just do it." She flashes me a smile that's more condescension than warmth. And in that rare moment when our eyes meet, I wouldn't be surprised if she were Agrath in disguise.

We make a line to the bathroom, youngest to oldest, and by the time Aaron and I wash, and we are seated back at the table, David and Abigail are canoodling in the hallway.

Bubbe sits down last and waves them both over. She addresses the rest of us. "Now we continue with the karpas, the bitter herbs." She grabs a sprig of parsley and a melamine bowl filled with salt water and dips the herb in the water. Each of us does the same, and once everyone has a salty, dripping bite of parsley that we pop into our mouths, she continues. "With this herb we remember the tears of our ancestors. We remember the pain that they were forced to endure."

David and Abigail and little Aaron at my side all scrunch their faces at the spicy tang of salt.

Then Abigail scoots her chair. "Excuse me," she says, then runs into the kitchen. David quickly follows. He swallows the last tears of our ancestors with a gulp.

Several minutes pass. I open my Haggadah to prepare for my part in the Seder, when I will ask the four questions that Jews have asked for millennia. Tradition dictates that the youngest at the table should read them, but Aaron is only five and doesn't know enough Hebrew.

My mother and father chug their Manischewitz. They look toward the kitchen, presumably to check on where their eldest son has gone.

"I'll go," I offer. I sneak around the corner against the room's back wall and duck behind the marble-topped kitchen counter island.

Muted laughter comes from the other side of the island, and when I peek my head around, I see an empty bottle of Manischewitz on the ground and two half-filled glasses of sticky purple wine.

Two glasses. A pair. The signal for Agrath. I feel the demon stir from her realm's nocturnal depths.

"What are you *doing*?" The wineglasses topple as I tip them with my fingers.

"Watch it!" whispers David.

"Go away," says Abigail.

"You can't drink in pairs. You *know* what that will do."

But it's already too late. The wine is half-drunk, the siren long since called, and Agrath turns her gaze on our cursed, withering family. She will come with her demon-spawned children of nightmare, and I can only hope that Lilith and Ashmedai don't follow.

"What's this?" says Bubbe, rounding the corner. "Don't tell me you finished my last good bottle."

I warn her of what's coming, but she doesn't seem worried. My parents don't either. Their patience for my hunting has faded along with Zayde.

We walk into the dining room as if nothing just happened. We sit down at the table. And we wait for the moment in which Agrath will arrive.

Rule number six: Avoid the roots, the trunks, and the shade of most trees.

"Now," says Bubbe, "it's time to reveal the matzah and hide the afikomen." The mention of afikomen captures Aaron's attention, and with tiny hands and twiggish arms he reaches over the table to grab the square of matzah. Bits of the unleavened bread fall behind. They cut across the tablecloth like the path that Moses carved through the waters of the Red Sea.

Aaron holds the matzah square high above his head. He smiles in delight. And with an exaggerated crunch, he breaks the square in two. One side is noticeably smaller than the other. He eats this piece and saves the larger half. This will now be the night's afikomen, the treasure to be found and eaten at the end of the Seder.

It's one hunt that we all know Aaron will win. He's the only one young enough to be eligible to search.

Then Abigail surprises me. "I know the perfect spot. Can I hide the matzah?"

Bubbe nods her head, and before I can even think, she and David are into the kitchen and through the porch door.

I suspect what she's up to. David should know better.

I rise from my seat and follow them outside. Aaron stays behind with Bubbe and my parents.

The buzzing lamp on the porch is swallowed by the night, but it allows me to see my brother and his girlfriend under the shade of the magnolia tree's branches. As if having one demon on their trail wasn't enough.

"Watch out for Rishpe!" I scream to David. "He lives in the roots! Don't get too close!"

But David and Abigail ignore me and my warning. She stuffs the afikomen, wrapped tight within a napkin, between two tangled and knotted magnolia tree roots.

They don't see the shadow that ripples up the tree trunk, the ghastly flickering fingers that slither from the branches, the twin midnight eyes that emerge from the darkness. The tree's white flowers extend into teeth, their incisors sparkling with the blood that will soon coat them.

And once again, it's me, the sole demon hunter, to save them from peril.

The porch's wooden planks groan under my footsteps, and without any pause, I launch myself forward. I knock into David. We both fall to the ground. And I push us as far as I can from Rishpe's roots.

Rishpe bends and strikes, but he's a second too late. The demon recoils. He seeps back into the roots, a reverse osmosis, and prepares to reemerge if we get too close.

Abigail, somehow, misses the whole attack. "What the hell are you doing? You can't cheat and see where we hide the afikomen."

David feigns ignorance. Instead of admitting that he disturbed a demon's realm, that his brother just saved him from becoming Rishpe's meal, he continues to seek the approval of a girl that cares nothing for him, nothing for Pesach, nothing for the generations of demon hunters before him that sacrificed themselves in order to learn their enemy's weaknesses. He lifts himself up and grabs Abigail's hand.

"Let's go," says David, with a roll of his eyes. "I'm starting to get hungry."

Abigail leaves the napkin-wrapped treasure where she placed it, between the two roots under Rishpe's eager eyes. She doesn't even offer to bring it back inside.

I grab the afikomen and retreat across the lawn. I can't see

Rishpe through the porch light's glare, but I know that he's awake. Waiting for me to return.

As I walk through the door to hide the afikomen, I am struck by a particularly worrisome thought. How many other demons will Abigail try to tempt?

Rule number seven, though this may actually belong farther up on the list: Don't trust your guests to do as you tell them.

The six of us settle back into the table—seven, including Elijah. His place mat and dinner tray and glass of Manischewitz still appear untouched, which leads me to believe that he hasn't yet arrived. And I'm not sure I blame him. I wouldn't want to be here either, if this weren't my own family.

I grab my Haggadah from the stack at the end of the table and distribute the rest of them so that each person has a copy. The picture on the cover is an idyllic ode to the Exodus—purple-robed Moses in the middle of the Red Sea, happy people holding up matzah in victory, the sad face of pharaoh Ramses II in defeat. Lilith and Ashmedai and Agrath are all absent. Whoever drew this book was not trained in the way of demons.

I motion for Bubbe to initiate the ritual.

"And now," she says, eyes roaming aimlessly, as if realizing yet again that Zayde won't need his copy, "we will hear the Four Questions. These will remind us of why this day is special."

Abigail stifles a yawn with the back of her hand. David follows up with a barely muffled belch. I can smell the dregs of wine on his breath from across the table.

I open my Haggadah to the page that I had bookmarked earlier that evening. "Why do we only eat matzah on this night, but on other nights we eat leavened bread and everything else?"

My family is silent. The wind on the roof sounds like Agrath tapping her feet, the clickety-clack of hooves against our home's brittle warding.

Abigail bites her lip. "Because our ancestors want to torture us until we starve?"

JEFF WEINER

David heaves with laughter and even my mother grins. The expression on her face looks so alien, so misplaced, like a fossil uncovered from centuries' worth of rubble.

I turn to Aaron, who smiles as well, but he at least answers. "Because the Israelites didn't have time to cook before their escape. They ran away from Egypt as quickly as they could."

Bubbe beams with pride. "Go on, then, next question."

But Abigail interrupts me. "Noam, how about we skip through the rest of the ceremony? I think we get the gist of it, and it's already getting late."

"Yeah," says David, "I'm hungry. Let's eat."

The glare that I give them is one meant to kill, and they are lucky that they aren't demons on my list.

To my horror, though, my mother and father agree. I can see the weight of the evening bearing down on their shoulders.

"Fine," I tell them. "If you prefer it that way, we'll move on to the feast."

That's all the permission they need to gorge on their plates, a frenzy of chicken shanks and oven-roasted brisket, soft potato kugel and slippery gefilte fish, haroset made from a mix of applesauce, nuts, and fruit. And of course, the meal wouldn't be complete without hard-boiled eggs, the food that most symbolizes the endurance of our people.

Abigail and David sneak more wine from under the table. They hide two goblets under napkins at their feet, each bending down to steal tiny, foreboding sips. They disobey my orders; they mock what they should fear.

Then Abigail again. "Mr. and Mrs. Yesowitz, I'm not feeling too well. Would you mind if I step outside for some air?"

"Of course," says my mother in her absentminded way.

"Go with her," says my father, pointing at David. "We'll wait to find the afikomen until you two come back."

David and Abigail slip away from the table. They may have fooled my parents, but Aaron and I aren't stupid.

I know she isn't sick. She wants to lead my brother out of the safety of our home, past the guard of the mezuzahs into the demon-filled night. It's as if she really is in league with Agrath and her brood.

Rule number eight: Never underestimate the power of your opponent.

David and Abigail are gone for some time. The rest of us sink into a black hole of silence, finishing the meal that Bubbe and I prepared. Aaron picks at a hard-boiled egg. He mixes the rubbery-yellow yolk with some haroset, smears it in circles around the perimeter of his plate. The image erases what little hunger I had.

"Can I be excused?"

My mother lifts her eyes and nods in agreement, but my father shakes his head. "Finish your meal."

"But I want to check on Abigail. What if she needs something?"

"Fine," he says, "but don't bother them too much."

I hop off my seat cushion and drop my Haggadah. The thick book lands on the carpet with a thump, the creased leather binding an indestructible shell.

The porch door opens, and I feel the night air, the crispness of winter giving way to spring. I couldn't care less how Abigail feels. My job is to protect David from the demons that she summons, and judging by the eerie quiet that smothers the backyard, it seems like she may already have him trapped.

But no, behind the tree. Just beyond the edge of its bough, hidden among the hydrangeas that Bubbe recently planted, where Aaron likes to go when we play hide-and-seek. There are two shapes wrapped in each other's freckle-smeared arms, one with a ponytail in a polka-dot scrunchie, the other with a royal-blue lopsided yarmulke.

David and Abigail do what they do best. They kiss in the spot that I told them to avoid.

An unnatural wind blows. The porch light flickers, the moths scurry away. And when I hear chitinous hooves clickety-clack against the roof, and my eardrums echo with a soul-piercing shriek, I know that she has come.

Agrath the succubus descends on our backyard.

She lands on the grass, a triple-headed fury with membranous wings like a duck's webbed feet, her talons sinking deep into the soft, muddy yard. Her body is that of an emaciated centaur, with a tail clipped by a brimstone blade. Each of her three wolverine heads wriggles its nose. They sniff in my direction through a cloud of her own ash.

When she turns her three noses toward David and Abigail, I scream at them to run. But they can't hear me through her shrieks.

I run back inside, searching for a weapon, anything that could possibly scare Agrath off. I'm not sure if such a weapon exists. Only Lilith, her mother, the queen of demons herself, is said to be stronger, and I pray to Yahweh that she doesn't come too. Zayde might have known how to kill these demons, but he left me before I could learn all of his secrets.

What could I use? Maybe something from the table. The candle from havdalah? No, too flimsy. The matzah to cut her? No, too brittle.

Then I have it. The karpas that we dipped in Bubbe's melamine bowl. The tears of the Israelites should smite Agrath's flesh.

I burst into the dining room to grab the rest of the parsley. I pick up the bowl of what's left of the salt water, cupping the rim with my sweaty, shaking palm, then return to the porch, weapons in hand.

Agrath has David crushed under her hooves. Abigail whimpers from against the magnolia's trunk. The demon's fiery breath incinerates the air, two smoking plumes that seethe through her nostrils. Her six eyes focus on David's trapped body, ready to break him. Ready to kill.

Then I see my chance, my one fleeting moment.

I charge at the succubus with all of Zayde's courage.

The salt water splashes onto Agrath's humped spine. There's a noxious, crackling sizzle as the water makes its impact, her skin first disintegrating then crystallizing in seconds, forming dense gray motes that float through the air. She stumbles and roars. The burn follows the curve of her spine down to her pelvis, seeps into the runnels of her bestial hide.

I motion to David to get up and run. He grabs Abigail's hand and the three of us retreat into the porch's fading light, past the mezuzah that hangs on the doorpost. We collapse in a heap on the living room floor.

"What *was* that?" pants Abigail. Her eyes pin down David as if this were his fault. As if everything that has happened tonight weren't because of her.

"I don't know," lies David, looking away. "Maybe a big raccoon?"

"A raccoon! That thing was bigger than twenty raccoons. And it had three heads!" She looks at me then. "How'd you know that the salt water would burn it?"

I avoid the question because she doesn't need to know. I'm still not sure where her allegiance truly lies, whether Agrath primed her months ago to slowly bring us down.

David breaks my silence. "Whatever it was is gone. We're safe inside the house." He looks past the door at the mezuzah on the other side, as if unsure whether he believes his own words. *I* know that *he* knows what we just fought. No matter what David would like to forget, Zayde taught us well.

Abigail fixes her scrunchie. "Let's get back to the table. I don't want your parents to get mad at me."

So, the three of us, pretending that everything is normal, that we didn't just fend off one of our strongest demons, return to the dining room. Bubbe and my mother and father are there. Elijah's seat is as empty as it has been all night. But so is another.

"Where's Aaron?" I say. "Did he go outside too?"

My mother answers hollowly through a mouth full of wine. "He started to get anxious. We let him go search for the afikomen a bit early."

David and I gaze at each other. David looks at Abigail.

"Where did he go?" I barely manage to say.

My mother points upstairs. "He went soon after you followed David outside. He's been up there for a while."

Rule number nine, which is really more of a warning: Demons are drawn to the pain of their children.

I grab the armored cover of my Haggadah from the floor and motion for David and Abigail to do the same. All the salt water is gone from our fight with Agrath, and even if I made more, the residual power of the kiddush wouldn't still hold. There wasn't any time. We had to act quickly.

The three of us creep down the hallway toward the staircase. I hear Abigail whisper something into David's ear. "Your family's pretty weird."

He cringes as if struck. He opens his mouth, probably to say that he isn't like us, just like he told Zayde that Hebrew school was a joke, as if he could cast off his heritage like an unwanted sweater then put it back on whenever it was convenient to wear again.

"Shut up," I say, a finger over my lips.

We synchronize our movements as we climb to the second floor, step by step, breath by breath. The silence around us is overwhelming, crushing.

If Aaron were all right, we'd hear him moving around, maybe playing with his toys. I didn't hide the afikomen *that* well, after all. Once David and Abigail had gone back to the table, I had put it under the covers in Aaron's race-car bed, one napkin-wrapped corner poking out at the top.

Something else must have found the afikomen first.

We mount the last stair and listen, still. The clatter of utensils on plates drifts up, the sound of Bubbe mumbling the night's final prayer.

Then a faint rustle like a wiry brush. Or razor-sharp teeth against a matzah cracker.

We slink down the hallway toward Aaron's open door. The mezuzah is on the ground, shattered in half, the klaf parchment shredded into a hundred wrinkled bits. Sulfurous holes line the ceramic casing's edge.

The three of us pause, take a deep breath. We round the last corner and charge into the room.

And are faced by Lilith, the succubus queen.

She sits on the carpet with Aaron in one hand, a many-jointed finger wrapped twice around his head. His eyes scream in terror while his mouth remains covered.

Lilith's other hand holds the rest of the afikomen, which she licks and crunches with a black, serrated tongue. She takes the last bite, shifts her pregnant belly, the skin over her thorax so stretched that it groans. The thousands of unborn demon spawn inside shriek and poke through with the rage of their mother.

Then Lilith turns. She sees us in the doorway, flaps two pterodactyl, skeletal wings, the wings of an angel gone horribly wrong, made of flame and ash and toxic, rotted flesh.

She approaches the three of us, sets down Aaron like a broken, forgotten doll.

David and Abigail break away to the side, avoiding the chasms in the carpet from her embers. They hold their Haggadahs like tiny paper shields, ready to strike if she comes too close.

I quickly weigh our options. If we meet her head-on, our chance at victory is slim. We have to work together to form a strategy, a way to circumnavigate the unfortunate reality that Lilith is mightier than all four of us combined.

I motion to David to circle around to her back. If he can immobilize one of her wings, that should distract her enough for me to feint and strike. Of all the grotesqueries of her unnatural body, her stomach seems the weakest, the most vulnerable to attack.

But my brother chooses glory.

He brandishes his Haggadah at Lilith's hulking form, screams at her to look only at him. At the same time, he shoves Abigail away toward the bunk beds.

Lilith doesn't hesitate. She flaps one of her gargantuan, bone-tipped wings and knocks him to the ground, Haggadah askew.

The membranes of her stomach stretch thin as she turns, steps across the carpet. Fingers poke through an ulcerous sac at her waist. Her unborn children reach out for a snack.

This is my moment. My chance to save Pesach.

I lock eyes with Abigail on the opposite side of the room, nod toward the upper bunk above Lilith's head. She follows where I look, nods in return, and I hope with all my heart that my instinct is true. Because if this plan fails, none of us will survive.

I charge forward, smack the demon queen with my Haggadah. The blow slips across one of her exoskeletal ribs, not enough to puncture.

She screams in fury and forgets about David, flaps both of her wings with gale-force wind. A gust knocks me over and I drop my Haggadah. She approaches me, eager to kill her daughter's hunter.

The demon queen stands over my paralyzed body, my Haggadah too far away for me to use in defense. The smell of her flame-coated afikomen breath makes me gag and choke, makes my eyes sting with soot.

She sticks out her tongue, ready for her meal.

But before she can bite, before she can end me, Abigail is there. She grips the cover of her Haggadah in one hand and swings herself from the top of Aaron's bunk bed with the other, leaping through the air, a ponytail warrior with a polka-dot scrunchie. She slams the Haggadah into Lilith's bare skull, bends her horns until they fracture and snap.

The demon queen bellows in unexpected agony. I take this opportunity to shuffle away. I grab the fragments of the ceramic mezuzah, hold them before me like a jagged, broken shield. Lilith backs away, inches toward the open window on the other side of the room. The one she must have opened with her over-jointed fingers.

David and Abigail approach with their Haggadahs. The three of us close in, pushing Lilith back, a *team* of demon hunters when there used to be one.

Lilith's head swivels, her obsidian eyes shine. She knows she is defeated. She bellows one snarling, threatening roar and retreats out the window into the cool, dark night.

I stand in disbelief. So do my companions. If not for the scorched carpet, the specks of afikomen littering the bed, the slowly fading terror that drains from my face, it's as if Lilith had never been there at all. The thought that we could defeat the queen of demons doesn't seem real.

Abigail smiles and tousles Aaron's hair. "I changed my mind," she says. "Your family's pretty weird, but that just makes you better."

And even though admitting it makes me want to scream, even though I'm not sure that I'll ever forgive her, I have to accept that she helped us win this fight. A part of me wonders if she isn't so evil.

Rule number ten: Fellow demon hunters don't have to be family.

This is one rule that didn't exist before tonight, before the overdue Seder that I thought would never happen. But demons never rest; they will always be out there, waiting and watching until summoned into existence. And I realize now that sometimes, people can learn. That it's better to teach them, to share with them our methods rather than blame them for not knowing what they never could have known.

The four of us, victorious, strut downstairs. Bubbe asks Aaron if he found the afikomen, but I stop him before he can answer and say that we did it together. This makes her happy, which makes us all smile.

David and Abigail clear their plates in the kitchen, drain the rest of their wine from under the table into the sink. Everyone except for Bubbe gradually floats into the living room. She sits, eyes closed, next to Elijah's empty seat, his glass half-filled with purple Manischewitz, his seat cushion lumpier than I remembered it being before.

"Bubbe," I say, eyes wide with wonder. "Do you think Elijah came?"

She smiles and nods, grabbing my hand, and we both hold our breaths at a whoosh under the table. A ripple of air tickles our ankles, and I see the front door mat shift to the side.

Bubbe cups my chin, softens her voice. "You did well tonight, Noam."

She winks at me then, shows me that she knows. That as long as I'm around, as long as I remember Zayde's demon-hunting rules, the Yesowitz family will be just fine.

Hemingway

written by
Emma Washburn

illustrated by
SETHE NGUYEN

ABOUT THE AUTHOR

Emma Washburn lives in Charlotte, North Carolina, where they attend Providence Senior High School and participate in both the yearbook and literary magazine programs. Emma is very grateful for the support and care from the advisors for both staffs, Ms. Mann and Mrs. Hutchinson.

Emma's love for stories developed at a young age, thanks to the people who surrounded them with books and tales since infancy. They began writing in the fifth grade because of a very supportive English teacher, their first short story was an assignment for the class called "A Single Envelope."

A bit of an eccentric, Emma collects crystals and hotel soaps, and absolutely loves candles. "Hemingway" was inspired by a weird dream they had about a house built on top of the ocean. They hope to continue telling stories into the future, whether it be on paper or screen.

ABOUT THE ILLUSTRATOR

Sethe Nguyen was born in 2001 in Ho Chi Minh City, Vietnam. Her love for art began while scribbling all over the walls as a kid, which lead to filling in the numbers in childhood sketchbooks. Taking inspirations from Japanese manga and anime, Sethe developed a great interest in all things art, from drawing and painting to singing and songwriting. She is currently in college to pursue dual careers in theater and the visual arts.

Hemingway

The little girl watched as the old man scraped barnacles off the bottom of his house, the small white shells dropping like fallen stars into the water dancing just below the floor. The ocean was inches away from soaking the worn hardwood barely visible behind the man. She frowned, her eyebrows pressed together as she tried to make sense of how a house could be built in the middle of the ocean. But, she had rowed to this nowhere herself on a plastic toy boat, so she assumed that the world must be a very interesting place, if one just cares to look around. She decided to get a bit closer.

"Hello," she yelled out, waving a hand up in the air. The sleeve of the jacket she'd stolen from her mother fell down her arm and bunched up around her shoulder.

The old man looked up from what he was doing, raising a hand so he could block the sun from his view. "Oh, hello there! What brings you here?"

The little girl rowed closer. "I'm exploring the ocean! I'm a sailor."

"Ah, the ocean! An interesting place. This right here," the man said, patting the side of his home with a wrinkled hand, "is prime real estate for an ocean lover."

She nodded. She didn't know what "prime real estate" was, but assumed he knew what he was talking about. Old people are wise.

"How'd you build it in the water?" the little girl asked.

"Ah, I didn't build it. But come inside, I haven't had a guest in years!"

The little girl knew that strangers were dangerous, but the old man seemed familiar, and she'd never seen such an odd house before. She rowed closer, stepped up out of the plastic tub, and stumbled through the open door. The old man began bustling about in the kitchen straight ahead, while two other doors flanked her sides. She pulled her boat out of the water and set it inside, since there was no dock to tie it to. Sitting down on her heels, she ran a finger along the scratched red plastic. The manufacturer's name had long since worn off.

"Would you like English Breakfast or chamomile?" the old man called. The little girl stood up quickly, walking toward the right to the kitchen. If she'd turned left, she would face the small dining room table and a window that opened to the outside. A teapot sat on the stove and the old man held two different metal containers of tea.

"Chamomile," the little girl said, mouth set firmly but eyes darting around the room. Almost every surface in the entire house was covered in stacks upon stacks of leather-bound books.

"Take a seat, take a seat! The tea will be done in no time."

The little girl tapped her heels together, sitting atop five different novels so she could see over the worn tabletop. Sipping his cup delicately, the old man took a deep breath as steam rose out to fill the thousand wrinkles that marred his skin. The little girl didn't touch hers. She didn't care for tea, but she supposed it was rude to deny a gift.

"What's your name?" she asked, drumming her hands over the table.

"I don't know. I haven't quite thought of one yet. You can call me Grandfather, if you'd like."

The little girl furrowed her brows. She'd never heard of choosing a name for yourself before.

"Grandfather," she repeated, "like the clock."

The old man's mouth was hidden behind the chipped ivory

of his drink, but the wrinkles that curled up around his eyes sank deeper than bowing waves, his eyes sparkling like sunlight glinting off the sea.

"Precisely."

The little girl smiled back. "Well, my name is—"

The old man stood up suddenly, hand outstretched and fingers splayed while his teacup rattled on the table, startling her into silence.

"Stop!" he said. "A name is a precious thing! It's best not to give it away so carelessly."

Static pricked at the little girl's eyes.

"Sorry."

The old man sat back down, shaking his head. He turned left to face the open window.

"There's no need to apologize for something you didn't know." He tapped the side of his cup. "You learn, and then you move on. Now, I must show you something. Follow me."

The old man rose again, his bare feet soundlessly carrying him to the front of the house. He turned to the door on his right.

The little girl leaned to the side, trying to peek out from behind him. The man turned the rusted knob and swung the door open. The little girl gasped. Harsh sunlight from outside streamed into the house, illuminating a few feet into the darkness behind the door. Stairs stood silently under murky ocean water.

"My basement," the old man lamented, "it's sunk under."

The little girl fidgeted with her jacket sleeves as she stared in disbelief at the water lapping slightly below the floor she stood on. A little fish swam up into the light before darting back down below. The old man closed the door.

"I'm afraid my whole house is sinking."

Biting her lip, the little girl contemplated his problem.

"Can you move?"

"I've lived here forever. I'm afraid I can't." The old man sighed. "And I doubt I'd fit in your boat," he added.

The little girl laughed. The old man laughed, too.

"Now, what time is it?" he said, turning back toward the kitchen. He squinted out at the sun dipping lower in the horizon.

"Don't you have a clock?"

"No, I don't need one. That way the only person who can decide the time is me." The old man squinted his eyes. "I'm afraid it's time for you to go, child."

She frowned.

"But, you can come back tomorrow," he said, turning around to smile down at her. "And every day after that. You can read my books, or help me patch up the walls to keep the ocean at bay, or talk with me over tea. I always listen."

The little girl held out her hand to shake his, which she'd heard happens when two grown-ups make a deal. And she did feel grown up. She had sailed across the ocean and discovered something new. The old man shook her hand. He had a very good handshake, she decided.

"Head toward the sun, and you'll be home before you know it." He clasped his hands together and smiled down at her. "See you tomorrow."

The next day, the water hadn't risen, but a few holes had popped up in the floor of the house. The little girl helped the old man patch them as he read *Treasure Island* aloud. She liked it because she wanted to find treasure, too.

In the following week, the little girl helped the old man clean all the barnacles off the sides of his house while reading *Where the Red Fern Grows*. She cried at the end, and her tears dripped down into the ocean to mix with the seawater. She told the old man she was sure that the ocean had come from the tears of angels. The old man nodded and said he always thought the ocean was made when god cried after making the world, so moved by the majesty of their creation. Holding a yardstick taken from her house, the little girl found that the ocean had risen a quarter inch since the first day she'd arrived.

SETHE NGUYEN

Within the first month, the water had gone up an inch and a half above the floor of the house. The old man read the little girl *Mr. Popper's Penguins*, *Pippi Longstocking*, *The Wizard of Oz*, and *The Swiss Family Robinson*. The little girl learned that she liked English Breakfast tea if she added a spoon of sugar to it.

Six months later, the water was to her ankles. The little girl liked that she could kick it around and splash her friend. The old man didn't seem worried about it. She helped him put all the books on top of the dining room table, so many that the stacks almost touched the ceiling. They'd read so many she'd lost count, but her favorites were *Matilda* and *Doctor Dolittle*. She wanted to go on adventures.

A year later, the water had risen to her shins. As soon as the boat rocked against the doorway of the house, she'd spill everything that had happened to her that day, and he would listen. The little girl felt like most adults didn't really listen. Whenever she told her mom or dad about her friend in the sea, they would smile in a way that meant they thought she was lying. But the old man never gave her that smile when she told him about how she fought a sea serpent on her way there or discovered aliens in her backyard. He'd tell her to describe them, to give him detail upon detail of what they looked like or how the battle had gone blow by blow. But he'd always call her "child" or "my dear." She wanted him to know her name. He always said it wasn't time yet and would stare at the ocean with jaw set and eyes narrowed, his grip on his teacup a little tighter than before.

Three years had passed in total. The day she arrived at his house crying, the water had gone up to her midthigh. The old man gave her tissues as they sat atop the table, the books pushed to the side or stacked on the kitchen counters to make room. Some kids at the little girl's school had told her that the tooth fairy wasn't real, so she shouldn't be so excited over losing a tooth. The little girl rushed home crying only for her mom to confirm her fears.

"It's not fair," she wailed. "Why would they lie to me? Why

would they make it up if it's not real? When they knew a day like today would happen?"

The old man squeezed her tight, as if the water below them was trying to wash her out of the house.

"It's nice to start out believing that the world has magic before you drift away with mundanity. That way, you can always find it again, if you want to look."

In the following months, the water level grew higher and higher. The boat was beginning to get too small, its plastic tub sinking deeper and deeper in the water with each day the little girl climbed into it. Before long, she was helping the old man transport books to his roof, barely big enough for the two. She was ten, now, but nobody had remembered her birthday but him. He gave her the water-damaged copy of *Treasure Island* they'd read so long ago, but she could hardly make out the words on the cover through the myopia of her tears. The old man made her promise she'd never stop searching for treasure and magic. She nodded, but stared down into the ocean as she did, the rise and fall of the waves synonymous with the sobs that rattled her lungs.

Another month passed. The roof was getting smaller and smaller, until the old man was stuck atop the chimney and the little girl had to stay in her shrinking boat. He could only hold onto one book, now, clutched in the withered hands that used to hold teacups filled with sugar and patch holes to stop their world from sinking. On the last day, he smiled at her as she rowed up. His eyes drooped and welled with phantom tears as he saw how cramped she was in her boat, and how far in the water the vessel now sank.

"What book do you have?" the little girl asked.

The old man handed it to her. Remarkably, it was untouched by the greedy waves. The little girl ran her hand along the spine, cracked and worn with age.

"The Old Man and the Sea," she said. "What's it about?"

The old man took his book back from her, staring down from

his perch. "It's about an old man, the boy who cares for him, and the great marlin he wishes to catch."

The little girl was used to the wise ways and mystery of her old friend. "So I'm the helper-boy, and you're the old man, but what's the marlin?"

The old man nodded, scraping his fingertips alongside his last book. "I suppose it's how we must part. Our names." He tapped his heel against the chimney. "It's time. You may tell me your name now, but then you can never return."

The little girl took a deep breath, a sigh that spoke more words than the book the old man held in his calluses. She had known the day was approaching. But she did not want it to be today. She wanted to stay afloat for a bit longer.

She remembered *Treasure Island* and *The Wizard of Oz*, and she recalled the taste of English Breakfast with a spoonful of sugar, and the stories of serpents and monsters she'd recounted to him with such an air of truth she'd almost convinced herself. And she could count the number of holes she'd patched in walls and the way the man's voice cracked after reading too long without something to drink. She closed her eyes, and dipped her hand below the waves, and knew it was time.

Carefully, she grabbed hold of the stones jutting out of the chimney, leaned close to the old man, and whispered her name into his ear. She sank back into her boat and closed her eyes, feeling the water rock her back and forth like a baby in a cradle.

"What a lovely name," the old man smiled. "May I have it as well?"

The little girl nodded, eyes still closed. "You've found a name, then. And you won't be able to forget me, either."

The old man's laugh rang through the air, ragged as sails on an ancient ship. "I'll never forget you. But you'll forget me."

The little girl's eyes snapped open, chapped lips parting, preparing to reject the old man's words. But when she took in the view of the ocean, she found she was only twenty feet from the shore near her house. The old man and the chimney were nowhere to be found, and her boat was scraping the sand at the bottom of the ocean floor. It was quiet. The little girl raised a hand in the air, her sleeve staying up at her wrist, waving an invisible goodbye to him and the house she'd spent her childhood in. Then she let herself fall out of the boat, waves cascading over her until she, like the house, was one with the sea.

Half-Breed

written by
Brittany Rainsdon

illustrated by
DANIEL BITTON

ABOUT THE AUTHOR

Brittany Rainsdon grew up as the only girl in a family with four brothers. She's reversing that trend with her own children—three girls and one boy. In 2008, Brittany graduated with her RN from Brigham Young University-Idaho. She received her BSN in 2010. Brittany has worked in both medical/surgical and rehabilitation specialties, but she currently enjoys work as a stay-at-home mom.

Brittany started writing at a young age, penning poems and stories, and filling an overstuffed nightstand with spiral notebooks, pens, and floppy disks (yes, those were still a thing in 2007). On entering college, Brittany lost touch with her writing and didn't come back to it for several years.

After having her third child in 2015 and needing a creative outlet, her passion for writing reignited. Once she found the Writers of the Future Contest, Brittany has not missed a quarter and has been a Writers of the Future finalist three times. "Half-Breed" is her first professional story and she hopes to publish many more.

Brittany lives with her husband and children near the Snake River in Idaho, where she swears it looks like a wintered Narnia for nearly half the year. She has many pairs of fuzzy socks.

ABOUT THE ILLUSTRATOR

Daniel Bitton is an illustrator from Fort Lauderdale, Florida, working primarily in science fiction and fantasy. His love for drawing began in early childhood as a way to connect with stories, worlds, and characters inspired by his favorite books and games.

He loves to depict fantastic characters and tell stories through his illustrations which are inspired by dreams, myths, and history. Through a mix of layered digital and traditional media, Daniel's work can be seen in both print and digital publications.

Daniel received a BFA in illustration from the Maryland Institute College of Art in 2019 and attended The Illustration Academy in Kansas City in the summer of 2018.

When not drawing, Daniel can be found running outside on the trails or thinking about his next project.

Daniel was a winner of the L. Ron Hubbard's Illustrators of the Future Contest and was first featured in Volume 36.

Half-Breed

The trees didn't trust Sequoia Asterlynn. They whizzed by as she stared out the window on the passenger side of Mom's pickup. With thick branches draped in Spanish moss, the old oaks reached across the road as if holding hands, forming a long brown and green tunnel. Sequoia could almost feel the press of their hard stares, united in judgment. *Filthy half-breed.*

Sequoia shuddered, and tugged at the frayed edges of her shirtsleeves, making certain to cover the five thin scars on her right arm. She'd carved one into her skin after each failed summoning, after they'd returned home and Dad had gone to sleep. The trees didn't know about those marks—neither did her parents—but if things went poorly tonight, she worried about keeping the secret much longer. If her own ancestors couldn't accept her, who would?

Mom broke the silence. "Principal Eklin called." She tapped a painted fingernail against the steering wheel. "He said there was an incident at school?"

Sequoia's face flushed. She could imagine what her high-school principal had told Mom. On the last day of school, someone had toilet papered Sequoia's car, wrapping it in an irreverent mockery of the summoning decorations dryads used on the trigani trees. Her windows had been muddied with dryad slurs. Someone had smashed ketchup packets on her hood. And it had all been topped with a beheaded stuffed animal strapped to the roof, marked as an "offering." She'd felt as if half the school was watching as she splashed water over the windshield and used her shirtsleeve to wipe away a slur so she could escape.

After she'd gotten home, Sequoia had realized they'd slashed a tire too. She'd been able to change it for the spare before Mom had gotten home. Sequoia had blamed the blown tire on road debris and Mom had lectured Sequoia for driving on a flat—and then promptly towed her car to the local mechanic shop.

But if Mom had learned what had really happened, that Sequoia had lied...

"It's not a big deal."

"No?" Mom frowned. "Mrs. Fritz accused you of plagiarizing your history final."

Sequoia's mouth felt like cotton and angry heat rose in her chest. She'd been falsely accused. Again. "I didn't cheat."

"That's what I told Mr. Eklin. He said he wanted to set up a meeting with you and Mrs. Fritz, but I told him you were leaving for your dad's, that you had a cultural ceremony, and that if he wanted to meet with anyone, he could meet with me."

Sequoia's pulse quickened. The first time she'd been accused of cheating, a boy had hacked into her online classroom account and stolen her answers for an English test. She'd had to show Mr. Eklin how to trace the IP before anyone had believed her. It wasn't fair that people automatically assumed she'd be the guilty party, but she understood why they did.

The humans in Walter Bay labeled dryads as tricksters and cheats, but the truth was simpler. Dryads were clever. It made sense a half-dryad like Sequoia would be clever, too—that she'd excel in academia. But no one liked to hear that. Instead, teachers would march her to the office, where Sequoia would frustrate them further by proving her innocence. Again. And again. It felt as if they could find a way to blame Sequoia for anything, perhaps even the car incident too, if it ever came to light. Maybe they'd say she deserved it. Why couldn't they just leave her alone?

The answer came to her immediately: Because she wasn't one of them.

"Sequoia?"

"I'm sure I could prove my innocence. *Again*." Sequoia hugged her arms to her chest. "*If* there were time. Not like I've got anything better to do."

"Oh, honey." Mom squeezed Sequoia's shoulder. "I just wanted you to know, in case they tried to reach your father or left a message on your phone. But I *am* taking care of it."

"Thanks." Sequoia swallowed. But as her scars tingled, she wondered if she'd done the right thing, not telling Mom about what the students subjected her to during class. And after. Words bubbled up her throat, threatening to spill until—

The truck shook as a white SUV *whooshed* past, thundering down the narrow road. Mom honked and Sequoia's stomach prickled as she caught sight of the picket signs pressed against tinted glass. Two boys pumped fists in the back seat. *Protestors.* Yes, her classmates had become more and more involved in dryad politics, citing flawed reasons why the ancient people should be evicted from their sacred land and have it annexed into the city. Sequoia slid lower in her seat.

"Be careful today." Mom's eyes stayed on the road as she spoke softly. "Relations with the dryads are more strained than ever. I don't know what happened with the fire . . . but people shouldn't take it out on you."

Sequoia's throat tightened at the mention of the spring fire that had ravaged the trigani trees in the ancient Balanos Forest. Mom had hardly spoken of it, but Sequoia knew more than enough. Nearly a fifth of the trees had been razed to the ground. Some of the dryad spirits housed within had been over a thousand years old. Two months had passed since the fire, and the dryads were still mourning.

Mom cleared her throat, changing the subject. "Rue should be at the summoning ceremony. Right?"

Sequoia shrugged. Rue was a feisty female dryad six months Sequoia's junior. As children, they'd raced through the river bottoms, made clover chains, and shared secrets about which powers they hoped their trigani seeds would hold. They'd spent many summer nights lying in the meadow, staring up at a star-spattered sky. But last year, after the ancients had spoken to Rue and given her a trigani seed, they'd grown apart. "I don't know if she'll come."

Mom tapped the steering wheel. "Well, your dad will be at the ceremony. And Auntie Cypress. I wish I were allowed, but—"

"You're not." Sequoia stared out at the trees again. Did they really hate her? Why did the trees hate her?

Same answer came again: Because she wasn't one of them.

"Don't let other people ruin this, dear. You deserve good things."

Sequoia turned to study Mom. Her gaze was on the road, blond hair falling perfectly over her shoulders. She kept talking, saying nice things about Sequoia. Mom was beautiful by any human standard, but the thought made something snap within Sequoia.

At seventeen, it was clear Sequoia had inherited dryad coloring: moss-green eyes, wiry black hair, and bitternut-brown skin, including the dreaded bark marks. The spindly bark-lines could almost pass as freckles when she slathered on a thick matte of foundation. Almost. But Sequoia's classmates had reminded her often of how very unhuman she was, that underneath everything she was still a freak.

If the dryads accepted Sequoia, she'd never wear makeup again. She'd toss out her electronics and abandon her online presence. She'd become whatever they wanted her to be. But...she'd approached the ancients five times already, and failed each time. She had the proof on her arm.

Mom kept rambling, but then caught Sequoia's expression. "Are you okay?"

"I'm fine." Sequoia smiled weakly, forcing herself to make the words sound true. They had to be. Because after this year's summoning ceremony, Sequoia wouldn't be allowed to approach the trigani trees again.

If the dryads didn't accept her tonight, they never would.

She vowed she would find a way to make them. This time would be different. This time, she had a plan.

Sequoia's heart skipped as Mom parked the truck by the sweet-smelling hydrangea bushes outside Dad's trailer. He met them by the front steps, holding a sweating can of soda. His gold peacekeeper badge was pinned to his handwoven ceremonial shirt and he'd rolled up the long sleeves, unashamed of his rippling bark marks that glowed bronze in the evening sunlight. As Sequoia hurried up the wood steps, Dad held out a calloused hand, his emerald eyes sparkling.

"I'll pick her up in three weeks." Mom gave Dad a look from the truck as he pulled Sequoia into a hug. His chest was as thick and hard as a tree trunk. Mom revved the engine and Sequoia watched her go.

"Better get dressed for the ceremony, Seque." Dad patted her arm. "Grandfather won't speak to you like that."

Sequoia wanted to say he wouldn't speak to her anyway but she held her tongue. Weaving and wearing her ceremonial dress, memorizing the ancient chants, familiarizing herself with dryad history, none of it had made any difference—but the information she'd gathered on her flash drive would. Her stomach knotted. *Hopefully.*

She let the screen door bang shut behind her and sulked inside. Clothes had been flung across the couch, waiting to be folded, and a maze of cardboard boxes littered the floor, as if Dad hadn't remembered which one had stored the ceremonial supplies. He was usually more organized, but it seemed everyone was under stress lately. Sequoia kicked past the mess to her bedroom, flinging her backpack onto the daybed and landing in a heap. Rolling over, she unzipped her backpack and pulled out the flash drive, flipping it over in her hand. Electronics weren't permitted in the Balanos Forest, but at least this was more reverent than a cell phone. She closed her eyes, hoping Grandfather would listen to her. That he'd respond.

She'd seen Dad "talk" to Grandfather, heard him whisper softly. Sometimes he would sing. Dad always said Grandfather spoke back, but to Sequoia it was as if he were chanting nonsense to a gigantic tree. But looks, she knew, were deceiving.

Trigani seeds couldn't be harvested. The trees offered them of themselves, and the power the seeds held tied the dryad to whichever tree had claimed them. Dad had been presented with a trigani seed from his father's tree when he was just ten years old. And Dad had worn the seed proudly on his neck ever since, the leather band that held it now buttery soft from wear.

Sequoia slipped the flash drive into her pocket, then stood and approached her dresser. She shook open the top drawer, eyeing the contents wearily. The empty leather band Dad had helped her braid six years ago rested on top of folded sheets. Wrapped inside the cloth lay her handwoven ceremonial dress. She'd outgrown her second dress, was on her third, and the thought made her cheeks heat. Five years of failure.

She shrugged off her shirt. Sequoia had only ever seen a trigani seed in banded form, like Dad's, dried and wrapped in leather to keep the magic potent until the bearer died and was buried deep in the Balanos Forest. Then their bodies became trees as well, spirit and seed bonding to pass magic on to the next generation. Most dryads had been offered seeds by their fourteenth birthday. Rue's seed had come late at sixteen. But unbound adults weren't allowed to approach the trigani trees, so nobody had ever been given a seed after eighteen.

Sequoia unfolded the linen and inspected her dress, a sweet vanilla scent flooding her nostrils. Made from the long grasses that grew under the trigani trees, her long-sleeved dress was more comfortable than it appeared, but the low V meant to show off her seed only showed skin. She dressed, inspected herself in the mirror, then fished the drive out of her pants pocket and slipped it into the side of her bra.

"Seque," Dad's voice boomed through the trailer, followed by the sharp snap of the screen door shutting.

392

Sequoia stiffened, making sure the drive couldn't be seen, then poked a head into the hallway. "What?"

"We have to go."

"Ceremonies start at sundown." Sequoia frowned. "We've got another hour."

Dad shook his head. "Protestors."

Sequoia tapped a finger against the doorframe. Dad never said much, but that was because of his magic. Truth. He could catch anyone in a lie, so it was no use telling one, but that meant Dad had to stay honest as well. Some dryads called it a cheap gift, but those were the jealous ones. It made his peacekeeping job easier. It was a clever gift, and all dryads valued cleverness.

"I'll stay here."

Dad shook his head, held up his phone. "There won't be time. Just got a tip: some human has a trigani seed and is showing it off at the border."

Removing a bonded seed was an unforgivable act, a cause for exile among the dryads. How could a human get one? Sequoia shivered. Maybe they'd raided the forest after the spring fire. She imagined cloaked gravediggers shearing a freshly rooted seed from a stiffening corpse. But as gruesome as stealing a seed would be, the uselessness of it made the act worse. Seeds bonded by blood. The magic associated with it couldn't transfer. Humans wouldn't know that though....

"Any truth to the claim?"

"Probably not, but I still have to check it out."

Sequoia frowned.

Dad shrugged. "The tipper certainly *believed* a human stole a trigani seed. But people, especially angry people, like to believe the worst."

Sequoia nodded but said nothing.

Dad gave her a once over, the faintest hint of a smile behind his eyes. "You look nice. Just wish your mother wouldn't make your hair so—"

Sequoia cut him off like she did whenever either of her parents started picking at the other. "I'll pack the ceremonial wraps, the water offering, and meet you and everyone else at Grandfather's tree." She backed into her room, dress swishing softly against her thighs, as she collapsed onto the bed and waited to hear the screen door slam.

Sometimes Sequoia wished Dad wasn't so honest. She knew that had contributed to her parents' separation—Dad either didn't say anything at all or he used a sledgehammer.

But then there were footsteps, hesitation at the bedroom door, and Dad's warm hand on her shoulder. "We should talk. Come with me?"

"Is it about the summoning ceremony?" Sequoia's voice tightened. She didn't want to be forced to reveal the flash drive. "Because I don't want to talk about it."

"It's about the fire."

Sequoia froze. Dad hadn't said anything about the April fire since the day it had happened. Grandfather's tree had blackened on the south side, leaves shriveled, but the tree itself would recover. Grandma's tree hadn't been so fortunate. It died that day, along with a few hundred others. That weekend—Mom had sent Sequoia home for a visit—she and Dad had walked among the ancients turned to ash, bark and branch still sizzling as smoke rose into a hungry black sky. Sequoia didn't need to be able to talk to trees to feel the loss of that place.

"What about the fire?"

"You didn't say much when it happened. Did you ever read anything, talk to Mom, watch the news?"

"A bit." Sequoia shrugged. Mom hadn't wanted Sequoia to watch what she called "skewed coverage," but Sequoia had sought what she could. And what she'd found disturbed her. There'd been an online article where the Walter Bay mayor expressed sympathy for the "tragic lightning strike." It detailed the devastation and concluded with the mayor's promise to stand in solidarity with their neighbors. A fluff piece. But then she'd scrolled through the comments section, where a keyboard-warrior dryad asserted it was arson and that the city refused to seek justice. He'd posted a photograph as proof, the charred remains of a road flare. That picture should have gone viral. Even now, if Grandfather would give her a seed, she'd make sure it did. She had more than a picture to support her conclusions. She had her info on the thumb drive.

Dad pulled his hand back. "The fire burned a lot more than trees, Seque. The dryads are furious."

Sequoia picked at the grass ends of her skirt. "It's their job to protect the land."

"This is different." Dad narrowed his eyes, gave Sequoia a hard stare. She stopped playing with her dress. "There's real hate in people's hearts, and any sort of spark cou———"

"I understand."

"No, Seque." Dad raised his voice. "You don't understand. You haven't heard the ancients speak. You don't know how things were before people like...before people like you showed up."

"You mean *half-breeds*?" The word felt angry on her tongue. She hated saying it, hated that Dad was pointing out her *otherness*. The scars on her arm burned and she rubbed her hand over the rough sleeve.

Dad nodded. "Dryads and humans have never truly gotten along. It's a miracle your mother and I..." He shook his head. "The fire has brought out the worst in people, rekindled old fears. Traditions. A few of the angriest dryads talk of poisoning the water table as retribution for the fire." Sequoia's eyes widened. Dad spoke quickly and held up his seed. "They won't. I—I'm sure they won't. But they talk about it."

"That's not comforting, Dad."

"This talk isn't about comfort. It's about helping you understand." Dad cleared his throat but this time he couldn't meet her eyes. "Dryads don't value sacrifice—never have. You see it in the gifts they give, the friends they keep. We're cunning, not loving, and that's what has helped us survive."

The bed squeaked as Sequoia shifted, feeling the weight in his words and the strange use of "us" versus "they." "But dryads are loyal to the trees."

"Because the trees give us power, Seque."

A lump rose in Sequoia's throat. Hearing Dad speak so plainly about dryad nature—it felt incomplete. She'd made dryad friends when finding human ones were hard. "You said the fire burned more than trees?"

"It burned tolerance, too." Dad took another breath. "And loyalty. Many dryads don't like you, Seque, and the ones who *do*, don't want to be seen with you right now."

Sequoia's stomach knotted.

"Rue isn't coming to watch you summon Grandfather tonight. Neither is Auntie Cypress. And unless something changes, they won't be visiting us again."

Dad hadn't needed to bribe Sequoia to come with him after that, but he'd handed her a soda anyway and she'd planted the chilled beverage between her knees. She'd use it as a cool pack on her skin while she waited for Dad to question the protestors.

She clicked her seatbelt in place and Dad started the jeep. The engine rumbled.

His jeep was even older than Mom's pickup, the cloth seats frayed and worn, with too much dirt trapped between the cushions. A cardboard box was shoved in the back with yesteryear's stained ceremonial wraps peeking out of the top. Guess he'd found them.

For about five minutes Sequoia remained poised for further discussion, but Dad's desire to talk seemed to have expired at the front door. They drove in silence until they reached the northern border.

A group of at least fifty protestors had gathered next to the barbed wire fence that sectioned off dryad territory. They shouted and shook handmade signs: "Tax the Trees or Ax the Treaties" and "Dryads Are Devils."

Anger twisted in Sequoia's gut as she read the slur. "Dad, why do they call us devils?"

Dad's gaze was on the road. Rows of vehicles lined either

side of it and more were coming. "Both sides contributed to that, Seque."

Sequoia frowned. "How?"

Dad shifted in his seat as they drew closer. "About sixty years ago, there were two tree fellers. They brought their iron saws and snuck into the Balanos Forest, looking for the oldest trees they could fell."

"That's horrible."

Dad nodded. "But one touch to the ancients left their brains addled. They came out of the woods screaming about dryad tree demons. Both fellers ended up in the sanitarium, never the same. For a long time, it was the talk of the town. Families wouldn't let their kids near us, not that we wanted them here."

Sequoia pursed her lips. "And now the humans want access to the trees for their pretty parks and bike trails. The ones that wouldn't be here, if the loggers had had their way."

Dad shrugged, but his face darkened as he watched a group of kids in matching "Dirty Dryad" T-shirts jump out of the back of a truck. "I understand why the city was angry then, but—"

Dad cursed. A lone dryad stood on a rickety wood platform, shouting down the crowd. It happened every year, at least one dryad trying to defend the "indefensible" and make humans see sense. It never worked.

Dad parked the jeep in a weedy patch thirty yards from the crowd and said, "Seque, wait here." He raised an eyebrow. "Things could get rough."

Sequoia nodded but rolled down the window to prevent herself from roasting. Dad slammed the door, clutched his seed, and stalked toward the angry crowd. Sequoia watched, stomach knotting and unknotting.

He'd be okay. Dad was smart. She tapped a finger on the soda can and shook her head. No, Dad was more than smart, he had magic. He'd know who had the seed *if* there was one floating around.

"Get off our land!" A beefy redhead threw a water bottle at

the dryad on the platform. The dryad ducked, and the crowd howled. Something deep inside Sequoia broke. Every year one or two dryads tried to make peace with the protestors, and every year they failed. But why didn't Dad try? He had a daughter—a half-human daughter. Why didn't he try to make the world better for Sequoia? Dad claimed truth was powerful, but he was too scared and selfish to use it for anything stronger than exposing lies during his peacekeeping duties. If dryad magic was so powerful, he should have been able to *make* the protestors see how they needed the dryads. The Balanos Forest filtered and cleaned the water that Walter Bay citizens drank. They'd been there long before the humans. If Dad wouldn't force the humans to see truth, she would. And maybe she'd finally be accepted by the dryads too.

"Hey, Seque," a voice piped from behind the jeep.

Sequoia sat up and glared at the teenage boy who knocked on the side door. "What do you want, Adair?"

Adair was a year younger, with a hooked nose and devilish personality. Just like humans, Sequoia had her least favorite dryads. "I wanted to see how you were enjoying the view. Come fall, this is as close as you'll get to dryad land."

Sequoia pushed her sweat-slicked hair from her face and rolled the cold soda can against her forehead. "Wow, Adair. Hope your summer feels as pleasant as your personality."

"Charming, then." He smirked, rubbing the banded seed on his leather necklace. "But it seems you're either ignorant or unaware that changes have been made." Adair didn't need to use his power—emotional manipulation—to make Sequoia's stomach knot. He grinned wickedly. "Guess I have your attention. Adults without a trigani seed won't be admitted to *any* dryad land." He nodded at the barbed wire fence. "That means eighteen-year-old you won't make it past the border. When is your birthday again?"

Sequoia frowned. "That's not true."

Mom had lived on dryad land when she and Dad were married—and she'd just dropped Sequoia off. Visitors had to be respectful, undergo a background check, and not go nosing around, but ever since the treaty, the dryads had allowed some visitors into their territory. The Balanos Forest that held the trigani trees—that was different. Mom had never been to a summoning, would *never* be allowed to a summoning, and if Sequoia didn't get a seed this year, her visits to the ancients would be halted as well. But she'd still be able to come home. After all, her dad *was* a full-blooded dryad.

"It will be true, come fall." Adair lifted his chin. "Times have changed and the ancients are expanding their restrictions accordingly."

Sequoia's heart squeezed. "You're wrong. And even if you're not, I am going to get a trigani seed tonight. My Grandfath——"

"Good luck with that."

She rolled her eyes.

"Ask your dad about the new restrictions." Adair grinned, dropping his seed to his chest. "He'll have to tell you sometime."

Sequoia leaned forward to roll up the window but Adair grabbed it and pointed. "Hey, aren't those your human friends?"

Sequoia twisted around the seat to see Mason Berger and Henry Lilinquest in blue and green Walter Bay High School T-shirts. Her face heated. She'd had a crush on Mason, but that was before her car had been vandalized. She hadn't seen Mason there that day, but his being at the border told her everything she needed to know.

"They're coming over." Adair gripped his seed again, eyes gleaming.

"Is that Sequoia?" The boys' voices traveled seamlessly across the air, the taller one pointing. Mason leaned over, said something to Henry.

Sequoia dropped the soda and finished rolling up the window.

Adair flashed another smile and then darted back to dryad land and into the trees. She counted the seconds as the footfalls closed in, waiting for the inevitable train wreck.

A knock on the glass. "Sequoia?"

She gave a little wave but didn't move to roll down the window. She'd rather endure the heat.

"Dude, she's in an actual dryad dress." Henry laughed. He pointed at her, talking loudly, like it didn't matter she could hear. But his next comment came quieter. "Maybe she can sneak us in. I hear once they're in the ancient part of the forest, they dance naked."

Sequoia shoved the door into him. Henry stumbled backward and landed in the dirt, face flushed with surprise. Henry was in her territory. This wasn't like high school.

"We don't dance until *after* we've feasted on human flesh." She climbed from the pickup and approached, glaring at both boys. "If you want to be a ceremonial sacrifice, we take volunteers."

"Sequoia?" Mason looked at her strangely, staring below her neck. Heat flooded and Sequoia crossed her arms over her chest, but the movement made the flash drive shift, slipping. Her cheeks burned as she shifted her straps to keep it from falling.

"Yours looks different," he whispered. His eyes hadn't moved and she realized he was staring at her necklace. His pupils were dilated strangely, as if Adair's magic worked on him, and Mason's fingers twitched, as if he wanted to reach out and touch the empty leather.

She pulled away.

"Come on, man." Henry scrambled to his feet, dusted himself off. "She's just another dryad tease. Not worth the ground she grew from." He punched his friend's arm.

Mason didn't move.

Sequoia stuck out her chin. "You should go."

"Dude." Henry had pulled out his phone and started snapping pictures. "This is going straight to the webpage Dillan created for half-breed hoes and—"

Sequoia slapped the phone from his hand; it tumbled into a prickle-weed patch. "Get out of here! You can't do that." But as she slapped it, the flash drive slipped again, tumbling down her dress and onto the ground. She swooped to pick it up.

"Better hope you didn't shatter my screen!" Henry dropped

to the ground. "You're on the wrong side of the border to think daddy can—"

"Stop." Mason squeezed his eyes as if he were fighting a headache, but when he opened them, his pupils were normal again.

"What's that?" Henry sneered, stepping forward and grabbing the flash drive from Sequoia's hand. "I thought dryads didn't use electronics. What's on here?"

Fear iced Sequoia's stomach. If he realized what was on that drive, her high-school experience was about to get much worse. Plus, it was her only way to bargain for a trigani seed. "Give it back!"

Henry held it over her head, taunting.

"You guys are such hypocrites. Spouting off all your tree-loving mumbo-jumbo." He snapped a low twig from a tree, waving the leaves and raining dirt on Sequoia.

Grit caught in her eyes as she blinked furiously. This wasn't high school, but it was beginning to feel like it.

"Aw, she's gonna cry."

"Henry, stop it. This isn't why I sai——" Mason caught Henry's arm, was pulling his friend to face him when Sequoia saw the opportunity. She lunged. Her knuckles cracked as they made contact with Henry's jaw. His head lolled backward and he dropped the flash drive. She scooped it up.

"What the hell is wrong with you?" Mason glared at Sequoia while he supported his friend.

"Ask that about yourselves." Sequoia's voice shook, but she stood tall. "You don't get to steal. My picture. My flash drive." She nodded at the protestors. "Or our sacred land."

Henry's face was pale, but as the stars in his eyes faded, his stance shifted. He struggled to lunge at Sequoia but Mason gripped his forearm, taking a deep breath and speaking calmly, "Go back to the border, Henry. I need to talk with Sequoia."

"I'm not leaving you alone with her. She's insane."

"She's right."

Something strange snaked through Sequoia's chest, but she

suppressed it. She hadn't expected Mason to agree with her, but she didn't like him thinking she needed his help. "Just go." She waved him off. "Both of you."

"Whatever." Henry rubbed his jaw, turned to Mason. "Are you coming?"

"In a minute." Mason scowled, motioning him away.

Sequoia clutched the flash drive protectively.

Henry rolled his eyes. "It's your funeral, Mason. If your dad knew who you w——"

"I said, in a minute." Mason's eyes flashed and this time Henry turned, trekking back to the protestors.

For a moment Sequoia wondered if the crowd had seen her punch Henry—and if they'd treat her father in kind. But it seemed they were too focused on arguing with each other to notice the teenage scuffle. Or maybe Adair had intervened there as well...

A breeze kicked through the trees, flapping the grass ends of Sequoia's dress against her thighs as she stared Mason down.

"Listen, I'm sorry."

"It's fine," Sequoia said. "You should go."

He shook his head. "I'm not saying sorry because of this. I mean, yeah *this* was bad but..." He took a deep breath, and his eyes shifted as if he couldn't quite meet hers. "I've been meaning to talk to you, but I—I didn't have a way to reach you."

Her stomach fluttered.

"I know who messed with your car."

Acid stung Sequoia's throat. "Lucky you." She should have known; a human like him couldn't be interested in a half-breed like her.

"It wasn't right."

"No, it wasn't." She nodded toward the protestors. "And neither is this."

He winced, still unable to meet her eyes. "My dad brought me here.... I'm not an activist." He shuffled his feet. "But you don't—you don't actually hurt people, do you? The rumors—that was a joke about eating hu——"

"Please," Sequoia scoffed, raising a brow. "The dryads hear things about the humans in Walter Bay too. But it seems people have a hard time understanding sarcasm if it fits their prejudices."

Mason's face reddened. "I'm not—"

"Hey!" Dad was blazing toward them, eyes full of fury. "Get away from my daughter!"

Mason's red face drained to white. "Sorry. I'll see you around. Promise," he whispered and dashed back into the crowd.

Dad watched him run and Sequoia used the moment to stuff away the flash drive.

"What were you doing with *that* boy?" He emphasized *that*, pointing out the difference, the otherness. The *humanness*.

Sequoia's anger shifted. If anyone owed an explanation, it was Dad. "*That boy* goes to my school."

His nose wrinkled, but he nodded to the car door. Sequoia slipped inside, still steaming as she yanked back her seatbelt.

Dad slid a hand over the steering wheel, breathing deeply. "You shouldn't have talked to him today. If anyone saw, it'll make things worse."

"It can't get worse."

"It can *always* get worse."

Sequoia jutted her chin. "Like how if Grandfather doesn't give me a trigani seed, I'll be banished from *all* dryad land?"

Dad choked. "Who told you that?"

"Adair. Is *that* true?"

Dad cursed, let out another long breath. "No. Not entirely."

Sequoia frowned. "So I'll still be able to come home? No matter what happens?"

Dad revved the jeep and backed into the road. "You'll get to decide."

Sequoia huffed. "According to Adair, the trees decide."

"Well, Adair doesn't always tell the truth, now does he?" Dad's eyes sparkled and Sequoia couldn't help the tingling heat that crawled up her neck. He was right about Adair, but there had been some truth to what he'd said too. Dad admitted that.

The jeep rocked as they drove over a pothole, but it felt as if it had rocked her confidence as well.

"Did you at least find the trigani seed?" The words bubbled up and out, anything to keep her mind from weighing on Adair's taunts and the ceremony.

"Yes." The heat from Dad's voice waned slightly, but his knuckles whitened as he gripped the steering wheel. "It wasn't real. The fraud had a nasty narrative in mind."

"Oh."

They drove in silence.

"Seque, it's fine. Things will work out."

"But what if they don't?" Sequoia's voice broke and with it came the flood of fears. "Grandfather's never even talked to me, and now, with everything else . . . he might blame me for what happened to Grandma." She shouldn't have brought up the loss, and yet as soon as the words tumbled from her mouth she couldn't take them back.

It was unreasonable, she knew, it didn't make sense—and yet the words felt true. The ancients despised humans, blamed humans. Was it really a stretch to include her in that mess?

"He doesn't blame you." Dad kept his eyes on the road. "I've already spoken to him about it."

"What?" Her hair flipped as she spun to stare at him. "When?"

"After the fire. He promised me he would speak to you . . ." Sequoia's stomach pitched. Dad went on. "And once he does, he'll see how strong you are. Realize your true potential, a bridge between worlds, not as—" He stopped short, but Sequoia filled in the blank.

A half-breed.

Dad pursed his lips and swallowed hard. "It's going to be all right. I promise."

It made no sense for Dad to promise that. There were no guarantees, even if Grandfather liked what Sequoia had brought him—but whenever Dad made promises she paid close attention. It wasn't just his words. It was magic.

The Balanos Forest had changed over the last few months. Although a black stain still sullied the once-emerald haven, patches of life were working their way through the ash. Purple Canterbury bells, orange poppies, and silver foxtails had laced their roots into the soil. Their floral scent mixed with the dwindling soot, blunting the impression of loss.

Sequoia knelt, barefoot to show respect for the trees, and fingered a tiny sprout that leaped from the center of Grandmother's ashy remains. Was it possible that Grandmother—

"That's not her." Dad spoke softly, kneeling beside Sequoia. "When the forest is full and alive there are seeds that fall but never sprout. When a fire comes, they have their chance to rise from the ashes."

Sequoia pulled her hand from the little shoot. "I'm sorry."

"Sometimes a fire is needed, Seque." He squeezed her arm. "Even if we loved what once grew there."

She nodded.

Dad lifted his chin toward the treetops, an orange-streaked sky peeking between the branches. "We should get to work."

Shaded by the ancients and cooled by twilight, they started. Dad pulled the bottles from the cardboard box and set up a circular water offering. Sequoia unrolled the ceremonial cloths—old and worn, painted red with dryad symbols. They displayed family names, favorite stories, and current events; things Grandfather could read after he'd woken.

Sequoia surveyed the branches. The saying went that blood was thicker than water, and perhaps that's why the trigani trees grew into such monstrosities. Thirty-six years had passed since Grandfather's body and trigani seed had been planted among the ancients, and his trunk had grown so wide Sequoia couldn't wrap her arms around him if there were two of her.

She draped the ancient cloths over the low branches, one by one, the pieces floating in the wind. She had over a hundred to tie before the ceremony could start. Pungent, sticky sap leaked from a branch on the burned side—and Sequoia took special care to bind that gently. Her fingers came back stained a sickly yellow.

Undeterred, she turned to the box, gathered another set of cloths, and stared back at the floating white strips. It had been just like that when they toilet papered her car—long white pieces floating in the wind.

Nobody likes you. Dirty dryad.

She shook her head, kept hanging the cloths.

Dad was counting on her, and Grandfather wouldn't be impressed by weakness or self-pity. Today she was a dryad and dryads were smart. Dryads were strong. Dryads didn't care what humans thought.

"Seque, what's wrong?"

"Nothing." She shook her head again, pulled out another strip. There were only a few left. Her dress whispered against her skin, her feet padded across the dry grass and ashy soil. She worked and let her heart freeze so it wouldn't hurt, so she wouldn't have to remember the painful prank, wouldn't have to think of the dryad slurs, or the unfounded accusations of her teachers, or of Rue and Auntie Cypress abandoning her.

She was strong.

"Seque?"

Dad gripped his trigani seed in his right hand, channeling his gift. He'd recognized her lie.

She smoothed the last strip, stared at the symbols, and kept her voice cool. "I don't fit in at school. In Walter Bay. The humans don't want a dryad there."

"You aren't *just* a dryad."

"I know." Sequoia grimaced. "That's the problem."

Dad dumped the last of the water into the circle and then stood to face Sequoia. "Who chooses who belongs, Seque?"

Sequoia rolled her eyes. "That's a dumb question."

"Who chooses?"

"I don't know. Whoever has power?" Sequoia waved a hand. "*Them.* The other people."

406

Dad frowned. "You had it right the first time, Seque. Those with *power* choose who belong. And you have that power. You choose to belong."

"It's not that simple."

"It is, Seque. You choose what you want and you take it." He nodded to the tree, roots gnarled and thick, still intertwined with Grandmother's. Black deadness, twisted hand in hand with life. "They did."

Sequoia felt the sour sting of acid as she swallowed.

"Seque, do you want this?"

She tried to imagine what having a trigani seed would be like. She'd sat under the stars with Rue and they'd swapped dreams about which powers would be best. Traditional abilities like wind whisperer, rain caller, and bee speaker had become rarer. Over the last few decades the trees had gifted seeds that would help their children protect themselves from a changing world: Adair's emotional manipulation, Dad's discernment.

Sequoia had never cared much about the actual powers that came with her trigani seed. Nothing was more powerful than belonging. Than knowing who you were and where you fit into the world.

"I do want this," she said.

Dad nodded. "Then tell Grandfather. Wake his tree."

He took a step back and made room for her to address the trigani tree. Sequoia stepped into the center of the water offering. She set her feet, toes squishing into the cool mud as she closed her eyes and started to whisper the sacred chant.

She placed her palms on the tree, the rough bark warm and grainy against her skin. The world around her became smaller and more focused as she chanted.

"Seque, louder. Show him who you are."

Her voice grew as she sang, trying to picture it. Trying to imagine Grandfather giving her a seed. Trying to show him what being a dryad meant to her. What she could offer. The flash drive burned against her chest.

There was a sharp flash like her flesh was melting into the

bark, a searing pain as her soul split and the spirit inside the tree dragged her within. Tingling waves of heat and light brought an amber image into focus like she was in a sepia-filtered photograph.

Sequoia's heart thundered somewhere separate from her consciousness.

This is it.

She quivered against the coming waves, trembling against a spirit flame that scorched hotter than glowing coals. She could see him now, his eyes so much like Dad's, the same face, though his bark marks were fully tree now, rough and flaky. His hair hung in wild clumps; leaves twisted through a thick, black mane.

Grandfather?

He didn't smile. *You are Sequoia, the half-breed, the girl the ancients despise.*

Sequoia's soul shuddered, wanting to protest that she was part-dryad, not just a half-breed, but she couldn't change how Grandfather saw her.

You seek a trigani seed. I promised your father I would hear you. Grandfather raised an eyebrow. *But I did not promise I would trust you.*

I will earn your trust.

His eyes gleamed unnaturally in the spirit light. *You've thought a great deal about what gift you'd like from me, what promises I will make. And I see your offering against your chest. It is an irreverent mocking to bring such things here.*

Sequoia's insides twisted. *You don't understand. I've brought proof of who started the fire. The humans are to blame.*

Bah! Grandfather howled. *You think the ancients do not know this? That your father doesn't know this?*

Sequoia stiffened. *The point is, I can prove it. I've gathered records from the police, hacked the mayor's emails. The fire didn't come from a lightning strike. I can make the humans liste——*

Like the humans listened about you not cheating on your schoolwork? Grandfather's eyebrows shot skyward. *They won't listen to a dryad, and certainly not a half-breed like you.*

DANIEL BITTON

Sequoia swallowed, hope crumbling. She'd been naive. *I—I just wanted...*

A trigani seed. Grandfather wrinkled his nose, as if the idea made him sick. *I don't want your proof that humans have malice. The ancients know this. I wanted proof of your loyalty. I've waited so long to see it.* His lips thinned. *Apparently, I must wait still.*

But I can show this to others, put it online, and—

And yet you haven't. You knew the humans were guilty, claim to have proof of it, and yet you did *nothing. How telling.*

Sequoia didn't answer. He was right, and a numbness spread through her chest as he went on.

I see the scars on your arm, the scores you make in your bark, the pain rejection has caused you. You wish to be accepted. You desire to belong. Whoever does that *has your loyalty.*

Sequoia moved to tug on her sleeves, but she was spirit and couldn't tug anything physical. Her soul was bare. Heat flushed.

Grandfather's lips twitched. *But I can make use of you still. If you promise to protect this forest from harm, I will be able to gift you a seed.*

I— Sequoia hesitated. Grandfather hadn't been impressed with her information or her inaction, but he was offering her a seed anyway? Dad's words from earlier speared her heart; dryads were cunning. They were loyal to the trees because they gifted them power—but dryads *were* trees, and so the trees must also be cunning.

Grandfather's lips split into a knowing grin. *I read your soul and what you think is true. There is often a motivating factor behind every gift.*

And you'll share yours?

Grandfather's smile faded. *Perhaps because you are a half-breed I should not expect you to understand.* Another wave of angry heat rippled through Sequoia, but Grandfather continued as if he hadn't insulted her. *I speak plainly. Your trigani seed will give you the hope of your heart. You will belong with our kind...but it will also poison any human that comes near it.* His voice twisted as he went on. *It is a costly gift, draining much magic, but I would happily bestow it to punish those who burned our forest. Those who—*

My mother? Sequoia's voice trembled. *What would happen to her?*

If you went home to her, she would die. Accepting this seed means you belong to us. He turned his back, waved a hand, and brought up two images: Mom and Dad circled in smoke. *Loyalty can be measured through actions. By what you* choose *to do.* He waved his hand again, brightening Dad's image. *Your father reminded me that humans revere sacrifice. Your mother would be your sacrifice to the dryads. Your proof of loyalty.*

That isn't proof of loyalty. Sequoia willed strength into her voice. *That's proof I'm capable of betrayal.*

A thoughtful twist on my words. Grandfather smirked. *But the choice remains. Every half-breed before you has made their peace with one world or the other.*

Sequoia knew he was right. She hadn't been the first half-breed to grow up between worlds. She'd seen an older gentleman with faint bark marks at the Walter Bay Market, minding his own business. She knew of two elderly women who had chosen the forest, magic darkening their bark marks to almost the same shade as the full-blooded dryads they'd chosen to stay with.

But Sequoia had been raised to believe she could live on both sides of the border. Why would her father say she was a bridge if that future wasn't possible?

Your thoughts wander. Grandfather's voice turned scolding. *Choose wisely. This offer won't return.*

As he spoke, a cold chill snaked through Sequoia. There was no way out of this. The ancients had thought of everything and made their point plain. Sequoia wasn't clever enough, wasn't dryad enough, unless she became one of them. And becoming one of them meant she'd have to cut out the human part of herself—including her mother. Somewhere distant, Sequoia's heart thudded, every pounding beat filling her with anger. Grandfather had seen her pain, her struggle to fit in, and had used it against her. The ancient dryads weren't just cunning.

411

They were cruel. Fury balled inside her. *You are asking me to become a murderer. There must be anoth———*

There is not. Grandfather's voice was fierce.

Then . . . I reject your offer.

Vicious half-breed! Grandfather's face twisted, the familiarity in his eyes evaporating as he advanced on her. *Traitor!* His eyes were red now, his teeth narrowing into sharp points, long amber fingernails clawing at her retreating consciousness. Sequoia tried to fade back out, but the angry eyes yanked her in, branding her mind with the images of Grandmother and her bark blistering in the fire. Of the hundreds of others cooked to cinders.

These are the crimes of the world you choose.

Sequoia's mind flailed, searching for a way out, but Grandfather only opened himself further, forcing Sequoia to burn in the ache for his wife and the friends he'd lost. She suffocated under his hurt.

His hate.

You will never belong. In this forest—or anywhere else!

He shoved her, her spirit finally thrown from the tree and into her body. She yelped as the momentum rocketed her backward, and she landed with a sickening squelch into the mud. Her hair fell over her face, and through grime-coated tangles, she glimpsed the flash drive, smoking and sizzling beside her. A numbness spread through her chest as she suppressed a sob. Grandfather truly hadn't cared about the information inside the drive. Had never cared for her . . .

"Seque?" Dad's voice came from behind as a whisper.

Sequoia didn't look up. How could she tell him? How could she admit what she'd done? What she'd chosen? She'd be forced to live in the human world now, forever banished from her dryad side.

Slowly, she stood, hugging her arms to her chest, and keeping her eyes on the dirt.

"Seque, it's okay." He kicked the flash drive and stepped closer, not even sounding angry that she'd violated a sacred space. He held out a hand. "It's not you—"

"Adair was right," she whispered, backing away. "I will be

banished. Grandfather gave me a choice, but I—I couldn't...Why did you make me hear it from him?"

Dad stepped closer. She could feel the weight of his gaze, and from the corner of her eye she watched his hand touch Grandfather's tree lightly, then pull away. "I was selfish. I knew what you kept on that drive. I also knew it wouldn't change anything. But I hoped your bringing it would help Grandfather see what having someone who understands both sides could..."

Sequoia closed her eyes.

"I had hoped he'd change his mind," Dad rasped. "There are few dryads who recognize what you are capable of. You could be a bridge—"

"How can I be a bridge, if I can't come here?" Sequoia spun to face him, hair flying, voice tight. "I am *banished* because I won't betray the human part of myself. And it's not like the humans will accept me, either. I'm not a bridge. I'm a raft stuck in a river between worlds and I'm sinking."

She ripped back her sleeve, the grass weave tearing, as she exposed the five thin scars from where she'd cut herself after every failed summoning. "I'm sinking because I will never be accepted anywhere!"

Dad stared at her, eyes drifting to the scars and then back to her face. "Does it matter if I accept you?" he spoke quietly. "If your mother accepts you?"

Sequoia didn't answer, staring down at the scars and wondering how she'd manage to make the sixth one tonight. Her throat closed and she yanked the torn sleeve back.

Dad's brow knit, but there was a softness in his expression. He took a breath. "Others can lie, Seque, but you know I speak the truth. I love you, and I would never leave you alone. I wanted to tell you about the trailer, but I sent you to Grandfather because I still hoped he would—"

"The trailer?" She remembered the clothes, the scattered cardboard boxes, and it clicked. He hadn't misplaced the ceremonial supplies. He'd been packing. "You're moving?"

"No child should ever be banished from coming home."

413

"You shouldn't have to leave for me." Sequoia's voice trembled as she nodded to the trees. "This is *your* home."

He touched her arm, and this time Sequoia gazed into his eyes. He said, "You are my home, Seque."

Her anger melted.

"I wish Grandfather," he continued, "could see what I see when I look at you. Such strength." He pulled his leather band from his neck, held the seed in his right hand and cupped it into hers. "But Grandfather is not the only dryad who can offer you a trigani seed."

Sequoia pulled away. "You can't—"

"I can." Dad held her hand tight and jutted his chin. "I have every right to give a trigani seed to my daughter. Bonded to my blood, born of my blood. You *can* take this."

She searched her mind, hardly daring it to be true. But it had to be because Dad had spoken it. "But *you'll* be exiled. It's cheating. It's—"

"Dryads are clever, Seque." Dad's lips twitched into a small smile. "The ancients left the door open because they didn't think I'd use it. Sacrifice is a human characteristic." He folded her fingers around the seed, pressed her palm shut. "The seed is yours. It should always have been yours." He let go.

And like a broken dam, dryad magic flooded Sequoia. The trigani seed rooted, tingling, and burning through her body as it opened her mind, expanding outward.

It was stronger than she had ever imagined—dryad magic that ignited her awareness of the world. It exploded to include the ancients in the Balanos Forest, the dryads wandering sacred land, and farther, past the border, where the protestors still stood with their angry signs.

She felt a steady stream of magic draining from the seed, pulling on the trees. She had to control it.

She urged herself to cut ties, to pull the truth tethers back. Her mind pounded under the weight, but as she brought the tethers closer, smaller truths touched and drew flame.

Adair was afraid of her and the change she could bring to

the forest. Rue felt guilty for missing the ceremony but had worried her family would have been ostracized if she supported Sequoia. Henry had been rude because he was trying to impress his friends—he'd been bullied before. And Mason's father had beaten him, forcing him to come to the protests.

She tugged on the truth tethers again, but they didn't budge, instead tying fast to a new understanding. People had a reason for their way of being, and taking the time to learn their truth—that was the way to empathy, to forgiveness, to peace. No one could force truth. They had to see it, to feel it, before they could change. The seed sputtered dangerously.

Sequoia yanked the tethers harder, and this time they obeyed, but as she wrenched the last one in, it crossed Dad.

She flinched as his truth blazed. Every time she'd silently chided him, he'd heard. He'd known she thought him selfish and scared for not building a new world with his gift. For not forcing the truth on others. He'd known her pain, and it had hurt him too. Hurt him badly enough to try something dryads considered unforgivable. He'd conserved the magic in his trigani seed, not because he was scared or selfish, but because he intended to save the strongest magic for her.

Guilt bubbled up Sequoia's throat. "Dad, I—I didn't understand. I'm sorry."

"I'm sorry, too." His face was paler now, and even in the moonlight it was clear his bark marks had faded. But Sequoia's marks pulsated deep bronze, a shade she would never be able to blend with foundation. The old Sequoia would have been worried about how to lighten the marks for school, figuring a way to taper off the magic. But the new Sequoia knew those marks were important.

They were supposed to stand out.

Sequoia's throat thickened as one last powerful truth pounded through her half-breed heart. She would *never belong* in the same way everyone else did—she wasn't meant to. And trying to be anything other than what she was wasted the gift Dad had given her.

She couldn't change what she was, but she could change the world around her. Bit by bit. Truth by truth. Through the gifts both parents had given her: sacrifice, understanding, and unconditional love.

Sequoia took a step toward Dad, knees still trembling under the new weight of her magic. She would learn how to wield this power. After all, she had Dad to help her.

"I'm so proud to be your father." Dad's eyes flashed in the dim light and he nodded to the wildflowers growing amid the ash. "I get to watch you change this ugly world into something better. A new tree must grow, Seque. *Your* tree must grow."

And because he was Dad, Sequoia knew he spoke the truth.

The Year in the Contests

Every year brings exciting growth and new changes to the Contests. In 2020, despite the global pandemic—or maybe in part because of it—we had a booming year!

LAST YEAR'S ANTHOLOGY

We released Volume 36 to huge success, and the trade reviews were excellent. *Publishers Weekly* reviewed it in their "Best Books" column and highlighted stories by Michael Gardner, Katie Livingston, Leah Ning, F.J. Bergmann, Storm Humbert, and David A. Elsensohn, declaring "Genre enthusiasts should take note."

Kirkus reviewers urged, "Don't overlook these wonderful short fiction reads being released this month."

Library Journal highlighted some authors and said, "With stories ranging from sf to fantasy, as well as some genre mash-ups, this collection offers something for both adults and teens to enjoy."

After reading Volume 36, the *Tangent Online* reviewer was "amazed that there are so many talented writers and artists out there."

And *Midwest Book Review* called the anthology "An inherently interesting and impressively entertaining volume that is quite literally the 'Best of the Best' in the current field of science fiction and fantasy...especially and unreservedly recommended."

Past volumes continue to stack up awards. Volume 35 won

the Foreword Indies 2019 Silver Award in science fiction, the New York City Big Book Award for anthology, the Benjamin Franklin Gold Award in science fiction and fantasy, and also the Critters Readers' Poll Award for best anthology of the year.

Though the awards season has barely begun for Volume 36, it has already won the New York City Big Book Award in fantasy.

In fact, last year's anthology was so popular, *DreamForge Magazine of Fantasy & Science Fiction* published an interview with Illustrators' Contest Coordinating Judge and artist, Echo Chernik, about her stunning cover art and the Contest.

CONTEST GROWTH

The Contests continue to experience explosive growth. In 2020, while everyone was stuck at home during the pandemic, many creators took advantage of the opportunity to write and illustrate. We had the highest-ever number of entries for both Contests.

As we've had entries from most countries on Earth, we rarely add a new country these days, but this year we had our first entry from Liechtenstein, a small country between Austria and Switzerland, with just over 38,000 residents. We now have entrants from 178 countries.

Winners in 2020 hail from China, England, India, Portugal, South Africa, the United States, and Vietnam.

A NEW WORKSHOP . . . AND AN AWARD-WINNING PODCAST!

The Contest launched an online writers' workshop in the spring of 2020 for anyone who would like to become a better writer.

The course is taught by Contest judges David Farland, Tim Powers, and Orson Scott Card, based on the timeless materials developed by L. Ron Hubbard. The workshop guides writers through the process of writing a story, from generating an idea to drafting a finished tale—and then shows how to submit it to the Contest!

Over 5,000 people have already begun the workshop. The course is free, and you can review the lessons at any time. To check it out, go to WritersoftheFuture.com.

Early last year, the sponsors of the Writers of the Future started a podcast and began interviewing writers, editors, and artists. The podcast has been an unmitigated success.

The 15th Annual People's Choice Podcast Awards recognized The Writers and Illustrators of the Future Podcast as a Finalist in the Storyteller category. You can listen to the podcast on our website.

NOTABLE ACCOMPLISHMENTS FROM ALUMNI AND JUDGES

The *Locus* Recommended Reading List for the year includes five Writers of the Future winners and judges, including Aliette de Bodard (Vol. 23), Ken Liu (Vol. 19), Nnedi Okorafor (Vol. 18), Tobias S. Buckell (Vol. 16), and Carolyn Ives Gilman (Vol. 3). (We've listed the Writers of the Future volume where you can first see an author's or illustrator's work.)

Author Martin L. Shoemaker (Vol. 31) released the novel *The Last Campaign* with 47North.

Contest judge and winner Nnedi Okorafor (Vol. 18) is co-writing the script for her award-winning novel *Binti* for Media Res studio.

Contest judges Brian Herbert and Kevin J. Anderson released the graphic novel *Dune* in preparation for the *Dune* theatrical release scheduled for 2021.

Contest judge Brandon Sanderson released the fourth book in his Stormlight Archive, *Rhythm of War.*

Contest judge Tim Powers released *Forced Perspectives*, the sequel to *Alternate Routes.*

Contest judge Orson Scott Card released *Zanna's Gift: A Life in Christmases,* just in time for the holidays.

Contest judges Larry Niven and Gregory Benford collaborated on book three of their Bowl of Heaven series, titled *Glorious.*

AWARDS FOR WINNERS

Our past artists and writers, along with our judges, continue to publish widely across many fields and in many mediums. We can't mention all their accomplishments, but here is a recap of notable awards:

Analog Analytical Laboratory (AnLab) and *Asimov's* Readers' Awards

Finalist: Best Fact Article—C. Stuart Hardwick (Vol. 30) with "Do We Still Need NASA?"

Finalist: Best Fact Article—Contest judge Gregory Benford, co-author with Albert Jackson of "Building a Gravitational Wave Transmitter."

Finalist: Best Cover Artist—Eldar Zakirov (Vol. 22).

Aurealis Awards

Winner: Best Fantasy Novella—Shauna O'Meara (Vol. 30) for "'Scapes Made Diamond."

Winner: Best Science Fiction Novella—Shauna O'Meara for "'Scapes Made Diamond."

Finalist: Best Science Fiction Novella—Cat Sparks (Vol. 21) for "You Will Remember Who You Were."

Finalist: Best Horror Short Story—Jason Fischer (Vol. 26) for "Of Meat and Man."

Finalist: Best Science Fiction Short Story—Jason Fischer for "Riding the Snails."

Finalist: Best Science Fiction Short Story—R. P. L. Johnson (Vol. 27) for "Canute."

Baen Awards

Winner, third place: Jim Baen Memorial Short Story Award—C. Stuart Hardwick (Vol. 30) for "Sample Return."

Finalist: Fantasy Adventure Award—Scott R. Parkin (Vol. 31) for "Who Will Know?"

420

Chesley Awards
Finalist: Best Magazine Illustration—Tiffany England (Vol. 29) for "Into the Wild Blue Yonder."
Finalist: Best Color Work: Unpublished—Bruce Brenneise (Vol. 34) for "If Stones Could Cry."
Finalist: Best Gaming-Related Illustration—Omar Rayyan (Vol. 8) for "Flaxen Intruder."

CILIP Kate Greenaway Medal
Winner: Best Children's Book—Contest judge and winner Shaun Tan (Vol. 8) for *Tales from the Inner City.*

Eisner Awards
Winner: Best Graphic Album—Nnedi Okorafor (Vol. 18) for *LaGuardia.*

Geffen Awards
Finalist: Best Translated Fantasy Book in Hebrew—Contest judge Brandon Sanderson for *Oathbringer*, translated by Zafrir Grosman.

Hugo Awards
Winner: Best Graphic Story or Comic—Nnedi Okorafor (Vol. 18) for *LaGuardia.*

Locus Awards
Finalist: Novelette—Nnedi Okorafor (Vol. 18) for "Binti: Sacred Fire."
Finalist: Short Story—Tobias S. Buckell (Vol. 16) for "The Galactic Tourist Industrial Complex."
Finalist: Short Story—Ken Liu (Vol. 19) for "Thoughts and Prayers."
Finalist: Anthology—Ken Liu for *Broken Stars: Contemporary Chinese Science Fiction in Translation.*

Finalist: Collection—Aliette de Bodard (Vol. 23) for *Of Wars, and Memories, and Starlight.*

Finalist: Artist—Contest judges Shaun Tan (Vol. 8) and Bob Eggleton.

Finalist: Nonfiction—Nnedi Okorafor for *Broken Places & Outer Spaces: Finding Creativity in the Unexpected.*

NAACP Image Awards

Finalist: Outstanding Literary Work, Children—Brittany Jackson (Vol. 24) for the illustrated book *Parker Looks Up: An Extraordinary Moment.*

Spectrum Fantastic Art

The Artist List for *Spectrum 27* includes Illustrators' Contest winners: Bruce Brenneise (Vol. 34), Laura Diehl (Vol. 20), Ben Hill (Vol. 36), Dustin Panzino (Vol. 27), Omar Rayyan (Vol. 8) and Contest judges Cliff Nielsen, Dan dos Santos, and Shaun Tan.

World Fantasy Awards

Lifetime Achievement Award for 2020—Karen Joy Fowler (Vol. 1).

Of course, with so many winners, we're at a point where we can't list everything here, but dozens of published short stories and novels can be found listed on the Contests' blog.

That's it for this year. Looking forward to next year and a spectacular future!

For Contest year 37, the winners are:

Writers of the Future Contest Winners

FIRST QUARTER

1. *Barbara Lund*
"SIXERS"

2. *Sara Fox*
"DEATH OF A TIME TRAVELER"

3. *K. D. Julicher*
"THE REDEMPTION OF BROTHER ADALUM"

SECOND QUARTER

1. *Christopher Bowthorpe*
"THE ENFIELD REPORT"

2. *Anj Dockrey*
"THE ARGENTUM"

3. *Elizabeth Chatsworth*
"THE WIDOW'S MIGHT"

THIRD QUARTER

1. *Trent Walters*
"SOUL PAPER"

2. *Luke Wildman*
"HOW TO STEAL THE PLOT ARMOR"

3. *Erik Lynd*
"THE SKIN OF MY MOTHER"

FOURTH QUARTER

1. *John M. Campbell*
"THE TIGER AND THE WAIF"

2. *Emma Washburn*
"HEMINGWAY"

3. *Ryan Cole*
"A DEMON HUNTER'S GUIDE TO PASSOVER SEDER"

FINALISTS

Elaine Midcoh, "THE BATTLE OF DONASI"
Brittany Rainsdon, "HALF-BREED"

THE YEAR IN THE CONTESTS

Illustrators of the Future Contest Winners

FIRST QUARTER
Jennifer Bruce
Isabel Gibney
Madolyn Locke

SECOND QUARTER
Rupam Grimoeuvre
Will Knight
Stephen Spinas

THIRD QUARTER
Mariah Salinas
Dan Watson
Jeff Weiner

FOURTH QUARTER
André Mata
Sethe Nguyen
Shiyi Yu

L. Ron Hubbard's
Writers of the
Future Contest

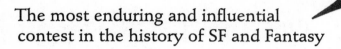

The most enduring and influential
contest in the history of SF and Fantasy

Open to new and amateur SF & Fantasy writers

Prizes each quarter: $1,000, $750, $500
Quarterly 1st place winners compete for $5,000
additional annual prize!

ALL JUDGING DONE BY
PROFESSIONAL WRITERS ONLY

No entry fee is required

Entrants retain all publication rights

Don't delay! Send your entry now!

To submit your entry electronically go to:
　writersofthefuture.com/enter-writer-contest

E-mail: contests@authorservicesinc.com

To submit your entry via mail send to:
　L. Ron Hubbard's Writers of the Future Contest
　7051 Hollywood Blvd.
　Los Angeles, California 90028

1. No entry fee is required, and all rights in the story remain the property of the author. All types of science fiction, fantasy, and dark fantasy are welcome.

2. By submitting to the Contest, the entrant agrees to abide by all Contest rules.

3. All entries must be original works by the entrant, in English. Plagiarism, which includes the use of third-party poetry, song lyrics, characters, or another person's universe, without written permission, will result in disqualification. Excessive violence or sex, determined by the judges, will result in disqualification. Entries may not have been previously published in professional media.

4. To be eligible, entries must be works of prose, up to 17,000 words in length. We regret we cannot consider poetry, or works intended for children.

5. The Contest is open only to those who have not professionally published a novel or short novel, or more than one novelette, or more than three short stories, in any medium. Professional publication is deemed to be payment of at least eight cents per word, and at least 5,000 copies, or 5,000 hits.

6. Entries submitted in hard copy must be typewritten or a computer printout in black ink on white paper, printed only on the front of the paper, double-spaced, with numbered pages. All other formats will be disqualified. Each entry must have a cover page with the title of the work, the author's legal name, a pen name if applicable, address,

telephone number, e-mail address and an approximate word count. Every subsequent page must carry the title and a page number, but the author's name must be deleted to facilitate fair, anonymous judging.

Entries submitted electronically must be double-spaced and must include the title and page number on each page, but not the author's name. Electronic submissions will separately include the author's legal name, pen name if applicable, address, telephone number, e-mail address, and approximate word count.

7. Manuscripts will be returned after judging only if the author has provided return postage on a self-addressed envelope.

8. We accept only entries that do not require a delivery signature for us to receive them.

9. There shall be three cash prizes in each quarter: a First Prize of $1,000, a Second Prize of $750, and a Third Prize of $500, in US dollars. In addition, at the end of the year the First Place winners will have their entries judged by a panel of judges, and a Grand Prize winner shall be determined and receive an additional $5,000. All winners will also receive trophies. The Grand Prize winner shall be announced and awarded, along with the trophies to winners, at the L. Ron Hubbard awards ceremony held in the following year or when it is able to be held due to government regulations.

10. The Contest has four quarters, beginning on October 1, January 1, April 1, and July 1. The year will end on September 30. To be eligible for judging in its quarter, an entry must be postmarked or received electronically no later than midnight on the last day of the quarter. Late entries will be included in the following quarter and the Contest Administration will so notify the entrant.

11. Each entrant may submit only one manuscript per quarter. Winners are ineligible to make further entries in the Contest.

12. All entries for each quarter are final. No revisions are accepted.

13. Entries will be judged by professional authors. The decisions of the judges are entirely their own, and are final and binding.

14. Winners in each quarter will be individually notified of the results by phone, mail, or e-mail.

15. This Contest is void where prohibited by law.

16. To send your entry electronically, go to:
www.writersofthefuture.com/enter-writer-contest
and follow the instructions.
To send your entry in hard copy, mail it to:
L. Ron Hubbard's Writers of the Future Contest
7051 Hollywood Blvd., Los Angeles, California 90028

17. Visit the website for any Contest rules update at:
www.writersofthefuture.com

L. Ron Hubbard's
Illustrators of the Future Contest

The most enduring and influential contest in the history of SF and Fantasy

Open to new and amateur SF & Fantasy artists

$1,500 in prizes each quarter
Quarterly winners compete for $5,000
additional annual prize!

ALL JUDGING DONE BY PROFESSIONAL ARTISTS ONLY

No entry fee is required

Entrants retain all rights

Don't delay! Send your entry now!

To submit your entry electronically go to:
writersofthefuture.com/enter-the-illustrator-contest

E-mail: contests@authorservicesinc.com

To submit your entry via mail send to:
L. Ron Hubbard's Illustrators of the Future Contest
7051 Hollywood Blvd.
Los Angeles, California 90028

1. The Contest is open to entrants from all nations. (However, entrants should provide themselves with some means for written communication in English.) All themes of science fiction and fantasy illustrations are welcome: every entry is judged on its own merits only. No entry fee is required and all rights to the entry remain the property of the artist.

2. By submitting to the Contest, the entrant agrees to abide by all Contest rules.

3. The Contest is open to new and amateur artists who have not been professionally published and paid for more than three black-and-white story illustrations, or more than one process-color painting, in media distributed broadly to the general public. The ultimate eligibility criterion, however, is defined by the word "amateur"—in other words, the artist has not been paid for his artwork. If you are not sure of your eligibility, please write a letter to the Contest Administration with details regarding your publication history. Include a self-addressed and stamped envelope for the reply. You may also send your questions to the Contest Administration via e-mail.

4. Each entrant may submit only one set of illustrations in each Contest quarter. The entry must be original to the entrant and previously unpublished. Plagiarism, infringement of the rights of others, or other violations of the Contest rules will result in disqualification. Winners in previous quarters are not eligible to make further entries.

5. The entry shall consist of three illustrations done by the entrant in a color or black-and-white medium created from the artist's imagination. Use of gray scale in illustrations

and mixed media, computer generated art, and the use of photography in the illustrations are accepted. Each illustration must represent a subject different from the other two.

6. ENTRIES SHOULD NOT BE THE ORIGINAL DRAWINGS, but should be color or black-and-white reproductions of the originals of a quality satisfactory to the entrant. Entries must be submitted unfolded and flat, in an envelope no larger than 9 inches by 12 inches. Images submitted electronically must be a minimum of 300 dpi, a minimum of 5 x 7 inches and a maximum of 8.5 x 11 inches. The file size should be a minimum of 5 MB and a maximum of 100 MB. Only .jpg and .jpeg files will be accepted.

7. All hard copy entries must be accompanied by a self-addressed return envelope of the appropriate size, with the correct US postage affixed. (Non-US entrants should enclose international postage reply coupons.) If the entrant does not want the reproductions returned, the entry should be clearly marked DISPOSABLE COPIES: DO NOT RETURN. A business-size self-addressed envelope with correct postage (or valid e-mail address) should be included so that the judging results may be returned to the entrant. We only accept entries that do not require a delivery signature for us to receive them.

8. To facilitate anonymous judging, each of the three photocopies must be accompanied by a removable cover sheet bearing the artist's name, address, telephone number, e-mail address, and an identifying title for that work. The reproduction of the work should carry the same identifying title on the front of the illustration and the artist's signature should be deleted. The Contest Administration will remove and file the cover sheets, and forward only the anonymous entry to the judges.

Electronic submissions will separately include the artist's legal name, address, telephone number, e-mail address which will identify each of three pieces of art and the artist's signature on the art should be deleted.

9. There will be three cowinners in each quarter. Each winner will receive a cash prize of US $500 and will be awarded a trophy. Winners will also receive eligibility to compete for the annual Grand Prize of $5,000 together with the annual Grand Prize trophy.

10. For the annual Grand Prize Contest, the quarterly winners will be furnished with a specification sheet and a winning story from the Writers of the Future Contest to illustrate. In order to retain eligibility for the Grand Prize, each winner shall send to the Contest address his/her illustration of the assigned story within thirty (30) days of receipt of the story assignment.

   The yearly Grand Prize winner shall be determined by a panel of judges on the following basis only: Each Grand Prize judge's personal opinion on the extent to which it makes the judge want to read the story it illustrates.

   The Grand Prize winner shall be announced and awarded, along with the trophies to the winners, at the L. Ron Hubbard awards ceremony held in the following year or when it is able to be held due to government regulations.

11. The Contest has four quarters, beginning on October 1, January 1, April 1, and July 1. The year will end on September 30. To be eligible for judging in its quarter, an entry must be postmarked or received electronically no later than midnight on the last day of the quarter. Late entries will be included in the following quarter and the Contest Administration will so notify the entrant.

12. Entries will be judged by professional artists only. Each quarterly judging and the Grand Prize judging may have different panels of judges. The decisions of the judges are entirely their own and are final and binding.

13. Winners in each quarter will be individually notified of the results by mail or e-mail.

14. This Contest is void where prohibited by law.

15. To send your entry electronically, go to:
www.writersofthefuture.com/enter-the-illustrator-contest and follow the instructions.
To send your entry via mail send it to:
L. Ron Hubbard's Illustrators of the Future Contest
7051 Hollywood Blvd., Los Angeles, California 90028

16. Visit the website for any Contest rules update at:
www.illustratorsofthefuture.com

BECOME
the next
WRITER
of the
FUTURE

Listen to podcasts with past winners, judges, luminaries in the field, and publishing industry professionals to get their tips on writing and illustration and how to launch your career.

Read blogs spanning the gamut from a novice contestant to a Grand Master of Science Fiction who will give you invaluable knowledge, guidance, and encouragement.

Join the Writers of the Future Forum moderated by former winners. Attend live Q&As with Contest judges.

Take advantage of our FREE online writing workshop featuring David Farland, Tim Powers, and Orson Scott Card.

Sign up for a monthly newsletter featuring advice, quarterly winner announcements, latest news, and accomplishments.

WritersoftheFuture.com

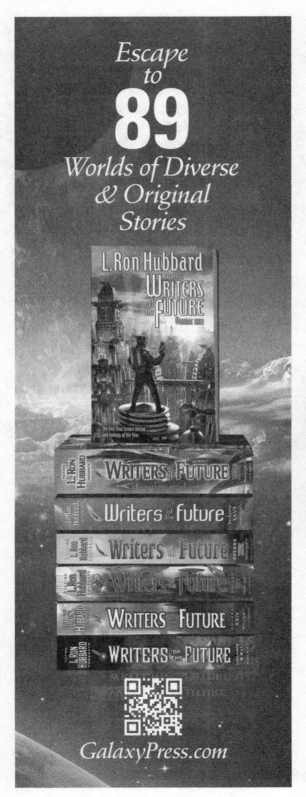